MW00416390

MULDOON'S MISFORTUNES

THOSE RESILIENT MULDOONS BOOK ONE

E.V. SPARROW

Copyright © 2024 by E.V. Sparrow

All rights reserved.

No part of this book may be reproduced in any form or by any electronic or mechanical means, including information storage and retrieval systems, without written permission from the author, except for the use of brief quotations in a book review.

ISBN: 978-1-962377-17-1

Celebrate Lit Publishing

304 S. Jones Blvd #754

Las Vegas, NV, 89107

http://www.celebratelitpublishing.com/

To my family's pack rats who saved every document, photo, and paraphernalia stuffed within
totes and bags for over a century. Then, handed the stash over to me.
Thanks to my unsuspecting great-grandfather, whose series of choices led to the birth of a great-
granddaughter who would become a novelist. Beware of what you do, for you never know if
you'll spawn a relative eager to write stories inspired by your life for all the world to read.

1

ME LOSSES HAVE NAMES

Mister Death seems stronger than You, God.
Michéal Muldoon

County Kerry, Western Ireland
Late Summer, 1866
Mister Death is a wily creature. He did it again. "Our prayers failed. That potato famine didn't kill enough of us, yeah?" Michéal stared at the shrouded bodies of his young family. "Mister Death overpowered God and stole the breath from me loved ones."

Michéal's sister, Orla, rose from a rickety chair in his chilly cottage where she'd mourned beside the bodies laid out on the table in the common room. "The famine? 'Twas over twenty years since."

"None can still do naught 'bout Mister Death. He always steals. Even so"—Michéal crossed himself—"I'll ask God to send His angels to accept me darlings' precious spirits." He ground his teeth. "Forgot to send them to battle Mister Death when they were yet alive."

"Hush." She tapped his shoulder and glanced above.

He gripped a chair, knelt, raising his stinging eyes toward heaven and the grimy rafters still stuffed with *bog scraw*. "Me *macushlas*, me darlings, are they released from purgatory? Been four days, aye? I had little to pay for penance."

Orla wiped her tears with her shawl's hem. "You're making me weep, brother."

He clutched a whiskey bottle, rose, and scuffed his boots across the uneven flagstones to the window. "You must love them, God. The church teaches us so, and You're watching for them, they say. Why do You not answer me laments?"

God's only answer was the rain pelting his thatched roof and the north wind that drove layers of water sideways, splattering it against a cracked window. *I'm not worthy of a response? 'Tis expected.* Leaning against the sill and grasping his comfort by its cold, glass neck, he sulked from another afternoon blanketed with gray clouds.

"Your Mister Death again? Sh." Orla looped her arm through his and tugged. "Come rest a moment, aye? God surely loves us, Mick." She looped her arm through his, then pulled a beaten-up chair away from the table and the bodies.

"'Tis so hard to feel God's love." He pulled his arm away. "The crucifixes on our walls are the rumor of it."

Orla glowered and glanced at the silver one nailed to the wall beside the hearth. "Brother—"

"And the rain. God's tears for Ireland, yeah? But God is good." He downed another burning swig from his bottle. "Is He good enough to care for us, sister?"

She held her fingertip against his lips. "'Tis the whiskey messing with—"

He jerked his head away, the room blurring. "No. 'Tis me heart battered within me."

"You're making no sense—"

"God's making no sense." Mick wobbled sideways. "We pray. We protest our oppression." He shook his fist. "Why does God not break the grip of the English Crown? God's helpless against them, as we are. Can He not deliver us from our suffering?" The pressure in his chest tightened, and he tugged at his shirt.

"Come now, you'll curse yourself for speaking such things. Sit down." Orla reached for the bottle. "Saints preserve us."

Mick wrenched his bottle from Orla's grip, sloshing droplets of the alcohol onto her hand. He waved toward his veiled family. "His perfect saints be ignoring us all. The church teaches us God loves children." His voice broke. "What's wrong with us? Me a cripple, and you . . . scarred. Have you felt His love?"

She crossed herself. "Hush, Mick. Don't bring a curse from heaven down upon us. Come rest, aye?" She pushed against him, but he resisted.

"I try to believe, I try." Mick mumbled so quietly even God wouldn't hear his complaints. "Do I deserve evil upon me? No, I committed only venial sins. Ah. I forgot to go to confession, don't you see? God is vexed I haven't confessed—"

"By all the saints. Go sit, will you? I need to get something. Sit." Orla hastened to the cottage door, drew her layered shawls up and over her head, and glanced back at her brother. "I won't be long. Sit there and wait." She slipped outside.

"You go, and I'll rest." Mick surveyed the quiet room. "Don't bother coming back." He fumbled with the door latch and locked it, then stared at his covered family on the table. "Mister Death seems stronger than You, God." He knuckled his eyes, then took another slug of whiskey. "You let him take both me wives, and all me children, one by one. Every year. Good women and sweet littles, they all were."

Mick staggered to the chair at the table and sagged onto it. "I'm beleaguered. Why'd You give me a twisted back like me Da?" He shook his fist at the ceiling. "Why'd You let me poor sister wound herself, and give people the frights?" Poor Orla.

He gazed around for his sister. Where'd she'd go? Oh aye, to get something.

He waved his hands so God could see him. "Here. Remember our potato crops got the blight? Terrible famine. Long ago, yeah, but we don't forget the misery. So many starved and died. Me own Pa, as well."

Folding his arms, he rocked himself in the chair, then tipped the bottle to his lips and gulped. "Whiskey," he whispered, "me friend. Where's your embrace?"

Splaying his arm across the battered tabletop, he rested his head on it, dizzy from his agitated breathing and whiskey's lavish effect.

"Where's me hope?" He crossed himself, then bowed his head. "I believe in God, the Father Almighty, Creator of heaven and earth…in Jesus Christ, His only Son, our Lord." *Um, what's next?* "Um, conceived by the Holy Spirit, born of the Virgin Mary. Hm…" He rubbed his face. "Suffered under Pontius Pilate, was crucified, died, and was buried…dead like me loves." He sobbed against his arm for a moment. "He descended into hell…the third day He rose again…He ascended into heaven." Mick tried to focus his mind and blurry gaze beyond the broken window.

A slanted ray of sunshine slid through the scuttling clouds and transformed the shadowed room with its light. He marveled at the glowing peach and gold chamber. "You sent a beautiful shaft of light? Your condolences?" He caressed the shrouded bodies. "Have mercy, Lord. Have mercy. Christ, have mercy. Make them breathe again." The cherubic faces of his children swam in his memory. "God's blessings, aye. But that wicked Mister Death, always the thief."

Mick slid his hands down the almost empty bottle and clamped onto the base. "Wicked cold. Hard as the English heart. Rotten to the core." His tears dropped onto the table beside his deceased family. "None can break those shackles. I never can."

The bottle swayed in his vision. "Whiskey, stop your moving like a ship on the waves." He closed his eyes to stop the motion. "Ships sail for escape, aye. Far away. I heard tales of a better life."

Pounding on the front door captured Mick's attention. Who could that be? Orla wouldn't knock.

"Michéal Muldoon? Here to collect the bodies."

"No." Mick stood and tripped over the chair leg. He spat. "You cannot take them."

"Michéal." The muffled voice increased in volume. "Open the door, man. We must make a report and take them for burial proper."

"No." He shoved the chair out of his way and steadied himself with it. Lifting it, he hobbled to the door to thrust its top rail beneath the doorknob.

"They been here too long. 'Tis the law," the voice spoke.

"Crown law, no doubt."

"And 'tis God's law, Michéal. Open it up, man." The pounding repeated.

"But Mister Death breaks those laws." Mick scrubbed at his moist cheeks.

"Mick? The storm's returned." Orla's lilting voice sounded beyond the door. "I brought them with me."

"So, God. You wrecked me plans to keep them here and sent me sister to do the job?" His bitter laugh reverberated in his ears.

"Mick?"

"You always best me, God." Lumbering toward his sister's voice, he yanked away the chair against the door, then opened it.

Orla stood in front of Undertaker Nolan and his assistant, with her shawls flapping in the relentless wind and rain. She turned her disconcerting, palest blue eyes upon him. "'Tis time to let them go. I'm fearful for your mind."

Mick grabbed Orla's shoulders and yanked her through

the doorway, against his chest. They held each other tight while sobs wracked his frame.

"Hush, now. They need to collect them." She grasped her brother's hand and towed him over to the bodies. Orla covered her face with her wet shawl, lifted the sheet corner from the infant, and gazed at the tiny boy. "'Tis sure you know this, Mick, heaven awaits the innocents?"

"Aye." Mick turned toward the men.

Nolan's assistant stood slack-jawed outside peeking in. He had retreated from the doorway. "Shall we return later?"

Undertaker Nolan shook his head.

"Have you never seen grief, man?" Mick ran his sleeve over his face. "Are you not an Irishman? We've been dying from persistent evil forever." He spat. "The English stole our land and let us starve." He indicated his deceased family shrouded on the table. "Even our little ones die. Not a care has the English Crown for us."

Orla stroked Mick's shoulder. "Anger and bitterness will not help."

"Even whiskey don't help much."

"I'll help you, I will." She clutched his elbow.

Mick motioned for the men to enter his home. "Take what you came for."

Undertaker Nolan and his assistant covered their faces with a cloth tied behind their heads and strode to the bodies. "Nigh a third of our village passed from the fever. I must check." He massaged his neck. "Been hauling them all away for two days, we have." The sheet corner trembled in his fingers. "Typhus fever. Blotches of red rash."

"Aye, 'twas." Mick ground his teeth.

"Mícheál, you got to tell me each legal name for the records." Nolan cleared his throat. "And sorry for your losses."

"Me losses. Aye, me losses have lovely names." Mick lumbered across the room. He peered past Nolan's hand gripping the cover over the face of his wife. "'Tis Fiona Muldoon."

Nolan's assistant scribbled.

Mick bent and kissed her white, cold cheek, avoiding the red rash on her face. He turned to the next, smaller body. "'Tis—" Mick pointed. "'Tis Rosie. She was two years." His voice broke. "And the little one, the babe, is our James. All me babes. All five lost to Mister Death, with both their mothers. Not me. He didn't beat me."

"Five?" Nolan's assistant froze his pen in midair. "What? Two or five children? Both mothers? He's too young to be married twice. That's too many—"

Nolan elbowed him. "He's talking 'bout the others, potato head, he's lost others before these."

Mick grimaced. "I'm twenty-six, and yeah, too young and too many. No matter how you count."

"Ah, um." The assistant blushed and lowered his eyes to his document.

Orla scurried to her brother. "I'm here for you." He rested against her side, and they wept, wrapped in each other's arms.

"Why do we always survive through hunger and sickness, sister? The little ones die, and we big ones live."

"'Tis the curse of the ones before us." Orla drew her brother away as she stepped back from his departed loved ones and wiped her nose. "Long life is supposed to be a blessing, so they say. Blame Uncle Thomas. Lived to one-hundred eleven years. And God has His ways. I don't get most of them."

"We'll be taking them now." Undertaker Nolan signaled to his assistant. They loaded the bodies onto fabric shaped like a hammock and carried them outside to the parked wagon.

Mick and Orla followed them to where the brown and white horses hitched to the wagon fidgeted and jingled their reins. "Those gentle *Cobs* don't like the smell of death. Poor creatures."

"Who does?"

The siblings waited for the open-bed wagon to depart, towing other typhus victims amid the showers.

Mick snorted. "Will death never end?" He yanked on his sister's shawl, tugging her beneath the cottage eves. "I cannot watch Mister Death steal away me heart again. Can you?"

"No, I cannot." Orla whispered. She grasped his sleeve, but her eyes sparkled. "I have a plan. Do you wish to hear it? We've been talking 'bout it. Me, Kathleen, and Ed."

He shrugged. "Talking 'bout what?"

"Getting away from here, from all our troubles. We plan to emigrate to America." Orla cradled his face. "Their war against slavery is over. 'Twas in the papers. 'Tis safer now."

"Heard the news. War is horrible, though 'tis one way to freedom." Mick knuckled his eyes. "Ireland knows 'bout oppression. We never won against England in all the wars we've had with them. But the Americans did." He wagged his head and dragged his focus back to her. "But Kathleen's going? With Ed? Our lamb will never survive a trip with him. Lamb's a gentle heart, God love her."

Orla huffed. "And am I not gentle, I'd like to know? She's wishing to find Aidan. You can be her guardian."

"Aidan Duffy? He's been in *America* five years."

"Her heart's desire is to find him."

"But we'd all be deserting Mam, and she'll be broken-hearted. She's accustomed to us being nigh every day."

Orla sighed. "Mam will have Rory and John. They're staying." She twisted her hands in her shawl. "John will visit Mam when the church allows."

"But four of us need money for passage. How?" Mick headed into his cottage. He left his front door open for fresh air, shuffled to his table, and grabbed a chair to slump onto it. "Whiskey." He brushed the empty bottle with his thumb. "You cost me, but you never last long, do you?"

"Give a listen." Orla dragged a chair next to him. "I've

plenty for all our vouchers. You've heard of cheap ships going to *America*?"

Mick flinched, and his chair tipped back, but she jerked him upright. "Cheaper? What's that you say? You're talking 'bout a risky transport in a coffin ship?"

She drew near his ear, and her breath tickled. "Not a coffin ship. More people survive the trip. Surely, you're not in such a stupor you can't grasp what I'm telling you."

"Head's clear enough, but you're daft."

2

BIRDS AND LAMBS

Hunger is worse than the fear of man.
Mick

Orla seized Mick's hand. "You wish to escape the horrors and memories here, aye?"

"Aye, if I can. But those boats are named coffin ships because too many died on them. And why'd you think I'd be sailing on one of those?" He crossed himself and shook his head. "I want to escape from Mister Death, not traverse the sea in a coffin with him."

"Stop calling them coffin ships, you dolt. Gives me shivers, thinking of them that way. Lots of folks make it across the sea nowadays. And stop speaking 'bout your Mister Death. The fare is cheaper for four vouchers on those ships, don't you know?" She raised her palm at Mick's grunt. "I saved up the fares for us."

He rubbed his forehead and neck. "Sure, you say you got cheap vouchers, but no passage is free."

"Aye, not free."

Mick's thoughts swam. "Some must yet be free, for how'd you earn enough money for four vouchers?

"Been saving."

"Since you were a babe?"

"A long time."

"Nah. Couldn't be that. We don't get paid enough for anything we do." He inspected her down-turned face. "Can always tell when you're hiding something."

"'Tis me secret. I'll keep it that way." Orla averted her face. "Escaping from here 'tis a good use of me money."

His heart pounded. "You didn't steal it, did you?"

"I'm no thief." Orla's pale-lashed, light blue eyes narrowed to slits. "I'll share me money with our family. 'Tis for our escape." She crossed herself.

"Where'd you get your money if you didn't steal it?"

Orla gave him a mischievous, dimpled smile.

She almost looked pretty that way—

"I earned it."

"What? You may work the numbers for the railway foreman on his ledgers, but he must pay low wages. Not enough for four passages to America. I'm no fool."

"Well, and I sold something. Not to worry, 'twas mine fair to sell." She folded her arms and raised her prominent jaw.

Mick's thoughts scattered to the villagers' idle talk he'd heard. "What did you sell?" His open mouth dried. Were those rumors 'bout her true?

She laid her hand on his arm. "I promise one day I'll share it with you. Let me be. I want to help us, and I can." She kissed his cheek.

"Our family wonders—"

"You four *boyos* do your best. 'Tis proud I am, to share me fair-earned money to keep us from shrinking into skin and bones. Aye?"

"'Tis. You earn your money from the railway then? We all felt the burden when Mister Death took Da away." He set his whiskey to his lips to wet his throat, then recalled the bottle was empty. If only he didn't need whiskey to forget his life's grievances.

"Da did fall ill. Even though he had enough bread and potatoes to eat." Orla cocked her head sideways and brushed at a wayward peach-colored strand. "I been helping you feed your families when you needed it, and you got your whiskey with me help. No asking where me money came from then."

"You know I always fed me family before I got me whiskey." He bent toward her, and his head swam. "You know that. They ate first, then came the drink."

"I know. You took grand care of them." She cupped his face and searched his eyes. "What do you say? 'Tis a new world across the sea with freedom from the Crown and work for everyone." Her voice intensified. "A free man. I can be me own woman. No being forced to do anything."

He jerked his face from her hands. "Cursed English. They—"

"Let's stick to the subject of leaving." She glanced out the window. "Once we're in America, we'll be free to do as we please. Not like here in the old country." They also capitalize Old Country. *But I can leave it this way.*

Mick cursed. He couldn't gather his thoughts well enough to continue following this droning conversation.

Faint sunshine crept in through his broken window. He blinked hard. The current condition of his once crowded cottage when his family was yet alive had altered into a burial *tuama*—silent, dreary, and foreboding. Why stay?

Orla tapped his hand. "Won't you come for Kathleen? Our lamb might need you to look after her until she finds her Aidan."

"That she will. If Ed goes with us, 'twill be even worse. I can't allow me sisters to traverse the perilous sea with a bully brother. And be in a strange country alone." *I must go despite me doubts.* "Naught left for me here." Mick scowled at her. "But beware the coffin ships."

"There you go worrying. Remember me friend, Maeve? She made it fine." Orla upthrust her hand to stop his words. "I know your objections. Village folks tell of getting letters from their family moaning 'bout the hardships on the voyage. But don't we have hardship in our own land? Don't we all die, here or there? But if we're free, we choose how we die."

He unfolded his shaky hands and picked at the callouses from hard work on the farm. "I'm in no mood to ponder it."

"Think of our lamb when you're in the mood. I'll find a ship leaving this month. So give me your answer in a fortnight."

He shrugged, although he knew what he should do.

She glanced out the still open door. "'Tis a good time to leave you, for there's a break in the clouds. And Mam will wonder 'bout me." She kissed the top of his head and strode outside.

———

Mick sat alone and lost track of time. As the deluge of alcohol faded from his brain, the pain in his heart increased pace with the stillness settling inside the cottage. No childish chatter or infant cries or sweet songs from his wife as she did her tasks. All the comforts of family life, which he adored, had vanished with their passing.

Through the cottage's open door, and the unrepaired broken window, a chill wind ruffled his hair. Mick shivered. He rose to latch it. "Give me a sign. Can You hear me, God?" He traveled halfway across the room when he spied a movement outside the doorway. He paused. A sly rat? Or a chicken, since they often pecked for bugs near the cottage door?

A sparrow flitted along the cottage's threshold, its brown and cream striped wings fluttering with each hop. It searched the sides of the doorjamb and jerked its head to glance at him before it continued.

He froze and held his breath.

The bird pecked at tiny specks, although Mick stood only a few feet away.

Hunger was worse than the fear of man. "Bravery."

The ordinary, tiny bird flew away from his voice.

Mick darted to the doorway, stepped outside, and followed piercing chirps. He searched the roof's corner and discovered the sparrow's nest tucked under the thatched overhang. "Ah, it must feed its babes. Hunger and need stoke its bravery." *Could I be that sparrow for Kathleen and Orla?* He'd never been a brave man.

Chills prickled up his arms and legs. His attention switched to the brisk wind battering his body, and the wet, emerald landscape beyond his bleak yard and stone wall. Poverty reduced the Muldoon family to tenant farmers centuries ago. *We toil to grow food from a cruel, cursed earth and beneath relentless rain.* The absent landowner, Lord Carrington, hadn't fixed the broken window, but had sent a letter saying his agent would arrive next month. Would he care if Mick was gone?

Probably not, for Rory is next in line to inherit, with Ed leaving as well. Who is Mick Muldoon? He was a tenant farmer with muddy boots and splattered cottage walls in need of lye wash. Did he have a care for snooty Lord Carrington? "He hides a heart of stone dressed up in his English finery."

He spit on the mud, then turned back toward the cottage doorway. A black robe flashed in his side vision. "And there's forever you to deal with, Mister Death." Mick peeked inside the cottage's dim interior for his spiritual enemy. "You enjoy torturing me soul. Can't see you now, but you're always lurking in the shadows, you are." *Hovering around me in the very air.* "I'll get away from you yet, wicked demon. See if I don't."

Would he ever be strong enough to fight off Mister Death? Mick propped himself against the door frame, reluctant to enter. He turned to scrutinize Orla's footprints in the muddy path leading up the hill to his mother's cottage. *Got me a bit of hope.* But will Americans be as superstitious about Orla's appearance?

Winning his struggle to clear his thoughts from the last remnants of whiskey, his hope grew with recollection of occasional help with repairing rails for the local train yard. He'd need to request a job reference. *They'll give me a letter.*

Could Mick desert his home and half his family? There were happy memories here as well, although overshadowed by tragedy. He'd be sad to leave them, especially John. But what of Kathleen? *Little lamb would never survive without me.* Those who left would never see each other again. Could he accept they'd not meet again until heaven?

He finger-combed his wet hair, entered, then closed the door against the chill. What would life be like without the arrogance and scorn of the Crown? *Am I betting on a fool's dream?*

What provisions did they allow on a ship? *What 'bout me whiskey?* Mick created a mental list of belongings he'd need. His clothing could be packed in a bag, and he had little else. He couldn't haul his mattress. He must burn the filthy mats because of the lingering pestilence.

Ambling to the rear of his cottage, Mick hesitated once inside the bedroom. Clothes hung from wall hooks or were hung over a line of rope strung across a corner of the room. His trousers draped over the iron bed. Soiled clothing lay in a basket tucked under the clothesline. He pinched a sleeve of Fiona's brown dress, then quickly released it as it sagged between his fingers. Hollow without Fiona.

Mick's vision landed on the tiny infant gowns. He stroked one with his fingertips, then whimpered and smashed his fist against his mouth, stifling a sob. He wiped his eyes with his soiled shirttail.

The departed rainstorm left a hush in the air with an occasional soft *drip, drip* from the eaves. He forced himself back into the common room. Through the narrow windows glowed the vivid sunset of gold and orange beneath the wind-blown purple and gray clouds. Would it rain much in America?

A knock sounded on his door. Mick swung it open. "Kathleen, little lamb. How's Mam?"

The youngest and slightest Muldoon sibling stood before him with her shawls wrapped snug around her slim frame. The wind tore the wrap from her head, exposing thick, curly auburn hair lighter than his own. "She's crabby, our mother. Why earlier this morning— But I had to come. Orla said you may travel with us. God's truth? I can be brave if you go with us and help me find Aidan. You must."

He puffed out his cheeks and stepped aside. "Glory be, Kathleen. Come in from the wind. You're shivering."

"You've not lit a fire? 'Tis as cold within as without." Kathleen hurried to the mantle, snatched the flint, and lit the peat bricks in the hearth. "I mustn't stay long. Mam dozed off, and I scurried out as quick as a mouse. Don't know where Orla is. She disappeared once more, although her scars frighten the community if her face is uncovered. She's never home, particularly when I need help. Do you know what she did—"

"Little lamb, you're skipping along scattered thought trails, and it won't get you home quick." Mick plopped onto a stool near the growing fire. "You came to beseech me. Finish it."

Kathleen smacked her forehead. "Oh. Where was I?"

"I must go with you."

"Aye, please." She dropped to her knees before him and carressed his hands, her sky-blue eyes swimming with tears. "Don't leave me alone with Ed. You know how our brother is. You always laugh at his taunts. I cannot. I've had nightmares of dying on the ship. I'll never make it across before I die of fright of him. And I need your help to find Aidan. I'm braving the sea, and your presence will strengthen me courage."

Mick's head throbbed. He wanted solitude and more whiskey. "Ed's your brother, not a ghoul or executioner." He squeezed Kathleen's hands before letting go. "I'd never let you go alone. Finding Aidan in that vast land may prove very difficult, sweet sister."

She clutched his arms. "You're dependable, and Orla isn't. She always disappears—"

"So, let's speak of Mam. What will she do with half of us leaving her? You're her caretaker, and her favorite."

Kathleen wrinkled her nose and removed her grasp on him. "You're the golden son. Why, when Mam and Da gave the rights of the farm to you over Ed—"

"Have you told Mam?"

She twiddled her fingers clasped on her knees. "Mam screamed, cried, and wouldn't speak to me for five days. 'Twas terrible." She glanced up at him and pouted. "Mam has three other children content to stay home, and they'll take care of her. I'm not content. I have me own dreams with Aidan. Why, only the other day—"

"Kathleen, surely Mam understands why we'd wish to go. This desolate house becomes more unbearable with the clearing of me head." He studied his sister's pale face. "What about Ed and Orla's reasons for leaving Ireland? Have they told you?"

"Those two *mummers*?" Kathleen laughed. "Always hiding something. Pretending to be what they're not." She stretched her hands toward the fire. "All will be well for me, should you come with us. I can't abide being alone with those two for days and years and—"

"Aye, little lamb. You'd detest it, I know."

Kathleen shivered. "'Tis so quiet in here. Without—um, that is—God's holy saints. Mam will be in a tizzy should she awake whilst I'm here." She scrambled to her feet and wrapped her shawls tight around herself, then twirled back to blow a kiss. "Good night, me brother. Join us please, for me?"

With the latching of the door, Kathleen's cheerful presence in Mick's heart and home shifted into gloom.

He clenched his jaw. Would his disappearance trick wicked Mister Death? News of shipwrecks flashed in his thoughts. Some were people they knew, even friends of his family. Hadn't Da's sister, Auntie Nora, died on a coffin ship in the 40s? An epidemic on that ship killed one-hundred people. More like Mister Death murdered them with pestilence. Ships couldn't be a safe way to travel, yet they were the only way to *America*.

Poor Auntie, trying to escape Ireland during *an Gorta Mór*, and what did she get for it? Slain onboard and dumped into the depths of the sea. Could that happen again? Mick shuddered. "'Tis the 60s. And Parliament is supposed to have improved the naval laws." He rose to gather something for supper and paused. "But when has Parliament ever fulfilled its promises?"

3

'TIS TIME

Must outrun Mister Death. That's what I must do.
Mick

T*he Local Pub*
        Two weeks after being convinced to emigrate, Mick rammed his hands into his pockets as Edward approached the group outside Donovan's Pub entrance. He expected strife with Ed joining them. How had Orla convinced him to join up tonight? He didn't wish to partake in the celebration this evening, even for its reopening after the vanquished typhus fever outbreak.

Mick huffed a breath. "Why'd we have to meet here on a rainy eve?"

Kathleen laughed. "What's your favorite saying now? 'If we waited for the rain to stop, we'd get nothing done.' 'Tis lively." She tapped her toe to the cheerful music drifting from the pub.

"Don't feel merry. Could've met at me home. 'Twill be hot and crowded within."

Ed scrunched his nose. "Why'd we wish to do that? Still smells of death in your home."

"Hush." Orla punched Ed's arm.

"Ow!" Ed's breath hissed through his teeth. "Blurted out the thought before I could catch it. Me apologies, Mick."

"Imagine, me bully oldest brother speaking his mind. Not a sensitive bone in you, yeah?"

"Now, now." Kathleen stroked Mick's clenched hand. "He meant no disrespect to your cherished ones. Aye, Ed? He got all of Mam's qualities and none of Da's fine ones."

"True, that," chimed Mick and Orla. Mick grinned for the first time in weeks.

Mick stared up at the pub's dripping eaves. Water sluiced over the edges and fell into puddles gathering in the mud near the entrance. "Always more tears from heaven's skies."

A group of men exited through the squeaky front door, increasing the volume of laughter, singing, and music from a flute, a *bodhran* drum, and a fiddle. The rhythm hovered and pulsed in the air.

One man tipped his *tam* in greeting. "Good evening, Muldoons." He bowed to the sisters. "Condolences, Mick, and me greetings to your mother."

"Aye, Mr. Gallagher." Mick nodded, and Kathleen gave a slight curtsy along with Orla.

Orla craned her neck to peek through the closing door of the pub. "Well, and are we entering? Must check for an empty *snug*. A pity the outside entrance was jammed."

Kathleen giggled. "Snugs. The looks of a confessional without the contrition and penance required to use them. Hiding the women or priests drinking. Although people and God will see us entering. Why should we use them?"

Ed snickered. "Lamb, here I'd been thinking how proper you are."

"Snugs hide us from the men, aye?" Orla scoffed.

Kathleen giggled. "Is it possible we'll discover Father Mangan sneaking a pint in one?"

"No doubt." Mick slid off his tam and gave it a shake,

then fluffed his damp hair stuck to his neck. "Let's get it over with. I'll not be doing this with pleasure."

Orla's brows went up. "Take a nip for your back pains then, and you'll be enjoying our meeting soon enough."

The squeaky door slammed behind the Muldoon siblings. They shuffled between their neighbors crammed inside the sizable, smoke-filled room. Men patted Mick on the shoulder and offered their condolences.

He sighed. "I wish to return to me home."

Ed spoke into his ear. "Be on the lookout for your Mister Death, yeah? He might be hiding under a table or behind the bar." He snarled and bared his teeth. Like a rabid dog.

Sweat dripped down Mick's back while the gathering hemmed him in near the hearth. Facing his neighbors' pity and questions would undo his hard-fought stability. "The entire community is here this night. I wished to avoid their merrymaking."

Kathleen looped her thin arm through his. "Aw, Mick, 'tis good for you to get out."

"It'd be good for me to have me family yet alive. Whilst we stand here waiting to make merry, the fire is baking me like bread on the paddle."

Through the aroma of pipe tobacco and alcohol, Mick inhaled drifting whiffs of Donovan's beef stew. His mouth watered and his stomach growled, but all his heart and aching body wanted was a drink or three. "Why must we meet here?"

"Hiya, Mick Muldoon."

He turned toward the gruff, booming voice during the lull between songs. It was near the bar. A group of railway men faced him with their cups upthrust in salute. The grizzled older man who spoke gave a nod and sipped his drink. Mick mumbled. "Ah, no, no. 'Tis Sean from the rail yard."

Sean approached the family. "Condolences from meself and the crew." He smacked Mick's shoulder and gave a slight bow to the siblings. "'Tis a wicked world, aye?"

"Sean." Mick gazed up at the taller man. "Was planning to ask you for an employment letter—"

"You were? I suppose the times you helped us to pound spikes counts." Sean outstretched his glass, rocked back on his heels. "But first, a toast. May it be that God Himself found your loved ones in heaven a half hour before the devil knew they were dead."

Kathleen gasped.

Mick gaped. "No call for such vile humor."

"Meant no harm. Thought to lighten your mood." Sean wiggled his thick, white brows. "Evening, Orla. Always a lady now, aren't you? And why're you wearing that scarf over your face? Not all women are beauties. God's seen it. Most of us seen it."

"Is that so?" Orla glowered. "From the tales I hear 'bout you, Sean, the devil himself has seen you many a time. Drooling until he gets his claws into you."

"Let's drink." Ed stepped between Sean and Orla. "Anyone else?"

Sean sniggered and returned to his crew.

Orla fluttered her fingers toward the two wooden-framed rooms reaching halfway to the ceiling with frosted glass windows, built to conceal anyone not wishing to be seen nipping their pints in public. "Think there's an empty snug there with the door ajar." She hastened away.

Kathleen jumped up and down to gain a view over the patrons around her. "'Tis not fair to be so short. God gave her all the height of a tree." She wound her way through the gathering.

Mick nudged Ed. "Where're those drinks you promised?"

After Ed headed to the bar, Mick gazed over the throng and spied Orla rattling a snug's knob. He slid between patrons to join his sisters.

Kathleen fidgeted with her long braid. "If 'tis locked, it's occupied, Orla. Ed can bring us our drinks outside."

"Won't suit our purposes if you and I must sit outside in the night whilst the men drink, will it now?" Orla tugged on the door.

"For heaven's sake, Orla, half the customers witnessed us standing here. It'll suit Mick's fancy to be outside."

Orla rapped on the frosted window. "Is someone inside this snug?" She placed her ear against the door. "Music's too boisterous to hear."

"Ah, well." Mick shrugged. "I'll get Ed. We'll go home, as I've wished."

"Which snug has the broken latch?" Kathleen sidled over to the second booth and lay her ear against a window. "Someone's snoring in this one. Well, and Mam would say 'tis rude to awaken them, aye?"

Orla stomped over to Kathleen and tugged on the broach clasping her cloak together.

Kathleen slapped her hand. "Stop it."

"I must pick the lock." Orla glanced at Mick. "What's amusing?" She turned her palm up to Kathleen.

"What's your rush?" Kathleen worked to unclasp her carved wooden rosebud broach. "Take care. Da made it for me." She gingerly lay the broach onto her sister's palm.

"Don't I know it? Our Mick is me rush. He'll start complaining 'bout his back and wish to leave before we set our plans." Orla twisted the pin in the keyhole at various angles.

"Got our pints." Ed handed them out. "What's the goings on?"

Mick grabbed his pint and gulped. "What good'll Guinness do me? Requested whiskey."

Kathleen raised her brow. "Any drink is grand, aye?"

"For the Irish, 'tis." Ed sipped his.

"No, Ed. Me drink is for me pain. To forget. To sleep without dreams."

Ed shook his head. "Keep telling yourself that one."

The latch gave way, and Orla let the door swing inward.

She pushed the door wider, then leaped backward, yanking the door closed. "Didn't take till Christmas, aye?" She rammed into Kathleen and bumped Mick's elbow.

Mick's pint splashed onto his face as he was about to take another swig. "Watch it." He wiped his chin with his shirt sleeve.

"Um. Did you see anything, Lamb?" Orla chewed her lip.

"Only you, smashing into me like a ramrod against a castle door. You were in a rush to unlock it, now you've shut it. I don't understand you at all."

Ed raised a brow at Mick. "I think I know what's up, aye? Think on it."

"They're coming out." Orla grimaced.

"They?" He grasped her meaning and pursed his lips.

Kathleen surveyed her siblings. "What?"

"Don't you worry 'bout it, Lamb." Orla pressed back against the frosted windows of the snug.

The door swung open to reveal a tousled couple in a hurry to exit the snug. The siblings made way for them.

"Isn't that a strange thing for them to ignore us knocking?" Kathleen cocked her head.

Mick held his breath to refrain from responding.

Orla nudged Kathleen into the snug and turned back to her brothers. "Sh."

"What's this?" Kathleen dangled a stocking above the booth. "She left this here. I know I'd miss me stocking. Wouldn't you notice if you had a bare leg?"

The siblings burst out laughing.

Kathleen raised her brows. "What's humorous 'bout an abandoned stocking?"

"God love you, Kathleen. We need the pure amongst us to remind us of our bygone innocence. Scoot over." Orla patted her sister's arm.

"Mick, sit in the booth next to Orla. She was that sure you'd wish to leave on account of your back pains before we could plan our travels." Kathleen snorted like a piglet and stepped aside.

Mick chuckled. "Your laugh. 'Tis always enough to bring me out of the pit of despair."

The siblings nestled around the table within the polished wooden booth and huddled over their full pints of amber liquid.

Orla leaned in. "Now, to get on—"

"Wait." Mick outstretched his glass. "Me pint is empty, thanks to Orla's elbow. Ed, will you get me a whiskey?"

"You wretch. I only just returned." Ed scrambled from the booth. "I'll be away then. No need to wait for me. And I'm only getting you one more."

Kathleen stifled a yawn. "Hope he makes haste. Been up with Mam since before dawn." She relaxed against the upholstery and closed her eyes.

"Ed's a creature. Sure, as if I asked him for the moon." Mick's crooked back and shoulders ached with a spasm. *Always in pain.* What about Christ's pain? "Do you think 'tis true, if we make the sign of the cross, it keeps evil away?"

"What made you think of that?" Orla grimaced.

"Christ's pain on the cross."

Orla shrugged. "If we don't do it, maybe worse evil would befall us. I know the devil hates the crucifix."

"By all that's holy, have you forgotten our catechism? 'Twas on account of the devil's conviction Jesus Christ died on it once and for all, then it shocked him along with the rest of the world to find Christ alive on Easter morn. The devil never saw it coming, did he? Imagine he'll never get over the fright of the cross."

Orla raised her brows and murmured.

Roused by her own snoring, Kathleen asked. "Fright of what?" She cleared her throat.

"You sound hoarse, Lamb." Orla reached out and felt Kathleen's forehead. "You feeling ill?"

"Only me throat." Kathleen swallowed a sip from her mug. "I'd say 'tis from raising me voice over the crowd earlier, though a persistent headache's been with me. Didn't mention it to anyone. Had it for nigh five months."

Orla's eyes widened. "Were you hiding your illness? Do you have a rash?"

"Not the typhus. Didn't wish to bother anyone, with Mick's family being dreadfully ill." Kathleen swiped her hand in the air. "I'm fine."

"Hm." Mick rolled his shoulders. "Maybe you need a whiskey, Lamb. Where's Ed? I wish to get home before Christmas Eve."

Orla frowned at her sister. "Kathleen. Fetch Ed." She slid open the drawstrings of her mother's hand-me-down, tattered reticule, dug inside, and counted out some coins. She handed them to Kathleen. "In case Ed didn't yet order Mick's whiskey, ask him to get you one."

"If I must." Kathleen turned back at the snug's door. "Fetching drinks defeats the secrecy of the snug, aye?" She exited the room, then sidled through the patrons headed for the bar.

Mick monitored Kathleen's progress. "She's a gentle creature, our little lamb. Confusion mixed with cheer follows her wherever she goes."

"Aye, but she has a point. Don't you suppose leaving the door open might injure the sensibilities of the men? The very ones who wish women to be hidden when patronizing the pub? Halfwits made the law and built the—"

"Sister, why is it you tend toward believing all men are dolts? Da was clever."

"True."

"That open door will help our true halfwit, Ed, to find us."

Orla lowered her face covering, revealing her jagged scars around one pale eye and cheek. She sipped her drink. "When they return, let's lay our plans. I heard tell of a ship leaving next week. Did you speak to the landlord 'bout going away?"

"Quit pushing me. Planned to speak to that creature, Sean, but now I'll ask Will for a letter, for he's a decent and fair fella. Even though I've only worked for the railway a few times. But warn that Lord Carrington?" Mick spit to the side. "He collects heaps of rent and does naught to help his tenants. Let me family die, he did." He swigged the last of his ale and thumped the glass atop the table. "Where's me whiskey?"

"Give them time." Orla lowered her voice. "You're right 'bout your landlord, they're rotten. Parliament enforcing land laws is like a mist on the moorland. Looks like 'twill become something productive . . ." She snapped her fingers. "Their goodwill disappears like fog, without helping us on our land at all."

"Aye. We're their subjects, but our welfare's not their concern." He inclined his head toward the open door. "Give a listen."

Beyond the snug's wall, the fiddle, bodhran, and flute band emitted a slow ballad. Folks in the pub's main room fell silent.

He crossed himself and folded his hands. "Hush, 'tis remembrance of the recent dearly departed in our village."

She clasped his hand tight.

The band played for several minutes. The mournful notes from the fiddle wrapped around Mick's heart and clamped it with a vice grip until the song ended. "I'm in dread to see our landlord, for I might do him harm. Been dreaming 'bout it. 'Tis evil, I know, but I can't—"

"Mick, no. Promise me." She clutched his sleeve. "We'll leave before you're tempted to do something dreadful. Pray to the saints for help."

"You pray to them then. I don't take up much with the saints. 'Tis a bother to remember who to pray to for what, and they help us little. Forget a priest telling us when and what to pray, for I rather say prayers right to God Himself."

"Hush." Orla's eyes flashed. "Father Mangan could be sitting next door. Lord, have mercy. Don't be saying such things out loud. People will believe you're a heretic, or worse, a loony."

"Don't I know it?" Mick squirmed on the bench seat. "Didn't realize you cared much 'bout what people think. Must confess me evil feelings to someone I trust. Lord Carrington's agent will come for the rent, aye? For he himself hasn't been to visit for a while, and I fear 'twill be Carrington himself this time, two Saturdays from now. Revenge is sorely tempting." He crossed his arms and rocked. Could he harm the man like in his dreams?

"There's terrible grumbling 'bout the landlords, and for good reason, but our best chance for survival is far away in America. 'Tis not a dream anymore. We must be away before he visits." She poked him in the chest. "Our Rory can handle things. You hear me?"

He nodded. "But Mister Death is whispering to me that no one will know."

"Stop thinking such things." Her jaw clenched. "Shove it out of your mind."

"God would punish me for murder. Don't wish to go to hell, but I'd deserve it." He gulped back a sob.

"Let your whiskey soothe you when it comes. What's that saying? God created whiskey so that the Irish wouldn't conquer the world. There's truth in it."

Kathleen entered and set Mick's glass before him. "Your whiskey." As she straightened, her heavy auburn braid slipped over her shoulder and thumped against his face.

"Watch it." Mick brushed his nose with the back of his hand. "God surely created sisters as a torment to their brothers. Bumping into us. Pulling and pushing on us."

"I like that." Kathleen stomped her foot and put her fist

on her hip. "As if you brothers did naught of tormenting your sisters. Yeah, you're angels all right."

"Aye. He could be an angel." Orla pierced him with her intense stare. "Choose to be one, yeah? For all our sakes."

Mick saluted with his beloved drink and downed most of it.

Kathleen chose a chair across from him. "So, Ed is speaking with that lout Sean."

"What?" Mick sprang up to interrupt him, then moaned and grabbed his back. "Did Ed spill our plans to him?"

Kathleen tugged on his shirt. "Sit. Edward said naught. Aren't we here to make our plans, Orla?"

"We are. We must depart next Friday."

"Glory be." Kathleen's eyes filled with tears. "Did someone tell our John? We must say farewell to him at St. Mary's. He'd be brokenhearted if we don't."

"Aye." Mick relaxed at last from the whiskey's quick magic and inclined against the booth's wall. "John has the soft heart, 'tis why he's a priest. We must see him on our way to the port, no doubt."

Orla smiled. "I wrote him. Let's be grateful we've time to visit."

"Seeing our John again will be lovely." Kathleen sighed.

He scrutinized Orla's downturned face. "What're your thoughts?"

"Leave it be, boyo."

Ed swaggered back to his siblings. "You wishing to be knackered, Mick? Your usual tippling, yeah?"

"You're the knackered one." Orla sipped her ale. "We must make plans for our family's farewell wake."

Kathleen clapped. "I'll plan it. Please let me. I got time to get the word out."

Orla tapped the tabletop. "Sure. Was saying there's a ship sailing next Saturday early. We must be on it and leave here by Friday. Can you all go then?"

Ed placed his elbows on the table. "How d'you hear when it sails, sister?"

"I got good connections listening for shipping news in Queenstown and Dublin."

Mick shook his head at what promised to be another tussle. She's the wildcat. The bully versus the wildcat.

Ed sneered. "What sort of connections are you speaking of?"

Bully yanking the wildcat's tail.

"Bona fide ones." Orla jutted her pointy chin. "I got many, so watch your tongue."

"I'd like to know how you got so many connections living in a little farm village." Ed folded his muscled arms and smirked.

"Meet people when I visit Aunt Mary and Cousin Tarah in Limerick."

"Hm, and whilst everyone sleeps, do you girls sneak away to the garrison?"

Bully. Mick shook his head. But could that happen?

Kathleen whispered to Mick. "What's he saying to her? Why do you let them go at each other? I always hate it. Do you think they'll act this way on the ship?"

"You know they've been quarreling since they were little ones. 'Tis amusing."

Ed sneered. "Or mayhap you ride over to Cork? Heard the garrison there takes any women who—"

"No business of yours whom I know or how—"

"Ho there." Mick nudged her hard and waved at the people staring at them through the doorway. "Go ahead with your spat and entertain the entire village."

Edward and Orla stopped shouting at each other to stare through the open door.

Orla thumped her fist on the table. "Enough accusations. We're wasting time." Adjusting her shawls, she rose and slammed the snug's door. "We must say our goodbyes to Mam,

John, and everyone else. I'm leaving on that ship with or without the rest of you, I am."

Kathleen cleared her throat. "Don't be that way. I said I'd go with you. I'm ready."

"I've gotten me affairs in order." Ed raised his glass. "Our sisters are ready, Mick. You're the only one left."

"I'll work to set me plans tomorrow, as I told Orla."

"You've left it for only days before we go? You've not much to deal with, have you?" Ed chuckled. "And you spend your money on drink whilst your family turns ill."

The sisters gasped.

"You're a—" Mick swung his fist at his brother and missed when Ed jerked back. Pain seared from his fist up his arm when it impacted the wall of the snug's frame. Orla had grabbed his arm just before it smashed full force. He yelled and held his throbbing fist.

Kathleen screamed and hid her face with her hands.

The pub went silent as a stone wall.

Orla shook Mick's arm. "Rein in your emotions. Reserve battle to escape, not wage battle amongst ourselves, aye?" She glowered at each sibling. "Finish up our tasks, then we hold the wake by week's end and away to America."

Mick massaged his sore hand, Ed grunted, and Kathleen sniffed back tears.

"Ow." Ed glared at Orla. "Why'd you kick me?"

"Because I won't be paying for your passage now, after your bullying Mick."

"I got me own fare. Saved me money." Ed fidgeted with his glass. "That's why I said what I did. Where'd Mick's money go?"

"Me money? You're a dirt clod. You only have yourself to care for. But me own responsibilities? I inherited the land rights and ~~paid~~ monthly pay the outrageous rent to Lord Carrington for the use of our cursed family farm. I'd four to feed and clothe, and you paid naught for living with Mam. None wanted to marry you because you're a—"

"Mam." Orla elbowed Mick. "Forgot to tell you 'bout plans for our Mam. Ed, here, told our Rory we'd be leaving soon, and he's next in line to inherit."

"Aye." Ed flipped his hand. "Good riddance to the farm."

Orla finished her drink, then turned to Mick. "And you?"

"Must outrun Mister Death first." Mick inspected his bruised knuckles. He took a deep breath. Once on that ship, no returning.

"Then what?" Orla lifted her glass.

"Get an employment letter tomorrow from Will. Then, ready the cottage for Rory, and hand over me donkey and cow. He'll have me plow and the hens as well."

"'Tis grand then, Mick." Orla nodded. "Rory's content to care for Mam, and now he can marry his precious Maureen. Settled grandly."

"Mam and Da shouldn't have given me the farm anyway." Mick tipped his head toward their older brother. "Should've always gone to Ed. Was willing to split the inheritance."

Ed choked on his ale.

Kathleen rubbed Mick's shoulder. "Even though you're not the oldest doesn't mean you couldn't have the rights to the farm. British law only allows for one to manage it, true? With six of us living, we were forbidden to split it between us."

"British law be hanged." Ed spat.

"Aye, but Da made his choice and gave it to Mick." Orla poked his arm.

"Because I'm the family's cripple?" Mick clenched his jaw. "A cursed land more like than a blessing." Hadn't his parents intended a blessing of inheriting the rights to the tenant farm? Yet Mister Death converted it into a dreadful curse with the deaths of his wives and children.

"Not a curse." Kathleen stroked his hand. "You're a hard

worker. Even suffering with your twisted back. You have a good heart, and your wives loved you."

"Aye. Hard worker." Ed sneered at Mick. "Who better than you, with the good heart? 'Tis sure, don't we all labor and sweat over our lands?" Ed's eyes narrowed. "Who could have done a better job, I wonder? If it were me, say—"

"Enough. Stop your squabbling." Orla growled. "We don't hold to your opinions, Ed. Your heart beats bitterness and jealousy, not a drop of familial blood. What difference would it have made if you were the tenant farmer? British law oppresses us all to keep us chained in poverty. We all got our reasons for leaving Ireland, and 'tis time for us to start anew."

4

MULDOON FAMILY WAKE

Mrs. Gilhooley's battered basket saved the day!
Mick

Mam Muldoon's Cottage
Late Summer
Mick gulped a sip of whiskey and concentrated on Kathleen. Their lamb flitted about the cottage like the sparrow on his doorjamb that awful day when the undertaker took his family. Now, he was at his own funeral observance.

His youngest sister paled and wilted one moment then flushed the next. Beads of perspiration trickled from beneath Kathleen's untidy, auburn hair as she ministered to their friends and neighbors at the customary farewell wake. She wiped her forehead. "Take a bit of bread with us, and would you like to have some stew?" She led the newest guest toward Mam's table, laid out with a darned and dingy tablecloth, her best serving dishes, and tasty morsels from the attendees.

Kathleen caught his stare and beamed. Wasn't Lamb always a sunny one? She and John were the most alike. Whenever guests visited their home, they perked up like kittens chasing mice.

Hadn't their cottage been a boisterous place with six living brothers and sisters, and him second eldest? Mick avoided crowds and enjoyed quiet unless he had a wife and children for blessed commotion. Tonight, he tolerated the vital gathering because it was for lamenting their departure in the morning. Forever separated. *Which is why we're dead.* Another loss for Ireland's families. He gulped against the sorrow.

Kathleen winked at him. He returned it. The week before, she'd announced their departure to neighbors, warned of their possible deaths crossing the Atlantic, and requested their attendance at the wake. She'd instructed each to bring a chair if they meant to sit and managed things very well without Orla's hovering and orders.'Twasn't like Orla to pass on such an important task to another.

Two neighbors, Mrs. Gilhooley and Mrs. Wiggins, arrived simultaneously. Both stepped through the open door and vied to enter first. He chuckled at their brouhaha. They ogled the offerings each brought for the wake then upturned their chins.

Mrs. Wiggins bent over Mrs. Gilhooley's offering. "You brought your shabby basket, I see. That lid doesn't sit straight, does it? Bread as dry as a cow patty by now. Cooks should be careful with their offerings, don't you think?"

Mrs. Gilhooley yanked her basket against her side, knocking the lid further askew. "I brought me a fresh bread in me old basket. 'Twill delight everyone."

"I'm fearful to try any of your concoctions." Mrs. Wiggins snorted.

Ah, no. He wasn't in the mood for the women's competitive and niggly ways. Both meddlesome creatures.

Mrs. Gilhooley turned away from her adversarial neighbor and called out to Mick's sister. "Orla, darlin, will you be looking for a man in America? 'Tis sure there's more to choose from there."

Harpy. Keep away. Mick sidled against the white-washed wall and stayed beyond the flickering candlelight's reach. He picked his way around people and chairs, avoiding the two bickering neighbors as they made their way farther into the group. He received a glare from one guest when he bumped into her hand holding her drink.

If he could just get nearer the door for some fresh air. Wasn't he glad he couldn't hear their nastiness through the cacophony of voices in the room? *How's Orla faring?* Mick scanned the room.

Orla had her sights on him and stepped in his direction just as Mrs. Gilhooley closed in on her. No escape from the harpy.

One mourner, a childhood friend, turned toward Mick as he stood near the doorway. Anne Brown. A small group of neighbors separated him from the Brown family.

Anne's dark green eyes glimmered with tears. She lingered by her mother, holding her youngest sister, Beth. *She must be 'bout two-years old now.* Beth resembled a younger Anne. Her youngest brother, Paddy, peered around his womenfolk's skirts.

Mick and Anne were of a similar age. They'd met each other weekly during Mass, and Anne always sat directly in front of him in catechism. She was still unwed, a pity that, since she was the third youngest of nine children of a neighboring tenant farmer.

He returned Anne's smile, and chuckled from the memories of her kicking him whenever he tugged her braid or scribbled on the table in front of her and the nuns blamed her. Or the time he took a bite of her bread when she wasn't looking and slid it back onto her plate. She was so dismayed he felt guilty. He snuck an extra slice from home to give to her the next time they had catechism. Why hadn't he ever married her?

Anne resituated Beth against her hip.

Mick jerked away from the wall. *By all that's holy.* Why

was he thinking about marriage? Because he enjoyed being married. Hadn't he done it twice before? Ah, but Anne's father was disapproving. He didn't want his daughter tied to a "lame" man. He wasn't feeble at all. Didn't he always work hard? *Always worked—always will.* Pains in his back throbbed down his leg. He stared down at his empty glass. He needed another whiskey. What would he ever do without it?

Ed strolled through the door as Mick took a step, and they collided. "Leaving, Mick? 'Tis just underway then, our funeral? Where're you headed?" His eyes narrowed.

"Empty glass and was 'bout to speak to Anne—Miss Brown."

"Fine girl, but her da?" Ed turned toward the Browns as they conversed with others. "He was a hothead."

The small group of mourners glanced at Ed and headed to Mrs. Muldoon's table.

Mick wagged his head. "You would know 'bout hotheads, 'tis sure. Have you any ideas on what's to be done with them?"

"Saints alive." Anne's eight-year-old brother, Paddy, leaned around his mam's skirt staring at Ed and Mick, his eyes wide and his jaw slack. "You surely don't look dead to me. You're alive. Why is there a wake for you—"

Anne shushed him.

"Are you right 'bout us being alive, boyo?" Ed moaned and swayed. He wiggled his hands above his head.

Paddy yelped then skedaddled out the cottage door.

"Aw, Ed, what'd you say that for?" Mick turned to peer outside.

"'Twas only funning with him." Ed followed.

"Edward and Micheál Muldoon, come away from that door at once!" Their petite mother had the screech of a seagull. High, piercing, and difficult to ignore. "Our friends are here to say thee farewell. You're not going out, or me name isn't Mrs. Martha Muldoon."

The mourners, dressed in black, fell silent and turned their faces toward Mrs. Muldoon's potential fugitive sons.

Mick's ears burned. "Mam, we aren't going anywhere. I promise you. 'Bout to explain to young Paddy Brown why we're having a wake though we're not dead. He thought he'd find us laid out here, being ignorant of our custom of holding wakes when we sail to the west—"

"Because you're as good as dead?" Mam Muldoon's pitch rose to that alarming note of hysterics all her children recognized.

He sucked in a breath.

Kathleen scooted away from a guest and over to her brothers. "Calm yourself, Mam. All's well. Those of us who'll be leaving are still here with you." She wiped her neck and pinched her brothers.

"Ow." Mick rubbed his arm. Women. Unpredictable creatures.

Since peace returned between the Muldoon boys and their mother, the attentive mourners returned to their conversations. *This tale will entertain the town gossips for years, no doubt.*

"Ed, what'd you say to Paddy? You upset him. Where's your chair, and where have you been these past few days?"

"You sound like Orla, Lamb. Didn't you ask her where I was?" Ed sneered. "Purchasing me ship's voucher. Told you all at the pub I'd get me own, remember? Took longer than I planned."

Mick pushed him. "Orla said you must. You just got it?"

"'Twas difficult shopping and comparing costs." Ed shrugged. "I got me one, so let it be."

"Are you on our ship?" Kathleen's eyes widened. "The *Mona*?"

"Don't recall."

Orla joined the discussion and stood next to Mick. "Let me see your voucher then." She put one hand on her hip and held out her other to Ed.

Ed growled. "Don't have it with me, and you're not Mam. Go manage people. Everyone's a-grieving for us tonight."

"Bully." Mick sneered. "Managing is what Orla's doing with you."

Two members from the pub's band entered the cottage with their fiddle and the bodhrán drum with its stubby *beater*. The fiddler bowed. "Evening, Ed. Mick."

Mick nodded in return. "Evening, Tom. Thanks for joining us."

Kathleen addressed the fiddler. "Where're the chairs I asked you to bring? Where's Jim?" Her face fell. "We need the pipe. 'Tis not a good enough tune without the pipe."

"Jim's running late. He'll be here. We plan to stand, Kathleen. No need for chairs. You know I play me drum standing to hold it at the best angle."

"Get yourselves a drink then and follow me, and take a spot near the table." Orla led them to it.

Kathleen fanned herself and headed toward Mam Muldoon. "So, we must wait for Jim, and I'm that weary. Mam's needing me as well. Pardon please, I must get through—"

"Ow! That's me foot you trod upon." A guest half rose from her chair.

Mick laughed while he refilled his cup. *God love her, our little lamb.*

"Hush, now. The band is here. Me apologies." Kathleen wound her way through the gathering sitting willy-nilly, crammed together, and approached her mother.

Tall, thin Rory clasped Kathleen's hand as they encircled Mam Muldoon near the hearth. Mick could just make out Rory's words in the hushed room. "I'll be seeing to your needs, Mam, since Kathleen's leaving us. And a good job of it I'll do. Our John will visit you when the church allows him time away from his priestly duties."

Mam Muldoon wept into the shawl draped over her head

and shoulders. Kathleen wrapped her arms around her mother and rested her face against her head.

"Mam's receiving comfort now." Mick turned back to Ed and discovered he stood by the table, speaking to the musicians. He took a swallow of his fresh whiskey and swung around in search of the Browns.

Anne remained nearby with her green gaze on him. She blushed and glanced down, still a demure person, even as a spinster. Then she screamed for all she was worth, piercing his ears.

Mick jumped away from her, splattering his full glass onto the floor. He searched for what frightened her in time to see a large rat scuttle across the toe of his boot. "Holy—"

Anne squealed again and slid behind Mick while still holding Beth. The tiny girl grasped his shoulder. "I don't like it."

Mam Muldoon's gray tabby cat tore through the open doorway in pursuit of the rat. Family and neighbors scrambled out of the animals' paths with such shrieks and nimbleness Mick never imagined he'd witness. People jumped out of the way, or over and onto chairs, then out the door—if they were near enough to it. They vacated the cottage quick as a wink in their panic.

The rat zigzagged amongst the furniture and between the feet of those who hesitated to move. It wiggled under Mam Muldoon's now-vacant, fancy stuffed chair.

The spectacle captivated him, and he froze against the wall with the Browns. He craned his neck to check outside for Mam's whereabouts. Orla accompanied her.

Even the screams of the crowd hadn't deterred the tabby's hunt. Single-minded, she focused on that rat without a concern for anyone who may trod upon her tail. She hunched into a stalk—tense, with her head down. The tabby flattened her ears. She scanned the floor, pupils dilated as her fuzzed-up tail twitched this way and that.

Anne remained behind Mick with Beth in her arms, shushing the young girl's whimpers. She peeked around him and whispered, "Think she'll get it?"

"'Tis sure. Mam's tabby is an expert hunter." Mick stared at the marvelous predator of rodents. "But I wish I'd Da's *shillelagh* with me to give it a quick whack upon its head."

"You'd surely crush it then. I couldn't. I abhor it when cats kill things. Yet I can't stop watching. Rats are the most detestable of all God's creatures."

"Aye, we all detest rats for being the devil's tools." Mick wanted to help the cat, then noticed his brother sneaking up behind her. "Ho—"

Ed pounced on the tabby, wound tight as a spring. Her reaction was immediate and vicious in her surprise.

The cat clawed, wailed, growled, everything cats ever do when foiled or frightened, causing the mourners to shout and laugh during the attack while dogs barked in the distance.

Mick glanced at Anne clamping her hand over her mouth, and at Beth with her eyes big as Mam's doily. He howled with laughter. Ed wasn't the brightest fella, was he? "Me brother's such a dolt. He deserves that."

Ed dropped the writhing cat beside the door, and the tabby raced outside, past all the people wobbling in hysterics. He wiped his scratched and bloodied hands on his shirt. His hair was mussed and his face bright pink as he inspected his tattered sleeves.

Orla poked her head into the cottage. "Why'd you do it, Ed? Did you think to be courageous or only your dim-witted, blockheaded self?"

"Something had to be done. Everyone's outside waiting for the *gall-luch* to leave or get killed. The *gall-luch* wouldn't move out of its hiding place if the cat continued to hunt it."

"Yeah, and where's the rat now, you fool?" Orla stopped within the doorway and scanned the floor.

"Underneath Mam's chair." Ed strolled to the chair and tipped it back. "What? That sly creature."

"Thanks, Ed. Now the family must get the rat. Tabby was the best way to find it." Orla stepped into the house. "Start your searching, everyone."

The Muldoon family examined every nook and cranny for the whereabouts of the rat, even in Mam's bedroom. They scooted furniture, pawed through clothing, and eyed cracks or holes in the walls for any traces of where it could've escaped but found nothing.

Kathleen waited inside the doorway with her mother. "It could've run out the door whilst everyone was hooting and hollering."

Orla bid the guests to enter, but even her mam wasn't attracted to Orla's enticement of food and drink until they found the rodent and dealt with it. Orla clapped her hands. "Saints alive. The food."

Mick stood nearest to the table of offerings. He budged the cockeyed lid of Mrs. Gilhooley's basket. "*Gall-luch.*" Inside, it feasted on her new concoction and didn't notice the curious human peering from above. Mick plopped the lid down tight. The basket jiggled beneath his palm.

Mrs. Gilhooley stomped to her basket. "That creature is inside? Chewing up me newest experiment before anyone could get a taste of it?" Her face reddened, her lower lip trembled, and a tear trickled down her cheek. "'Tis a crying shame."

Mick clamped both hands over the lid while Orla, Ed, Kathleen, and Mrs. Wiggins circled him and the jerking basket.

Mrs. Wiggins raised her face to heaven. "'Tis God's will, methinks."

Mrs. Gilhooley glowered at her neighbor. "Shush your mouth. You're not a true friend."

"Now, Mrs. Wiggins. You're joking with her, aye?" Mick forced the basket to be still.

Mrs. Wiggins folded her arms. "Well, now. Think on it. 'Tis a new recipe, she said. We should watch over the *gall-luch*. If it dies, then we'll all be saved and celebrate our brush with death."

Mrs. Gilhooley clasped her throat. "I'd never do such evil by poisoning our neighbors."

Orla patted Mrs. Wiggins' shoulder. "Whilst 'tis true we detest the loathsome creatures, 'tis untrue that we believe Mrs. Gilhooley would poison us."

Ed dabbed at claw marks on his neck.

Orla scowled at him. "'Tis your fault, Ed. Carry the basket outside and deal with it."

"Don't blame me. I tried to help. Always blaming me, you are." Ed took the basket from under Mick's hands and kept his own hand clamped over the lid.

Mrs. Gilhooley followed Ed to the doorway, and Orla turned to Mrs. Wiggins. "'Tis a shame for you to say such things to your long-time neighbor. You went too far with your jealousy." Orla glanced over her shoulder. "I'm that glad Mam didn't hear you. 'Twas mirthful though. You're me favorite friend of hers."

"Always thought so." Mrs. Wiggins hugged Orla. "I'll miss you, I will. And you, Mick. You've been hatched too long a time to be alone, Orla. We'll be praying to the saints for you both to find spouses."

Mick grit his teeth. *Orla's scarf covers her face in public.* Without it, how would a man be interested in her?

"Thanks ever so, Mrs. Wiggins." Orla turned to the gathering outside. "Come in. The hullabaloo is over." She spoke above the commotion as they reentered the cottage. "'Tis sad to miss out on Mrs. Gilhooley's offering, though there're plenty of other tasty dishes and drink left for us."

Kathleen and Ed returned towing Mam Muldoon, and

Kathleen murmured to Orla. "Will you take over the wake? I wish to rest." She led their Mam to her favorite and only stuffed chair and sat in another beside her.

Orla gave her brothers a puzzled expression.

"Poor Lamb. It seems she's ill." Mick scowled, as Ed shrugged.

With the rat and cat gone, folks meandered back into the Muldoon home, along with Jim the piper. He wove his way through the group as they chose seats. "Evening." He nodded to Mrs. Muldoon. "Pardon me tardiness. Me wife took ill. Hear I missed a rumpus."

Mam nodded. "That you did."

The group settled into their seats or took stances against the walls and hushed, looking to Mick as he extended his glass for a toast.

"Such fantastic stories will forever be told 'bout the Muldoon siblings' wake. When the cat and the *gall-luch* did battle, and of Mrs. Gilhooley's battered basket saving the day. 'Tis sure, Listowel won't ever forget us." He aimed his glass toward his neighbor and smiled. "To Mrs. Gilhooley."

Mrs. Gilhooley perked up and beamed.

Mick gave her a wink because even harpies need praise and notice.

Everyone but Mrs. Wiggins extended their glasses and toasted, "To Mrs. Gilhooley's battered basket."

Orla stood by the hearth and faced the mourners. "Well now, everything 'tis fine and ready. We're grateful to you all for coming to grieve us before we go. We're glad to hear your wise advice and pass on messages to your family in America." Orla took a deep breath. "As you know, Ed, Mick, Kathleen, and meself leave at dawn for Killarney. We'll visit our own brother, our Father John, for the final time. Then we're away to Queenstown to sail westward on the sea."

Mam Muldoon arranged a black shawl over her head and wailed as though her heart broke. "Four of me babes. Never to be seen again. Never again." She made the sign of the cross over her body then swayed back and forth. Her friends and neighbors followed her lead. "Lord, have mercy on us, Christ have mercy. May Saint Christopher watch over you, me precious babes."

Mick approached his mother, bent down, and kissed her cheek. "Sorry to grieve you so. I know how loss stabs the heart and rends the soul." Tears pooled in his eyes, and his mother's face swam in his vision.

"Me boyo, me frailest babe. You're well acquainted with suffering and grief, aye?" She squeezed his hands. "Promise me you'll find new love? And be watchful of the drink. 'Tis the ruin of many an Irishman. I know why you do it. Pain 'tis a terrible affliction." Mam Muldoon wiped her eyes. "You and Ed take care of Lamb." She glanced over at Orla. "And keep watch on that one. That girl keeps secrets."

"I know, Mam. But Orla always manages us well, aye? She's a dutiful sister."

"Aye." Mam Muldoon tugged him closer and whispered into his ear. "But who is there to manage Orla? God gave her the hard task of looking strange. Don't sit well with men to look at her scared face."

"Ah." A spasm seized Mick's back, and he released his mother's hands. "Me back."

Kathleen shushed him. "'Tis time for a song."

The fiddler readied his bow. He gave a nod, and the trio played a sad ballad, low and slow. The guests hummed along while candles flickered, and shadows fluttered against the walls. Mick headed for those shadows to hide from his memories.

Remembrances of dearly departed loved ones and stories of shipwrecks and troubles in foreign lands circulated amongst the gathering. He caught snippets of their comments.

Propped against the wall, Mick drifted between wakefulness and sleep, under the influence of drink and the lingering exhaustion of grief from leaving his home country and all he held dear in his heart.

Wails broke into his slumber. He jerked upright, bumped his head against the wall, and caught his empty glass before it landed on the earthen floor.

Villagers with family members who had earlier sailed to America called out their messages. They requested the Muldoon siblings to please pass them on, should they find their lost loved ones. Their list of known towns had peculiar names—New York was the only English name in the bunch, but Manhattan, or Massachusetts, Minnesota, Chicago, and Ontario?

Mam Muldoon wagged her head. "What could the strange names mean? A foreign land with foreign names, saints preserve them, if they hadn't already died on the ship."

"Who'd want to go to a place called Ontario?" Mrs. Gilhooley snorted.

A heated argument arose when two mourners couldn't agree if Ontario was in Canada or America.

The sleepy attendees mumbled and sat up, alerted by the kerfuffle. Joining sides about the whereabouts of Ontario, the game of knowledge ebbed and flowed around the room and split the group. His people knew little about the world outside their island and might have mispronounced the names—they weren't British or Gaelic names after all—but some declared the places were terrible.

"What does it matter?" Mam Muldoon wailed. "Wherever they go, they're still gone from me." She rocked back and forth with the shawl over her head, while the group joined in her wailing.

Mick's eyes burned, and his throat tightened. This custom of staying up all night created tired travelers in the morning. He was forsaking his wives and children. *Buried in the cold, damp ground.* Deserting the living and the dead in search of a better life. *Forgive me, macushlas.*

When the stars faded away and the cottage's interior lightened to gray with the impending sunrise, the mourners' wails stilled as the band sang a farewell song. The group hummed along to the end of the tune.

Mrs. Gilhooley approached Ed and his siblings then handed him a note. "'Tis for me nephew, Charlie," she whispered. "You remember him? 'Tis going on fifteen years since he left us, during the terrible Great Hunger. Charlie was fifteen. He'd remember you, surely."

"Aye, we knew each other."

Mrs. Gilhooley blew into her kerchief. "We got one message from him. Did I tell you?"

"You did." Ed slid her note into his grimy coat pocket.

"He settled in a place called the Manhattan." She shivered. "Sounds dreadful. Thought you could look him up. If he's still alive. For pity's sake, whoever heard of a British colony without British names?"

Orla laid her hand on Mrs. Gilhooley's shoulder. "America isn't a British colony now. They went to war a long time ago and broke away from the British. You remember that. 'Tis one reason we wish to go there, along with many others." Orla glanced at Mick.

"So, 'tis one grand reason to like America. And, if Charlie's still alive, then 'tis another." Mrs. Gilhooley turned away and sat beside her sleepy adult daughter.

"Sunrise at last." Orla stood and crossed herself. The gathering followed her example. "Time for us to go. Mam, we love you, and we'll always remember you in our hearts." She and her siblings hugged and kissed their mam. They spoke farewells to their other siblings remaining in Ireland.

"Rory." Mick smacked his younger brother on the back. "I know you'll take good care of Mam and the farm."

Rory tousled Mick's hair. "Me brother is now a dead man.

Never believed I'd see the day you'd emigrate, 'tis sure. May God be with you."

"And also with you." Mick smoothed his hair and donned his scruffy, woolen tam with its low brim. He glanced at Anne near the doorway, still holding her sleeping sister, and she gave him a tiny nod. Her green eyes shimmered with unshed tears.

Orla nudged Mick's arm and addressed the group. "Those who want to follow us, we're away to the station."

The mourners who remained until sunrise donned their coats and capes, while the emigrants collected their few belongings tied up in various sorts of carriers.

Kathleen dabbed at her tears and hugged their mother for the final time. Both women shook with emotion.

Orla stuffed her tattered coin purse into the bodice of her dress and smiled at her mother. "I'll forever treasure your reticule, Mam. You're the best mother a girl could have." She turned to follow Ed and Mick. A few feet outside the entrance, she took a sidestep. "Kathleen, watch your step. Don't slip on the tail. Looks to be our tabby's breakfast."

"Holy saints." Kathleen shuddered. "I hope there won't be a *gall-luch* on the ship."

The gray tabby licked her paw then cleaned her whiskers under a bush near the rat's remains.

"Good tabby." Mick took Kathleen's hand after she waved back at their mother. "Come with me, Lamb." He limped after the group heading down the hill.

Orla huffed. "Why didn't you kill the creature, Ed? Or is it a different *gall-luch*?"

"Me plan was to kill it. Took the basket inside the barn to grab a shovel. Guess 'twas when me back was turned, it escaped, for when I smashed the basket, 'twas empty." Ed called out, "Mrs. Gilhooley, 'tis sorry I am for destroying your basket trap. Left what remains of it beside the barn door, should you be wanting to keep it as a shrine for yourself. After all, you saved the day."

Mrs. Wiggins fluttered her hand. "Needed destroying, that thing, so it wouldn't become a shrine for saving the day. That loathsome *gall-luch* climbed inside. And if we ever saw Mrs. Gilhooley bringing that basket to another gathering, she'd be the one hit with a shovel, becoming a noteworthy murder in our village."

"True, that." Mick chuckled.

Powerful gusts of wind fanned puffy clouds across the late summer sky. Their shadows crossed over the faces of the small convoy of family and friends headed down the hill toward Listowel's new train station.

Mick paused and turned back to capture a last memory of his family's farm. His mother fluttered her scarf from the doorway, leaning on her shillelagh, with Rory supporting her. Would it be worth the leaving? Would he find a thriving life without the curse of Mister Death?

5

METAL MONSTER RIDE

There's no straight road in Ireland, 'tis true, nor tracks neither.
Mick

L istowel's Train Station
Mick halted to remove an object from his boot's
sole. Wasn't his limp bad enough without a stone
making him wobble? "Go ahead, Kathleen. I'll catch up." He
waved his siblings towards the train station. With their backs
turned, he snuck a swig of whiskey and sealed the bottle tight.

Amid farmland in the Muldoon's town of Listowel, the
train switchyard directed travel in Ireland. *Would've starved
without some employment with the rails.* Listowel's hub lay in the
southwest portion of Ireland, a crossroads to switch and direct
trains going north, even as far as Belfast, the British-ruled
section of Ireland. Mick spat and wiped his lip with his sleeve.

Metal monsters with incredible horsepower, trains. Riding
south went to the seaports, and further down the tracks on
Ireland's Southwest Coast lay the Muldoon's destination of
Queenstown. *Will be aboard the ship tomorrow.* Once there, the
trains switched eastward to the capital city of Dublin located
further up Ireland's east coast.

This first leg of their trip headed south, toward Killarney, the home of Mick's favorite brother, and priest, John. Excitement bubbled inside his spirit. Mick straightened and joined up with the convoy of family and friends approaching the station.

Orla, in her usual manner of covering her face with her shawl when out in public, climbed onto the platform first. Ed and Kathleen joined her. They thanked the well-wishers, gave handshakes or hugs as requested, and said more fare-thee-wells.

Mick pointed toward the board listing all the departure times. "I'll be getting our tickets to Killarney. Return in a shake of a lamb's tail." He left the swarm of travelers and the chaos on the platform to scan the list and found the train to Killarney. After giving the ticket agent his name, he counted the four discounted tickets Will had left for him.

"Where do we go?" Ed adjusted his tam.

"Track three, Ed. Departs in five minutes." Mick's siblings hastened to him. The four wove through the small gathering of travelers who watched for or boarded transportation to their own destinies.

Most passengers on the platform waited for the train to Queenstown, but the train going to Killarney attracted a smaller group.

Woot, woot. Steam swirled overhead and circled around the traveler's legs while the Muldoon friends and family stepped away from the train toward home.

Kathleen yawned. "To bed for the fortunate ones, or to work for the other poor souls."

McDonnell, the conductor, stood at the doorway. "All aboard." He helped older folk with their bags up the steps. Would he miss the smell of coal and grease, or would he smell it again in America?

Mick glanced at Kathleen. "Plan to get work on the trains in the city of Manhattan." He stretched and resituated his horse's old feedbag to his other shoulder. His bottles clinked. He must be careful not to break them, or he'd end up with wet pants and smelling like a drunk in the pub on a Friday night.

After the conductor punched their tickets, they settled on hardwood benches facing each other. The passenger cars of third class were wide open and without storage for bags. Orla set her former seed bag on the floor between her feet. Ed had packed his items in a threadbare and patched shirt. He propped it against the seat for a pillow. Kathleen placed Mam's old quilt, which she said held a change of clothes and a few loaves of bread, on the bench between her and Ed. *Only God knows what Ed packed in that shirt. Him and Orla keep secrets.* Those two were more alike than he'd realized.

Mick searched for a place to stash his smelly feed sack. Settling it between his leg and the wall, he supported it with his calf to keep the bottles from rattling.

Kathleen and Ed dozed off soon after departure. *The train rocks and rolls like a cradle with a babe.* Kathleen was flushed with her head against Ed's shoulder. Ed snored softly, his head tilted back and his jaw slack.

Orla glanced around and loosened her shawl from around her face. An infant cried, and a young girl across the aisle squealed.

The girl scrambled onto her mother's lap. "A witch over there, Mam, look. She has white eyes."

"Hush, girl." Her mother hissed. "She's no such thing. Having strange eyes and being disfigured don't make people witches. Don't look at her."

Mick cringed and waited for Orla's response. He stared at her hands gripping her shawl with white knuckles, then at her face. Her focus was on something far away in her thoughts. "Orla—"

"Am accustomed to it. Children speak their thoughts." She pursed her lips and took a deep breath. Her scarf hung free across her thin shoulders, ready to snatch up.

Best change the subject. He cleared his throat. "I must confess something to someone. Might as well be you."

Orla's eyes widened. "What? Go to confession then. For heaven's sake."

"Nah, isn't a sin exactly. More of a surprise. Happened last night. I want to tell it and get your thoughts. Will you hear me out?"

"Last night?" She fluttered her fingers. "Go on then, if you must."

"I nearly asked Anne Brown to come with us."

Orla's pale brows disappeared under her lace cap, and her mouth dropped open. "Why?"

"Always liked her. She's a kind woman. Pity her, being a spinster." He placed his elbows on his knees. "I feel guilty for thinking of marrying anyone only a month after losing me beautiful Fiona. What's wrong with me? I should be wallowing in me sorrow still." He gulped hard. It seemed he had a whole egg with its shell intact stuck inside his throat.

"Boyo." Orla fingered her pointy chin for a few seconds. "As far as I could tell, you always enjoyed being a husband, aye?"

He nodded. "I enjoy marriage very much. Don't wish to be alone."

"You're made for it. You've been married twice since you were eighteen and had a family soon after. You've not been alone. Pity they all departed this world so young." Orla crossed herself. "Mam and Da wanted you to have the advantage of the provision from the farm. Sure, and the law says inheritors must rent a parcel of land from an English landlord—"

Mick spat.

She snorted. "Spitting won't rid us of the English. So you'd an entire house for your family, not like the rest of us all crammed together inside Mam's and Da's cottage. Me heart wants to burst with joy from the thought of no longer sharing a bed with Kathleen. What was I speaking of?"

"How I was the beneficiary of the land and family cottage. Terrible thing being that the Crown forbids the rest of you to own land as Catholics."

Orla grimaced and smoothed her shawl. "Aye, with our family system in Ireland being what 'tis with the rest of us siblings striving through life with no work or meager pay at best. And without marriage. What's left for us? The work-house. Or to immigrate. You have the choice of remarrying and caring for a spinster and her family."

"I know not to remarry here, or I couldn't go to America."

"Made sense you chose to go. Give your heart some time to heal. You always were the best choice for our village women, brother. Add your handsome face to your farm—your looks being like Mam's. And a kind heart in your chest. Well, it all means no lady can resist you. Your painful condition never kept you from working and providing. Even with your limp. You fathered several children, so no doubts you can make a family."

"Who all went away to heaven because of Mister Death's curse. Shall I be daft to remarry?" He breathed in deep to keep grief at bay.

"Ah, now, Mick. They're all gone because of the illnesses and hunger killing off our people."

"Wicked Crown. Must've been their plan. They've split our family and created havoc between us as well."

Orla glanced across at Ed and lowered her voice. "Good thing Ed is fond of you. Always dreaded to visit your home and find a knife in your back. He wanted the farm that bad for himself."

Mick recoiled. "Sister, you have a dark side I never knew of, don't you now?"

She shook her head. "And you have a bright side I never

understood. Let nothing change you. The world needs people like you to find the best in them."

"Ah, go on with you." He swiped his hand at her.

"Don't wish for me praise? Well now, me and Ed, we're tougher. Had to be. We learnt wariness. You were sheltered from most of the evil in the world."

"Sheltered? I experienced many horrors."

"You should rest up, Mick." Orla folded her shawl into a pillow, placed it on the bench back, and laid her head against it. "Me own eyes feel like burning coals from that sleepless night."

He rested his shoulder against the chilly wall. *Please God, no nightmares.* He closed his eyes, then let the train soothe him to sleep with its rocking.

———

Sharp pains in Mick's shoulder popped him out of a sound sleep. Squirming out of his corner, he unfolded his arms and forced his eyes open.

Orla stared through the window at the lush green landscape and stone walls rushing past. She caught his gaze. "Couldn't sleep much meself, I'm that excited to be away." Her glance slid to Kathleen and Ed.

They still slept. It was as good a time as he'd ever get to question Orla about thoughts that niggled at him. "Been wondering, why d'you let Kathleen take on the plans for the wake? 'Tisn't your way."

Orla pulled out her delicate lace travel cap from a hidden pocket in her skirt and slipped it back on. "For all the love in me heart for her, I can't take her on as a dependent."

"Dependent?"

"Aye, we must all earn a living when we arrive." Orla stared at her hands. "We won't have a farm or family members to support us. We're the first there. All of us, and I mean Kathleen, will need to work our own way. I told her so before we left. She looked shocked at first, then she agreed."

"Of course she would be alarmed, having never supported herself."

Orla folded her arms and tucked her cloak tighter across her body. "You seemed to think ahead 'bout how you'd earn your way. You didn't think you'd live on me money, and I was planning to take care of you." Her eyes narrowed. "I promised to get us away, but not to house and feed us forever. Have me own dreams."

He blinked. "Truly, I don't expect that from you. Got me reference from Will. The letter doesn't spell out 'twas temporary help. Plan to find work with the trains in Manhattan."

"Aye, there's that. You got your letter. But Kathleen has none. She took care of Mam and the house, helping to run a home with the ten, then eight of us. Should count for experience. Told her she ought to apply as a housekeeper or scullery maid, with those being her only skills. God knows she's an innocent."

"Sounds reasonable. Will you do that as well?"

Orla pursed her lips and shrugged. The train chugged along the tracks with its load of sleeping passengers while she fixed her gaze out the window again.

Why was his question difficult for her?

She cocked her head. "I may do, as Kathleen and I shared the duties. I can manage a staff. Don't have much trouble speaking what's in me mind, do I?"

"And me sisters never needed to kiss the Blarney Stone for the gift of gab." He winked and relaxed again.

"Nah, never did. Been thinking of me number skills being good. As you and Ed know, I secretly kept the books for the railway." Orla glanced behind her then turned to Mick. "Answer me this. Why are men flummoxed at women knowing how to work numbers? Why should we not have their business skills?"

"Don't know. Never bothered me. What does puzzle me is how you can see, read, or hear something once and never forget it. Now that there is pure fright."

Orla smiled. "Da was like that. Me mind works the same way. Pity 'tis naught anything I can teach. Wish I could earn a fancy living and make lots of money by teaching others how to do it."

"You often speak of living fancy. Why?"

"Money is freedom. If I could teach people how to remember everything they read or hear, I'd have enough money for the rest of me life. I'd never need to work or . . . Got a glimpse of living with lots of money—"

"Lots of money?" Ed held Kathleen's head against his shoulder. "What did you glimpse?"

Orla lifted her chin. "No business of yours."

"You said it with us sitting where we could hear you." Ed smirked. "Women. Irritable creatures."

"And that's why good women don't like you. You're a tyrant, even to your good sisters."

"Yeah, let's talk about good or moral or shameful. What do you say, sister?"

"Let's not." Mick squirmed in his seat. "Don't like the tone of this conversation." *What's Ed doing taunting Orla?* He must suspect something bad.

"Let's speak of good men." Kathleen pushed against Ed's shoulder and righted her crooked lace cap. "Our da for instance. I'm reminded of something I want to ask 'bout."

Thank God for Kathleen's sidetracking ways. "What is it, Lamb?"

"So, 'tis 'bout when you were born, Mick, on the Night of the Big Wind, before an Gorta Mór."

Mick gasped. "The cursed black years of blight and starvation? 'Twas shocking how Grandfather had the 'sight' and got the warning of that hideous time and dreadful night before it happened. Aye?"

Orla snorted. "Haven't we've all heard the tales of his gift of the 'sight?' If you—"

"Me question is not 'bout the 'sight.'" Kathleen huffed. "Me memory 'tis always a skittish thing at best, but I was born long after the storm. And the family tales have faded, just as those of our John's poor twin. Daniel died at one-years-old. God rest his soul."

Mick crossed his chest in unison with his siblings. "Aye, God rest his poor soul." His brain swirled like Mam's hands mixing bread as he tried to track Kathleen's thought patterns.

Kathleen rearranged her cloak then held up her fingers. "So Ed was three, and Rory wasn't born yet." She ticked off their birth order. "How old was James when he died?"

Orla scrunched up her face. "James wasn't born yet. He died as an infant during an Gorta Mór when England allowed us to starve. Why must we relive the tragedy of the Great Hunger as we're leaving Ireland? And why in heaven's name are you going through our siblings? You're as confusing as the flight of a fly."

"Alright then. Let me ask this. When I packed, Mam told me to fetch her old cloak to take on our journey. I dug through her storage chest. You know, the one by her bed? And look at it. The cloak had a few holes, but I darned it—"

"Kathleen." Orla glowered.

"Oh, aye." Kathleen plucked at her darned cloak. "Where was I?"

"Lamb." Ed smacked his head. "Get back to *Oíche na Gaoithe Móire.*"

"Edward don't shout at me. I'm trying to ask."

Ed glared. "Do it, then. We'll be a-wondering till we're dead what you want to know 'bout The Night of the Big Wind."

Mick massaged his temples. "I'm getting a headache whilst we wait."

Orla curled her lip. "Ed, your impatience is me least favorite characteristic. Without patience, you'll make horrible mistakes and harm other people."

"Me?" Ed's face reddened.

Kathleen hopped in her seat. "Now I remember what I was telling you. 'Twas when I found Da's diary."

"Da had a diary?" Kathleen's three siblings chimed together.

"Aye, he had real nice handwriting, easy to read—"

"Lamb." Mick swiped his jaw.

"Right. Me thoughts are all a jumble. Mam dozed off, so I wrapped Da's diary in her old cloak and snuck it into the chicken coop to get a glimpse of it."

"You took it from Mam?" Ed's mouth fell open.

"You always seemed such an angel." Mick grappled to come to terms with Kathleen's new persona.

Ed shook his finger at Orla. "There. That's why I don't trust women. First you, then her. Me good sisters are truly the devils—"

"What're you saying?" Kathleen asked, wide-eyed. "I didn't steal it."

Mick upthrust his palm. "Stifle it Ed, will you? Let's get back to Da's diary, Lamb."

Orla closed her eyes. "And if she doesn't ask now, we'll not hear it till Easter in *America*."

Woot! Woot! The train's brakes squealed as it slowed to a stop. The conductor announced, "Tralee. Off for Tralee." He addressed the Muldoons. "No need to switch trains for Killarney. You can stay aboard, for we're going straight through."

The young girl and her family across the aisle stood and gathered their bags. They frowned at the Muldoons as they moved toward the exit.

Kathleen brooded. "What did we do?"

Mick rummaged through his memory of their conversation for anything offensive they might have spoken. The young girl turned and stuck her tongue out at them as she exited. He waved at her.

Orla grunted. "Well, she's a creature. Mam would've popped us if we behaved in such a way."

Mick shrugged. "Aye, though when we're all together, we forget to mind our audience."

Orla draped her shawl over her face and folded her hands in her lap while the train idled. Greetings between the conductor and new passengers boarding the coach grew louder with footsteps and skirmishes amongst a few school children. They scrambled for seats near the entrance, under the watchful eyes of a nun.

The train whistle blew three times and the train jerked forward.

Orla lifted the scarf from her face. "Saints alive, Kathleen, let's get to your question."

"I wanted Ed to tell us what it was like on the Night of the Big Wind. Da wrote about the death and destruction, especially up north and in England."

Orla slapped her hands on her legs. "That's it? For heaven's sake, why didn't you just say so?"

"I did. I tried . . ." Kathleen stuck out her lip, and her eyes shimmered.

Mick scowled at Orla. "See what you've done to our little Lamb? Who's the impatient one? You'll get your answer, Lamb."

"Aye, me apologies." Orla wagged her head. "Go on, Ed, tell her what you remember."

"Being young, I only recall the terrifying parts of that devil's night." Ed moaned like a ghost. "I'll recite Da's tale of that wicked night as I can recall. It began with two bundled-up women strangers who arrived at our cottage. The sun dipped low, and the wind whistled down the chimney. I sat near the hearth with Da where we usually had a fire blazing."

Kathleen's eyes widened. "Where did the two women go?"

"They'd be with our Mam, you goose. Mick was born that night." Orla chuckled. "Must I tell you what they'd be doing?"

Ed frowned. "Ugh, don't you dare. Well, the two women blew through the door when Da opened it. It banged against the wall. I got a glimpse of the trees outside. Blown sideways, they were. That's when I became frightened."

"Who were the women?" Kathleen tipped her head.

"They were the village midwives. Don't know how they knew to come."

Orla grinned. "The town is small, and messages travel easy enough."

"Aye." Ed shrugged. "Those women were talking 'bout how they could barely walk in the wind. Even birds smashed into the cottages. The wind drove them against the stone walls and impaled them in the hedgerows. Some were never seen before. Such strange and bright-colored birds."

"Holy angels." Kathleen's eyes were round as the full moon.

Ed nodded. "'Twas believed they came from heaven itself, they were so peculiar. Then we heard they came from far-off countries. Anyways, Da said, 'You're shaking, me boyo. Come sit with your Da.' He took me up on his lap. Da held me tight all night long while the wind screeched louder and trees fell over with a crash. Well, 'twas mostly tree branches."

The train brakes screeched as it took a long curve. The siblings swayed to one side and grabbed the edges of their bench.

Mick huffed. "There's no straight road in Ireland 'tis true, nor uncurved tracks neither. But by all that's holy, this engineer can't calculate his speed well enough. 'Tis the third bad turn he's taken. I'm checking me whiskey bottles."

Ed grimaced. "We could've reported him if we were staying. Timmy would've written him up if he heard of an engineer driving this way."

Kathleen nudged Ed's arm. "Keep telling your tale. The wind felled branches."

"Aye, it blew all night. I asked Da if it was a *Bean Sidhe*."

"You knew of banshees as a small boyo?"

"Sure. I'd heard someone speak of them. We always remember what frightens us, aye? I thought it would come down the chimney and snatch us away. Da said God's own angel was guarding us and not to be frightened. When we heard wind whooshing in the chimney, he'd say, 'There's the angel's wings, flapping hard, whilst doing battle with the banshee.'"

Kathleen gaped. "Glad I wasn't born yet."

"I'd lean against Da and stare at the dark opening where our fire should've been. Da said, 'We can't have a fire, for the angel's wings will blow it out.' He was always a quick wit. He shouted above the wind, ''Tis only the wind, not to worry.' Then, we'd hear such a howling as never before, and I shivered with fright. He'd say, 'There's that foolish banshee a wailing, but what does the angel do?'"

Kathleen's mouth dropped open. "What?"

"I'd answer him, 'Battle the banshee to keep it away.' Then Da asked me to guess what was making the sounds we heard. Was it the wind, the banshee, or the angel? We made a great game of it. Then, near sunrise—"

"You didn't ever sleep?" Kathleen scrunched her face.

"Nah, 'twas noisy. Then came an eerie sound, a different kind of crying. Da took me from his knees and set me on the floor. I grabbed his leg to steady meself. Da stood just as Mam's bedroom door opened. A woman came towards us with a small bundle. He inspected what was in the blanket, took it from the woman, and brought it to me. High-pitched wails came out of it, and Da said, 'Here's your new brother.' Had the frights of you, Mick, for quite a time."

"*Eejit.*"

Ed patted his cheek. "Nah, thought you were a baby banshee. And that bright red fuzz on your head gave me jitters."

Mick pushed Ed's hand away. "Get away with you. Didn't you know your hair is the same as mine? You dimwit."

"Stop it." Orla raised her hand. "Ed, a brother is a boy. He couldn't be a banshee. They're females."

"All I knew was it screeched like a banshee, and it came during the battle with the banshee and the angel. Didn't pay much mind to a brother being male." Ed turned to Kathleen. "And banshees warn of approaching death. Many people died from that storm. Made sense."

Mick jolted in his seat and smacked his forehead. "Oh, ho! That explains it. Never occurred to me before. I was born on a night of death, and Mister Death has pestered me ever since." He was doubly cursed. "Born on the cusp of an Gorta Mór and the potato blight. I wonder if Mister Death sent that blight ahead for more destruction during Oíche na Gaoithe Mire?"

His siblings gawked but didn't comment.

"Can't you see it?"

Orla and Ed glowered at each other, and Kathleen snorted. "I see the coincidence." Kathleen patted Mick's knee. "But death comes to everyone. No one escapes it. Ed, how many died from the storm? Anyone from families we know?"

"Hundreds. Mostly up north and over in England. Think it was mainly Manchester where 'twas bad. We all had thoughts of judgment upon the Crown." Ed spat, joined by Mick.

Orla rolled her eyes. "As if spitting aids in resolving the Irish plight."

Kathleen rubbed her arms. "Holy saints, I've chill bumps. No one ever speaks 'bout it anymore. Maybe since 'twas nearly twenty-seven years ago?"

Ed shrugged. "Don't you remember? Mam mentions it every year on Mick's birthday."

"I remember that she mentions it." Kathleen pouted and turned toward the aisle. "No one tells the entire tale as you did."

Orla tapped Kathleen's shoulder. "I'm wondering what you did with Da's diary."

"Holy angels." Kathleen cupped her mouth. "I left it in the chicken coop. Rory came out to get eggs. I stuck it under a chicken in its nest. I meant to get it later."

Ed and Mick burst out laughing. Orla shook her head. "You and your forgetful ways. Might still have the chicken sitting on it, covered with chicken—"

"Hey ho, we're slowing down." Mick shifted on the bench to peer out the window.

The brakes squealed, and he craned his neck in search of the sign declaring their location.

Hedges, then vines of yellow flowers wound along a stone wall blurred past the window. A white wooden sign with black, hand-painted lettering appeared on the end of the wall. *Killarney*. The area opened wide onto a platform of slightly warped and weathered wood as the conductor entered their car and announced their stop.

Orla wound her shawl over her lace-capped head, tucking it tight across her face below her eyes. "Kathleen, put your lace on. We'll be going into the church. And may Christ have mercy upon me."

Kathleen donned her lace cap. "Mercy for what?"

Orla averted her face.

Ed and Kathleen scooted out of their seats, collected their various bags, then toted them on their shoulders down the aisle toward the exit.

Mick resituated his bag, careful with the bottles, while Orla inspected her re-used seed bag. "Orla, when was the last time you went to confession and Mass?"

She clasped the edges of her frayed bag with shaky fingers. "Don't recall. Hope this bag holds up on the trip. Me money is inside me bodice."

"Changing the subject, yeah? Do you expect John to be waiting for us at the station?"

"Nah, he's a priest now. Must we go straight into St. Mary's?" She shoved her face inches from his. "If so, I'll be keeping watch for lightning strikes, and don't stand nigh me."

KILLARNEY KIN

Limping along and holding up a droopy woman, I am
Mick

Killarney, County Kerry
Mick slid his shabby tam over his head as he
and Orla shuffled down the aisle, past the empty
seats toward the exit. The two thanked the conductor as Orla
strode onto the wooden platform and Mick limped down the
steps.

Orla waited for him while she checked her scarf
shielding her cheeks and hid her scarred eyebrow with her
hair. Her long pale lashes glinted in the late summer
sunshine.

"Over there." He pointed toward the yellow-trimmed
stone ticket house partially covered with purple floral vines. Its
sweet aroma wafted past his nose. Ed and Kathleen stood near
the station house and reviewed the train schedule posted next
to the open ticket window.

Orla surveyed the area. "No John."

Mick embraced his sack against his chest and slowly
swirled in a circle, searching the entire platform. Not another

soul in sight. He rolled his neck to wiggle out the stiffness. "Was hoping he'd meet us."

Ed turned away from the train schedule to Orla and Mick. "We should return by half past two o'clock for the connecting train to Queenstown. Gives us 'bout three hours to visit with John."

Kathleen traced the departure times with her finger. "'Tis true. Or else we must wait till the last one at five o'clock. Orla, you said the room in a boarding house you reserved for us is at the harbor, aye?" She grabbed her lace cap as a gust of wind attempted to steal it away and coughed. "Me throat is dry. This wind makes it worse. Do you think John will set us a tea?"

"I dearly hope not." Orla scrutinized the sky. "We must go inside the church to have tea. Won't go inside for anyone."

"Should be inside the presbytery, Orla. You'll not go in? Even for our John?" Kathleen's eyes widened. She slipped her hand inside her blouse, tugged out her rosary, and fondled the beads. "Lord, have mercy on us."

Ed smirked. "You're such a contrarian, Orla. Like your confirmation name. Mary, Mary, quite contrary. 'Tis sure the rest of us would like a bit of tea, yeah?"

"Aye, Ed, and stop calling Orla that horrible nickname from schooldays." Mick sneered. "Our John always minds his manners. We can expect tea with him. Let's be on our way then." He jerked his head toward the carriage route to their left.

The four Muldoons rearranged their bags and sacks to more comfortable positions, either onto their shoulders or backs for roving. The women's cloaks and shawls flapped in the breeze as they headed toward the center of town. Mick shuffled behind, his boots scraping on the worn pathway and against the pebbles along the roadside.

"'Tis not a quick jaunt. Nor is it a very long jaunt. Been here a few times before." Ed glanced back.

Mick scratched his ear. "Didn't know you were. When?"

"Aye, don't never tell you all me business, now do I? And not going to tell you it now."

"Sheesh." Mick bumped his elbow against the stone wall. "Narrow carriage roads have little room for pedestrians if a cart or two comes through, aye? Forces us to keep to our carts and horses to avoid banging up our limbs." He twisted around to catch sight of his sisters. "Let's all keep a listen for carts."

Ed slapped Mick's shoulder. "You got to be quiet enough to hear them coming, brother."

A moment later, two carriages approached from both directions. The Muldoons flattened themselves up against the stone wall, like Mam's tabby flattening her ears, and greeted the passerby. He chuckled. The passing carts hauled chickens and eggs, and milk to sell at market. The Muldoons greeted a few shepherds moving their flocks and women wearing voluminous skirts covered by aprons. Vegetables filled their baskets tied to their backs on their return from market. *How do they manage such heavy loads?*

"I feel warm." Kathleen dabbed at her face.

"A sunny Irish day, yeah?" Mick removed his cap and wiped his brow. "Be needing a drink soon. How much further, Ed? Lamb is wilted." He stopped for another swig of whiskey from his sack while he waited for her.

"Not far, now." Ed shook his head. "Man, can't you wait for that? Guess not. 'Twill always be the drink for you, aye?"

"And you know why, Ed." Nothing will ever change about his twisted back or the tragedies he'd witnessed.

"See those trees above the thatch?" Ed indicated them. "We're coming upon the edge of the woods. 'Tis a marker for St. Mary's, grandly nestled there. We'll see the spire soon. Last time I laid me eyes on it, they were renovating."

Orla halted and inspected Kathleen. "You don't look well. I can purchase you a ticket home." She turned to Mick and Ed. "Let's hold up a moment, aye?"

"No need." Kathleen unclasped her cloak. "Just a bit warm. I'll be fine." She dragged her feet, and her dusty shoe skipped a stone. "How much longer? I need me thirst quenched something fierce."

"Do you have a fever, Kathleen?" Orla lay her hand against her sister's forehead. "Oh, aye."

"Take a swig of Mick's whiskey." Ed reached out and jiggled Mick's feed sack. *Clink.* "Sure enough, he has plenty to share."

Mick twisted away. "Don't be offering Kathleen whiskey. Lamb, you're shivering."

"Take hold of me, Lamb." Orla offered her elbow. "Ed says we'll be there soon." She stared at the distant horizon and fidgeted with her face covering.

Kathleen followed her gaze. "You don't feel well either, Orla? Are you in dread of—"

"What I got making me ill differs from yours and make no mistake."

"You may rub my worry pearlswhilst we say a prayer." Kathleen fondled her beads.

"Worry pearls?" Orla cringed away. "Those are for praying. You do it, Little Lamb. No need for me fingers to touch those."

Kathleen pouted. "They're for all of us. Prayers and worries are the same things."

The group went three hundred feet more where the stone walls parted. The carriage road led to the center of Killarney and the town's marketplace. Even though it was late morning, stragglers still meandered in search of bargains. In the distance stood the great, green woods, and farther away, the blue hills.

"There." Mick pointed at the church spire. At that moment, the bell chimed eleven o'clock. "'Tis like a greeting to us, just when we arrived to see our brother. It beckons us closer."

Orla laughed. "And you're a fanciful man."

"Can we sit for a spell? I'm hot." She wiped her damp temples with her shawl.

Ed scoffed. "'Tis only a few more steps, Kathleen. Surely, you can wait. We have little time before we must head back to catch our train."

"Here." Mick offered his elbow. "I'll hold your left arm, and Orla can hold the right." He switched his bag and wove his arm through Kathleen's, tugging his sisters forward. He surveyed the market.

The townspeople stopped their activities to stare at the foursome. *Are we the curiosities of the day?* Mick switched his attention to his family. On a sweet summer's day, Orla half covered her face, and Kathleen withered like a thirsty flower. Then there was Ed, scowling at people. *And meself, limping along and holding up a droopy woman, I am.* He chuckled at his imaginings of the townspeople's opinions.

"You find something enjoyable?" Orla glared at Mick over the top of Kathleen's head. "'Tis naught anything humorous here."

"What would that rude group of women, all huddled together and whispering whilst they point at us, think if I shouted out, 'Hey-ho, she's our own lamb whose lips never touch the drink,' yeah?" Mick grinned.

Orla smirked. "I care little for village women's opinions."

Ed beckoned them in the direction of the church. "Keep moving. Time's a-wasting." He passed the market and the shops, took a turn at the corner of Keoghan's Pub, and continued down the street. The steeple served as a perfect beacon and compass for the travelers. Once they passed through the town's center, a pastoral scene with St. Mary's in its center appeared. The nearer they drew, the more imposing the church grew.

Mick reached under his cap and scratched his damp forehead. *Imposing churches make you feel the size of a lowly ant.*

The four halted outside the black iron gate and gawked through the iron bars of the fence to survey St. Mary's well-manicured grounds.

"Look at those." Mick indicated the cemetery on the western side. Many headstones appeared new and only slightly weathered compared to other markers. Moss grew on the north sides of the new stones.

"Headstones." Orla shivered.

"Mister Death strikes again. Don't like this at all. May God send His holy angels to protect us." Mick's body tensed. He shook his head, released his grip on the fence, and stepped back as his heart pounded. He craved to run away, but he wanted to see John even more. He trembled with the battle.

Ed slapped him on the back. "Ho, Mick. Steady there. 'Tis only the Great Hunger victims in those graves. Been here 'bout ten years. We know many died, don't we now? Shouldn't shock you senseless."

Kathleen clutched her bag against her chest, her eyes wide. "Do you have frights of the graves or of dead people, Mick?"

"Naught to be frightened of, is there?" Ed shook Mick's shoulder. "No need to run off now."

"'Tis not the dead. 'Tis Mister Death himself who frightens me. Don't trust him."

Orla faced the stone building. "Maybe I'm not in dread of the graves, or Mister Death, but there's more to dread than the dead." She examined the scarce wispy clouds then the cathedral's roof. "'Tis God's house. He lives there. Get John and bring him out. I'll wait here."

"You believe in Mister Death, Orla?" Kathleen's brows went up. "I never knew. You never said before." She stood on her tiptoes while she surveyed the cemetery. "Does he live in cemeteries then?"

Ed snarled. "Ninny. They're having you on—"

"Mister Death lives in the sky." Mick scrunched his sack in

his fist, and the bottles clinked. "Not on the ground and not in the graves neither."

Orla shrieked. "'Tis God, I fear, not Mister Death. I'll not tempt God to strike me dead should I dare to enter His own house. Me and Him are not friendly."

"I'm not entering His house neither." Ed folded his arms. "I agree with Orla. 'Tis God's place. Not been to confession in years, so God and I aren't on right terms. Not budging in case He's in there today."

Mick hissed. "You said you'd been here before, but you didn't go in to see our brother?"

"No. Not me reason for being here."

"What was your—"

"Me own flesh and blood shaming me." Kathleen jabbed Ed and Orla with her skinny finger. "Da should come back and get you from his grave. Never mind what Mister Death might do to you. God would forgive you of your sins if you did your duty, He would. 'Tis what comes of not going to confession and Mass regularly." She reached out to Mick. "Are you coming in with me?"

"Staying here." Mick darted glances around the church and graveyard. "Must stay alert for Mister Death or an angel."

"Angels would be inside the church, Mick. Come on, 'tis safer inside from Mister Death, aye?" Kathleen pulled his hand.

Mick shook his head.

"Wait till our John hears of this." Kathleen dropped her bag and stomped off toward St. Mary's door, calling over her shoulder, "And I must be the one to tell him of our family's disgraceful condition." She stopped to cough. Nearly to the Gothic doors, she twirled around and hollered, "'Twill shame his priestly heart, 'tis sure." She coughed again, marched up the steps, and disappeared through the arched doorway.

Mick chewed his lip. "Well, he's our favorite brother, yet we can't tolerate entering. For shame. He's truly the best of us." His own affection for John was almost enough to keep him in Ireland.

Orla's eyes widened, transfixed on the church.

A flash of black material from behind the left corner of the church caught his attention. *Is John playing with us?* Mick stepped forward and paused. Black fabric flashed by the right corner. Was there more than one priest hiding behind the church?

Mick pointed. "Did you see that? Did you see John playing with us, a-hiding back there?" He craned his neck for another sighting. "He's a bit swift. Unless there's someone with him."

Ed jeered. "What's that you say? There's nary a person to see."

Mick turned to Orla. "You didn't see him? Hoping the angels see him then, if that's the devil."

Orla scrunched her shoulders and searched the sky. "Naught to worry 'bout yet."

"He's addlepated." Ed tipped his head toward Mick. "And he calls me dim-witted. You're not having us on, are you?"

"Saw him."

Ed sneered at Orla. "And you. Why're you staring at the sky? God lives inside the cathedral. No worries if you stay out here."

Mick turned around to inspect the building. No one outside. No one came through the doors. The sun shone in a now cloudless sky and the blackbirds flew their erratic patterns between the trees, where robins hopped beneath for worms. Finches chirped, and sheep bleated in the distance. "Aye, having one on you".

The world seemed right, but something felt wrong. Chill bumps prickled up his arms and neck. Mick spied another movement at the cathedral's entrance and held his breath. Kathleen beckoned. He let out a sigh and relaxed his shoulders. He'd best be careful with John. Mick cradled his sack tighter. *Must I explain me bottles? A new worry for me.*

Kathleen poked her head around the doorframe then reached behind her into the shadows. Mick shaded his brow to see better. Sure enough, she had ahold of John. They stood in the doorway, arm in arm. His John. Mick chuckled, and his heart swelled with joy.

John smiled back, and his blue eyes twinkled. Of all the Muldoon children, John was the most handsome, like their dark-haired da. Tall, gentle, kind, and tolerant, quiet-natured but quick-witted. John's clerical garb rendered him more distinguished than ever. He approached them, his black robe swirled around his legs, and his large silver crucifix swayed across his chest. He raised his arms wide. "Here you are at last. Welcome to me home at St. Mary's."

The three took a few steps toward John and Kathleen then stopped. *There may be a standoff here.* Ed had removed his cap. Mick yanked his off.

"Kathleen tells me you won't come in." John tsked. "I suspect something's amiss. Priests are knowing ones, don't you know? God tells us things, aye? Naught can sneak past us." He clasped his hands and tapped his foot.

Ed gulped and Orla turned paler than usual. Mick burst out laughing. "John, our own Father John. Can't believe they let you be a priest. 'Tis the church's gain and our loss for sure."

John skipped down the steps, and Mick almost forgot about his bag with glass treasure inside. He gripped it tight and embraced John with his other arm. It had been far too long since John was within reach.

Orla and Ed shuffled their bags and followed Mick's example. Kathleen joined in from behind for a family hug.

John sniffed. "I smell me some whiskey. Who could it be?" He ogled Mick. The siblings chuckled while Mick's cheeks burned.

When John asked about various families in the village and

friends from school days, they started to update him about the goings on.

Kathleen wilted again. Strands of her hair stuck to her forehead.

Mick rubbed her shoulder. "May we sit somewhere? Outside. Under the shade of the largest tree?"

John shared his plan to have tea with them in the rectory. "'Tis not exactly the church, although nigh and connected by a hall, but not the same, aye? Will it work?" He winked at Orla,

Orla blushed, and John offered his arm to Kathleen. "Then come, me macushla. Our little lamb." He led the group around the back of the church and showed them features of the cathedral's restoration work. They were nearer the graves at this point. "The graves of the Great Hunger victims. We shall never forget them." He made the sign of the cross, and the siblings copied him.

"Ah, John." Mick frowned. "Were you outside earlier, just before we arrived? Thought I saw a black robe behind the church."

John twisted sideways to peer back to Mick. "No. I'm the only one here today. I was in the confessional and came out when I heard footsteps. Believed 'twas me family fetching me. Such strange goings on lately. I'll share a bit 'bout it during our tea."

Orla glared at Mick. "Please, tell us your bits of news 'bout your church life, Father John. We have our own from home."

John led everyone into the sparsely furnished but efficient rectory. It contained four chairs, a table, and a small kitchen off the hall to the bedrooms. A plaque of the Ten Commandments, the Apostle's Creed, a large crucifix, and a portrait of Pope Pious IX adorned the walls.

"I expected this sort of room." Mick nodded.

John led Kathleen to a comfortable chair in the corner of

the room. A statue of the Virgin Mary stood on an altar of lit candles beside a closed door. Mick observed Orla for her reactions from being trapped in this religious setting.

Orla ogled a closed door. "Is that the door into the church?"

John grinned. "Orla, 'twill remain shut whilst you're here. Please take seats, and we'll have tea together."

After her serving of tea, Kathleen dozed off.

Their visit began sweet enough until John brought up the subject which he considered recent goings on. "Have you heard the church is sending a flood of priests to America? Although not all are welcomed. The need is great since countless Catholics emigrated there during the Great Hunger."

Mick's hopes swelled, and he touched John's hand resting on his knee. "Will you be going?"

"Not I."

Mick's hopes dissolved like a woodland mist running from the sun.

John folded his hands. "Bishop Moriarty got into the political fray last Sunday. He's sympathetic to the Crown, don't you know? His position is precarious between God, the church leadership, Crown politics, and the laity." John took a sip of tea and a bite of biscuit. "Need sustenance for this story I'm 'bout to tell. So, Bishop Moriarty preached a fiery homily about the recent trouble with the Fenian Guard, you know, planning an uprising—"

Ed choked on his tea, spewing it over Mick's shirt. Ed's face reddened to a purple hue, and Orla pounded his back.

Kathleen, roused from sleep, joined the siblings. "What's this 'bout the Fenians? Why's Ed coughing and purple? A sore throat?"

Mick scrutinized his brother. Ed had some mighty radical political ideas. Could he be a member? Maybe sympathetic to their cause? But what Irishman didn't want freedom? *'Tis always at high cost.* "Ed, you could get yourself arrested. The

Crown will kill Fenians during uprisings or lock them away forever in prison."

"Sounds like Ed, yeah." Orla sipped her tea and glowered at him.

John's eyes narrowed. "Things have settled down for now. Got something to tell me, Ed? Not as a priest but as your brother?"

Ed shook his head. "Nary a thing." He pounded his chest. "Swallowed down the wrong pipe."

Orla smirked. "There me brother goes, a-lying to a priest. And God Himself in the next room."

"But you'd tell me if you were a Fenian? I have a report with names from witnesses." John steepled his fingertips. "One man was named Edward and fit your description. 'Twasn't you then?"

Ed jumped to his feet and spat. "We shouldn't protest the Crown's treatment of us, their oppressed subjects, yeah? Should we roll over and take—"

"Enough." John raised his palms. "I understand your sentiments, but I don't condone the Fenians' actions. 'Tis a precarious and perilous thing being persecuted and oppressed."

Ed slumped onto his chair. "Leaving tomorrow anyways. I'll be involved with them no more."

"Take heed, me brothers and sisters." John regarded each one and folded his hands as in prayer. "Avoid the criminal element in *America*. I've heard tales of the Irish ruffians in New York City. Beware of the wicked who emigrate mixed in with the good. Not all people have pure motives for leaving their homeland. Bitter and angry people take all their ugliness within them to new lands as well." John shook his finger in the air. "Going to a better land doesn't improve a bitter heart. The wicked cause heartbreak wherever they live, and their targets are the weak and needy. Guard yourself from them, 'tis me warning to you."

A clock chimed once from across the room. "'Tis half past one o'clock—we must be away." Orla stood. "Kathleen, are you revived now? You're looking better for your rest."

Shattered pieces of Mick's heart dropped into his boots, with sorrow grasping and choking him. He rubbed his throat and chest. The farewell to John was one of the saddest things to do. How could he ever forget his own beloved John? It was another death. His thoughts blurred with the tears in his eyes, and he craved a drink.

John rose and reached out to Mick. "I feel the same, me brother. There's nothing to be done, is there?"

"No."

The four siblings were silent as they left the rectory and rounded the cathedral toward the cemetery. They'd head to the town center and then for the train station. Never to see their John again.

John led his family past the graves. Mick caught a flash of movement on the edge of his vision. He scanned the area and spied a swift swoosh of a black robe or cloak, a bright light flashed, and the robe disappeared behind a large headstone. His siblings continued ahead. No one else reacted to the supernatural display. Chills crept up Mick's back and neck then down his limbs. Was it Mister Death, and an angel doing battle behind the church? Had Mister Death come for John? *But he's found me. Must outrun that devil. But first . . .* He grappled for a bottle of blessed courage.

7

BELLY OF THE S. S. MONA

Our brother John was right, he was. There are criminals amongst us.
Mick

Qﾠueenstown Harbor, Ireland

At sunrise, a heavy blanket of fog cloaked the harbor, hushed and shrouded. Mick had visited the sea a few times as a boy. The pungent salt air caressed his face, the gulls screeched above, and waves pounded the shore, all announcing the whereabouts of the sea within the mist.

Kathleen followed Mick as they exited the boardinghouse near the docks amongst other travelers. "Terrible disappointment with it shrouding me first view of the sea. What if we can't catch up to Ed and Orla in this fog? Why'd they leave us so early?"

Mick shivered. He reached behind for Kathleen. "We'll find them. You needed your rest, and they went on ahead. Watch you don't take a tumble down the stairs. You've been a bit wobbly." Someone elbowed him in the side as they sped past while another jostled Kathleen into the stair rail. "Ho, watch yourselves, dolts."

"What's their rush?" Kathleen pulled out of his grasp. "You're squeezing me arm." She checked the pin clasping her layers of shawls. "Don't you ruin me favorite shawl whilst saving me."

"Well then, hold tight to me. With all the pushing and shoving going on, 'tis treacherous. Let's find Orla at the docks, as she instructed." He yanked off his cap and stuffed it into his pocket.

Kathleen clutched the back of Mick's coat.

"People want out of that God-forsaken boardinghouse, 'tis me guess. Horrible night. Hard floor. No mat, no heat."

"Feared for you, Mick. 'Twas a blessing to have a room, not like the other poor souls who went God knows where. Me bed sloped to one side, the feather mattress had lumps, and it itched. I suspect bedbugs. 'Twas not much better than the floorboards, I imagine."

"Hmm." He thought better of the floor after hearing about the mattress.

"Are we late? Orla left hours ago to secure a place in line for us. Do you know where Ed is?"

"We aren't late. Ed was off early to do business, he said. We're to meet them both at the docks." Mick glanced back. "Keep nigh."

Kathleen trailed him in the hurried crowd and tucked her bag between their bodies. "Did you know Orla didn't come to bed until the wee hours? Just as the cock crowed. She rolled against me till sunrise. Where did she sneak away to?"

Mick's head throbbed as if church bells rang inside his ears. He'd already drunk half a bottle of whiskey to keep the nightmares away, but the pain in his back persisted. "When we get to the docks, ask her yourself. See there, the mist is lifting."

In a swirl of fog, the S.S. *Mona* loomed before the two siblings. "Glory be, 'tis another monster made of metal for the sea." Mick's jaw slackened, but he kept up his uneven pace with the throng of fellow emigrants.

"Mick and Kathleen!"

Which Mick and Kathleen in this Irish crowd? He stood upon his toes in search of Ed.

"Muldoons." Ed jumped up and down.

Mick shouldered a large man to the side. "Let us through, you bruiser." With all the kicking, shoving, and yanking of clothing, it was a wonder he and Kathleen weren't scratched and naked when they reached Ed. Mick had never experienced such a tussle between the Irish to get from one place to the other.

Ed met them halfway. He grasped Mick's arm to raise him higher above the throng. "See our Orla there? Nigh the ship's clerk. 'Bout two dozen people between you. She'll get you a safe place aboard ship."

"Ed—"

"Good luck." Ed whacked Mick's shoulder, then embraced Kathleen. "Maybe I'll be seeing you. Maybe not. I'm away to Canada on that clipper." He indicated a smaller ship nearby, partially shrouded by fog then the crowd engulfed his progress.

Mick swore. It was as though Ed had dumped icy water over his head, and the cold pricked throughout his body, freezing him still. *He left me with the care of our sisters.* His temples pulsed with each heartbeat. "Has he no conscience?" Or family devotion?

Someone thumped Mick from behind. He twisted around to find the culprit but got jostled again.

A voice from the *Mona* announced all aboard.

"Come on, Mick. Ed only cares for himself." Kathleen yanked his arm. Her eyes brimmed with tears, her pink nose ran, and her cheeks glistened with moisture. "We must leave him be. May the saints preserve him."

"Ed's ship is half the size of our steamer. Bitterness has led our brother onto a cursed coffin ship." As he removed his cap from his pocket and pulled it over his forehead, a ruckus exploded at the ship's dockside. Such curse words and screams pierced through the commotion.

The genteel folks boarding the ship on the upper plank to the saloon rooms halted and ogled the steerage plank below them linking to the cargo hold.

"Oh, by all that's holy, 'tis Orla." He clamped his hand over his mouth.

A ship's official halted the throng. "Steerage, step back."

Orla's getting us kicked off before we get aboard.

The official cupped his hands around his mouth. "Mick and Kathleen Muldoon, come up."

The woman in front of Mick studied the people surrounding her. "Muldoon? Didn't we hear that very name earlier? Troublesome creatures, they are."

He tapped her shoulder. "Troublesome. 'Tis me." He winked when the woman scrutinized him from head to toe before stepping aside.

Mick emphasized his limp for the crowd and pity's sake. Avoiding any eye contact, he drew Kathleen forward through the masses.

The lower deck's steerage plank swayed beneath his foot with his weight. "We'll be leaving home with our final steps. Go slowly, Kathleen. Shifts with your feet, it does." He adjusted his sack, steadied his balance, and held onto the rope with his free hand.

"Oh my, it does. I don't like this at all." Kathleen gripped his arm.

"Grasp the rope instead."

They reached Orla and the irritated purser with his monumental, dark-eyed glare. *Keep your mouth shut, Mick.*

"Here. These are me brother and sister." Orla jiggled the papers under the purser's prominent nose. "Owners of these two vouchers."

Mick nudged her. "Did you know 'bout Ed's plans then?"

"He purchased his own passage, didn't he?" Orla

addressed the purser. "I paid for us three. As you can see here, me brother moves slow with his lameness, and so I came early to get a place for us." She upturned her face to the gray-haired man. "I paid you. And I'll remember me other promise."

The purser's slanted dark eyes glinted with malice. "If you do not, I will find you. You cannot hide." He turned to Mick. "Name. Work." He scribbled the word "laborer" in all caps instead of Mick's answer of "farmer" on the manifest beside his name.

Mick dared not correct the irritated clerk with strange speech, who held the power to alter his uncertain destiny.

After the purser sneered at Orla when she answered, "business owner," which he then wrote as "housekeeper," he added the same occupation next to Kathleen's name. The clerk stepped away from the Muldoon siblings and jerked his head to the side. "Go now, your kind, to steerage. With cargo. Belly of ship." He turned away toward the impatient horde. "All aboard."

Mick snorted. "What did the clerk mean by 'your kind?' Does he think we're vermin?"

Kathleen whimpered. "Orla, his words to you were harsh. Why?"

"Don't be concerned, Lamb. 'Tis nothing. And now's your final chance to leave us. I'll purchase you a train ticket home if you wish. I'm thinking you're ill."

Kathleen shook her head and stifled a cough. "No. I want to go with you."

"Then make haste." Orla hustled down the rungs into the dim and musty cargo hold called the steerage deck. She swung to one side of the ladder beside the base, staked out one of the bottom bunks lining the walls, and claimed it with her sack.

Distant squeaking with scuttling sounds scraped along the wooden crates and the berths.

"A *gall-luch?*" Kathleen hid behind Mick. "Must be. Familiar sounds. God's angels, have mercy on us."

Poor Lamb, her worst fear.

"We're with you, macushla." Orla patted Kathleen. "They'll hide, and then we'll be watching for those dirty creatures. This ship should have a cat somewhere. Bottom berths are best. The uppers are wobbly." She shook it. "No one can climb these shaky things. Yours looks to be rickety as well, Mick. They must've hastily added berths to carry more passengers for profit."

"Aye." He shook the frame. "'Twill be a wonder if it doesn't collapse with me upon it."

"Plop down with your bags and sit on the bunks on either side of me till the ship fills up with passengers around those crates in the center."

Mick and Kathleen obeyed Orla when voices drew near the hatch and feet appeared on the first rung.

"Should be the crates will be a shield for us. Hard telling what's inside them." Orla lowered the shawl from her face. "The air in here is stifling." She patted the bunk's hard planks then spread her hand on her skirt. "Wished we could've brought some bedding to avoid sleeping on the damp wood."

"But at least we'll be off the floor." Kathleen wiggled an upper bunk. "I suppose no one will climb in above me then?" As she surveyed the mass of strangers swarming the cargo hold in search of berths among the crates, her eyes widened.

"Poor lamb." He gaped at the worn, slimy planks used for makeshift bunks in the shadows of the ship's belly and dared not touch his. *Don't relish sleeping upon them.* He grimaced and squelched back thoughts of where the slime came from.

Kathleen wiped her hands. "'Tis a blessing, being above the muck, aye." Her voice trembled.

"What country sails this ship? 'Tis a strange flag, and the steward speaks odd. And what did you promise him?"

"Mediterranean line of some such." Orla shrugged.

"Worse conditions than some, not as bad as others, but 'twas cheaper passage on a merchant ship than the fancier and newer lines. Booking a safe, affordable passage is a game of chance."

Nausea swept through Mick. "By all that's holy. You didn't get us on a coffin ship, did you? You couldn't have forgotten me fear—"

"Course not. What do you take me for?" Orla flashed her dimpled smile. "We got a ship with sails and an engine. Not like Ed's ship." She shook her head and sliced the air near her neck. "Has only sails, so that could be a coffin ship. Tried to tell him. He's a nitwit."

"He always was."

Orla glanced around the nearest crates atop risers. "All worked out according to me own plans. And you limped for the crowd. At times, we think alike."

"Falser words never were spoken."

Orla smirked at him, then turned toward Kathleen. "Lamb, I'm asking you again. You going back home or staying with us?"

Kathleen shivered. "Staying."

"Then hear me. From the tales told, the best air is here by the hatch, and best access to the deck. Easiest way to get above the damp and filth sloshing across the floor."

Considering the fellow passengers in the shadows, Mick cringed at what he imagined their future might hold.

Kathleen covered her face behind her hands. "God's angels, have mercy on us."

"Let's hope." Orla shook her finger. "But remember our goals for leaving our home? We'll get through this journey and clean up fine in *America*." She whispered, "Be mindful of John's warning. Watch for thieves amongst us. I'd say 'tis the best light here to guard our belongings." She slapped her knees then rose. "Let's move some of those crates nigh to us and make a blockade. People will become hungry and thirsty, you know? Desperation turns good people into sinful creatures."

Orla turned her gaze to where the hatch lay open for steerage passengers. "Something truly terrible happens during storms, I'm told. They'll lock us all in so the water can't fall below and sink the ship." She narrowed her gaze at her siblings huddled together. "Change your minds now or make the best of it."

The horde's movements dipped and swayed the massive ship as they awaited the hundreds of passengers to come aboard. Kathleen's face turned a green hue in the dim light from the open hatch. "Hold on, Lamb. I'm glad for those high windows." He pointed near the top of the cargo hold.

"Nah, Mick. Those are for ventilation. Heard rumors that seawater will seep through those gaps into the cargo hold here, especially during storms. There'll be little light piercing through those holes. Get accustomed to the dark."

Kathleen whimpered and joined Mick on his bunk.

"Sounds close to hell itself. Maybe when we die, we'll avoid purgatory." With all his might, he committed to memory whatever he could decipher of his surroundings before they shut the hatch to the ship's belly.

———

Aboard the S. S. *Mona*
The First Day

Mick feared for Kathleen's revulsion for rats that evening. *Poor macushla.* She had spied rats on the ship, as she'd dreaded. Worse, Orla was gone all day. His back ached more than he'd remembered it could. The damp from the walls and floor penetrated his bones. He planned to daily mete out his whiskey on the trip, but Kathleen might need a share to break her fever.

Mick covered her with her cloak as she reclined against him. Her sleep was fitful, and he wished she'd gone home. Could she survive in this hellhole? Would he get ill? He didn't want to catch whatever illness was making her worse. The one time he dragged around the crates to search for another berth, he discovered the cargo hold was packed as solid as peat stacks with passengers. *Did Mister Death follow us?*

Seawater trickled through the open hatch. He listened to the retching of passengers in the shadows. Kathleen joined them. He plugged his nose from the odors in the poor ventilation and sighed. *Saint Christopher, bless us with calm seas.* Mick changed his mind about which was worse—the stench or the periodic engine's noise—and he covered his ears. *This racket's scrambling me brain.*

By day two, there was still no Orla. Where'd the hellcat go? She took half their total food. True, Kathleen wasn't hungry. Mick had shuffled through her quilt bag and found her favorite rosary was mingled among the items. There was also partially eaten bread, a book of Psalms, and some herbs. He knew naught 'bout herbs. He didn't pray with a rosary, but their mother used both.

"Little Lamb." Mick struggled to force a portion of whiskey into her mouth. "Take a swallow." She closed her lips, and it dribbled out. "Please. It could break the fever, macushla."

Kathleen moaned, and her teeth chattered. She slumped back onto the filthy, damp bench. Her clothes were drenched in sweat, her shoes and skirts stunk of human waste.

Mick cuddled his sister's head and looped the rosary around her neck. "Christ, have mercy, Lord, have mercy on our ill Kathleen. I'm not the one for nursing. Didn't I lose me wives and children?"

Something dark stirred nearby. He stiffened and peered

into the gloom. "Mister Death? You stay away from us, by all that's holy." He crossed himself. "Orla lied. Must be a coffin ship we're on." Mick fingered Kathleen's rosary, then laid his coat over her. "Hope your worry pearls protect you, Little Lamb."

He mustn't get discouraged. Didn't his sweet sister deserve his best efforts to help her? "Lamb, I fear you've depended upon the worst person to save you." A sob escaped his throat, he caressed her face, and cradled her in his arms. "Hold on tight to hope, macushla. Remember, Aidan is waiting for you to find him."

The following day, Orla slipped into the shadows next to a groggy Mick. "I'm here."

His head was fuzzy, and shivers went through him. "Where'd you get to, Orla? I've needed your help."

"I suspected so. 'Tis sorry I am but had to leave you. There's a storm warning now." Orla checked Kathleen. "Bad, aye? Tried to find a doctor, amongst other things. Fresh water." She pulled a cask from her bag, wrapped it in her shawl, and sipped. "Take it quiet-like or they'll mob us."

"Aye."

"Give it over for Kathleen." Orla held Kathleen's head and tried to force open her mouth.

Kathleen clamped her lips tight and turned her face away.

"Saints alive, she won't take it. She's hot. Her face is flushed." Orla lay Kathleen's head down. She pulled two apples and a cheese wedge from her skirt's hidden pockets. "Don't ask me questions. Hunch down behind the crates and chew without a sound."

A shadow dimmed the feeble light through the hatch above. "Storm." A young, brown-skinned ship's mate poked his face through the hole. "Must batten hatches." He slammed and sealed it with a *clunk*, trapping everyone in the steerage's gloom.

"Haven't slept for two nights." Orla plopped onto her

bunk near Mick. "Must try now. 'Twill get rough in here soon."

"Get rough? 'Twas bad enough before, now 'tis a dungeon with the hatch shut." Mick rummaged for his bottle. *Put me to sleep, me friend.*

Whiskey fulfilled Mick's request. He dreamt of being rocked inside a rowboat, with his da smiling down on him and speaking something in Gaelic, the ancient language outlawed by the English Crown. Da patted Mick's belly and ran his hand under his shirt. Mick tried to say he was fine, no need to worry, but he couldn't speak. Da rocked the boat faster, as a wave tosses ships in a storm. "Stop, Da." A violent heave jolted him awake.

Retching and gagging echoed around the ships' dark cage. Mick dry-heaved, joining the chaos. Would the crew survive? What was happening above deck? The rancid stink in the ship's belly increased overnight while the S.S. *Mona* rolled over high waves. He opened his eyes, then touched his eyelids to be sure, for the darkness didn't abate. Seawater sloshed through the narrow vents. He reached down with his fingertips and discovered a shallow pond against his bunk.

Time was untraceable in the dark, until Mick tracked it through the vents which revealed time by the color of light— faint blue for day, invisible at night. *No faint glow. Must be night.* There was no glorious sunup or sundown, as on his farm. No moon or stars. He also missed his mother's old wind-up mantle clock, a gift from Mrs. Wiggins. Mick longed for the farm he'd been desperate to leave. His back and leg ached like never before.

He groped around his wibbly wobbly berth for his sack, wanting a sip from his bottle and to use his extra shirt for a mask. The sack wasn't behind him. Mick sat up and smacked his head on the rickety base above. He clambered out and ran his hands along the empty bunk above.

"Mick," Orla whispered in the dark, "what're you doing? What's wrong?"

He turned toward Orla's voice. "Me sack is gone. He clawed around his feet for his bag. "By all that's holy, what happened to it?"

"I'll reach out me hand. Follow me voice and step nigh. I'm with Kathleen. She doesn't feel—"

Mick seized Orla's hand. "Where's our sacks? I need mine."

"You're crushing me fingers. Let go. Me head is atop me sack. Don't have any bottles in mine to dent me head. Don't you remember we put yours with Kathleen's bag and shoved them behind her for safekeeping?"

Mick bent forward and bumped his forehead on the frame again. "Devil it." He followed Orla's instructions and held onto the frame with one hand as the ship tossed on the sea. His angst turned to giddiness. "Here. Glory be, 'tis here." He jiggled each sack. "Hey, something's not right. Not at all. Me whiskey is gone. Gone, I tell you." Mick squished both bags and swore every cuss word he knew. "The thief took Kathleen's bread and left the Psalms. We must find—"

Orla seized Mick's coat and yanked him down toward her. Her stale breath assaulted his face. "Listen well. We can't see. We can't start a fight. We can't start accusing folks. We aren't amongst only Irish, there're others from places we never heard of. What if they have knives? What if they have no scruples 'bout killing?"

He groaned.

She gave his collar a tug. "Be the man here. You got two women to protect, aye? We must make it to *America*, then we'll be safe. We must stick together meanwhile. Don't go attracting attention. I've been out in the world all those times I was with Cousin Tarah. Know what I'm talking 'bout, aye?"

"Aye. You're right. Our brother John was right, he was. There're criminals amongst us." Mick restrained his panic with all his might and clutched his sack. He slid with it to the filthy floor. He propped himself against a crate.

"Evil surprises naïve ones, but I've always been amongst offenders. You haven't."

"Orla, how have you . . . Nah, I need me whiskey. 'Tis all I need. Only that. What'll I do without it?" Panic again swelled in Mick's soul. "Never been without it."

Kathleen moaned in the dark amidst the crashing waves churning the massive S.S. *Mona*.

Orla caressed Kathleen's brow. "You'll both make it, you will. Maybe six days more. I'll try to get you another bottle after they open the hatch. 'Tis most important to care for Kathleen. She's breathing strange. We must sleep in watches."

8

ENDURING STEERAGE

Orla, Mister Death is here. He grabbed me feet, and I fought him off.
Mick

On the Atlantic Ocean

Mick's stomach roiled, his head throbbed, his body shook, and he dreamed of clawing his way out of a deep pit with trembling hands. "Do I have typhus?"

Orla whispered. "Me guess? 'Tis your lack of the drink. You're well into it. Been nearing a week since you've sipped it."

A hairy creature flitted up his arm, and he swiped it away. "Vermin."

"No, 'twas me hand."

"I see them, don't lie." Mick's heart raced at high speed. "How'd we get trapped in this web?" He couldn't catch his breath but dreaded to breathe in the horrid stink. *'Tis rotting me brain.* Someone moaned. Infants and children cried. He jolted upright. "Me babes?"

"No, no. We'll escape soon." She pushed him flat. "Lie still. Saints alive, which is more torturesome? Being thrown 'bout in the dark with nary a warning or hearing me brother and sister die with the raging sea tossing us?'"

"Die? Burning hot. Churning pit. The noise, 'tis terrible. Where's me whiskey?" The motion aggravated his back and leg. He tried to relax his muscles on his wooden berth.

Orla fisted his shirt into a bunch against his chest. "'Tis gone. Stop asking for it."

Wicked Orla. Pure agony.

Day 7, Steerage – Now, deadly and silent Mister Death hovered over Mick in the dark. He sensed the evil presence. Mick groaned and tried to speak. Lights sparkled in the air around his bunk. He knuckled his eyes, but the lights flashed above him. Had God sent His angels?

A dark figure floated past, then Mister Death gripped his feet and pulled. The creature yanked and tugged while Mick fought with all the strength left in him. His boot thumped against Mister Death.

"*Oof!*" At last, Mister Death released his feet.

"Stay away." Mick croaked like a frog. "You steal too much. Always taking." His heart thudded in his ears while sweat dripped down his back. *Spiders.* He picked at his legs, swiped at the creepy-crawlies, strained his eyes in the dark to no avail, and lay back against the hard plank.

"Mick." The voice was like Orla's. "'Tis early morning. Must bring you a doctor. Many have gone above deck. I'll be leaving you, 'tis sorry I am. Guard Kathleen."

"Mister Death is here." He rocked himself. "He grabbed me feet. I fought him off."

"Nah, 'twas most likely a thief. I must leave you, now. Only a moment."

A hand as soft as a feather and sweet, fresh air wafted over his face. He breathed in deep. The muted sound of bells tinkling above made him open his eyes. "Fiona?" A shimmering light beside his bunk dissolved. The cargo hold darkened except for a silver ray through the open hatch piercing into the compartment. He extended his arm behind him, and sure enough, Kathleen lay pinned between himself and the wall. Mick drifted back into nothingness.

A sound awakened him. Faint, golden sunshine extended down through the hatch into steerage. Seagulls screeched above. A ship? *We left Ireland, aye.* His hands shook, and his belly ached. He retched, but his stomach was empty. *Where's Orla?* Mick shifted and glanced over his shoulder. *Kathleen.* His heart shattered, and the shards stabbed his lungs. He couldn't breathe. *Mister Death stole her from me.*

Kathleen lay uncovered and pale. Her cloak, favorite shawl with her prized pin, shoes, and bag all gone. Turned toward him, her sweet, white face held unblinking eyes. *Holy heavens.*

"Little Lamb." He stroked Kathleen's icy skin with his shaky fingers. Sobbing, he closed her lids, lay his head against her chest, and lost consciousness.

A man's low-timbered voice pierced through the engine noise and revived Mick. It was calm with a clipped inflection. It approached his bunk.

Mick lifted his head from Kathleen's chest and twisted as far as he could to glance behind him. Twilight came through the hatch.

Orla, her face swathed in a scarf, approached him with a man in tow. "Here they are, Dr. Ross."

Dr. Ross had his arm over his nose, his eyes darting around the shadowy cargo hold. "The conditions down here are dreadful. Poor souls. Someone must do something. You've been trapped here for the better part of nine days? I feel chagrined regarding my complaint about my saloon room. It is decadent compared to this . . . this filthy hell."

'Tis well said.

"Many were trapped here. Dr. Ross, we know the world has nary a care for the poor." Orla shook her head. "We don't pay much for passage, and they don't care much what happens to us. I couldn't find anyone who'd agree to come down. 'Twas only you who would."

"I suspect you speak the truth, Miss Muldoon. And I am grieved for it." Dr. Ross bent under the berth above and drew closer to study Mick's face. "Hello there, Mr. Muldoon. I am a surgeon returning from the mission field to America. I brought some medical instruments with me, and I would like to examine you and your sister. May I?"

"Aye, see to Kathleen first." Mick whispered. "Our little lamb is gone, Orla. An angel came to guard us. But—"

"Gone? You must be mistaken." Orla shook Kathleen's bare arm. "Kathleen, wake up." Orla recoiled, covered her eyes, and sank onto the grimy floor.

"Please, Miss Muldoon, arise from the filth and step aside. I am very sorry, but I must see to her." Dr. Ross set his bag on the end of the berth. "Mr. Muldoon, can you stand? Or I can move you."

Mick scooted away and gripped the decrepit bunk post. He wept while Dr. Ross examined Kathleen, then wiped his eyes and nose with his sleeve. "Curse you, wicked Mister Death."

Dr. Ross turned to the siblings. "Who? I am truly sorry for your loss." He replaced his instruments into his bag and unfolded a rag. "I must take her above and list a reason for her death. The law requires it. She may have survived if it weren't for the storms delaying us from reaching America and getting medical attention earlier. I assume you had no freshwater access here?"

Mick shook his head. His voice was raspy. "Couldn't ask. Nor get above deck. Orla brought us a bit."

Orla wrung her fingers. "'Twas the typhus? Couldn't find a doctor until I found you. I couldn't."

"I know you searched. You did what you could. We should have already arrived in port if not for getting off course. Miss

Muldoon, come stand here, and please block the view of your sister from curious passengers."

Mick blinked hard at blurry human shapes behind the bank of crates.

Orla followed Dr. Ross's instructions and waved her hands above her head before spreading her shawl to arm's width. "Shoo. All of you ruthless creatures. Have some respect, will you?"

Dr. Ross examined Kathleen's arms, and raising her skirt, checked her legs. Unbuttoning Kathleen's bodice, he inspected her torso. "Hmm, need some light." He removed a small box from a wrapper in his bag, which Mick couldn't make out. "Hope I kept these dry." He struck the thin piece of wood against the box. After two attempts, a spark of flame burst forth with a pungent odor.

Orla stepped back, and Mick flinched. The odor stung his nostrils. "Glory. You have lucifers with you."

"Fire is a shipmate's terror, but for me, lucifers are an occasional necessity." Dr. Ross shielded the flame while he hovered the light over Kathleen's torso. He thrust the stick into the watery grime on the floor. A thin wisp of smoke twisted upward. "It does not appear to be typhus. Please tell me how she was feeling leading up to the time you left Ireland. Did you notice any symptoms?"

"She mentioned a sore throat for a long time." Mick murmured. "Don't know how long. Do you, Orla?" He stared at Kathleen's face, willing her to open her eyes. He yearned for his little lamb to sit up and say she was only sleeping and ask why they were upset.

Orla shivered and sat next to Mick. "Five months." She swiped at her tears, then described Kathleen's complaints. "Said naught 'bout a rash."

"You three appear malnourished. Makes it difficult to fight off illnesses. What is hopeful is that you have no symptoms after being with her for months." Dr. Ross turned to Mick.

"I'll see to you now. You've had a rough time of it, I hear. Miss Muldoon says someone stole your whiskey and that you drink daily?"

"I must. It numbs me pain so I can work. And I'll not sleep without it."

After Dr. Ross examined Mick, he asked questions about the past seven days. "The worst should be over, but it will take a few more days to be completely clean of the alcohol. That is why you are so ill, Mr. Muldoon. I will send food and water with Miss Muldoon and return tomorrow."

"Thank you, doctor, for your kindness to us," Orla murmured.

Dr. Ross stood. "Your sister must be brought above. You are Catholic, right? I caught sight of Kathleen's rosary tucked beneath her bodice." He patted Orla's shoulder. "Would you like the last rites performed? I have not seen a priest onboard, but there might be one." He clasped his hands. "I am Methodist, but I am willing to say a prayer for her. Miss Muldoon, do you wish to have Kathleen's rosary?"

Orla jumped up from the bunk. "What?" She wagged her head. "No, 'tis hers. Our mam gave it to her at her First Communion." Her voice shook along with her hands.

Mick reached for her, but she recoiled. "Orla, everything was against us. You and me—"

"'Tis all me fault. If only I found a doctor before today. I never found a priest either. If only I forced her to go home, if only—"

"Miss Muldoon." Dr. Ross squeezed her shoulder. "You are a dutiful sister. You said they locked steerage passengers down here for almost three days. How could you do anything more?"

Mick shook his head. "And me, her brother, all messed up with me own afflictions. Didn't protect her, did I now? We failed Kathleen, the both of us, we did."

"Come, come, you two." Dr. Ross released Orla. "Often

circumstances are out of our control. I am sure Kathleen is with God as she seems to have had faith in Him, as you do. Try to take comfort in that."

Mick gulped. *Me own meager faith would put me in hell.* But not Kathleen's.

Dr. Ross wiped his bag of instruments off with the rag. "Sorry to leave, but I must ask some of the crew to come down for her. I have never sailed with this shipping line before, but it was the only passage I could secure. From its mismanagement of things, it may be some time before we arrive at port." He turned away and headed toward the ladder up to the deck.

Orla curtsied. "Thank you for your kindness, Dr. Ross. I'll be cleaning her up as best I can and readying her for burial whilst Mick takes his rest."

Dr. Ross bowed, then climbed the ladder.

———

Day 10, Steerage – Since the ship was delayed it grew more terrible inside the hellhole. Mick held the crook of his elbow over his face. His soiled clothes added to the intolerable stench. How could the ship's owners believe two toilets above deck could suffice for hundreds of people? The cans and jars passengers used slid around and fell over in the storms, sloshing their contents onto the floor to join the seawater. What good were those?

He wanted to claw his way through the ship's wall, but his weak, and smelly body had entrapped him until journey's end. Everyone stayed away from his bunk. They must have heard the news about Kathleen's death since the kind doctor's visit. Thieves should keep their distance.

At sunrise, two crew members with Dr. Ross approached Mick and Orla, bringing two mats and three wool blankets. The men halted to wrap linen pieces snuggly over their faces.

"I need one. May we have some? The smell is something dreadful." Mick outstretched his palm, and Dr. Ross handed a cloth from his bag to each sibling. "Thank you, doctor."

"I brought extra cloths to ease some of your discomfort here."

Orla replaced her scarf with the linen. "Thank you."

"What're those blankets for?" Mick asked from behind his new covering.

Dr. Ross closed his bag. "I requested them for you and Miss Muldoon. I am very sorry it took so long to return for Kathleen. They embroiled me in quite a battle. Everyone refused to come down. Cowards. Except these men." He tilted his head at the men behind him. "They took some convincing with a bribe, and I explained several times that she wasn't infectious. I also threatened to report the shipping line on the legalities of leaving a, um . . ." He cleared his throat. "When the captain heard my threats, he hopped to it. No need to bore you with more details."

Mick soaked up his tears with his facecloth. Why were people cruel?

Dr. Ross's men passed the mats to the siblings. "I believe they should provide blankets and mats for steerage passengers. It's not possible to carry every item aboard that you would need for transatlantic journeys. This should minimize your suffering."

"Aye," Orla accepted hers.

"My apologies, Miss Muldoon, that a priest is not onboard. They often were on my other voyages. Have you prepared for this?"

Mick closed his eyes. "We have." He must always be ready to deal with another death.

At Orla's nod, Dr. Ross directed the crew members to roll Kathleen's body in a blanket. "You people, over there." He addressed the crowd assembled to gawk at the tragedy. "Please step away and leave them in peace."

Most of the curious passengers obeyed Dr. Ross's request and faded into the shadows.

"That's better. First, would you like to say farewell to your sister?"

Mick and Orla clung to each other. "We did, doctor." Mick snuffled. "We recited many prayers." They made the sign of the cross.

With great care, the stewards handled Kathleen's enshrouded body.

"I'm going up. Me only sister. How shall we ever tell Mam?" Orla scrambled after the stewards as they hauled Kathleen above deck.

"I say we don't." Mick shook his head. "'Twould break her heart. Our sweetest lamb, gone. Dear God, Aidan. Shall we toss out her letter to him? And I've no strength to climb that ladder." He trembled and sobbed.

Dr. Ross stayed behind and sat on Orla's berth. He waited while Mick grieved and pulled himself together. "We should arrive in three days' time, the captain told me. I expect your strength will return by then. I must check you as well, Mr. Muldoon, and then get above deck. How are your symptoms today?"

Another night of troubled sleep, but Mick's nightmares had lessened some, although he fought sleeplessness from guilt. He shuddered and tucked the new blanket under his chin. *Was Kathleen thrown overboard and torn asunder by sharks?* They wouldn't do that, would they? "May the saints preserve her."

A sudden streak of light poured over his bunk, and he flipped over. Was it an angel? Mick's muscles cooperated in their usual way, his headache had abated, but not his back pain. The bright light shone through the open hatch, silhouetting a form on the ladder. He blinked. Something moved in the corner of his vision.

Orla skittered onto her berth, laden with fruit, cheese,

water, and chicken. "From the kind doctor." She laid the food on top of her clean blanket. "There'll be naught left for the thieves by now. Eat and drink small amounts. Doctor said try it, and he'll be down to see you soon. He says Kathleen probably had scarlet fever. Her poor heart was weakened." Orla took a bite of bread and cheese while she gazed at him. "I didn't think I could eat after watching the horror of . . . but me stomach is so empty." She chewed while Mick nibbled at the bread and sipped water.

"This water is sweet as honey. Never knew it could taste so good." He sighed.

"I got something to tell you." Her voice shook. "Don't know how, really." She gulped hard and lowered her cheese wedge. "Well, they tossed Kathleen overboard. I was there. 'Twas so horrible. But for Dr. Ross, I'd be despairing."

Mick gagged on his bite of cheese and coughed. "Had a nightmare 'twas so. 'Twas true? How could they do it?"

Orla shuddered. "'Tis how they bury at sea. Can't leave corpses aboard." Orla crossed her torso and wiped her tears. "Dr. Ross says God can find her soul in the water. Lots of people are at the bottom of the seas." Her chin trembled.

"May Christ have mercy on her soul." He shivered, envisioning the icy water swallowing Kathleen's body wrapped in the wool blanket and sinking into the dark depths.

Orla clenched her fists. "Besides Kathleen, I heard rumors of three others dying on this trip. Recall hearing people retching with seasickness around us? I've seen pale ones on deck in their soiled clothing, holding onto the rails or their family, trying to get in line for the toilets above."

"Imagined 'twas better above."

"Moving air and water are the graces. And Dr. Ross isn't the ship's doctor, for they haven't any. He only came down for you and Kathleen. Steerage passage counts for naught. We're like sheep packed together for slaughter."

"By all that's holy."

Orla gripped his arm. "'Tis more awful than I was ever told. Takes all me strength of will to return here away from the fresh sea air. Seen people on deck, shivering with the cold and damp, lips turning blue, and refusing to come back down."

A shadow blocked the light from the hatch, then traveled backwards down the ladder.

"Good day, Muldoons." Dr. Ross rearranged his face covering. "How are you, Mick?"

"Good morning, doctor." Orla stood and turned her back to her brother. "We're grateful for your care."

Mick shoved aside his folded blanket then unbuttoned his shirt for the examination.

Dr. Ross finished and inserted his stethoscope into his bag. "You are almost sober. I encourage you to refrain from any more alcohol use now that you have survived this nasty process. Do you think you can avoid the drink?"

Mick didn't want to lie to the good doctor, so he folded his arms and said nothing. How could he ever work, or sleep peacefully without it?

"No? Ask a doctor for laudanum if you need something to help you with pain or sleeplessness. Right? You would have to endure this all over again. Also, you might feel strong enough to climb the ladder to the deck tomorrow."

"Aye, Orla says . . . Well, that's a thing to look forward to."

"One more issue." Dr. Ross clasped his bag under his arm. "If you have not heard, someone should warn you of the social difficulties for Catholics in America. It is not fair or right, but it is best you know the truth. There are Americans who revile Catholics. They do not understand your Christian sacraments or practices, and they fabricate repulsive stories which the weak-minded believe. Some have burned down Catholic churches. Here is my address if you need any help in New York City. Godspeed." He handed Orla his card and left them.

Mick cocked his head. "Do you think what he says 'bout America, is true? All we hear are good things back home. I hope what he says isn't right. Or we've suffered for naught."

"We must hold to our hopes, brother."

Another storm hit the S.S. *Mona* in the night. A crew member again locked the hatch. Mick's head had cleared enough for him to understand the ordeal of Kathleen's death. What was disturbing now was how Orla had finally hit her limit of tolerance during this dreadful voyage.

Orla screamed at people one by one and on into the darkness. "Was it you who took me sister's treasures? Let me see your bags. Shame on you all, stealing me poor sister's shoes and cloak off her dead body. Do you think God and all the saints missed seeing it? They know, you dirty dogs."

Me pitiable sisters. It was especially tragic to hear a woman's voice wailing in the dark, and the way it blasted off the walls of the ship's belly. *Shaming the banshees, me sister is.*

Orla raged on about the thieving passenger's attempt to steal Mick's boots from his feet, while he hoped Kathleen would haunt the thieves forever for their black hearts and deeds.

———

The hatch stood open when Mick awoke, and seagulls screeched outside. He flipped his blanket off, splashed his boots into the muck in the cargo hold, and tested his strength. "Glory be to God me legs support me. Orla, the hatch is open. Let's get above." He rolled up his now grungy mat and blanket.

Orla blocked the light with her arm, then raised onto her elbow. "'Tis arrival day. The bedding was such a grand gift from the fine doctor, but 'tis filthy. Should leave it behind." She donned her lace cap, her cloak, then wrapped her shawl over her kerchief. "Hold on to me or the walls.

The sea seems smooth today, but I don't trust the contrary thing."

Most passengers avoided close contact with Orla and Mick as they shuffled to the ladder to exit the putrid belly of the S.S. *Mona*.

Excited voices carried down through the hatch. Mick tugged his tam on, and tried ignoring his muscle pains. More passengers around them stirred and packed their sacks. These progressed as slow as he did. "We must be nigh to port. Have many already gone above? Steerage is half empty."

"The wise and healthy have, 'tis sure. I'll follow behind you once you grab a rung." They climbed the ladder at his slower pace.

A chill misty breeze slammed into Mick's face, and he took a deep breath of tangy salt air. He grabbed his cap as the wind fought to snatch it. He shielded his eyes while they adjusted to the light. Weak sunshine glowed behind the mist, outlining the ship and passengers with silver and gold.

"Glory be. 'Tis nigh to heaven, aye?" He studied the sails and rigging. It was a magnificent mercy to be freed from the cacophony of the engine below during their approach to America. "Will forever remember this day of deliverance."

While the ship made a slight turn, a robust wind smashed waves over those near ship's edge. The hundreds of passengers on deck stood packed tight with their bags lodged between them. "Like sheep herded to market. Could we be in peril of tipping this cart over?" He focused on the horizon's increasing dark spot for his first glimpse of America.

"It wouldn't dare dump us." Orla clutched his coat sleeve. "Wish Kathleen was here. She braved the trip to see it. She wanted so much more."

A small child holding a woman's hand and sitting on the shoulders of a man squealed. "See the dolphins, Mam?"

"Is that land? In the distance. There. Do you see it?" The shorter man in front of Mick pointed.

The emigrants hushed while they strained to gain a view around the horde on deck.

Head and shoulders above many men, Mick stood upon his tiptoes and craned his neck to search beyond the masts and over the bulwarks.

"What is over there?" Orla tugged on his arm.

"Some shapes are on the horizon, and gulls are circling 'bout it. We must be nigh to America."

The single screw steam engine switched off. There was a welcome quiet, and the crew scrambled to unfurl the sails. "Land ho!" shouted a mate. The S.S. *Mona's* forward power dragged a moment, she jolted then eased into a glide over the sea. The sails fed the ship's speed, deceptively quick on the smoothness of the sea's surface.

Gulls swooped and encircled the *Mona's* foremast. To their right, another ship approached. Farther off, another sailed away from the growing shape. Scattered exclamations broke out, and people jostled each other for a better view.

"Blessed America." Mick focused on the horizon as the dark spot drew closer. Enthusiastic chatter perculated throughout the horde. He spied a peninsula, docks, and a round building with ramparts. "'Tis a strange sort of castle there. Didn't expect to see castles."

"Must be why they call it the Castle Gardens." Orla stood on his booted toes to see better.

Cheers erupted around the siblings. Some passengers hugged each other and laughed. They'd all survived the terrible trip, arrived at New York's Castle Gardens, and were finally about to begin the promised abundant life in their new country.

9

LIBERTY'S LACK

I stink. Ashamed to be in public.
Mick

Castle Garden Entry Point, America
The S. S. *Mona* cruised toward port. "Surely, we're almost there, sister." Mick grasped her shoulder. "Can you see the docks? I shall forever be grateful to remember this date, September 13th, 1866, when our terrible journey freed us from Crown tyranny. Thanks be to God." The pair crossed themselves, along with others surrounding them.

Castle Garden lay on the tip of a peninsula jutting into the Atlantic Ocean and along the Hudson River. Seagulls swooped overhead as Mick and Orla disembarked with the mass of mainly Irish emigrants. People danced a jig, sang a song from the old country, or hugged and congratulated each other.

Orla nudged Mick's arm. "Me friend, Maeve, wrote me that Castle Garden was a fort in 1855, then used as a cultural center, and a theater." She indicated the flag atop the tower.

"No longer will we be seeing the Irish flag. Americans, we are."

Officials directed the new arrivals onto the wide dirt path from the docks. Mick's knees trembled, and his belly churned. The ground beneath his feet rocked like the sea, though he wasn't walking upon the water like Christ. He followed the hushed crowd ogling their surroundings and being funneled between long wooden buildings on the one side and docks along the harbor on the other. Odd structures. They approached the Emigrant Landing Depot.

"We're stinking up America." Mick whispered near Orla's ear.

The crowd slowed their pace and murmured to each other as they surveyed the various trees with tall trunks and high branches and other unfamiliar plants in the nearby garden area.

Chills crept up his arms, so he searched for Mister Death, hoping he wasn't following them from the ship. No shadow or a black robe flitted about. Maybe he was still on the *Mona*. "Orla, 'tis the same blue sky above us and earth below us, but why is this air sticky?"

"Don't know."

He pointed ahead. "So, 'tis a castle, as I thought." He surveyed the low circular tower constructed of chunky red bricks with a high, carved frame around the entrance. "Well, bless me soul. 'Tis well built, aye? Solid. What do you suppose that tower— Look there. Are those cannons? They beat the Crown with them, no doubt."

"And how would you know that? We only learned bits of their history in school, I'd say."

He glanced down at his sister, her shawls encasing her head and face. "Never made it to the toilet up on deck the entire time being stuck in the ship's belly for near a fortnight. 'Tis lucky you are, being wrapped up with your shawls, not I."

"Me? Wouldn't say lucky, a bit warm, but aye." She shuddered. "Such a dark time of it you had. And unable to get up the ladder when the hatch was open."

The sea wind carried away most odors until it fanned them into Mick's face. "I stink. Ashamed to be in public."

Orla shook her head. "Warned you. The times they locked us in, none could go." Her eyes twinkled above her veil. "Now switch our thoughts to what a glad day 'twill be to wash ourselves and our hair."

"I'd plug me nose but 'twould mistakenly offend me fellow Americans. 'Tis what we are now, aye?" He gave a hop, and pain shot up his leg. "By all that's holy, I need some drink."

"You're done with it, yeah? Dr. Ross said to be done. Best to leave it alone after—"

"What's that?" *What's she thinking to be nagging at me?* He stopped moving with the crowd, and people stepped around them. "We're away from home, and now you'll be me mother? I'll not stand for nagging me, not at all. I've reasons for me choices, I do. I can't stop. The drink is better than not being able to work. And the terrible nightmares."

Orla frowned. "Don't get yourself into a bother. 'Twas possible you didn't remember, is all. Let's keep up with the others and get to the processing." They joined the pack of immigrants entering through the fort's narrow doorway and into an open area. Someone called it a courtyard.

"Let's get processed, as you say." *Does she have me pains? No, her back and leg don't pain her.* A foul odor wafted up Mick's nose. *Well, and who could tell who stunk the most?* All of them were unbathed. *Our own waste upon our clothes.* The officials had packed the immigrants together again in winding rows. A gale from the sea couldn't part them.

The pair waited while officials questioned hundreds ahead of them before waving them into the fort. Once inside, they wound between scattered benches. Light filtered through the narrow windows centered high and deep within the short tower's ceiling. Wood beams and joists crisscrossed above their heads inside the circular fort. The crowd's voices merged with crying infants, or children yelling before being hushed by their parents, all magnifying the discord.

Mick's stomach growled. All he wanted was a meal and a swig of his friend. And a bath. His knees shook from the unknown, hunger, and need for alcohol. He ground his teeth against the pain that writhed up his torso from standing for hours and attempted to ignore his own stench.

Officials separated some poor souls into another room, escorted others to the side, and told them to wait for something. Mick couldn't hear what. Surely, they couldn't come so far to be dealt with unfairly.

He drew close to his sister. "Aren't you frightened?"

"Learned never to show fear." Orla stepped up next, and a processor asked for her name, country of origin, and to state her plans.

Mick strained to hear her last answer. He'd never asked her exact plans. Thoughts of survival consumed him on that hell-hole voyage of a demon ship, where Mister Death stalked them.

She bumped Mick's arm. "He's with me. Me brother, Mick Muldoon. He'll be joining me and me friend, Maeve O'Donnell, owner of a home on Rose Street."

"Is he a mute?" The processor wrinkled his nose and sneered. "Or can you answer for yourself, man?"

Mick slid off his cap and wadded it in his fists. "Yes sir. Michéal Muldoon, of County Kerry, Ireland. I—"

"Welcome to Manhattan then." The processor stamped their vouchers and shooed them toward the exit. "Next."

"We're through." Orla clapped as they exited the fort. "Fresh air is me new love."

"Aye. Never thought to treasure it as I do now." He tugged his tam on and followed Orla toward the noisy street beyond the harbor and garden. The pair made their way between small groups of processed immigrants headed toward the city. Some sat on the grass to rest.

He stopped and pivoted to survey the surrounding port activity of ships entering and exiting with sails of all sizes—each made good time with the wind. "I'll be that glad to never see another ship for the rest of me life. Nor Mister Death, neither, but ah, Kathleen. We're here without her."

Orla backtracked to him and crossed herself.

"The truth is terrible." Mick stared at the sea, yanked off his cap, made the sign of the cross. "Farewell, Kathleen, me macushla, our little lamb. 'Tis a sorry thing he stole you away from us." He wiped his nose on his sleeve and slung his sack over his shoulder.

"Who stole her? Oh, your irritating Mister Death, yeah." She swiped at her tears then resituated her sack to dig inside to remove a wrinkled envelope. "Got Maeve's letter here and her map."

"O'Donnell, you said. I recall her from years ago. She was your school chum, aye?"

"Maeve left home with her parents sixteen years ago during the Great Hunger. Says she runs a boarding house situated in the tenements." Orla lay her sack on a grassy area at the garden's edge to study Maeve's map. "The lower east side of Manhattan, she writes." She tipped her head. "That way's east, away from the lowering sun."

The city teamed with motion and noise. Drivers with carts and wagons shouted at heedless shoppers or other drivers, horses clip-clopped and whinnied, merchants called out their wares from their doorways. Mick longed for the familiar sound of his cow lowing or a robin's song. *Me ears could burst with this man-made cacophony.* "Will it always be boisterous?" Could he adjust to living in this land, under these conditions? Yet here he was. Maybe there was nothing to worry about.

"Maeve's address is 22 Rose Street. Nigh to the seaport." Orla turned the map sideways. "The port is here." She transferred her sack to her other side. "Head east to Pearl, cross Maiden Lane, then left on Rose. There's Pearl, straight ahead."

Mick scrutinized the mayhem before him. "Was Dublin or Limerick like this?"

"Well, 'twas and 'twasn't."

"By all that's holy, must we walk through all that commotion? Following that map she drew? What happens if she missed a street? How shall we find our way then?"

Orla stashed the letter in her sack, clutched the map, and shrugged. "We ask for directions."

Foot travel took far longer than Mick and Orla expected. Nigh to the port—hooey. The long streets wound between two- or three-story buildings. Once, when Pearl became Hanover, they lost their way. A kind, unkempt woman selling wilted roses showed them where to pick up Pearl again. Mick asked for a rose and offered her Irish coins.

"No, no. Take it as a welcome gift from a fellow Irishwoman."

Instead of blending in with the masses of humanity, the filthy pair flared like a fire in the night and smelled worse than a barnyard. A fancy-dressed man with a fashionable woman stared at the Muldoons. "Such pitiful creatures. They will probably add to the crime in the area."

Mick's face burned, and his heart raced with his efforts to not respond to the insults.

Other people grimaced or side-stepped around them when they hesitated to cross Maiden Lane. It was the busiest street Mick had ever seen, where traffic came from all directions. *Need a magic cloak to hide meself.* He glued his eyes on Orla's skirt and ignored people's reactions as much as possible for several blocks. He knew his face was bright red with the heat of summer and his disgraceful condition.

Orla hadn't spoken another word. How was she faring in all this? *Glad she covered her face, for it could be even worse.* He buried his nostrils in the wilted rose to hide his own odor. "Not to bemoan finding Aidan, but I don't see how we will."

Orla turned to him. "We're after finding Maeve first. Such a relief to be through the tangle."

It seemed hours since they'd departed the ship. Cramps seized Mick's leg and back from so much walking, and his stomach growled again. His thirst for whiskey grew so intense he feared his tongue might loll out of his mouth like a hard-working sheep dog. He wanted to growl and snap at the hordes of people. *To think, we must live amongst them.* He inhaled his rose's aroma again, and it restored his spirits enough to forge ahead.

"Left on Rose next. Roses win the day, aye?" Orla turned down a narrower lane. Fewer horses and buggies traveled past. Disheveled and sparsely clothed children played in the street next to a dead horse in the gutter. Barefoot children waded and splashed in foul smelling, brownish water.

Orla stopped, and Mick bumped into her. "Watch it. You bruised me hip. We're here at last. Thanks be to God."

Mick tore his gaze from the bloated carcass, murky water, and grimy children. He forced his imagination away from the origin of where that awful water came from to where Orla jabbed her map.

A shabby, faded, hand-painted sign hung cock-eyed above the doorframe. *Rose's Boarding House.* The main window had a long, glued-together, diagonal crack in its middle. "This is Maeve's? Twenty-two Rose? Doesn't seem a good place, Orla. Did you see the children in the muck? I'd never let me children play in—"

"Must warn you. You're 'bout to see things you never seen. You're no longer on the farm in Ireland, brother." Orla faced the door, its black paint peeling in strips. She knocked. "Remove your cap, Mick."

"Me cap is the least of me offenses." He scrunched it and

ran his fingers through his oily, matted hair. "No use combing it," he muttered. "Best to cover it."

The dilapidated door creaked open. An untidy young woman whom he guessed to be around fifteen and clothed in flimsy unmentionables, yawned as she blinked at them. "Yes?"

"Orla Muldoon and Mick, me brother. We're looking for Maeve. She expects us. Who are you?" She inspected the girl.

"Annabelle. I'm Maeve's, er, helper. She's asleep. Shall I wake her? She mentioned friends were coming over from Ireland." The brunette girl stepped aside as she opened the door wider. "Come in out of the heat. It's not much better inside. What's that stink?"

Mick flinched.

Annabelle pinched her nostrils shut and giggled. "I smelled worse before." She wiggled her bare shoulder and ogled Mick. "Brother, you say?"

He stared at her red-smeared mouth. He had a bad feeling about the place. This woman didn't look right. Something was off. Besides her clothes. "Orla," he murmured, "we—"

"Hello there." A husky voice called out from above the stairs. A woman, who appeared around thirty-years old, bent over the banister. Her long hair tinged with an unnatural yellow color swung back and forth. "Glory be, 'tis me old chum. You made it across, so you did." She hurried down the stairs, and her buxom figure, wrapped inside a scanty robe, jiggled. Purple outlined her eyes and red smudged her lips.

Mick forced his attention to the cracked window beside him. The room was decorated with dusty and faded red-velvet curtains. They might have been thought beautiful once. The soot in the fireplace spilled onto the hearth, and scorch marks tinged the floor. A scratched upright piano, a worn sofa, two patched up chairs, and a threadbare rug completed the musty parlor. Housekeeping wasn't important here. Though steerage was worse.

Orla dropped her sack and extended her arms out for Maeve. "You're such a loyal friend to help us out, dearie."

"Aye, aren't I?" Maeve held her palm between them. "I'll skip me hug for now till you've had your bath, if you don't mind." Her hand remained outstretched after Orla squeezed it. "Do you have it with you? The sum we agreed upon, I mean. A woman must earn her way in this world one way or the other."

Rude landlady asking for payment without us yet inspecting our rooms.

"Yeah, Maeve, me chum." Orla slid her hand inside her bodice and tugged out her reticule. She dropped Irish coins into Maeve's palm. "Exchange them for us, aye?"

Maeve counted the coins. "I expected payment for three. Where's your sister?"

Orla gave a shortened version of Kathleen's illness and death on the voyage. Orla and Mick crossed themselves while Maeve and Annabelle did the same and murmured their condolences.

"Certainly 'tis tragic news." Maeve pouted. "Such luck. I must say though, 'twas no fault of me own, so I'll still be needing the payment we agreed upon. Rent is dreadful in the city, so me price is the lowest you'll find for two of you." She counted the coins Orla added to her palm.

I'll need me whiskey to drown out the evil in this place. Mick coughed to hide his growl and objections then compared Annabelle to Maeve. Was she Maeve's daughter?

"Mick." Maeve cooed as she drew nearer. "Such a handsome man you've grown into. Last time I laid eyes on you, you had the looks of a lad. Now, under all that dirt and whisker, you're a handsome one."

Flatterer. He recoiled. Never trust a flatterer, Da always said. He offered his wilting rose and balled his other fist to refrain from strangling her. Why was he so angry? Or troubled. He'd never met such a woman as this creature.

"Such kindness, to think of me." Maeve inhaled the floppy rose's perfume.

Orla unwound her shawl from her face. "So——"

Annabelle gasped. "Such gruesome scars——"

Maeve pinched her. "Mind your manners, girl."

Annabelle yelped and shrunk away from the newcomers in the parlor. The worn stairs creaked with her every step as she sped up the staircase.

Mick cleared his dry throat. "May we have water, Maeve? We're also in dire need of supper and a bath."

"Ah, 'tis sure, now." Maeve slid a damp strand of hair off her face. "The summer heat is stifling. So which shall you wish for first? I'd say a drink, then a bath, and supper last. You may use the kitchen and stove as you like or purchase your supper items down the lane at the corner market. Your board doesn't cover meals."

"Right." Orla smiled.

Maeve led the siblings into the messy kitchen. "We bathe in the kitchen tub. If the weather is fine, we wash out back in the evenings by the row of water closets. Americans call them outhouses."

"Bathe in public?" He almost chose to remain in his own filth.

"Course we do." Maeve giggled. "Behind the curtain. There's a rope strung between two pipes we use." She escorted them to the common area out back, pumped water into chipped cups, and handed one to each. "You can keep your cups in your room and wash them as you wish. We don't pay a cook or a housekeeper."

Orla asked where they could find their rooms. "We're a bit worn out, you know."

"Surely. 'Tis best to hide, uh, keep your monies and food in your room. The girls sleep during the day, so you must be quiet. Seeing as how I thought there'd be two women, I had the larger room set aside for you, Orla. We'll tiptoe up the——"

A crash above and laughter startled them. Maeve smoothed her robe. "Ah, so the others are awake. Follow me. We'll have such a grand time."

Four whispering young women clustered together. They wore scanty slips or camisoles, their hair mussed from sleep. Various acrid perfumes lingered in the hallway.

Mick hesitated, then sneezed. As Maeve introduced her boarders to the newcomers, the girls sashayed down the hall and behind him. They ignored Orla. One girl retrieved a pair of black lace stockings hanging on a make-shift laundry line near the closest room. An argument broke out when each claimed ownership of the hosiery.

He retreated a few steps.

The tiff spiked into hair-pulling and name-calling, and Maeve screeched threats of murder. She slapped the girls in turn and shoved them toward their rooms before turning back to Mick and Orla. "Don't you pay any mind. The girls always have scuffles over naught. They'll settle soon enough. Follow me." They ducked beneath undergarments strewn over a few thin ropes. "Here 'tis." She opened a door and beckoned Orla inside.

As Mick dodged a slinky unmentionable dangling beside him, he waited for Orla and considered the condition of the hallway's cracked floorboards with the hazy little window at the end of it. *This house could fall atop us.*

"Mick, come see what you think of it." Orla's expression was stony.

It was more of a stuffy, windowless storage room, about six feet by eight feet, stuffed with a cot, narrow bed, and a dresser with a candle. A mop, two buckets, and a broom each covered with cobwebs, were propped in one corner.

Giggles erupted from a room down the hall. Someone screamed, then sounds of another tussle ensued. Maeve excused herself to investigate.

Orla plopped her sack onto the bed. "The upstairs is even worse than the downstairs. Mam and Kathleen would be ashamed to have their home in such shambles."

"None of me wives would allow it neither. Your Maeve wanted three of us in here with one bed and a cot? Terrible. You're aware of what this house is, aye, sharp-minded as you are."

"Me apologies. We got no choice till we get accustomed to the city and find work. Me money won't last forever. 'Tis why I'll offer to be a housekeeper for our room and board."

"I have money in me boot. I can't abide these women. Must ask 'bout the other room." He fingered the tattered cot. "I'll be needing this, 'tis sure."

Maeve returned, and he made his request. She shrugged and led the pair through the kitchen. "Do you want it?" The other available room was a five by seven covered back entrance and more humid than upstairs.

"Me height is six foot-three inches. Might I fit on the cot?"

"Should."

"Done then." He agreed for the sake of privacy and solitude.

Maeve situated a metal tub in the kitchen. "You can take turns. Must be off to supervise the girls. Oh, and their clients arrive by eight o'clock. Could be raucous."

After Mick bathed, his mood improved. *Although living in this house of ill repute is disgusting.* He wanted to escape, but to where? He knew nothing about New York City. Mick left his filthy traveling clothes and sack on the floor beside the tub as Maeve requested. She told them she planned to burn their clothes and bags in the fire-barrel by the water closets in the common yard.

He donned his one change of clothing left by Maeve's customer who had departed in a hurry. He declined the story she wished to tell. Mick entered his tiny room and centered the cot over a hole in the porch floorboards. Exhaustion and overwhelm from his circumstances overrode curiosity about what might live below. Today's only care was for the supper and whiskey Orla brought home. And a fine sleep.

―――

Loud voices, laughter, and off-key piano music awakened Mick. *What's that scratching sound?* He sat up, and his whiskey bottle rolled under his legs. *Did Mister Death find me?* There wasn't a black robe nor any grasping hands in the dark.

A *scritch-scratch* came from beneath his cot. He slowly leaned over the edge. "By all that's holy."

Two large rats scuffled into the hole. Tufts of their hair stuck within the splinters. "No hiding, you little hell-borne beasties. What I'd give for Mam's tabby." Mick yanked his old mucky boots on. Maeve had no leftover shoes for him. He exited to the common backyard and searched the area for supplies. The full moon highlighted a perfect-sized piece of wood that lay over two adjoining porch rails. Other smaller pieces of wood and metal pipes were piled together by the washtubs and near the barrels for burning trash. It was more of a junkyard than a play yard. No wonder those children played in the streets.

He hauled the piece of wood to his room and placed it over the hole. *Get through that, you filthy beasts.* He settled on his cot and took a swig from his bottle.

After his recurring nightmare about Kathleen's body being attacked by sharks, Mick never thought it could happen to him, especially on land. The first attack jerked him awake from a sound sleep. What? The second hit slammed into his cot. His groggy brain and whiskey-induced sleep evaporated. His attacker wasn't a shark. It was a scraggly brown mutt biting him with a crazed old woman, wild as a demon, shrieking and whacking him with a cane.

"Thief!" The woman was quick for her age. "You stole me roof." She thrust her cane for another strike. "Came home to find it beneath you."

"By all that's holy, what's going on?" Mick's head throbbed. His heart pounded as he used his arm for protection. "Ow! I didn't know." Was she a looney? "I didn't wish to wreck your home. Take it back." By the time he flipped off his cot, used it for a shield, and shook her mutt loose from his arm as he escaped to the yard, the entire neighborhood had assembled to gawk at the wild scene.

Close to the outhouses, the neighbors questioned the old woman dragging her roof away. A brawl began over Mick's innocence or guilt, with neighbors taking sides.

Maeve urged her girls past him, all armed with kitchen utensils, the unused broom, mop, and four buckets. She screamed at the crowd. "He's no thief. He's my new tenant."

If his arm wasn't bleeding and he didn't have welts on his legs, he would have laughed to see such a sight. "Why must women always protect me?" Wasn't right, but there it was.

Orla dabbed his arm with her nightgown hem. "What's happened? Looks to be bite marks."

"Am ashamed to say 'twas her little mutt which got the best of me."

The mutt barked nonstop, ran in circles around the swarm of neighbors, and snapped at any leg within its reach.

Mick examined the bites. "First believed he was a shark in me nightmare. What are they arguing 'bout? Can't make out their jumbled words."

"Thief is one word. They're too far away to hear more." Orla elbowed his arm as they viewed the rabble throwing rocks at Maeve and her fierce army of girls. The girls smacked the brawlers with the mop and broom, drenched them with water, then refilled the buckets for another round. People slid and fell in the slippery mud just as the police arrived.

Orla tugged on his uninjured arm. "Back up quickly now, into the kitchen. We don't need to be a part of this."

"Aye, we don't. America, you're not what I imagined." *And here I believed the Mona was as terrible as it would get.*

10

MISCREANTS OR RUFFIANS

Secrets can be kept, but not forever. There's no lock can keep them hid.
Mick

Maeve's *Boarding House*
Mid-Spring, 1867
Manhattan's oppressive air lingered through the summer, but Mick grew accustomed to it, then to the more frigid temperatures of winter. No matter how he tried, he couldn't adjust to the close living quarters of his tenement. He craved open space, green hills, lakes and rivers.

Mick battled unemployment woes, but since the neighborhood tussle, his neighbors appreciated him for his watchful guard over their little ones while they played in the common area near his room. *Though they mightn't trust me if they see me bottle.* Why must he explain his drink to everyone? It wasn't unusual for an Irishman. If they ever invented something besides laudanum to help with nightmares and sleep, or to dull pain you're born with without knocking yourself unconscious and useless, he'd consider it. If he could pay for it. For now, he was glad the whiskey helped and gave him courage.

He wasn't useless or lazy from it, was he? Hadn't Mick

stopped a possible thief when he bellowed, "Who are you?" and raised a shovel in the air, startling the thief into dropping his bag of spoils? And the time he herded the littles up the steps and into his room when that rabid dog entered the yard, growling and frothing at the mouth. That won them over. Now his neighbors invited him over for tea and sometimes offered supper.

Mick shivered and swigged a bit more whiskey. He didn't like Maeve being right about the housing situation. *No rooms I can afford, aye?* Especially since the railroad employment letter he brought with him from Ireland didn't help him find a job, even in Manhattan with all its construction. Same as always, that. Managers and foremen took one look at his gait or posture and laughed outright or pitied him. They claimed they weren't hiring, despite the *Now Hiring* signs. *Rotten liars.*

He tucked his quilt tighter, intending to set the bottle down, and changed his mind. "Wicked Mister Death, where have you been since the voyage?" He had evidently shaken off that invisible devil from his trail. "What do you think, Mister Death? The genuine devil now is Maeve's beau, Digger."

Orla burst through the kitchen door onto his porch. "Digger's here with Maeve—"

"What?" Mick choked on his sip and tucked the glass bottle inside his blanket.

"Was that whiskey?" Orla rubbed her arms. "I suspected. Dr. Ross said you should stop. Are you warm enough?" She bounced on her toes.

"Devil it, woman. Does Dr. Ross have a painful back? Does he have nightmares? Can't a man have peace, even in me own paltry room? Told you, I must have it. It lessens me pain."

"There must be something to be done 'bout your pains."

Mick wiped his mouth with his quilt. He rubbed his blurry eyes. "Mayhap one day. Truth be told, thought I could find work easily with Will's letter. At me wit's end. 'Tis me limp once more destroying me hopes. You don't understand—"

"And you don't understand me."

He flipped back his blanket, scooted over, and cradled his bottle. "Join me. I've suspected you've got your secrets, aye?"

Orla wadded her apron into a fabric ball.

"Tell me 'bout your secrets, me sister." Mick scooted over on his cot. "Help me to understand. I suspected by villagers' hints and tales, 'tis something to do with men?"

She sagged next to him and covered herself. Orla confessed her introduction to the physical relations of men with women, which began at age sixteen. "Cousin Tarah knew many soldiers, and no one at the garrisons had a care 'bout me scarred face. Did it to feed our family and save for me future. I knew marriage wasn't in it."

He swallowed a gulp of whiskey, hoping to force down the massive clump of shock in his throat. Did this news surprise him? *Many destitute girls earned their living that way.* He took a deep breath. Abused and disdained. Sold for a pittance. She's worth much more than her body.

"Mick?"

He forced his voice to work through the frozen wheels of his mind. "That's your story? Did Aunt Mary suspect?"

"She never said a word. Tarah helped her own family survive as well, what with Aunt Mary being an invalid and raising four of our cousins. Mam always let me visit and didn't ask questions."

"Mam must've known. You wanted to help the family. Thus, you did." He banged the back of his head against the wall to shake his thoughts loose. "But I wouldn't want you to do it that way. Why do you continue—"

"Don't you shame me 'bout me choices—and I won't shame you 'bout yours." Orla wagged her finger, then flipped off the quilt and straightened to her five-foot, ten inches.

"Orla—"

"We make a pact here today. We got our reasons for who we are. How we live. We understand each other, yeah?"

He ran his hand through his hair. "Can't you stop and become a housekeeper now? Change your life, aye? That's why we come here. A new land, a fresh start."

"Aye, 'tis what I'm doing. But you got no right to make me future choices. I'll make no promises if this don't work out. Now, 'bout Digger. Hide out here quietly or go visit Sally and Joe. I'm thinking she's making supper."

"Why should I always hide from that loutish, pimp of a—"

"I know, Mick, 'tis a shame he won't believe us 'bout you. Why he thinks you'd be sniffing after Maeve is beyond me imagination. Don't Americans honor their wedding engagements? Back home, we're as good as wed by our promise." Orla glanced behind her. "Must go back inside. The floors need sweeping, and I'll arm meself with a broom. Now get away."

"Yeah, yeah." He unwrapped the blanket and tugged his boots on. "Digger thinks all men are like him. Ne'er-do-wells. I keep to me vows. I've never been without work before." Mick donned his coat, then trudged through puddles across the common yard before he dumped his empty bottle in a trash barrel. He refreshed his spirit by studying the first evening stars. The city's dirt, dust, and myriads of laundry lines crisscrossing between himself and the sky obscured the sunsets. Unlike his farm in Ireland.

Dishes and pots clinked from inside the tenement's walls. An infant cried, cats shrieked in a fight, and the Fitzgerald couple argued over how much Mr. Fitzgerald spent on drink.

Mick stopped beside a fire barrel. *'Tis a mercy there's no trash burning tonight.* He wasn't in the mood for socializing either, after Orla's confession. The aroma of beef stew and cabbage wafted past but didn't entice him.

Sad memories of what happened to Orla filled his mind. He'd heard comments about her from his boyhood. Children at school bullied, ridiculed, and abused her because they believed she was evil with her almost-white eyes. There were kind nuns who'd defended her, and some who didn't try. Rory, being next to her in age, got into fisticuffs over her. He came home with a black eye more than once.

Another sad thing about Orla. Born with a sweet nature, a gentle sort of girl, never created to endure cruelty. Her hair was the most glorious color with the glow of a peach-tinged golden sunrise, and she had deep dimples in her snowy skin. Angel kisses. The perpetual complaint was her disquieting, tilted eyes of the lightest blue with a dark outline and pale lashes. Eyes like a demon, they said. Who ever saw a demon? But wanting to gouge out her eyes with Mam's scissors? Nausea swept through him at the memory of his little sister with bloody gashes in her soft skin.

Mam told Orla children would stop bothering her as they grew older. *But her eyes wouldn't change.* After her injury, Mam finally allowed her to cover her face in public. No wonder Orla chose a path of being wanted, or needed, or what substituted for love. In truth, 'twas another road to hell. Mick couldn't save her. He never could rescue the women in his life, not from any enemy. Especially not from Mister Death.

He shoved his hands into his pockets and eyed Sally and Joe's backdoor. Should he knock, or hide from Digger in the shadows?

————

On the road to the city docks, horse's hooves clopped as they tugged creaking carts past Mick. Avaricious merchants loudly enticed their wares to arrivals, and bells clanged from a train station. He covered his ears. He craved tranquility, solitude, and the aroma of earth with green, growing things. And his donkey. Plus, a cow, chickens, and a home. Mayhap marriage?

He hustled across the street, hands stuffed in his pockets, and quickly side-stepped out of a fast-moving carriage's path.

"Dirty Irish!" The driver spat over Mick's head. He had never hated his auburn hair before, but he did in America. He didn't blend into the crowds unless he was in the Irish Quarter or inside the pub. He adjusted his cap lower on his forehead and stuffed strands of loose hair inside it.

How did Orla tolerate the bustle along with the bullying and bigotry? She'd insisted the Americans didn't react to her appearance. He hadn't left his home and come across the vast ocean on a perilous voyage to be treated in such a manner.

A freckled-face boy Mick had seen before shook a newspaper near his face, assailing his nostrils' with the pungency of fresh ink. "Here, sir. You can have this creased one for free and don't tell. No one should be that rude."

"Aye." Mick fumbled with a few coins in his pocket for pennies to hand to the boy. "Your kindness is grand, though I think I can pay for it."

"Yes, sir." He turned back to the masses of humanity, most much taller than himself. "Today's news! Read it for yourself." He swished a paper in the air.

Could I sell newspapers? Mick walked on, found an empty spot under a shop awning, and inclined against the wall to read. "God bless you, Sister Margaret, for making sure we learned our letters in school." He smoothed out the help wanted page. "'Dock workers needed'. Could try that one, 'tis nigh to here." Folding the paper under his arm, he headed closer to the western docks.

Standing at the port, with the screech of the seagulls overhead, the ships, and the water, Mick froze. *Terrible idea to come here.* Being near anything resembling the S.S. *Mona* brought back the terrible experience he never wanted to relive again. Battling the nightmares from his voyage was bad enough. His heartbeat revved, palms turned clammy, and his chest tightened. He breathed in shallow spurts. The newspaper fluttered to the ground. He backed up, almost into an alley behind him, keeping his focus glued to the monstrous hulk of a ship at the dock.

Something dark flashed to his left, and he turned in time to spy a black cloak disappearing. Was it Mister Death?

Thump! Arms encased Mick, pinning his own tight against his torso. A large hand covered his mouth and nose. Flesh and blood. Mick twisted his face every which way to loosen the calloused palm.

The man with the vice grip snarled into his ear. "What have we here? Fresh off the ship?"

"Freshly off, but shall we help him back on? A cripple's not worth much to us." The raspy voice spoke from behind Mick.

He couldn't breathe. The ship and dock blurred. He kicked behind with his good leg and twisted to escape the brute's grip.

A rough sack covered Mick's head as he shouted, and they tackled him to the ground. Everything went dark.

———

Pain seared up Mick's legs and back, then through his chest and head, forcing him into consciousness.

Booted feet kicked him. "We don't want your damaged kind. *Oof.*"

Dirt and gravel crunched beneath several feet. "Get away from me brother," bellowed a familiar voice, "and don't mess with Irishmen, you dogs. Skilled boxers we are." More curses followed the warning.

Ed? Mick's head throbbed, followed by ringing in his ears. How— Footsteps approached.

"Why'd you leave the hood on, Mick? You didn't wish to watch me fight?" Ed yanked it off. "Ho there, they gave you the once over, didn't they?" He drew close to inspect Mick's face. "You'll be ruggedly handsome now. Not such a pretty boy."

"What?"

Ed extended his hands. "Grab them and let's go. 'Tis a rough part of town." He tugged Mick onto his feet.

Mick moaned. "Wished I'd had Da's shillelagh. Could've clubbed them." He hunched over while his muscles in his chest and side ached and burned. His left eye throbbed. "Thanks be to God, you stymied them. How'd you find me? You were in Canada."

"Was. Been searching for you. Orla came down this way last night. Saw her from me boarding house window. Thought you might have as well, so was on alert. Watch your back. Our farm didn't teach you 'bout street life. Me and Orla? We learned to make our way." Ed rubbed his knuckles. "Me own vice is gambling."

"You saw Orla here?" Mick spat and tasted blood. He wiped his lip. "Why must people always be reminding me I was a farmer? I'll not forget."

"Did they knock out a tooth? Didn't see one."

"Nah." Mick searched around his feet. "Just me pride. I'm the perfect victim." He pivoted. "Me tam. Those miscreants stole it, thinking there'd be money in it, no doubt. Those dimwit dirty dogs. 'Tis inside me boot."

Ed snickered. "As I taught you. Two against one are terrible odds for most of us, me brother."

"Despise the city. Me and Orla have been here for half a year. No way will I settle here. 'Tis mean, dirty, and worse than being under the Crown, yeah? Seen some bad ones of our own people mixed in with the good. 'Tis just as John said."

"You fearful?"

"Nah. Mostly feeling I can't breathe. Noise never stops." He limped a few steps down the alley toward the street. "Leg's fine enough to walk."

The brothers turned from Fulton onto Pearl and headed inland toward the business district.

"Guess I should be a good brother and ask how Orla is faring. Found you by following her uh, nightly activities, though she always went to an upper crust part of the city. Immoral alley cat."

Mick stopped. "She must be hunting Aidan to deliver Kathleen's letter."

"Aidan Duffy? Could be a chauffeur at most. Nah, always knew 'bout Orla's secret life. Got to be a numbskull not to know." Ed kept moving.

"None of us knew you were a Fenian, did we?" Mick caught up with his brother. "Until you confessed 'bout it to John in Killarney. Secrets can be kept, but not forever. There's no lock can keep them hid. God must prefer it that way."

"Fenians still have the right of it. Fighting for freedom from the Crown. So, have you seen Mister Death lately? You're always nattering on 'bout him."

"And you're always a bully." Maybe a helpful one, but there he was. "I spied him in the alley before the men attacked. Wondered why he was there."

Ed chuckled. "Me own fearsome arrival frightened away Mister Death, yeah? You owe me one, little brother. Well, you're the same. America hasn't changed you. Yet."

"And you're the same bully."

"Aren't you the perfect one? At least one of us Muldoons in this land is good. You shouldn't compare me with Orla. 'Tis unfair. I done naught like her." Ed shuddered. "Disgusting."

Mick grabbed Ed by the collar. "Will you be her judge? Can you rightly be?"

Ed's face turned red. "Let go. You're taller, but I'm a trained boxer. I'm warning you." He glared at Mick, inches from his chin.

He shoved Ed. "Thinking 'bout Orla from me da's heart.

Be heartbroken, if me Rosie had survived childhood only to become what our sister is."

"Point well made." Ed rolled his neck and cleared his throat. "Recalling Orla as a little girl chastises me attitude. How's Kathleen? Is she a grand housekeeper now? Cleaning and entertaining the staff with her rabbit trail stories?"

"Ah, Ed." Mick smacked his forehead. "How could you know? Kathleen. She didn't make it off the ship. That hellish voyage." Perspiration trickled down his temples. "The terrible nightmares of that now added to previous grievous events in me life."

"Sweet lamb." Ed paled, grabbed Mick's arm, and yanked him nearer. "What happened to her?"

"We all knew she was ill, didn't we? She denied it, but 'twas clear enough. We didn't wish to believe our eyes, did we?" Mick crossed himself and trembled. "Christ have mercy on our souls."

Ed crossed himself. "Kathleen died of a sickness then? Was it typhus?"

"The doctor on board said 'twas scarlet fever most likely. Remember her sore throat? He said we're all malnourished, so sickness took over. Lamb planned to find Aidan. She had her dreams." Mick dabbed his eyes. "Orla and I been asking 'bout Aidan's whereabouts to no avail. She wrote to Mam 'bout Kathleen, though I said not to."

"Poor Kathleen, our little lamb. Unbelievable." Ed sniffed. "Never meant me harsh remarks to her. Only having me fun. God rest her soul."

The brothers fell silent while they wound through crowds of shoppers. They avoided steaming horse manure at the street crossing, passed a shoe store wafting fresh leather, then grocery stands of crates piled high with bunches of yellow, orange, and green produce.

"I'm that glad our loves in heaven never know of the awful

things we do." Mick turned to Ed. "Aren't you glad Da never knew what you or Orla became? Da didn't approve of gambling. Since he died before Orla took a turn into adultery, he can't know 'bout either of you."

"Maybe 'twould never have happened with Da here. In our own ways, we tried to help the family without his earnings to support us."

"I suppose so." Mick's stomach growled. "Hey, there's me favorite bakery." He led Ed inside and purchased meringues for them. "Lemon. Me favorite."

They bit into the slightly tangy cloud concoction. "God bless the French's bakery skills. Must tell you something. Orla still gives me money whilst I search for work." He smacked his lips. "We had a chat 'bout me whiskey. She don't lecture me, I don't lecture her." He wiped his sticky hands against his pants.

"Must confess something to you, Mick. You weren't to blame for getting the farm. Bitterness led me to desert me flesh and blood in Queenstown." Ed swallowed his last bite of meringue. "But I been looking for you and Orla for some time, once I heard the unsettling news of Manhattan's Irish gangs."

"Aye. Heard rumors as well. Never seen them. After searching for work in the mornings, I spend me time in the tenements with the littles whilst they play."

"Been asking all around the city for you. Even went to the trains. A chap remembered your limp and told me to check the docks. They'll take anyone for odd jobs. Don't mean it bad." Ed turned his attention toward the tinkle of the doorbell.

A plump elderly woman with a deeply lined face entered the bakery with her natty lined basket. She approached and passed between the brothers as they exited the shop.

"Think she was a slave?" Ed stared after her.

Mick peeked back in the window. "Could be, and now

free." He considered another treat, then decided it might ruin his supper. "Me friend from the pub, Josiah, was an ex-slave. Freed in '63 by President Lincoln's Emancipation Proclamation, they call it here. God bless him. Tragic 'twas, his assassination by a villain."

"Lincoln? Aye. Heard some pitiful stories whilst up in Canada of slaves attempting escape. Other sorts of stories—"

"Aye. Josiah's wife is Sheila, a housemaid from England. She could've helped Kathleen. So, they dance most nights in the pub. Josiah sure enjoys the bodhran." Mick rested his shoulder against the bakery window. "He says the freed slaves have naught, and I told him we came here with naught. We understand each other because we're together amongst the downtrodden masses in this city."

"Downtrodden, aye."

Mick licked his fingertips. "Josiah says lots of Irish and freed slaves marry here. But intermarriage offends some people. And why should it? No business of theirs. Didn't God create us all? The powerful have the say and always demand to have servants—"

"Are you having me on?" Ed's mouth hung open. "Not the same at all."

"What's not?"

"The Crown never shot Irish servants who ran away. We weren't put in chains neither."

"Shot? Josiah never told me stories 'bout being shot. Says he won't talk 'bout the past, only the future." Mick wiggled his sore jaw. "Did people kill slaves here in New York?"

"Don't you know anything 'bout it, man?"

"Naught but little." His stomach growled again. He tugged Ed's elbow. "Let's get back to Maeve's for supper."

"A better notion." Ed jerked his head. "Let's get to that pub there, McGinty's. Sit with your back against the wall. Being messed up, they might mistake you for a hoodlum."

Mick laughed. "They know me there, man. Been speaking of McGinty's pub all along."

Customers were scattered inside McGinty's. No lively music played, as there was in the evenings, but it contained a flavor of the old country. Patrons paid no attention to the chiming bell or the Muldoon brothers' entrance.

"Hey there, Muldoon," the bartender called out.

Mick flicked his hand.

The brothers chose the only empty table against the wall, and Mick settled onto a chair. "'Tis grand to sit." A mirror hung behind the length of the bar, and the shelves over it held various sizes of colored bottles. Men occupied several barstools.

Ed ordered and delivered their whiskey. He sat next to Mick and tilted his head. "Bless me soul. There's the man I need. Can't believe me eyes, but he's been staring. Mayhap he recognizes me?" Ed patted his clothing in search of something.

Mick scanned the room over the top of Ed's head.

A man puffed his cigar and gazed at the brothers through the cloud of smoke. Gray streaked his dark hair, and his eyes were as hard as flagstone. He rapped his knuckles on the table, and the two large men sitting with him stood. They moved to the sides of his chair, slid their hands into their pockets, and fixed their gazes on Ed.

Mick glanced at Ed for reassurance.

"Ah, here 'tis." Ed rose and scrunched his shirt pocket.

"Even a farmer knows those men are a threat to good fellas, and 'tis not a brilliant idea to call their attention to us." Mick shrank lower in his chair.

The men blocked the cigar smoker from his view.

Ed called out, "Charlie. Charlie, I have a letter for you from your aunt in Ireland."

"Charlie Gilhooley?" Mick swung his stare to the tattered

letter his brother flapped in the air which Mrs. Gilhooley gave to Ed at the Muldoon's farewell wake. He turned his attention back to Charlie and his men and hoped this peculiar confrontation wouldn't end in bullets flying around the room. Bad top-off for this day.

Someone hidden behind the menacing men shoved them apart. The smoker's cigar jiggled on his lip. "Ed Muldoon? Upon me mam's grave, 'tis truly you. Couldn't believe it for a moment there. Come talk with me." He shoved the men farther away. "Can't you see he's me chum? Get us some drinks, you ruffians."

Mick remained in his chair. He didn't care to meet more ruffians.

Ed hurried to his chum. Charlie mumbled to Ed, who then beckoned Mick. "Come on over, me boyo. He wishes to talk with you." Ed handed the letter to Charlie and beckoned to Mick.

A hell's devil with guardians. This was bad. Mick scraped back his safe chair and joined the three fearsome men. Colder eyes up close. The guards set whiskey and glasses in the middle of Gilhooley's table.

Charlie studied Mick. "Ah, Ed's brother. You have an unfortunate limp, don't you?" He gulped his drink. "How do you care for America?"

Mick met Gilhooley's stare. "Not much so far. Except for me freedom."

"Aye, the coveted freedom."

Ed shook Mick's shoulder. "Miscreants by the dock messed up me little brother. Having a bad time of it." He sipped his whiskey. "He had the family farm. Searched months for Mick. Knew he'd be in trouble. Up in Canada, we heard of the gangs in New York City."

Charlie puffed his cigar. "Aye, and you should join me own gang. Proved your loyalty by delivering this letter."

"Nah, came to take care of me brother, the farmer."

Charlie Gilhooley inspected Mick then smirked. He stubbed out his cigar. "Yeah, Mick's not cut from the ruffian cloth. He's cut out only for farming. Not tough enough."

Mick's mouth dropped open and his face heated. *Curse me fair skin. Glowing for all the world and this hooligan.* He switched his gaze to the colored bottles on the shelves behind the bar. The lone ray of light through the entry door's window lit them to shimmering. A black shadow fell across them, blocking the sunray. Mister Death?

Ed hit Mick's shoulder. "Aye, me brother here's been sheltered all his life. Me, now? I was a Fenian back home." He crowed and puffed his chest like a rooster.

Eejit. Mick scrunched his face.

"Learned how to box with Fenians, along with other things." Ed slammed his fist into his palm. "Haven't much care for Crown law and all."

"Fenian, you say?" Charlie thumped the table. "Heard tell of those patriots back home. Could use those skills in me gang. Irish criminals, we're called. Well, and what's a criminal in America?"

Ed shrugged.

Charlie clenched his fists in front of him and stared at each brother. "Not the same as Ireland's. No, not at all. Here they must catch you doing something. Trick is not to get caught. Here you can say what you like, for no Crown is after squashing your speech. No Crown arresting you for being an Irishman wanting to be free."

"Me own freedoms shouldn't be used for busting up people here. 'Tis not why I left me loves buried back in Ireland."

Charlie snorted. He emptied his bottle, then shooed his two guards back to the bar. "Lucky thing Ed left Canada, Mick. The Crown has reach there. Here? Well, we still got problems. Irish Catholics are reviled, and prejudice is alive. The bigots burned a few churches as well. And the tales 'bout us are disgusting. Think we're superstitious with a strange religion. They've even spread it 'bout that the priests rape the nuns, strangle their babes, and burn them. As if they'd ever do such terrible things."

"We were warned 'bout it by the doctor on the ship."

Charlie took the fresh bottle offered by his men and poured three more glasses. He flicked his hand. "Be off with you, men. Wait by the bar. I want to chat with me old chums alone."

"Got called a dirty Irish when I went looking for work." Mick surprised himself for speaking up, and he glanced at Ed, who raised his brow.

"That's all you been called here?" Gilhooley wrinkled his face. "The saints preserved you. I'll catch you up on the doings in our city. The Irishmen were an unruly lot here. Thus, the police and fire departments recruited us. I wasn't interested. No money in it."

Mick straightened. "Would they take me then?"

"Nah. Your unfortunate limp." Charlie turned to Ed. "We're fighting Irish from the centuries of oppression and abuse back at home. Would they blame us if they endured what we did? Fought for everything, aye. We brought our old history to a new country. We're a tough breed, a fierce people who laugh, sing, and dance. And drink." Charlie arranged the glasses on the table. "Now, what have you done to me? Chatting poetic, I am. 'Tis speaking of the old country that did it. What was me original point?"

Ed extended his empty glass. "Subject of criminals."

Charlie bobbed his head. "So 'twas. Here we got gangs for protection. Much like the Fenians back home, don't you know. Gangs offer group power and wealth. Money comes in, and 'tis a glorious thing. Who amongst us wishes to live powerless again? Do you?" His black gaze slid back and forth between the Muldoon brothers. "I'm asking you."

Mick shuddered. He thought of the ship and his filth then

his tenement. But this wasn't the way to freedom. "If you have your ear to the city, have you heard of an Aidan Duffy?"

Gilhooley's hard eyes narrowed. "Why would you be asking 'bout him?" His stare burned into Mick's soul through the thick cigar smoke.

"Me sister Orla has a letter for him, and she's been searching—"

Gilhooley sliced his thick hand across his neck. "Dead. Tragically slayed three years ago. Tell her to look for his tombstone and deliver it to him there." He sneered.

Black fabric flashed past Mick's side vision and slid into the shadows near the bar. He squeezed his eyes shut. Kathleen's face hovered in his mind. Was she with him in heaven, then? He blinked.

The hoodlum facing Mick puffed a smoke ring, and his icy stare was more lifeless than any of his dearly departed's.

"And me offer?" Gilhooley clenched his jaw.

Mick shivered. How could a living man have a dead soul? "Don't understand your offer to Ed."

Gilhooley turned to Ed. "Did you understand it?"

"Aye, and 'tis generous of you." Ed wagged his head. "Came here for Mick. We'll go west for farmland from me gambling winnings. Think I'll stick to me plans."

Mick whooshed out a long breath. "Glory be, Ed. Farming?" He hopped on his seat. "Green grass, earth, and open sky?"

Gilhooley chuckled. "Excited like boyos we all once were, yeah? The world needs you, Farmer Muldoon. Keeps us jaded men remembering our innocence." He stubbed out his cigar with vigor. "Break free now, whilst your heart desires wholesome things." He gulped the last of his drink then hissed. "Get out west before the city sucks out your soul. And don't ever rat on me. I'll hear 'bout it, and I'll hunt you, I will."

Mick flinched at Gilhooley's hard tone. He didn't want a cold heart like him.

Ed stood and offered his hand. "Charlie, 'twas fine to see you."

"Aye, 'twas grand, for old time's sake. Now get out of me sight." Charlie stiffened his shoulders like a bull ready to charge. "Get. And don't tell tales or look back, for you might find a devil with a gun's barrel against your head."

11

BUFFALO HUNTER'S ASSISTANT

I swear to God, if you do it again, I'll bellow loud enough to knock the clouds down.
Mick

Upper Midwestern Prairie
Late Spring, 1867
Vast sky above, the smell of prairie earth below, and fresh air in Mick's lungs brought him to within a hair of complete contentment. All his soul needed was a road on the open plains. He hadn't seen so many green growing things since his ship arrived at Castle Gardens. "Over a year since we planned to leave Ireland and since landing in America."

Ed grunted.

Feels like a lifetime. How could Mick guess his bully brother would appear in Manhattan loaded up with gambling winnings, share his unexpected financial freedom, and release Mick from another oppression—despised city life—and back into farming?

"How much longer till we find our cheap farmland?"

The wagon creaked and groaned then hit a hidden stone. Ed cussed, and his poor dog, Danny, dug his claws into the wooden bench seat to keep from sliding off. The spotted mongrel hung on as Mick wrapped his arm around his torso. Danny just missed Mick's nose with an appreciative lick.

"Ed, watch it, will you? That's the fifth stone you hit in a hundred yards." He clenched his jaw and massaged the upper thigh of his bad leg. "Can't take much more of this. I swear, if you do it again, I'll bellow loud enough to knock the clouds down."

"Get out and walk or try driving yourself, yeah? Stones and ruts and holes are hidden beneath the grasses." Ed spit over the side of the buckboard. "Be patient."

Mick massaged his leg. "Well, and 'tis sure you're too blind to miss a one of them." His back, hip, and leg burned like a blacksmith's rod in a fire. "Been wondering 'bout Orla and how she is. Think she'll keep her promise to visit us after we're settled?"

Ed shrugged. "Don't know and couldn't care less. Orla does as she wishes. She'd irritate me. You're doing enough of that with all your complaints."

"I'd enjoy seeing her. She provided for me. I wish to pay her back one day. But I'm glad she stayed behind. Couldn't have tolerated you and her bickering every minute, like—" *Thunk.* "By all that's holy." Mick bellowed.

Danny bumped his skull as he scrambled beneath the bench and wedged himself behind Ed's legs.

Stormy and Rusty jolted in their harnesses. They flung their heads, twisted, and backed up, shimmying the wagon into a cockeyed direction. The jostling and bumping shot more pain up Mick's lower back. He ground his teeth and clamped his hand over his mouth. He'd had enough whiskey for one day.

"Woah, there, boyos." Ed clicked his tongue. He worked to get the horses under control and switched to crooning. "Settle there, settle. 'Twas only me numbskull brother making noise. Those clouds are still hanging in the sky, brother."

"Eejit. Come up, Danny. Me apologies for giving you the frights." Mick scooted sideways on the bench and rubbed Danny's head.

Ed handled the horses then glanced at the sky. "Getting nigh sunset. 'Tis good a time as any to stop." He put the brake on and climbed out of the wagon, followed by his dog. "I'm his owner, yeah? Stealing me dog's affections, you are." He opened a canteen and poured water into Danny's cup.

"Easy to do."

"Another day of traveling tomorrow." Ed turned to unhitch the horses while Mick stretched his legs and back.

It was difficult for Mick to sit hour after hour, day after day, on a wooden wagon bench. He should have realized the challenges ahead on this cross-country trip before he agreed to their plan. *Escapes can be excruciating, aye.*

Ed spoke over his shoulder. "Will you unhitch Rusty whilst I care for Stormy?"

"Aye. Rusty's me favorite." Gentle and cooperative, Rusty nuzzled Mick while he brushed the horse's copper coat. *Like me own hair.* He regretted not having a carrot to give him. "Apologies," he crooned near Rusty's ear. "Never meant to startle you. Needed to let off some steam is all."

They tethered the geldings with long ropes tied to stakes, set up camp, and set out their rations. Mick lay on his blanket with his whiskey atop the aromatic grass. He'd found a soft comfortable spot on the ground and relaxed. The relief from the worst pain gave him chills. Danny curled up by Mick's side. "Are you sure you want me instead of Ed?" He winked at his brother. "I'm all for it."

Ed grunted and stirred the canned beans in a pot over the meager fire.

The cool of the night spread from some point east, as if searching for the sun, and crept over their camp. Gold, orange, and lavender glow faded into turquoise and peach then navy. The full moon rose at last amongst a myriad of stars twinkling from afar. Insects sang their various lullabies carried by the breeze.

Mick wished he had a musical instrument. He longed for his family's old piano, even though it had two broken keys and some missing strings. Orla or Kathleen had always played when Da was alive. They all sang together as a family. Family. All in pieces, now. Some here, some back home, and too many gone to heaven.

Danny rose and turned in a circle then resettled with his head on Mick's chest. He fondled the dog's silky, wavy fur and ears. *Ed's an odd one, to name a dog after Da.* He shivered. "Ed, wouldn't it be grand to have Mam's old piano?"

Woo! Ah, woo! The noise broke the stillness, followed by yips.

Danny leaped off Mick and to a stiff stance on the first note, his ruff on end, his low growl menacing. Stormy and Rusty whinnied and sidestepped. They were nearest Ed, so he seized their ropes.

"Take Rusty." He approached the wagon. "Danny, up." The dog hopped aboard, quivering. His ears perked forward while he examined the dark prairie.

Mick's heart raced as he released a snorting Rusty from his stake and led him toward the wagon. "Quiet now. Settle. Do you think 'twas tribal men?" He whispered, "Heard they imitate creature sounds." They tied the horses to the wagon's hitch and covered them with blankets. "Nothing now. Think they're gone?"

"Perhaps."

The horses' ears twitched. They jerked their heads and shuffled sideways. Danny's hackles still stood on end, and he growled. Mick breathed hard, as if he ran. He swiveled as he searched. "No, there's something lurking around. Our creatures can hear it or sense it." Sweat dripped down his back.

"Away, over there." Ed shook his finger. "A small pack of wolves." He retrieved his rifle from the wagon, checked that he'd loaded it, then yanked on the wagon's brake. "I'll fire a warning shot to scatter the wolves. Brace yourself. The horses won't like this." At Mick's nod, Ed cocked his gun upward and fired. The shot echoed across the night sky with a zing.

Rusty and Stormy reared, joggling the wagon, and Mick clutched their ropes tight while Danny scuttled under the wagon bench. Mick's hands stung from the ropes pulling across his palms, and his arms ached. "Easy, now, boyos. Never fear."

As the echo faded, Ed helped settle the horses.

Mick's ears rang, and his mouth was dry. He searched the prairie's horizon. "I hoped 'twould be the tribal men with their feathers and furs." *What's that?* His breath turned shallow. "Over there." He pointed. "Do you see shadows moving?"

"No." Ed squinted. "There's nothing. You're spooked, and you've been drinking. Careful what you wish for. The tribes travel in groups for safety, and they're skilled at survival. Did you think it was your Mister Death?"

"Mister Death doesn't make those sounds." His breathing slowed as he observed Ed's dog. "Aye, Danny settled. He wouldn't if there was something there. What'll we do now?" He adjusted Rusty's blanket while Ed settled Stormy with another.

"We must sleep in turns and keep the fire up. I'll take first watch. Something could spook the horses again." Ed climbed onto the bench.

Twice more on his watch, Mick heard howling, though much farther away. He drifted in and out of sleep, and the chilly night dragged him toward dawn with fits of broken rest.

Ed shook Mick awake before sunrise. "Up and away time, brother."

Mick tugged on the canvas and blanket covering his face and frowned over the edge. "Naught ever happened then? 'Twas only the wolves that once?"

"Right. Don't you think if I had to shoot again 'twould awaken you?"

"Aye. Ed," Mick yawned. "What were your plans if we got attacked?"

"Me rifle. Did you see Mister Death last night?"

"Nah." His face heated.

"Then you had naught to worry 'bout, yeah? Heard there's not much trouble with the tribes since the Civil War. Up in Canada, everyone lives together. If you're traveling, you must stay up on news. Native peoples value new, useful things, like anyone. 'Tis why I brought leather goods, furs, and food-stuffs in me chest beneath me seat. Learned it in Canada."

"Are Americans empty headed? They spoke naught 'bout native peoples."

Ed guffawed. "Your innocence is shocking. They're consid-ered inferior." He spat and stomped the spittle into the dirt with the sole of his boot. "Governments say we're all inferior, senseless, and unmanageable if we don't agree with them and from not wanting to be ruled by them."

"You still talk like a Fenian. The truth is Irish and native want to be free and have our own land."

"Part of the truth." Ed whistled for Danny. "You must be hungry after all that whiskey." He handed Mick a chunk of bread with a canteen filled by their water barrels, urging caution to mete it out until they found another water source. "I fed the horses. They're watered and hitched, so let's be away."

Mick snatched his whiskey, climbed over the seat, and settled himself with Danny by his side for another long, painful experience. "How many more days till we get to Iowa?"

"One or two is me guess. We'll be nigh civilization soon. Open the map and get the compass, will you?" Ed slapped the reins against the horses' backs. "Get a move on, boyos. I want to find a card game tonight. Need us more funds for land."

———

Iowa

Early Summer

At last, he could stretch his legs. Mick enjoyed Frogger's numerous trees but didn't care much for what was considered the town—or what he could see of it in the night. A saloon, where Ed joined the poker game, a stable, a store, and a church. Mick whistled Danny to his side when he strayed too far and sipped his whiskey while he meandered up and down the rutted street. *How many wagons pass through this God-forsaken place?* He'd peeked through the saloon's lit up window when they first parked the wagon out front and counted eight men with two giggling, painted doxies amidst a lot of smoke. *Well now, Orla would fit in.*

Ed's dog barked at something underneath a watering trough.

"Danny, ho. Leave it. None of that, if you please." *No doubt a rat—the bane of me life.*

Mick scrutinized the heavens. The stars winked, secretly plotting something, as the air grew chilly. How much longer would Ed be? All he wanted was some blessed sleep. Mick returned to the wagon. The uncomfortable chill didn't compare with his pains from bumping on a hard seat for hours. Mick shuddered. He stashed his empty cask inside his shirt and fumbled for his gray blanket. "Farmland, you'd best be worth this misery."

Groans and shouts burst from beyond the saloon's open door. He spun around in time to catch Ed swaggering through and whistling Danny onto the wagon.

"'Twas a good haul. Drive and be quick 'bout it." Ed retrieved his rifle tucked behind the wagon's buckboard.

Mick jiggled the cart as he quickly climbed in beside Ed,

which made the horses as nervous as himself. "Hey now, Ed, what's your gun for?"

"Insurance. For safety. Won the kitty, so best be away. Head east and turn right there. Pull up behind the mercantile, beyond the edge of lantern light."

"You said be away, and now you're telling me to hang around?" The horses tugged them away from the saloon, and they parked behind the store.

Ed clenched his jaw. "Stop nattering on. I know what I'm 'bout, I do."

"No doubt." Mick scanned the black wooded area beside them. He tensed. Was that a footstep? A corner of Mister Death's robe swished past the wagon, and Danny growled. Mick stroked the dog's back and ground his teeth. Blood rushed to his head with the racing of his heart. "You get away from us, Mister Death. Nothing for you here."

"What?"

"Mister Death, he's always lurking in the darkness of dire circumstances." Mick murmured to not be heard by the others, while he kept a watch out for spirits or men. He seized the wagon's side and bent over the edge to search beneath it.

Ed smacked Mick's shoulder. "Sh. You're a daffy taffy."

Boisterous male voices blended with horses' clip-clops and drew near the street side of the store. Someone yelled. "The missus will kill me dead. We must find the cheater and take my money back."

The ruckus faded away as the riders headed east. Crickets chirped in the woods beyond the brothers, and frogs croaked their nightly tune.

"Told the men we were headed east, not west, Mick. You hear anything now?"

"Besides creatures? Did you cheat those men? Is that why they're after you?"

Ed snorted. "No need to cheat. I'm that good with me card playing. Won it fair. 'Twasn't enough for land yet. Maybe one more game." He half-stood. "Move over, I'll drive. We're closer to getting our farm, aye? So I asked the men 'bout farmland, and they confirmed a rumor of who's selling it cheap in Minnesota as I'd heard back in New York. Newspaper stories, you know, but 'twas early in the game. They'd no reason to lie. And no more talk of Mister Death, yeah? You give me nightmares."

"Aye. You have me promise." He handed the reins to Ed and stroked Danny.

"Glad to hear it."

Mick glanced at the heavily shadowed fields. *Why does no one want to know 'bout Mister Death?* He took a swig of drink. No matter how much he drank, Mister Death persisted. Stalking him, ever since the day of his birth. Though he was still here, wasn't he? *Mister Death slays me darlings, not meself.* He was yet alive with dreams for America.

"Walk on." Ed slapped the reins. "Away through Iowa first."

"And another thing I'll be promising you, Ed. I'm helping pay for the land with me own money. I'll be finding a job on our way to Minnesota to add to our pot. Done with others paying for me dreams."

———

Northwestern Iowa

The railroad was nearing completion in Iowa when the Muldoons arrived a week later. Mick read a sign posted in town by the railroad promising three meals a day and good pay. From the boarding house where they took a room, he limped his way to report to the railroad's office. He'd patted his pocket with Will's crumpled and wilted employment letter from Ireland and applied. They'd offered him a buffalo hunter's assistant job. Mick expected manual labor, but this sounded exciting. He was to join up with a Mr. Conch. The one with a gun. *Never shot one in me life.* With his hands in his pockets, he whistled a jaunty tune. Things were surely improving.

Finally, he could earn his way, and add funds to his boot. It now only stored a meager $1.25 left over by Orla's goodwill and earnings from things he refused to imagine.

Mick thought he'd been a victim of trickery, although Mr. Conch told him there were yet buffalo as sure as mosquitoes, but not as many as before. After four days on the plains, the buffalo hunter hadn't found a herd. A thickset grizzled character in his mid-forties, Mr. Conch told tales of how ten years earlier the plains swarmed with vast herds like a dark and wide river. Now it was a trickle. He'd been shooting them for over a decade.

"'Tis only the railroad who hunts them to such low numbers?"

"Mostly. Tribes still follow the herds. Buffalo is their main sustenance. One will feed many men for a month." Mr. Conch loaded his gun and checked the site. He adjusted his wide-brimmed leather hat lower on his forehead and scanned the prairie hills. He called over his shoulder, "Sure, we feed the men—the crews—with the meat, but rumor has it the railroad kills the herd to subdue the tribes and clear the plains." Mr. Conch strode toward a low hill and turned back to Mick with a wide grin. "Feel the ground vibrate? A herd's coming. Must settle on that hill for the best view. Plan to shoot at least nine." He chuckled.

Nine buffalo? Mick's head throbbed. He almost fainted from the horror of what he'd heard. Starvation and slaughter were their goals? By all that's holy. He crossed himself. How well he knew the effectiveness of starvation, and taking a people's land away. He'd come to a brilliant and beautiful land to escape cruelty. *To a country that purports to accept every immigrant from its seaports.* But this behavior resembled England's.

Mick couldn't catch a breath. His mind fogged with the billowing brown clouds rushing toward him. He covered his eyes. The earth turned to water beneath his boots, and he dropped to his knees. The rumble increased, and dust went airborne. It swirled like a dense mist on the moorland, clogging his nose and throat. The shroud of flying dirt threatened to obscure Mr. Conch from his view. Mick rose with his knees bent for balance and tucked his face into the crook of his elbow while he joined Mr. Conch. He couldn't tell where the herd was and didn't want to get stampeded. Once or twice, large horns blurred past, not twenty feet away. They were nothing like the cattle in Ireland. *Such a shyster was the man who hired me.* He cowered behind Mr. Conch and strained his eyes in the dust but only caught dark flashes. Still, the buffalo hunter waited to shoot.

He, the hunter's assistant, shook with terror. There was nowhere to hide.

While the dust clouds settled, earth and sky negotiated their peace with the thundering of buffalo fading.

The first rifle shot broke apart the impending truce with silence and echoed across the dry plains. Then the next and the next. Mick hunched on the hill behind the hunter with his hands over his ears. He couldn't tear his gaze away from the dark hulks lying on the prairie below as he counted four more shots. So the buffalo hunter only killed seven. Nausea churned his stomach.

"An excellent day's work. We can return home soon." Mr. Conch sat on the hill facing his kills and fished for his flask.

Mick recovered his wits while he surveyed a higher hill to his left. Through the thinning dust, he spied a bare-chested man armed with a bow on his horse. His gaze bore holes into Mick's heart.

Never had he seen such an expression on a man's face.

Even back home. Maybe his own was like it at the deaths of his darlings. *That man is me own mirror of angst.*

Mr. Conch jerked his hand over his shoulder. "Get your knife and the rest of the supplies out of your pack. Choose one and start cutting. I'm going for our horses at the outpost. Did you hear?"

Mick shook his head, held out his hands, and faced the man on the hill. "I'm sorry."

The buffalo hunter slugged Mick's shoulder, knocking him sideways. He cursed through clenched teeth. "Never you mind that filth, and don't apologize for anything. Get to working or we'll lose daylight. You got this one chance before I report you." Mr. Conch smirked. "Plus, I got the gun."

Mick gulped back his retort and groped inside his pack. Now he wanted his own gun and didn't have one. He had hatred in his heart and didn't want that. What a tragic world.

"Got it?"

"Aye." He gripped the hunting knife in his fist while he waited for the buffalo hunter to leave. A knife pitted against a gun wouldn't do. He approached the nearest brown, motionless hulk. It was close to the height of his cottage's lowest eve.

The killing of magnificent beasts appalled him. He stared at his glinting blade and the hide. His hand shook. He searched the hill for the stoic man. Gone. Mick gritted his teeth and crossed himself. He'd finish this hellish, bloody job. Ed's idea of farming in Minnesota was in his mind an ardent hope and the only viable plan for his life.

What Mick had expected to be a glorious day—finally working for pay, his wish to see tribal people with his own Irish eyes, plus a buffalo to boot—ended up on his list of his worst days yet in America.

12

RANCHER'S WOMAN

Must be a dire circumstance, or is it a warning?
Mick

Twenty Years Later
St. Paul, Minnesota
Early Spring, 1887

Mick kicked a piece of wadded up newspaper blowing past his feet as he trekked toward home on a layer of thin, crunchy snow after his railroad shift. "Bah. Wheat farming in '67 Minnesota with the railroad's 40,000-bushel capacity grain elevator had promised us success. Dolts to believe it." *What was I thinking?* Ed wasn't the best person to make plans with, even though he rescued Mick from Manhattan. Didn't it thrill Mick to split from his eejit brother after those cursed farming years? Who knew tuberculosis would ravage the area? *Only God Himself.* Mister Death cursed him again with losing Shauna and their four children during those eighteen years.

He studied the full moon skirting behind fast moving clouds. The same moon here rose over his homeland. Sunrises and sunsets, as well. The years hadn't lessened the terrible nightmares of his family's misfortunes in Ireland, or the stark memories of their suffering and deaths when he was awake or asleep. Nothing had completely erased the sight of their misery from his mind. Mayhap one day someone would create something that could take it away.

"Shauna, me heart's own beloved." He jammed his hat tighter over his head and hunched his shoulders against the chill. *Me broken heart showed itself 'tis best to live life alone.* Why did it take years to get the message he shouldn't marry or have children?

The odds were in his favor he never fell ill. Didn't the crew avoid him at the pub after he blamed Mister Death for all his losses? Wasn't whiskey partially to blame for that slip up? No, 'twas Mister Death. Couldn't blame whiskey for the tragic curse of tuberculosis. Whiskey gave him courage to face life's possible tragedies.

Icy snowflakes fluttered against his face. Like on the farm. Mick arrived at his dwelling, turned the key inside his door's lock, and it swung inward. "Peculiar curse, that tuberculosis. Someone powerful should investigate that affliction, aye, Grey?" He fingered his dog's soft gray-and-white patchy fur as he entered his compact railroad housing, then slid on an envelope laying on the floor beneath the letter slot.

Grey leapt away from his scrambling feet, as Mick seized the door's edge. "By all that's holy, nigh to breaking me neck." He clicked the door shut and examined the envelope's address. "Ontario? No sender name." Removing his gloves, he slit it open with his pocketknife and slid out the smudged note paper. "So, Ed, the tenacious gambler, plans to pay me back for the sale of me farmland? Shockers, that. Bringing me money." He edged to his desk for his calendar propped under his tiny front window. "In two days? Money's the only reason I'd welcome him, Grey."

Grey yipped and wagged his stub of a tail.

These past five months as a switchman for the Chicago,

Milwaukee, and St. Paul railway at least earned Mick a living. Wasn't independence what he'd hoped for? Dreamt of? But losing a third family was the stuff of more nightmares. *Three wives. Nine children.* What happened to them haunted his dreams. Not the Irish American dream Mick wanted for himself, was it? *I wish to forget what happened, aye?* He'd never forgotten yet. It was all as fresh as yesterday. He refused to ever risk his heart again except for loving a dog. He'd never give up dogs.

"Must get to making supper." Mick removed his outer clothing then entered his narrow kitchen with a potbelly stove. He added wood and kindling then struck the flint and lit the kerosene lamp as well. He'd have time to mull over his life some more while he warmed his place and waited for the water in the teakettle to heat.

"What'll satisfy our hunger tonight?" Scanning his two shelves of jarred and canned goods, Mick found nothing to entice him. Maybe Mrs. Chilcott's gift? His neighbor's berry jam with bread and another bit of beans with bacon could do the trick.

A train rumbled along the ground, approaching the switchyard. Like a buffalo herd. The metal hulk grew louder in its nearness, rattling his kitchen window and items on the shelves. "Holy heavens. The slat across the shelves." He laid his arm over the broken slat up against the jars and cans, until the monster slowed and passed farther down the track.

"Grey, remember when the shelf crashed to the floor, and you had the frights for days? Now you don't pay any mind to the trains at all. But I can't abide the ruckus."

He stepped away from the shelves and set the lamp on the table. Then he pumped water into Grey's bowl, dropped some bacon from breakfast onto a cracked dish, and served himself the last two pieces while the beans heated in the pan. Sitting in the twilight, Mick tugged out his pocket watch. Six o'clock. He could fill the evening hours thinking about the past or the future. Which would it be? Mick yawned. The future.

What he wanted most was a quiet place with earth and sky, open land, and fresh growing things to eat. "That desire never changes." Should he save or spend the money Ed would give him? Should he try farming again, and if so, where? "Naught will come of it."

———

~~St. Paul, Minnesota Five Months later~~
Late Summer

"St. Paul won't do, Kelly." Mick swigged his last drop of whiskey. "Not the same as New York City, but nigh enough. Too many people and not fond of the chaos. Me railroad chums been pleasant enough to run with. Well, nah. Lost their appeal altogether."

Kelly, the barkeeper, smirked. "And where would you be going to, eh? What is it you want, me friend?"

Even this, Mick's favorite pub, lost its charm. "Been in the United States for nigh twenty years, I have. Am I settled? Any the wiser?" He shook his head and nearly toppled off his stool. "Only wise choice was leaving that cursed farm and the railway."

"So 'tis wise leaving now?" Kelly propped his weight onto his elbows on the glossy polished counter.

"Thinking so." Mick plunked his tumbler down. "Thinking 'tis wise to return to Iowa."

"What for?"

"Was there before with the railroad. Hunted buffalo." Mick shuddered. "Dreadful job. I'll not be doing something like that again."

Kelly scoffed. "There're no buffalo left. Were you dreaming, man?"

"Wasn't a dream. 'Twas a nightmare. A few herds were there in those days. Gimme another, Kelly." He outstretched his glass.

"Not I." Kelly tidied some glasses. "You've had the limit you made for yourself. Away home with you and get some rest."

"Home? Rest? Both are elusive for me grasp." He stretched his arms, then kneaded his sore shoulders and back. "I'll tell you an eerie dream, and should you make a good explanation of it, I'll pay me entire tab. Then you'll gimme another splash, aye?"

Kelly shook his head. "And why should I be wanting to hear 'bout your dream, man?"

"You simpleton, to have me entire tab paid."

"Don't I know the railroad is good for it?"

"Well, and you're me only friend of a sort." Mick folded his arms. "I wish to tell of it and have it explained."

"Go on, then." Kelly shifted his weight and wiped the counter. "Give it a go."

"Always begins this way. I'm sleeping sound, but something hits me window. 'Tis birds crashing against the pane with a fierce wind. I go outside—"

"Why?" Kelly slapped the counter. "Stay in bed and your nightmare will burst."

Mick growled. "'Tis not our deal that you tell me what to dream. Tell me the meaning only." At Kelly's nod, Mick continued. "Once outside, there's laughter from beyond the hedgerows and a stone wall. Shauna calls to me. There're other muffled voices. I hasten into a maze of hedges to follow the laughter and then I recognize Maura, Fiona, and Shauna's voices—me three wives passed on before me." He crossed himself and cleared his throat.

"Hold up. You've had three wives? A nightmare of its own."

"You can count. Such a brilliant one you are." He wiggled his glass. "Apologies. Need that drink, Kelly." He swallowed his tears and wiped his nose. "Out of your fond heart?"

Kelly fetched another bottle and poured. "Only a bit till you're done. Per our deal."

Mick gulped his ration. "I follow the women's voices, turn a corner of hedge, and there's a barred, padlocked metal gate. Beyond the bars is another wooden gate. From behind that comes children and women's laughter. I hear *Da* a few times. 'Tis all me children, Kelly, I know it. I feel it in me soul. There're nine of them. Lost to Mister Death. I'm thinking 'tis heaven beyond the gates." He wiped his tears with his sleeve.

Kelly's mouth opened. "Ah, Mick. 'Tis too many." His voice sounded choked. "I see why you keep company with your whiskey."

"Yeah, but whiskey doesn't help." He glanced into the bottom of the empty glass. "So I shove me arm through the bars to reach the second wood gate. 'Tis just beyond me fingertips."

"Ends there?"

"Nah, that's when I notice the clearest brook ever seen flowing underneath both gates and beyond the wall. There's splashing and music. Shauna's voice whispers to me between the closed doors of the gate as they crack open. I hear a foot-step and turn. Whoosh, someone throws a black cloak over me. I yell and awaken. Dreamt it three times now."

"Dagnabbit." Kelly straightened. "The black cloak ends it?"

"Dagnabbit? Strange word."

"Heard it from an old California gold prospector. The cloak?"

"Oh, aye. Aye, 'twas the end. What do you say? What's the answer to me nightmare's riddle?"

Kelly pursed his lips. "How would I know? But you're doing it for a drink. Hmm. Me answer is more whiskey. Hey, did you say something 'bout a Mister Death?"

For the next hour, Mick slurred his way through tales of Mister Death. Then, after Kelly flipped the open sign around, he slid off the barstool.

"Farewell, Kelly. Grand knowing you. Should've stopped when you said." Mick swayed, then righted himself.

Kelly wiped snifters. "See you tomorrow night. Watch out for your Mister Death."

Mick shook his head and swaggered through the doorway into the moonlit early morning, and Grey rose from his guard post by Kelly's entry. He slid his hand over Grey's head. "Me one true friend, you are. Better than whiskey. Home to the boarding house we go then off to Iowa. Must make us some plans, God willing."

———

Iowa

Mick patted Grey on the bench beside him a week after speaking of his restlessness and nightmares with Kelly. "What do you think, boyo? Shall we stay?" He slowed his new horse, Scout, as they approached the general store on Main Street in the rural township and pulled up to a boardwalk connecting the storefronts. He surveyed the surrounding buildings and bonneted women. Their skirts swished in their hurry to cross the dusty street or swayed around their ankles as they stopped to peer into a window.

He tipped his cap and gave a nod to passersby to test the town's welcome. A few mothers escorting their older daughters glowered, as though he had wicked intentions toward their precious ones.

Grey stood on the seat and licked Mick's face. He stepped on the wagon's rail and circled back, wagging his tail. "In need of a break, aye, Grey? Down you go." Mick stretched, stashed his rifle beneath the bench, and collected his sack. He tied Scout to the hitching post near the trough and turned toward the store. A curled, yellowed sign painted with red letters of "Help Needed" hung beside the door. *Red letters, eh?* "Must be a dire circumstance."

He waited until the walkway emptied of shoppers before he climbed three steps for a closer inspection of the faded sign. Grey plopped beside him, and Mick massaged his ears. "Grey, should we give it a try? I suppose I should go inside to inquire—"

"No need."

Mick glanced up at the woman's voice. A near-to-middle-aged, tall, sunburnt, and full-figured woman stood three feet away. Her wide, blue-eyed stare was level with his, and her messy hair was as copper as his own. It was like seeing a feminine reflection of himself in a mirror. She wore a shabby work dress with a tight bodice missing a button. The woman inspected him from head to toe. "You'll do."

He removed his cap. "I'll do for what?"

"Working at me ranch." The woman tilted her head toward the window. "'Tis why you're reading this sign, yeah?" She stepped back, set her hands on her generous hips, and glowered. "Are you a simpleton? Or a laze-about? Don't need those."

The red letters had been a warning. *Don't need a disagreeable wretch of*—

"Your face shows your thoughts, mister. Thought you should know." The woman scowled. "Away with you then—"

"No." *Why'd I say it?* He sighed. "I'm needing work, 'tis true."

The wretched woman cocked one auburn eyebrow. "Me name's Molly Doyle. I'm a, on a, well on me own."

By all that's holy, not another boarding house Maeve, is she?

"Noticed you have a limp. An injury?"

"No, was born with it."

"Can you work hard?"

"Aye. Always do. On me farm, then for the railroads."

She aimed her gaze at his left hand. "You got a wife and children?"

"No. They all passed on." He crossed himself. "I should—"

"Birthed eight children, five living and grown up enough to live on their own, but we're estranged. You won't be meeting them. I have a sheep ranch. That your dog?" Molly indicated Grey.

Mick's face warmed at her frank speech about birthing to a stranger. "Is this a contest? Me name's Mick Muldoon. Married three times, lost me wives and all nine children. Grey here is me best friend, so you'll not get me without him."

"*Hmph.*" Molly's ample chest jiggled as she turned. "Me cart is down the way. Follow me if you've a mind to." Her curvy rear end jostled as she strode down the walkway, and he couldn't look away. His ears burned with the heat of his thoughts.

She turned around. "Mr. Muldoon, your dog, Grey, is why I'll be taking you home with me. I've a fondness for dogs."

Mick flipped Scout's reins to move along. "Grey, me boyo, Iowa's rolling green hills aren't Ireland's, but it soothes me spirit anyway." They followed Molly while he soaked up the countryside. He'd learned he couldn't thrive without the earth's aroma, or his spirit dried up like that dead garden in his dreams. Strange how, when he finally got behind those stone walls and gates in his recurring nightmare, he discovered a forlorn and empty garden overrun by weeds.

The Doyle farm lay a few miles out of town. A windbreak of elm trees surrounded a building, a whiteboard ranch house was hidden until they turned onto the drive. Mick's spirit dried up like the paint chips off Molly's porch. A two-story outbuilding held on for dear life in worse condition than the home. The red barn was the jewel, being in the best shape of all three buildings. *Suppose 'tis grand for Scout.* His horse would be sheltered well if Mick stayed on.

Two horses whinnied and trotted to a trough. *Must be nigh suppertime.* The small flock of sheep lifted their heads as the wagons approached.

Grey fixated on the flock and flattened his neck and head.

He's gone sheepherding in his mind. Mick chuckled. "That's it, keep up your image, boyo. She likes you best."

Molly called out as she climbed down from her cart. "Help unload supplies before you settle in."

"You're so sure I'll be staying then?" He snorted.

"You're here, aren't you?"

After they unloaded, cared for the horses, and fed the livestock, he headed with his sack toward the dilapidated outbuilding. *Dodgy carriage house.*

"And where do you think you're off to?" she screeched.

He whipped around. "Eh? To me housing. That building there." *Is this wretched, rude woman also daft?*

"Well, and if you think that building's safe for you, get away with you, for you must be empty-headed."

"Me?" He stomped toward Molly. "Woman, you have gruff ways 'bout you I don't much care for. Wasn't it you that asked for hired help? Make it worth me time by being polite."

Her shoulders slumped. "Me apologies. When a body's exhausted, it don't care 'bout good manners."

"Right. Exhaustion is a thing I know." He headed toward the rickety porch. "Is this building in better shape than the other? Appears not." Mick stepped up the stairs and one gave way. Pain shot up his back with the slam of his foot onto solid ground below. His sack flew sideways and knocked into Molly. They both burst into laughter.

Grey woofed and wagged his nubby tail.

She held her ribs. "Shall we start our introduction over? Name's Molly Doyle and this is home. Been in me husband's family for generations. He's gone." She glanced away. "Nigh four years. 'Tis why there's work to be done. Before they left, me sons did what they could. Me youngest left for the city two months ago. She was fifteen and took up as a maid. Not many jobs here for the youth. Let's go round." Molly headed to the back door. "Me sons worked on the barn and made some repairs inside our home but had no time or interest in the carriage house."

They passed a water pump and trough, approached the back door, and entered the simple kitchen. "Your dog can sleep in here for now."

"Stay," Mick commanded Grey. "He'll need food and water."

"Aye. I'll fetch two bowls." She retrieved the chipped crockery and handed them to Mick. "One more thing before you settle in. This deal we're making. There're other duties." She scrutinized Mick. "You look to be younger than me. I'm thirty-five, and you're?"

"Forty-eight. Last January."

"*Hm*, but in fine shape. Been a widow for some time now."

Is she saying? He gaped. *Nah. She wasn't blushing.*

"I'm speaking of the ways of a man and woman. Clear enough for you?" Her contempt for him shimmered in her bright blue eyes.

He recoiled. "We aren't married, and I gave that up." A flush rose from his chest to his hairline. His mouth went dry. Could he do such things without marriage?

"Glory be." She shook her head. "Mick Muldoon, fresh from Ireland, are you? No one cares for conventions in this land. Wild ways are what we'd say back home, but not here. We do what we please. Law officers are scarce, and the church isn't into our business as in the old country." Her intense gaze locked with his. "What'll your answer be then?"

Mick's objections swirled and vanished. Was Molly right about this? He clenched his eyes shut, shoved away Christian teaching, and squelched any guilt from all his beliefs to see if they'd stay buried. *Numb.* There was no reaction. He shrugged.

"Think on it a bit. Follow me to me eldest son's room." Molly ambled down a narrow hallway. A door stood open. The dim room had one window covered with a white curtain, a large bed with a quilt of various blues, a washstand with a basin, and a high dresser with crystal knobs. "You can stash your clothes here and shave using this." She showed him a round brass mirror hung on an otherwise empty wall.

He crunched his hat's brim.

"Must get our supper ready." She left him to consider his decision.

Mick's nightmare began the same. He found the path around the stone wall, entered the garden, and mourned its untended condition. He fought his way through dry under-brush while Shauna sobbed and called to him. "Mick, what's happening?" She backed away into the shadows.

"No. No."

"Mick, wake up. Muldoon." Someone shook his shoulder.

He jerked awake and sat up. Sweat dripped down his back. His eyes focused in the moonlight. Mick gawked at the white, ample figure of a woman a foot away. "Molly?"

"Well, I ain't this Shauna you been yelling for. But I'm here, aren't I? Move over now." Molly upturned Mick's quilt.

Mick didn't object, although he was unsure. *Molly made it plain what she's after.* Two lonely people living together, what did he expect?

———

~~Several Months Later~~
Mid-Spring, 1888

. . .

The next lambing season, Molly birthed their own little lamb and named her Moira. She had curly, copper hair and the looks of her mother. When their daughter was old enough to eat solids, Molly encouraged him to take part in Moira's care.

Mick would have none of that. Didn't Mister Death always steal them? He'd locked his heart up safe behind double gates in the dead garden in his nightmares. He resisted Moira's allure with all his strength and ignored her as much as possible. Could he avoid his daughter until he was sure Mister Death wouldn't take her?

———

We're finally away to the Justice of the Peace. Mick stood before the shaving mirror to wet and comb his dark auburn waves smooth. He dipped his comb in the basin of water. Two-year-old Bridget napped on the bed behind him, and four-year-old Liam sleepily studied his da. "These gray streaks are taking over with each addition to me family, boyo. A da of four in me fifties. Never expected such a gloriously ridiculous thing." He also never expected Molly's reticence about marriage. He shouldn't have trusted in that. Or focused on only being a good da to children who had survived Mister Death. But that had been worth Molly's deception. Thanks to sweet Moira, now six, who had changed his walled-up heart.

Baby Cara cried from the other room. Molly crooned to her and asked Moira to bring her a cloth. *Must be feeding time.*

Mick slowly sat on the bed beside his other sleeping children and stared out the window, mesmerized by the clothesline of diapers flapping in the breeze and reflected on the past. What would he have missed if he'd kept his heart locked up tight against ever loving anyone again?

. . .

He had feared for Molly and their second unborn child that fateful day when he opened his heart to young Moira. Molly had been so ill with a fever. He had faced some of his fears. He hadn't glimpsed or sensed Mister Death for nearly a decade. Nor seen any angels. *Strange, that.* Molly called to him, and Mick had entered their room.

Molly's face had glistened with perspiration, and her eyes were dull and unfocused. "You must take Moira. Feed her. I can't. She's helpless. You must do it. I need some water."

Mister Death hadn't taken her yet, he had thought, so mayhap there was hope in that. Mick took a deep breath, scooped up the whimpering Moira, and poured another cup of water for Molly. He glanced down at Moira, her wild curly hair tickling his nose. He jerked his face away. "Dagnabbit."

"Bit. Da." Moira's rosy lips pursed as she played with his shirt buttons. "Da."

"And you would have those dimples to bewitch me, yeah? By all that's holy, how can I take care of you?" He carried his daughter into the kitchen and set her in a chair. She screeched like a banshee until he lifted her from the chair and patted her back while she snuggled against his chest. "Sh, Moira. Why must you cry? Mam is ill. Sh."

Moira crunched his shirt in her tiny fists as he jiggled her. "You have the looks of one of your sisters, aye? Didn't think so at first. Her name was Maggie. She was your age when Mister Death . . . Can I speak this way to a child?" Mick hadn't gotten beyond two years with fathering his children. Mister Death had taken them all away before then.

He had considered Moira while she nibbled on a biscuit chunk. *Can I be a ' to her, should she live?* He'd need to find out quick. Maybe he could think back and follow his own da's behavior? He'd try to be a better da with their next child. *Sweet Moira's survival changed me hopes for me new family's future.*

Applying how his own da treated his children was a grand notion. Following most of that had helped Mick to be a good Da to Moira, Liam, then Bridget. He'd thrown his whole being into learning what his children liked and how to help stop their fussing or squelch their fears, hadn't he? The terrible thing was, he'd stopped paying attention to Molly and her odd behavior. He should have asked more questions. *How could I have been so trustful of her, and unaware of her deception and struggles?*

While cradling their awakening newborn daughter, Cara, in his arms, Mick had urged Molly to marry. "If there are going to be children, the church would want this done right."

"We can't. We'll be damned. The wrath of God shall come upon us." Molly's voice shook. She cuddled hungry Cara closer to her bosom.

"Wrath of God? Now you mention His feelings 'bout us? You said you didn't care what the church says 'bout marriage, only baptism."

Mick almost didn't catch Molly's muffled words behind her hand. He sagged onto the rocking chair beside the bed. "Did I hear you right? Did you say you've already a husband?"

Molly handed Cara to him. "He left us six years ago. Don't know where he is. 'Tis why I couldn't marry you. So ashamed." She covered her face again.

He shifted the tiny babe to burp her on his shoulder and checked the blanket for snugness. "I don't understand why you'd deceive me, Molly. Why did you feel you should lie? I haven't been a practicing Catholic for years now, and neither have you, aye? Couldn't you have explained yourself better?"

Her pale and tired face with reddened eyes from crying tweaked Mick's heartstrings. "Aye, we both forsook our faith because we easily can do so here in a land who mostly shuns us. Why did I lie? I didn't wish to be left alone." She sniffled. "I couldn't. Not again."

He kissed her hand. "Do you think I'd desert me own children? I'm not such a rotten man as that. Not all men will do such things, aye?"

"Not all. But I've seen enough. I deceived you when we had no children, then trapped us within the lie." Her eyes slowly closed. "I need rest, Mick."

"Truly, I think it wouldn't have mattered to me. So we wait, Molly. Go on as we were, aye. We'll know where your dishonorable husband is someday." Mick wondered why he didn't feel angry, or sad. He imagined his heart was a goose down pillow that was torn up by a fox—a tattered, empty sack.

He had been too content to wait things out. Neither were practicing Catholics. Although the priest in town knew their situation because they had Moira baptized, then Liam, so their children wouldn't be damned.

Mick avoided the church. He didn't want to attend confession, for not everything was his fault. He knew he couldn't give up his whiskey. He'd never sleep or provide for his family without it. Useless laudanum. It had knocked him out so he couldn't work, and it left his head fuzzy. Maybe worse, He didn't want God to be extra offended and get angry from his unholy presence inside His church. Not after his shameless arrangement with Molly. How could God forgive him that?

The following week after Cara's birth, Mick caught a dark flash. It turned out to be a delivery man at their gate with a telegram. It was from Molly's husband's family solicitor.

Mick stood beside her as she read it.

"All me letters to his family from long ago were returned unopened. Thought they must've moved somewhere." She scanned the paper and held Mick's hand against her shoulder. "So the gambling da of me ten children died from the influenza, it says. I'm a true widow. Why would the solicitor send this? Why not his family?"

"Curious thing." Mick shoved his hands into his pockets.

"More important, 'tis time we get married as we discussed earlier. We'll go into town tomorrow."

"Aye. 'Tis time." She folded the letter and closed her eyes.

So, on this day in 1894, the Muldoon family shall become legitimate and blessed by the church at last. Mick studied the bedroom and his sleeping children. "Mayhap Mister Death gave up on hunting me, aye." Could he try not drinking as much? He may not need the boost in courage it provided him. But the pain and nightmares may not allow the loss of it.

13

UNWANTED IDENTITIES

'Tis a tragic happening.
Mick

Eight Years Later
Doyle Ranch
Late Summer, 1900

A black, hooded shadow flashed through Mick's dream, awakening him with a drenching sweat before dawn's light. *A new century, and here's me old nemesis.* Why had he believed Mr. Death was no longer hunting him or his family? What made him appear now? *Last time I thought I glimpsed him was in '94, after Cara was born.* But his American children thrived.

Mick surveyed his bedroom for any movement then flipped off the blanket, careful not to awaken Molly. She'd been testy and tired of late.

Was Mister Death truly in his imagination? Couldn't be from his whiskey. The demon seemed real enough when sneaking around during troubled times. Was trouble brewing? *Shouldn't be.* His heart's garden flourished in his dreams.

The day went smoothly enough, nothing unusual. A day like any other. Before suppertime, Mick hung the pitchfork and shovel on the spikes near Scout's stall door. Something black whooshed past. Chills bristled the hair on his arms. What brought that devil around? His family was healthy and content, except for Molly. She had been acting strange.

He hastened from the barn into the twilight up to the house with Grey following him. They burst through the front door and approached his children at the kitchen table doing their schoolwork or reading by lamplight under Moira's guidance. The dog slid under Liam's chair.

"Ho there, macushlas. Where's your mam?" Mick swiveled around the kitchen and peeked into the unlit common room.

"In bed again." Moira lay down her book. "Mam was in bed when we got home. She's always going to bed before supper, and I must cook it. I'm only ten." She bit her lip. "Sister Mary told us at school that sometimes mothers get tired and not to worry. Am I complaining, Da?"

Liam bent over his chair and petted Grey. "Mam ignores us after school—"

"Only a little." Bridget kept her voice low, while she watched Cara draw a picture of a horse.

Or is it a dog?

"See, Da? I drew you. Do you like it?" Six-year-old Cara held up her artwork.

Mick patted his children's heads. "Aye, macushla. 'Tis perfect. All will be fine. I'll go speak with Mam."

Moira stood. "Shall I bring her a biscuit and tea?"

"If you'd like to. I'll call for you should I need something else." He forced a smile. "She's wanting a rest, I'm thinking."

Cara giggled and squirmed as Mick took a step. He glimpsed something moving beneath her dress bodice.

Grey growled, but stayed where he was by Liam's command.

"Ho there. What's happening inside?" Mick patted the small roving bulge. Definitely something alive. "Cara, open it up."

She unbuttoned the stirring material, revealing a tiny, gray bunny. Its pink nose wiggled, and its whiskers jiggled.

"And where did you get that? Outside, aye? It belongs there with its mam." *By all that's holy.* "We're safe enough with a bunny, but when you brought in the baby snake, it 'bout did Moira in. No more, aye?"

"Yes, Da. But it's dark outside." Cara cuddled the bunny and rocked it.

"All the more reason. Its mam will be sad and looking for it. Liam, take the bunny outside, and I'll keep Grey with me."

Dark outside, she says. Nothing's darker than Mister Death. That evil creature didn't appear for no reason. His heart pounded with every footstep as he and Grey headed down the hall and entered the dim bedchamber. Highlighted by the rising full moon's beam, he found a note lying on the quilt against the pillows.

"Gone to visit parents." He flipped it over. The paper was blank. An icy chill swept through Mick's body. Gone. Without warning? No, 'twasn't true. Hadn't she given him warnings by her withdrawal from him and the children? He should have paid more attention to her struggles. But what did she struggle with? If he'd loved Molly, he would've noticed. *'Tis all me fault.*

The room swam around Mick. He closed his eyes and collapsed onto the bed.

Grey laid his muzzle on Mick's leg.

How can I work and care for the children? No blaming Mister Death this time. Would the children blame him for their Mam's disappearance? They'll think she doesn't love them. How could he explain her frailty when he didn't fully understand it?

Shall I hide me shame? Mick's breath came faster than his thoughts. *Me only wife who lived, yet she deserts us.* He spun in circles in search of Mister Death. "I know you're nigh, you bloodsucker. You-you, life-stealer."

Moonlight spilled through the window sash and lit the

shapes in the bedroom with silver, but nothing stirred in the shadows. Mick's legs shook and gave way. He crawled along the mattress, peering further into the shadowed corners. "You took her alive. Still robbed us, you did."

"Da?"

Mick spun over and sat up. He struggled to control his breathing. "Liam."

"What are you doing?" Liam's eyes were wide.

Mick gulped. "I, uh, I was . . . um. Well, and what did you hear me say?"

"You said something was took, Da. Somebody robbed you?"

"Yeah, I lost me bottle. Do you know where 'tis? The one under the bed is gone."

Liam shook his head. "No, Da. You didn't tell me where you put your new one. You said you were trying to drink less. And we know not to touch your bottle unless you ask us to fetch it for you. Where's Mam? Do you know?"

Mick slid off the bed, snatched the note, and approached his ten-year-old son. "I do. I do know that." He drew a deep breath and ruffled Liam's hair. "Shall we go to the girls, and I can read Mam's letter once, for all of you?"

"Letter? Yes, Da."

"Alright, then. All will be well. Worry naught."

He ambled down the hall after Liam while he unscrambled his thoughts. Half of his prayer to God was answered— four children lived. But Molly's tragic desertion? Mick wiped his brow as his son entered the kitchen before him.

"Girls, Da has a note from Mam." Liam extended his hands. "I knew she wouldn't leave us."

"She's done it." Moira burst into tears.

"What?" Liam turned back to Mick, his face pale. "Da? Did she?"

Mick sucked in a breath and pulled up a chair. He settled Cara on his lap. "So you suspected trouble, macushla? Of the five of us, Moira, you'd be the one to catch on. You were the best helper for your Mam."

Moira nodded. A tear slid down her cheek.

He let out a sigh that pricked like thorns inside his throat. "I paid no attention. Owe you all apologies and more. Come here, Moira. Liam. Bridget, did you have worries as well 'bout your Mam?"

Bridget had buried her crumpled face in her arms on top of the table. She rolled her face sideways to peek at him. "Yes."

The stunned and panicked expressions of his children clawed at Mick's heart. There was nothing to be done but face this together. He'd tried to squelch his fears. He was never much of a man or a da, but dread now crashed against him like a stormy wave broken free from the sea.

He breathed deep. "The unexpected happened. Your Mam made up her mind to leave us. For a visit, she wrote." Mick pursed his lips to restrain more words.

The two older girls sobbed while Cara wailed. Mick rocked her writhing body and held her tight against his chest until she tired herself out. What could he say to his children to make this disastrous situation better?

Liam rose from the table and stood rigid—his large blue eyes aimed at his da until a fierceness crept into them.

Mick extended his hand. "Liam, me boyo—"

"Leave me be." Liam darted out of the kitchen.

"Don't worry, Da, Liam will be okay. He'll return. God and the saints will look after Mam, and you know He'll take care of us all." Moira comforted her sisters with embraces and kisses.

Mick cleared his throat after the girls calmed. "Mam left a brief note to explain her absence. Shall I read it to you? It says, 'Gone to visit parents.' Now there's a way to look at these things." The paper trembled in Mick's grip. He laid it on the table. "Mam isn't ill unto death. No, Mam is alive and—"

"Da." Liam returned to the kitchen with Mick's empty traveling bag. "Will you go after her?"

"Ah, no, son. Mam needs some time away from us. You all noticed she was very tired? Let's give her some rest, shall we?"

The girls didn't speak, but Liam did. "No."

"I'd say Mam told us where she is and didn't just disappear into the mist. She wants us to know she'll be safe. She wrote of visiting her parents. I promise to go visit her soon, aye." This wasn't the time to share his suspicion with the children she might not return, and this wasn't his ranch to keep if she didn't. *That family Molly married into cares nothing for her wellbeing.* They hadn't answered even one of her letters over the years. Would she return? What if those heartless people heard of her desertion? Gossip is a peril like wildfire. He'd better act fast to keep his family from getting burned and set a plan in the works for their welfare. *Dear holy Christ, please have mercy upon us.*

"Da, can you hear me? Can you go tomorrow?" Liam upthrust his chin, and his lip trembled.

"Ah, well, you see, I must work each day, aye? I must feed us all."

Moira folded her hands as if in prayer. "We can take care of the ranch, Da. We know how. At least, Liam and I can do it while you go after Mam."

He addressed each youngster. "I know you can do most of the chores. Schooling should continue for all but Liam. Sadly, I'll need you here, boyo. And hear me on this. I'm the only one who can get a job with the railroad. We may need the money, well, to plan for troubles. Can any of you do me jobs?"

The children gaped at him and shook their heads.

"Me boss will be the one to give me the time off to check on Mam. But I tell you this—the five of us all together must be strong." His voice shook. "We are gifts to one another. I love you, macushlas."

Mick's children scrambled to embrace him. Their thin

arms enfolding him helped lessen his fears, but he craved an entire bottle of his liquid comforter tonight. As soon as he could find his new bottle, and everyone was in bed.

———

Early Autumn

Mick clocked out after working the rails and rode Scout home. The day had been horrible, marred by a foreman's debilitating injury. His chum, Flash, had been the one to swing a pick and missed his mark, hitting the foreman's foot. Who could say where the blame lay? The steel gangs worked as fast as possible.

The only certainty was the risks of the job. Mick's thoughts wandered into disastrous events in Minnesota. His neighbor, Cal, was impaled by that pitchfork when he fell backward from the hayloft. There was the boy who fell into a grain silo and suffocated before they could dig him out. *Then, that panther nigh got me.* He no longer blamed every terrible thing on Mister Death, did he? He slumped from exhaustion in body and mind then caught his balance and hung onto Scout a little too tight.

Scout skittered and threw his head from Mick's confusing signals. "Whoa, gentle now. Settle." He pulled Scout up for a moment and repositioned himself firmly in the saddle. "Me apologies for entertaining dark memories. I'll pay better attention, aye? Get us on home."

The stress of parenting motherless children had built itself into a round tower fortress, like Castle Gardens, within Mick's mind. No amount of whiskey numbed the fears and doubts for his family's future. He found no escape from his current reality.

Guilt from pulling Liam from his learning at school to help

work the ranch weighed down on Mick like a rancher's knee shearing a sheep. There was no clever way to break his brilliant son out of the shearer's grip in this situation. What could he do to stop this madness?

When they arrived at the barn, Mick dismounted Scout and led him into his stall. While he gave the horse a good brushing and tended to its needs, it temporarily soothed his worries. "Mindless tasks to be sure. But aren't they comforting for us, Scout? And don't you deserve that treat for dealing with a dimwitted, knackered owner?"

The horse chewed a serving of oats before switching to his portion of alfalfa.

"Da." Cara entered the barn, ran up to Mick, and tapped his waist. "You got a letter today. It's all fancy with a seal on it. Hurry and come see."

"So I will. How'd you get so muddy?"

"I was playing in the creek. I caught a salamander, but Moira made me put it back." Cara sighed and hopped on one foot toward the barn door.

"No doubt. Wait for me, macushla, darkness is upon us."

Although Cara thought the seal was exciting, Mick sensed black clouds on the horizon bringing a storm of some sort. An envelope with a seal often represented an official communication from someone you'd rather not hear from. He selected a lantern from the hook beside the door, lit it, and exited the barn.

Cara sang as they sauntered. "'Come, Holy Ghost, Creator blest, and in our hearts take up Thy rest; come with Thy grace and heav'nly aid, to fill our hearts which Thou hast made. To fill our hearts which Thou hast made.' Do you like it, Da? Moira sings it all the time and Bridget taught it to me." She skipped ahead, surrounded by the lantern's gold light, toward the shadowed house.

He'd not heard that hymn, "Come, Holy Ghost," for some time. Ever since he took up living out of wedlock with Molly.

Going to Mass without confession and penance would've been offensive to God. Didn't he choose rightly to avoid Mass? But sweet Cara's song about God reminded him to thank the kind neighbors for faithfully taking his children to Mass most Sundays. He wiped his eyes. Should he or could he return to church?

The aroma of stew swirled around Mick, and his stomach growled. He whispered, "God, bless me children. Moira, for feeding us, Cara and Bridget, for singing songs for us. Me boyo works hard for us, he does." *Good children.* He had much to be grateful for.

Cara hurried up the porch steps and through the door, letting it slam behind her.

Mick swung open the door to find Grey wriggling and wagging his tail as Liam greeted him with the letter. Liam's eyes flickered with fear and unspoken questions.

Dishes clinked in the kitchen. Moira and Bridget were almost finished with supper preparations.

Cara hopped back into the common room. "See, Da? I can hop like a bunny. Do you see the seal?" She tugged on his sleeve.

"That I do, macushla. Here now. Give your Da a moment alone to read it, aye? Go help your sisters to put supper on the table."

"Yes, Da." Cara turned toward the kitchen, dragging her feet.

Liam stiffened and straightened his shoulders. "Can I stay with you, Da?"

"Aye." Mick read the addressee's information, and his heart plummeted into his boots. An attorney's office. The envelope shook in his hand. He lowered it, grappled for the chair back, and let himself slump onto the seat. Grey waited near Mick's knees.

Liam shuffled his feet. "Da?"

"Let me read it first." Mick scanned the lengthy, indirect

sentences twice to make sense of the message. He turned to Liam. "'Tisn't good news. I'll not lie 'bout it. 'Tis a notice to vacate the property." *That hardhearted family must've heard 'bout Molly.* A rushing sound rang in his ears. The room spun. He clenched the letter in one hand and the arm of the chair with the other.

"What's happened?"

"What did I expect? This. Kicking us off the land." Molly's husband's family were unknowns. He was a stranger and nobody to them. They had no family ties to his children. Without her living on their land and the death of her husband, they had no reason to care, no doubt. Christian charity should've done the trick.

Liam gripped Mick's arm. "Why, Da? I don't understand. Who is kicking us off our land?"

"Strangers to us. An attorney for the family who owns it. A rumor of our situation reached that family, wherever they live." Mick attempted to swallow with a dry mouth and throat. "Will you fetch me bottle?"

"Isn't this Mam's land—"

"No. I'll explain soon enough. I need me drink now."

Liam hurried down the hallway.

How will I explain? Would they blame him or their mother? *Think, man. Fix this before it goes too far.* Cara's song entered his thoughts. Heavenly aid. "That's it. Aid. Molly needs me aid. And we need hers. Haven't gone after her, have I?"

Grey laid his head on Mick's knee, and he fondled the dog's soft ears. "Bless me soul, Grey. I let her alone for nigh a month." He stood as Liam returned.

"Here, Da." Liam handed him the bottle. "You look better. Are you?"

"Aye, I am. I've got a plan to share with you all, and I'll tell you 'bout this letter. Let's go to the table. Time for supper."

Father and son entered the kitchen with Grey trailing behind them. The dog slid under Mick's chair. A roasted chicken, a fresh loaf of bread, and a bowl of shucked and boiled bright-yellow corn on the cob waited on the table. The children scrambled for their seats. Mick laid the letter next to his plate. Once the family of five settled, he asked Cara to say grace.

Cara straightened in her chair, checked each family member's readiness, and crossed herself. She folded her hands and recited. "Bless us, oh Lord, for these Thy gifts, and for . . . That, eh, what we are about to receive. In the name, uh, from Your bounty. Through Christ our Lord. In the name of the Father, the Son, and the Holy Ghost. Amen." She crossed herself, bit her lower lip, and looked to him.

Mick winked at her and urged his children to eat their supper in silence as he had taught them. When everyone finished eating, they lay down their silverware and waited for their Da. He took two swigs of whiskey and wiped his mouth. Would Molly be open to listening to his pleas or believe he'd attempt to pay more attention to her? Could he truly change? *All but the whiskey. Mustn't promise that away.*

Moira cleared her throat.

"So, here's me plan. I'll go to your grandmother's home to see Mam. Then we'll have a chat—"

"About Mam returning or about the land?" Liam frowned.

Mick thrust up his hand. "What did I tell you about interrupting adults when they're speaking?"

Liam stared at the table and traced his finger along a deep gash in the surface. "Sorry, Da."

"First, I must speak to your Mam 'bout her feelings. Let her have her say. I'll address the land issue with her, to be sure. This land belongs to your Mam's first husband's family. You know she was married before me and has grown children, aye?" He took a breath. "Well, 'tis a landowner's right to do as they wish with their property. As 'tis in Ireland." Mick's face warmed with his repressed resentment for England.

Cara's lower lip trembled. "You're bringing Mam home, Da? I want Mam."

Moira pulled Cara onto her lap. "Sh, now. Let Da tell us his plan."

"You heard me correct, and now . . ." A brilliant idea entered Mick's thoughts. If he told his children their Mam might be in St. Paul, he could take Molly there to be alone with her, woo her a bit to convince her he'd changed. Then she would be more likely to return with him. Surely, he could convince her. St. Paul was an exciting city, and since it was farther away, he could request more time off work from his boss.

Bridget clapped her hands. "I knew she wouldn't be away forever. We all love each other."

"Your Mam could be in St. Paul. I'll go find out. If we don't return within two days, you'll know I went into the city for her. You'll be fine together, aye? Moira's nearing eleven. I'll put her in charge of you." Mick glanced around the table at his children for their reactions.

They nodded.

Moira attempted a smile. "You should go, Da. I'll take care of everyone."

He stood. "I'll tell Mrs. Cook down the road I'll be away and ask her to keep an eye on you until me return. Liam, take her extra eggs and a bucket of milk for her trouble, aye?"

"Yes, Da. I will."

Mick clapped his hands together. "Well, then. That's settled. All will be well, macushlas. You'll see your Mam and bring her home in the shake of a lamb's tail, you have me promise." He hoped it was a promise he could keep.

14

SHATTERED VOWS

Hadn't he dreamt of ways to escape his own pain?
Mick

Iowa, 1900
Late Summer
'*Tis a blessing, working for the railway.* Mick not only supported his family, but it was a means of free transportation for employees as well. He rolled his tense shoulders to relieve some pain and anticipated Molly returning home where she belonged.

Passengers settled around him, including a young woman with a small boy. The boy, dressed in short pants and a cap, scratched his upper lip while he studied Mick's long, curled mustache. He wrinkled his nose.

Mick slipped his train pass from his shirt pocket and examined the cream-colored ticket while he waited the conductor to punch it. *Employee. For the Chicago, Milwaukee, St. Paul, Tacoma. ... Idaho East & Western R'wy Co.*

He chuckled. "A very long name for a very long track." He read on. *No. 9939 Pass—*

"Muldoon. Bust me buttons with the sight of you." The conductor, Bill O'Reilly, stood next to him and slapped his shoulder. "Haven't seen you down at Cleary's Saloon in weeks. Not like you. Are you still working Section 9?" Bill took Mick's ticket and punched it.

"Aye. Nigh to finishing it. Taking a few days off."

Bill punched tickets from the passengers nearest Mick. "When you're done with your rest, come on back to Cleary's. You're missing out on things."

"Sure, Bill. See you there." He'd hoped to keep his trip quiet for now. His boss hadn't asked many questions but stared Mick up and down like he'd find some answers pinned to Mick's shirt.

"See you." Bill headed to the car's entrance. "All aboard. Last call for Green Valley, Black Oak, Summerhill, and points beyond."

A pretty brunette woman across the aisle smiled when she caught Mick's glance.

He spun around to face the window. None of that. He shook his head and focused on the passing scenery.

The train jerked forward and picked up speed. Mick relaxed and let the train's rocking motion lull his body and mind. Trees, crops, barns, and cows, all where they should be —under late summer's cloudless, blue sky. But the players in his life weren't where they should be, were they? He wearied of the passing scenery, wiped his eyelids, and situated himself against his bag on the hard bench's back. One day, he might have the riches to ride in parlor, not in coach.

The train jolted and awoke Mick. A black cape swished through his corner vision. He stiffened. Then, he scanned every bit of the car, the passengers, and even under the benches. No Mister Death. Must've been a leftover dream.

From over the seat ahead, the curious boy stared at him again. "Did you lose something, mister?"

"No. Just looking at things."

"One time I lost my bear. Mama found him. He rolled down to the steps." He pointed to the front of the car. "Maybe what you lost is there."

Mick tugged on his mustache. "You may have the right of it. I'll be checking the steps as I leave."

"Tommy, let the man alone." The woman next to the boy pulled him down to sit beside her. "Mind your manners."

"Summerhill. Next stop, Summerhill." Bill called out from the rear of the car.

Mick gathered his bag and waited to exit the train as it squealed to a stop. His seat was near the back of the car, for he didn't care to be ogled as he climbed down the steps.

Two rows of passengers exited ahead of him. Nearing the steps with his mother, the friendly boy turned around. "I don't see anything. Hope you find what you lost, mister."

"As do I." As the mother tugged him down the steps, Mick stood and tipped his hat to the boy.

Standing on the platform, he consulted his map. By the looks of it, Molly's parents' home was about two miles away. Not a bad wander. He'd have extra time to partake from his bottle and rehearse his speech. Mick retrieved his whiskey and slung his bag over his shoulder. With his hat lowered against the sun, he headed east.

Mick halted before the Quincannon's home. *Shame how dilapidated 'tis without Mr. Quincannon.* The ranch style home's low roof had missing shingles, a cracked window or two, and its siding begged for a thick coat of paint. Comparing this place to Molly's slightly rundown, two-story home for their family made him feel privileged indeed.

The widow Quincannon answered the door. Tall and plump with a messy bun atop her head made her an older version of Molly. Mrs. Quincannon gasped, warning him Molly hadn't mentioned his visit.

Mick tipped his hat. "Morning."

"Oh, holy Mother." Mrs. Quincannon wrung her hands on her grimy apron and groaned. "Holy Saints preserve us. Holy Christ, have mercy—"

"Please, Mrs. Quincannon." He must stop her list of holies. "I'm that grieved if Molly didn't mention me visit. Didn't plan on staying overnight if that's what you're worrying 'bout."

"No." She stepped from behind the screen door, and onto the porch. She glanced at one of the curtained windows. "'Tis only that Molly hasn't been herself and is making no sense. Says she came for a bit of a rest." Mrs. Quincannon lowered her voice. "If 'tis all the same to you, please take her away. Something's not right in her head. Something's not right with leaving her husband and children. She won't speak of it except—"

"I know 'tis hard for you and for us." Mick lay his hand on her shoulder. "'Tis why I'm here. To take her home." He transferred his weight to relieve pain in his leg. "Truth be told, a Doyle attorney discovered we're on their land. They know Molly's not living there, and they've no loyalties to me and our children—"

"Such a shame." Mrs. Quincannon held her chest with one hand and fumbled for a rocking chair next to the front door with the other. She plopped onto it. "I've no room here for them. Come sit with me." She indicated another rocker. "Woe is me. What've I done? The poor littles." Mrs. Quincannon switched her gaze to the heavens then covered her face and head with her apron. "Never a thought in me head 'bout them."

And she thinks her daughter is daft? "Please explain."

Mrs. Quincannon dropped her apron onto her lap. "I hope you'll forgive me, but I do run off with me mouth at times." She bit her lip. "Here's the truth of it. I think I know how they heard 'bout Molly. I told Mabel, who must've told June, and she would tell Maggie, who may've told Maureen Sheahan down at the store." Mrs. Quincannon threw her hands up. "And once Maureen hears anything, well, the entire town knows 'bout it. But for certain the Sheahan's are good friends of the Doyle's, don't you see?"

What I see is me world spinning out of control.

His mother-in-law clasped her hands as though in prayer, and whispered, "'Tis worse of course, for I mentioned Molly claims she wishes a divorce." Tears trickled down her rosy cheeks and hung onto her jaw. "Will you forgive me for gossiping 'bout it?"

Her tears mesmerized Mick, and his thoughts froze from the shocking news, erased by the sensation of ice water being splashed over his brain.

"Can you forgive me? The only thing Molly said that's worth the hearing is divorce."

That word reverberated around him, forcing him to stand. His own mother would die of shame if she knew. "I can. I heard you. But I must speak to Molly. Where is she?"

Mrs. Quincannon rose. "She's in her room. Been sleeping away most days." She led him through a sparsely furnished room with a tattered green rug, faded blue curtains, and unpainted walls. They stood before a closed door. She knocked. "Molly. You got a visitor."

Bed springs squeaked. Footsteps on the wood floor approached the door. The latch clicked, and the door cracked open. In a filthy nightgown, Molly's oily red hair hung in long strands over her chest. Her stench wafted over him. "You?"

Mick scrunched his hat and stepped back. "'Tis me, true. Your husband." He took a deep breath and almost gagged. "Will you get dressed and come outside with me for a moment?"

"No. I feel ill." She stepped aside. "Well, come inside then."

Mrs. Quincannon dabbed her damp face. "I'll be in the kitchen."

He entered the dim bedroom, tugged apart the dingy curtains, and opened the window. Sweet fresh air wafted inside, and he inhaled.

"Who said you could do that?" Molly's voice twanged like an off-key piano note.

Mick swiveled around. He'd heard her like this before. "'Tis a fine day out." He kept his sights on his wife as he scooped soiled clothing from a chair under the window and cleared a spot for his bag on her dresser. He grappled for his whiskey, sat on the edge of the seat, and took a gulp. *Seems to be bad timing, coming here today.*

Molly stomped her foot. "Did I tell you to put your bag down? And I see you've brought your bottle." She shook her head, perched on the bed, and muttered, "Yeah, always the whiskey. Always drinking, he was."

Mick paused the whiskey bottle inches from his lips. "Aye, I know that. I do. I worked as well. But you understand me need for it, don't you?"

"Hmm." Molly hummed a tune. She rocked back and forth, like a leaf in the breeze.

Now I have the reason her mother is frightened.

"But did he ever understand me?" Molly mumbled, twisting a strand of her lank hair, and separated each piece. "Did he ever love me? Did he have a care for his wife? Not so. Not him." She glowered at her husband then brooded. "You came here. Who asked you to—"

He held up his hands. "Now, Molly. I came here to listen to you. Can you tell me of your welfare? I know I never asked how you were. So tell me." Maybe she must speak of her feelings. What did he know about that? He'd tied his own up in the grave with his macushla, Shauna.

Molly hesitated with her head cocked, studying him through the straggly hair covering her face. "Then here's me story. You never loved me, for 'twas only ever Shauna. You said her name in your sleep, you did." She rose from the bed and moved near the door. "Don't wish to be anyone's Mam. Birthed fourteen children. Do you hear? And I don't want to rear more children up to adults. I'm weary of it."

"Molly, I—"

She turned and beat her fists against the wall. "I don't want to be nobody's wife. Don't want to work no ranch. I want to just be Molly." She twisted away from the wall and growled through clenched teeth. "Want to be left alone. You hear me desires?"

Hadn't he been desperate to escape his own pain? But he'd promised the children their mother. He ventured closer to his wife. "I do hear you. I come to make things right between us. To take you home with me. Things will change for the better. I'll drink less. Accept me apologies, Molly. Never meant to harm your sensibilities." He thrust his unsteady hand toward her.

"Sensibilities?" She stiffened. A wild look, like that panther hunting him in the Minnesota woods, entered her eyes. She lunged at him, clenching her hands around his neck. If her eyes were gold instead of blue, he would've responded quicker.

Mick lost his balance and knocked into the dresser before they landed on the edge of the bed. Molly still clung to him, and he tried to pry her fingers loose. She'd transformed into a murderous devil.

"Molly, stop!" Molly's mother burst through the door and swiped at Molly as her daughter writhed and screamed on the bed with Mick pinned beneath her. Mrs. Quincannon tugged on her daughter's arms from behind and broke Molly's grip on him.

He tumbled to the floor, scrambled up, and backed away to escape her reach.

Molly snatched a hand mirror from the dresser and flung

it at him, shattering it when Mick deflected it with his arm. She seized the pitcher from the washstand and tossed it at his head. He ducked, the pitcher smashing on the floor behind him. It smashed to bits on the floor when he ducked. Next, she grabbed her boot and hit his rump as he skipped out of the doorway.

"*Oof.*" Mick ignored the pain and retreated outside to the front yard. He glanced back at the house in case she was in pursuit, in time to catch a corner of black material disappearing behind the house. "By all that's holy."

Mrs. Quincannon scurried onto the porch, then joined him. "She's in such a state. 'Tis been years since I've witnessed such a tantrum."

"'Tis recent for me."

Screams accompanied by the shattering of breakables carried out of Molly's open window. She yelled out the window. "Leave me be, Muldoon. I want a divorce. A divorce!"

Mrs. Quincannon seized his arm, and her voice shook. "Do you see? Woe is me. What shall I do with her?"

His knees trembled, and he fingered the sore spot on his rump. "Unsure. Such a quandary, 'tis. Seems me visit made things worse. But what to do with her is the question of the day, aye? I'm miserable to ask this, but me hat and bag are in Molly's room. I'll need them to get home." He squeezed Mrs. Quincannon's arm.

Molly continued screaming curses from the window. "You need your bag?" She disappeared for a second, then launched his hat and bag at him through the opening. "Take your rubbish."

The bag smacked Mick in the face, knocking him off balance. A trickle of warm fluid ran from his nose down into his mustache. He swiped it away with his arm.

A tiny object nicked his forehead and landed in a clump of grass.

Mick rummaged through the clump. Her wedding band. Still worth something. He turned to Molly's mother as he pocketed the ring. "May God and the lucky shamrocks be with you, Mrs. Quincannon." *And me. A divorced man. Raising me children alone.*

15

UNCOMMON RESCUERS

No child should be twice deserted by their mother.
Mick

Mick napped before his anticipated suppertime arrival. He awoke, gripping his now empty bottle, and huddled against the train's wall with his sack. He transferred his hat from his face to his lap to gaze out the window. Neither the sunset nor the passing scenery impressed him. Everything blurred in his numb brain.

He listened to the solace of the train—the *clickety-clack* of the train's weight on the rails, the locomotive's steam, and the whistle as it neared a crossing.

A young child wailed behind him, shaking Mick from his reverie, and he peeked back over the seats.

Various passengers were scattered throughout the car. Two read the newspaper with the headline, "McCormick Reaper Makes Farming Profitable." *'Bout time, that. Wish I'd invented it.* One woman knitted while she glared at the distressed child and his mother, who rocked her crying boy.

What should he tell his own distressed children? Their faces and reactions flickered across his mind when he'd first

190 I E.V. SPARROW

told them their Mam left. No child should be twice deserted by their mother. How could Mick tell them of Molly's condition?

Moira at almost eleven may understand, but what of Liam? And sensitive eight-year-old Bridget, or six-year-old Cara, could they grasp their situation? If Mick told his older children the truth, they'd spill the secret eventually, and guilt would consume them for injuring their younger sisters. *Terrible quandary. Sometimes, deceit is best.* But what deception could he tell?

As the train slowed and its wheels squealed, a conductor Mick didn't recognize navigated his way down the aisle. "Glennis. Arriving at Glennis."

A couple across from Mick readied their bags for departure. They discussed some challenges with their jobs in St. Paul, as though the woman worked outside of the home. The man tipped his hat at Mick, and the woman upturned her nose. She held her leather satchel in front of her like a shield.

I may smell of whiskey, but she smells of money. Mick reviewed her well-constructed hat as she passed him, with her tailored outfit and her nicely polished boots. No country girl, that. What sort of job did she do? He clamped the back of the bench seat in front of him. A job. He'd tell the children their mother took a well-paying job in the vast city of St. Paul. She's living far away in Minnesota. She might send her address. Maybe she'd visit sometimes.

"All aboard." The conductor leaned out the door. "All aboard for Lime Springs."

Steam hissed and billowed past his window. After a few moments, when no one boarded, the train jerked and chugged forward with a *clunk.* The shrill whistle warned the waiting passengers on the platform.

Home in an hour. At last, his new plan eased his burden. He must hide the secret that their mother needed institutionalizing. Deception was the way. He'd never used it and hoped he was good at it.

Mm. Mick awoke to the aroma of pancakes for breakfast and an odd chirping sound coming from somewhere. Must be a bird nest nearby. He turned over and stretched. Hadn't his tale about their Mam done the job well? The children accepted it much better than expected. Mick arose, splashed his face at the washstand, dressed for work, and limped into the kitchen. His back ached more than usual from being jolted on the train.

Grey scrambled up from his place in the entryway with a stiff gait as he approached. He greeted Mick with a lick on his hand and received a welcoming pat on the head with an extra rub on his ears.

"You're not a pup anymore, aye? You've aged like me. Ho there Moira, you're making me favorite." He turned the corner into the kitchen with Grey beside him to the sight of his daughters cooking. The chirping was louder in the kitchen.

Sunlight streamed through the window between the flour-sack curtains Molly had sewn. Moira hovered over an iron pan on the pipe stove, Cara held the metal spatula in her mitted hand, and Bridget, with flour on her face, sat at the table stirring batter inside the chipped mixing bowl.

Moira held Cara's hand over the spatula and flipped a cake. "Watch the edge of the hot pan. Don't touch it."

"Thanks, machuslas, for such a delight. And you're kindly helping your big sister. What's that chirp sound? Cara?"

Bridget tapped her spoon against to bowl's edge. "She found a baby bird. We're keeping it in the wood box by the stove nested in one of Mam's old stockings. Can I have Mam's old clothes, Da? Moira said she'd show me how to make my costume for the school play. I just had a scathingly brilliant idea. It'll be good practice for when I'm in vaudeville—"

"Tell me more 'bout that later, macushla. Cara, put the bird outside where you found it. What did I say 'bout bringing wild creatures into the house, aye?" Mick peered into the box. The brown sparrow was half grown and hopped in short bursts while flapping its wings. "Little fella's down is gone, and he's grown his feathers. 'Twas probably trying to fly from the nest."

"I know, Da. I only just brought it inside to make sure it wasn't hurt. Bridget, you tattletale."

"Forgetting your Da can yet hear at me advanced age? And where's Liam? Was he here before me to enjoy your cakes?"

Moira indicated the bucket next to the sink. "No, but he left us fresh milk. I haven't seen him this morning."

"Me neither." Bridget stopped stirring. "I got up with Moira at five o'clock, and he gets up at four-thirty to milk Daffodil. I like that name so much. Glad I learned at school that it's a yellow bulb flower. Yellow is my favorite color. Can we plant some by the front porch, Da? Sally says—"

"Ho, now, that's a discussion for later, macushla." Mick curled his mustache. "I'll sit meself down to break me fast. Found Grey sitting by the front door. 'Tis strange Liam didn't take him along and he's not here to join us. Grey always accompanies Liam on his chores every morning."

Moira plopped a stack of cakes onto the plate Cara handed to her. "It'll be heavy, Cara. Da, I only had two eggs leftover and used them for the pancakes this morning." She poured more batter from a cup into the pan. "It's surprising how late Liam is in fetching us the eggs. So unlike him. He did say the other morning how our poor Grey is slowing down and seems to be in pain when he follows him around during chore time. Maybe Liam left him inside where it's warm."

"True. Uh, I meant 'bout Liam. But Moira, you're responsible like him as well, at taking care of your sisters."

"Well, I know you have troubles with my moodiness." Moria scrunched her face.

Mick shrugged. He finished his pancakes, drank a mug of

milk, but refused the coffee Bridget set before him. "Must go find Liam, since he hasn't brought us the fresh eggs."

Grey struggled to stand.

"Stay, boyo." He gave him the hand signal, palm down, to sit. "You've earned the right."

Grey slowly sat.

"Keep him close to you, Bridget. He likes your gentle ways. Give him some milk." Mick grabbed his hat on the peg by the back door and exited into the morning sunshine. He headed for the chicken coop hoping Liam might possibly be collecting the eggs.

Scout was at pasture, so Liam hadn't gone into town. The rooster crowed from a nearby tree, even an hour past sunrise, and the clucking of hens increased as Mick approached the barn. Liam wasn't anywhere. Mick neared the coop and rounded the corner to peek through the wire fencing. "Liam?"

No new feed lay about for the chickens. They squawked inside the yard and skittered with their wings fluttering or ran up the ramp to enter the hen house.

"Liam?" His heart pounded faster. Mick scratched his cheek and stepped forward, jiggling the coop's door. He unlatched the framed door to more squawking and knocked on the henhouse wall as he rounded it toward the rear entrance. "You're hiding from your Da?" But that wasn't Liam's way. He was a serious boy.

Mick opened the door and ducked inside the henhouse. Feathers, nests on shelves, a few spider webs up high, then a piece of smudged paper nailed to the wall. He yanked it off, and the note quivered in his fingers.

Dear Da,

Mam could be lonely in a big city like St. Paul. I went to fetch her. I hope you will forgive me for not telling you.

You tried, but she might still be angry with you. I hope she loves me enough to come home.

Your mostly good, and only son,

Liam

P.S. Tell Bridget she can have my turn collecting the eggs. She likes it.

"Dearest Christ, have mercy upon him." Mick crunched the paper and dashed outside. He latched the door shut and fumbled with the lock. "By all that's holy . . ."

As he turned toward the house, the rooster intercepted him with flapping wings and outstretched talons. Mick scooped up a rock. "Don't you think 'bout it. Your death wouldn't grieve me at all."

The rooster veered sideways and dropped to the ground, as though he understood the warning.

Mick headed home as rapidly as his legs would move. He burst through the back door. "Moira."

The girls startled in their seats. Silverware clanked against plates, and Cara spilled her milk on the tabletop.

Moira shot up from her chair. "What's happened?"

"'Tis Liam. He's run after Mam." He paused for breath. "I must go away to find him. Come with me whilst I pack a bag."

The girls hurried after him to his bedroom.

He dug under the bed for his bottle, Moira searched for his carpetbag, and Cara laid a shirt on the quilt.

"Can you find him? I'm afraid." Cara bit her lip.

"Sure I'll find him."

Moira hugged her youngest sister. "He probably took the train since we're allowed to. Da has friends on the trains because of his job. They know Liam, and God's angels will watch over him, right, Da?"

"Aye, 'tis their job."

Bridget stacked his underclothes. "Liam took his coat from

the peg. Will you need a coat in St. Paul? At school Tammy said it's colder in the winter than in Iowa. Billy Jean said it gets below zero degrees there, too. It freezes the hairs inside your nose. Isn't that awful?"

Mick pulled himself up from the floor by gripping the iron bed's post. "*Oof.* I'll take me long johns for warmth, Bridget. 'Tis not yet winter." He nestled a bottle of whiskey on the stack of clothing. "Moira, are there more clothes on the line?"

"I'll check, Da. Cara, come help me."

Bridget sat next to Mick's carpetbag. "Da, do you think Liam is alright and Mam is warm enough? They'll be so happy to see each other. Can you take her clothes? What if she—"

"Macushla. Mam took a job in the city, aye? Meaning, she'll earn enough money to purchase what she needs." He smoothed Bridget's hair then stashed money in a handkerchief and tied its ends before inserting it into his boot. Mick glanced back at his middle daughter. "No need to worry 'bout Mam, aye?"

"I suppose not." Bridget kicked her legs on the edge of the bed and contemplated her swinging feet. "Mam took her boots. They aren't here."

Didn't he know it. He listened for Moira's return then sat beside his concerned daughter. "So, you come into our room now and then without asking?"

Bridget shrugged. "Sometimes. It makes me feel closer to her when I wear her dresses. They smell like her."

He'd be needing to keep Molly's things then. There were many details to keep in mind when telling a falsehood. "I understand. You have permission to come into me room and wear her garb until she returns. Now, I must hurry." He hugged Bridget and kissed the top of her head as Moira and Cara returned with a pair of stockings and a shirt.

"That's all there was, Da. Do you have enough for your trip?"

"Aye. Moira must take me to the train station. Bridget, yourself and Cara should go tell Mrs. Cook I'm away on an urgent matter. Ask her to keep watch on you. You all know what to do and how to behave for Moira whilst I'm away. She'll return with the wagon. Say a prayer for your da and Liam. With God's help, we'll return quick as a wink." He embraced the younger girls.

At the station, after Mick climbed down from the wagon seat, Moira scooted into his empty place. She took up Scout's reins with trembling hands. "Do you think he'll follow my commands, Da? I've only ever driven him twice by myself. You're usually with me."

What choice did a father alone have? "You'll do a grand job, macushla. Do like I taught you. Reins firm and sit straight. You're no stranger to him. He knows your voice. Keep your eyes on the path home. You've done this before." Mick loosened his tight collar.

"Yes, Da. He knows me and my voice." Moira slapped the leather against the horse's neck. "Walk on, Scout."

Old Scout plodded ahead with Moira and the wagon and around a waiting carriage.

He wanted to rush away, but parenting multiple children had its challenges. *Each one needs something at the same time.* Liam needed him most, though Moira was fearful of her task. Mick was glad there was little commotion today with people or carriages. He hefted his bag onto his sound shoulder and rearranged his wide-brimmed hat.

A train whistle blew. Mick slid the train schedule and pocket watch from his vest to compare—*8:00 am.* "Next train to St. Paul is . . ."

"Glory be. Me very own chauffeur." A familiar feminine voice spoke over the noise.

Mick searched the faces of the meandering group of passengers on the platform. A tall woman fluttered her gloved fingers. Clothed in purple velvet with a matching wide-brimmed hat full of white feathers twisting in the wind, her long, brilliant peach ringlets bobbed below the purple veil. Her pale blue eyes were highlighted with a dark outline beneath darkened brows, and her scars were barely discernible beneath powder.

His train schedule fluttered to the dirt. "Orla? By all— what are you doing here?"

"Fine greeting. You'll not be wanting that paper then? 'Tis soiled like me?" She grinned, deepening her dimples. Her fuller face softened the sharpness of her chin and nose. *She's looking nigh pretty.*

"Uh." He stooped over to gather the schedule and stashed it back into his pocket with his watch. "Was thinking you've changed, but no. Still me painted sister, you are."

She sauntered to Mick with most of the mingling passengers stopping to stare at this flamboyant and extravagant woman carrying a bulging floral carpetbag.

"Hello there, me sister. Such a delightful surprise." Mick yelled to be heard over the train and for the busybodies' benefit, hoping to squelch their speculations. He lowered his voice. "Orla, I must be away quickly. Liam's run off to St. Paul, I believe. Will you stay with me girlies until we return?" His heart pounded with the thought of Liam's head start.

She didn't blink. "What?"

"You've just missed Moira with the wagon. I'd no inkling you'd be visiting. Had I sent you me new address?"

"Aye. So you've lost Liam, both of me latest letters, and I've no way to get to your home? You're truly a trouble magnet, exactly as that blockhead Ed always claimed, aye?"

"Will you watch them for me, sister?"

Orla tilted her head sideways. "Sure, and I took some time away from me own family. They'll not miss me after the big dustup we had. Brought your new address with me and I'll find a way to your home. I'll get acquainted with me nieces, but will they know to trust me? Only Liam was home the last time I visited. Have you mentioned me name to the girlies?"

An incoming train whistle blew, and he glanced at his pocket watch. "I have. That's me train. Tell me girls you're Little Lamb's older sister. They know the story 'bout the *Mona*. I owe you, sister."

"You do."

He scurried away to wire the train depot in St. Paul to be on the lookout for an unaccompanied boy with red hair named Liam Muldoon, son of one of their brakemen. *By all God's saints, hope Milton catches me wire.* He'd met Liam a time or two.

After his wire request, Mick hustled to catch the train to the bustling city of St. Paul, where a youngster could vanish forevermore.

16

A NOSY SAWBONES

Only this, a nosy woman with a spyglass.
Mick

For the first time since Mick rode on trains, the rocking motion didn't soothe him enough to put him to sleep. Perhaps a nip of whiskey for courage. *No, 'twould numb me wits.* He must remain sharp and aware for Liam and Mister Death. This sort of event could cause the vulture Mister Death to appear.

Mick bent over into the aisle, searching beneath the seats. Tension spread up his neck and to his shoulders. Was that devil ready to pounce? Not a hint of a black cloak swished around the car.

Liam, where are you, boyo? He balled his hands into fists to stop them from shaking and tried taking deep breaths, but rapid heartbeats tricked his body into thinking of running. He couldn't tolerate it much longer. "We must go faster."

"Oh dear, you think this is not fast enough?" The older woman dressed in black sitting beside him twisted slightly to stare at him. "I believe we are doing a rapid speed. We must be going thirty-five miles per hour." She held a newspaper that quivered with every *clunk* of the wheels on the track.

"What?" He panted. "Aye. No. Aye, 'tis fast." *Like me heart.*

"Hm." The woman adjusted her silver lorgnette, magnifying her eyes, then tipped her head, her wrinkled face peeking from beneath a black wide-brimmed hat. She studied Mick and twisted the black ribbon tie flowing across her lap from within the folds of her skirt.

Only this, a nosy woman with a spyglass. He glanced away seeking a distraction and wiped his palms on his legs. "I'm in a hurry." What nasty plan had placed her beside him? He only chose this second-row seat to be nearest the door. He didn't wish to have a thousand personal questions shot at him from a shriveled old lady dressed in garb from fifty years ago.

"We will be traveling companions for a while, so let me introduce myself. Dr. Dora Lampert. Please call me Dora. I like to travel third class for the adventure of it." She held out her black-gloved hand.

Doctor? That explains it. "Mr. Mick Muldoon."

Dora's fancy buttons on her black glove jabbed into his sweaty palm. He jerked his hand away and brushed it against his work shirt.

"I see. You are nervous. Are you one of those who does not like to be confined within small places?"

"No."

"Hmm." Dora flipped open her lorgnette, and her eyes grew twice their normal size.

He turned away but sensed her inspection. Busybody. Was he sorry he hadn't changed out of his work clothes? *Nah, make your judgements.* Mick scanned the nearby passengers. Most read newspapers or a book, ate a snack they'd packed, or were involved in conversation. A few dozed. He envied them. Trips always flew by while you slept.

Dora sighed.

He tipped his hat over his face, propped his head back,

and pretended to sleep. Maybe she would be silent for the rest of the trip. Dizziness overtook him. He fought it with all his strength, but his heart thumped as fast as the train, while he tried to slow his breathing. He massaged his chest. *Me heart can't take this madness.* He'd never wished to live as long as his revered Uncle John. Who wants to be 111? At this rate, Mick only wished to make it to his sixty-second birthday.

A delicate hand lay on his forearm. "Mr. Muldoon?"

Good heavens, woman. He budged his hat brim enough to glare at Dr. Dora.

"Poor man. Does your chest hurt?"

"No."

"Let me help you." Dora handed him a page of her newspaper, *The Davenport Weekly Republican.* "You cannot escape bodily, but you can mentally. Read it to me, please."

"You want me to read to you? You're a doctor, you can read it." He thrust the page beneath her nose.

Dora smiled. "Do you know how to read?"

Heat circulated from his pounding heart upward to the top of his head. "Aye."

"Go ahead. Concentrate." Dora folded her hands in her lap.

Her poor, suffering patients. He shook a wrinkle out of the page, and lacking his spectacles, held it at arm's length. "Nothing interesting here."

"Choose something. Anything will do. We have a long journey ahead of us. Then we can discuss the article."

Mick shot Dora a glare, then cleared his throat and shook the page again. His gaze captured one of the briefer articles. *Here's a quick read.* "Taken from a hospital, he was—"

Dora shook her head. "Word for word, not a synopsis of events."

"By all that's holy." He jerked the paper and jabbed his finger against it for an article. *"Wednesday, May 23, 1900.*

'A Missing Child Sought For. Catherine Gorman, Ten Years of Age, Strays From Her Home.

Matt Gorman reported to the police this morning the disappearance of his sister, Catherine, ten years of age, which occurred last evening after school. The Gorman's live somewhere between Farnum and LePage Streets on East Sixth street. The child is a niece of ex-Alderman-at-large Matthew Gorman. The police are looking after the missing girl.'

Holy angels. There're more missing children? How could this be? He crumpled the paper with his fists. "Did a wicked person take her? Wonder if Mister D—"

"Calm yourself. It might be helpful to read another news article, Mr. Muldoon."

"First off, this is months old, and they could've found the girl. But 'tis a terrible thing. Such a tragic story, and I'm determined it won't happen to Liam. I've lost more than enough . . ." *Anxiety must've loosened me tongue.*

"You have lost children before?"

Mick wrapped his arms around his chest hoping to keep his pounding heart within his body. "Don't wish to discuss it. I've dealt with me losses—three entire families of wives with our young ones." Confessing his many losses to a stranger? *What's this?* His throat ached with the effort to squelch his memories, grief, and terror. *Liam, you must come home to me.*

Dora took a deep breath. "Mr. Muldoon, I am acquainted with grief. I lost five infants before they could live apart from me. Miscarriages, they call them. That word makes women blame themselves. We must choose a different term."

"Ah." *Wicked Mister Death's curse.*

She dabbed her nose with an embroidered handkerchief. "Each infant was perfectly formed externally, but with something wrong internally. Or it could have been something wrong within my womb." She turned to him with tears in her eyes. "It is not the same as a kidnapping, although they were unexpected deaths of my dreams for motherhood just the same."

He couldn't swallow or speak from the shock of Dora's words. Shauna's face and that of their infants flashed through his mind. He'd never spoken about their stillborn, Rory, to a stranger. *Who speaks of such things?* He'd not even discussed it at length with Orla nor Ed. The nightmares were enough to remind him. Unless he drank to lessen their sharpness. Mick dug his fingers into his knees as tears choked him.

"I see that you may understand my losses. I must confess, it almost destroyed my faith in God. Do you believe in God, Mr. Muldoon?"

"Well, I went to Mass for many years. Not so now."

"Such losses shake our faith to its very foundation. No one has answers for their deaths, do they? Not ministers and reverends. They might answer, but the why is elusive."

He blinked around tears. "Nor priests. They've no satis-fying answers for me about the tragedy." He glanced around for Mister Death. Surely, he was lurking about from their discussion of death.

"Ah, so you are a Catholic. No matter. We all struggle with our faith in God in the whys of suffering and death."

Mick smirked. *Rich, nosy, and a confounded Protestant to boot.* Why should he listen to her? "Is your heritage English?" That would further sink her opinions in his esteem.

"No." Dora shook her head and clasped her hands together. "One day changed my long-held grief in an instant. I was reading my Bible, as I do most days, and came across a hopeful Scripture. To be absent from the body is to be present with the Lord. Don't you see?"

"I don't."

Dora gripped his arm. "All those tiny people I lost, each with a spirit. Does it matter to God what size they were? You can be three inches long or six feet tall and still be with the Lord in heaven." She covered her face and wept without restraint.

204 | E.V. SPARROW

He swiped at his surprising tears. How could he cry over his stolen macushlas again?

Passengers in the seats ahead of Dora glanced over their shoulder. They murmured and shook their heads. He glared in return. Didn't they know you can't control grief? It sneaks up unexpectedly.

Dora dabbed her eyes. "Beg your pardon. It is indecorous for one to cry in public. I wish to encourage you with the hope I found. I will never be a mother of the living on earth, but one day I will be with them in heaven."

"Ah." Mick brooded. Straight to heaven? No time in purgatory to pay for lingering sins? His head spun with the effort to make sense of her belief. "And how do you know for sure you'll be in heaven then? Not to insult your beliefs, Dr. Dora. And what about purgatory? You're so certain to be getting out of it quick, are you?"

"Oh, dear."

"We know the innocents go straight to God if they're baptized. Purgatory—"

"I forgot about your church's sacraments of baptism and purgatory. My church doesn't teach that. We say once saved by grace, forever saved from hell. Believe in the name of the Lord Jesus Christ and He shall save you. You know, Christ's blood shed on the cross for all who believe?"

"Aye, the cross. We have it. Well, I'll think on what you've said." Mick's face heated. There was no place to hide. Hadn't he ignored Christ's cross for decades? He lay his head against the wall and closed his eyes. What he wanted most was a drink. With righteous Dora next to him, how could he sneak his bottle out of his sack?

Woot, toot! The whistle announced a stop. Mick and Dora awoke and rearranged themselves in their seats as a cloud of steam fanned past their window. The passengers ahead of them prepared for the stop.

Dora yawned, then asked, "Where is your stop, Mr. Muldoon?"

Groggy, he resented that he missed his chance to snatch his whiskey bottle by not awakening before Dora. "'Tis the train to St. Paul. You know that."

"And why are you traveling there?"

Mick rummaged in his tattered sack. *Who cares if she sees me?* He popped open his bottle and took a good swig. "Dr. Dora, you're a nosy sawbones."

Dora laughed. "Yes, I know. It is no secret among those who know me. I will tell you about my business first. You are an astute man, so you must have noticed I am dressed in mourning." She smoothed her black skirt then peeped out the train window as they pulled away from the platform. "Mine is a common enough story, really. My only sister and I were estranged over some silly misunderstanding, and the last time we spoke was in anger." Dora turned back to him. "Twenty years ago. Now I must attend her funeral having never made peace between us. What about you?"

He huffed and popped open his bottle for another swig. "Need a bit more." *Should he tell her?* "Me son ran off." He stuffed his bottle back into the carpetbag.

"Oh, dear. A runaway. It is no wonder how that article disturbed you. When?"

"This morning. Found a note in the coop. He's gone to find his mother. I failed me children, you see, because she wouldn't return to our family. Couldn't bring her home as I promised." His throat tightened with fear, but he tamped his anguish back into its pit of despair. "Then, I lied 'bout where she went. To keep them from worrying, I did. They might believe she didn't love them you see. Could I let that happen?"

Dora touched his shoulder. "No. No, any parent might do the same to protect them."

Fear and distress burst out of his chest. Mick clutched his head with his hands and wept as silent as possible. He was glad the car was noisy with the rail commotion, conversations, and children's gaiety, all a suitable cover for his distress.

A few moments passed. Dora cleared her throat. "I ran away once."

"You did?" Mick mumbled into his hands.

"My parents did not allow me to go to a birthday party. No reason to go into more detail. I ran until I stopped at the edge of town where my grandmother lived." Dora chuckled. "Grandmother found me near her garden gate. I had forgotten to bring food with me. Her strawberry patch enticed me."

Mick wiped his nose with his soiled bandana. "What was your age?"

"About eight. My reason for running away was silly compared to your son's. Your son must be a brave boy or one who loves his mother very much."

"Both."

"When you told him a falsehood about his mother, do you recall if you told him a specific place or address that she lives? That may aid in your search."

"I didn't. Wish I'd added that to me lie. What if I can't find him?"

"I am sure you will. When you do, I suggest you tell him the truth immediately. Falsehoods and misunderstandings grow out of control and are threats to relationships. Believe me, I know." Dora opened her bag and handed him an apple. She bit into one herself. "Here, I will give you another for him."

"Thanks." Mick dropped it into his bag. He smelled the sweet tang of his own then twirled it, studying the red, slick skin. "I wonder if Liam took any food with him."

"Young boys are ravenous creatures. I recommend you find the nearest store or diner after we arrive, and you will find your boy, or at least information regarding a sighting of him."

"Aye, 'tis a place to start." He accepted a piece of cheese from Dora.

"Children forgive much easier than adults. In my practice, I encountered many children. You will not believe what—"

"Do you believe whilst someone's alive, there's always time to correct things, so there's always hope? And once they're gone, we've missed our chance?"

Dora nodded. "You have lost many people you loved, and you must wish you had just one more chance to say you loved them, correct?"

Mick stared at his half-eaten lunch. "Lost me macushlas to Mist—to death. I'm now on me fourth family, but this time me wife left us through me own fault." He finally admitted this aloud. *Is the woman a magician?* He'd told her more tragic stories of his life than he'd dared tell anyone.

"Did you admit this to her?" At his nod, she continued. "And yet she would not return with you. And you are about to make all the corrections you can with your children, right?"

"Aye."

"It is all that God requires us to do in these situations. He will help you. You will see."

The train whistle blew twice, then the conductor announced a stop before St. Paul. What a blessed relief to have a plan of action with hope.

Dora pointed her cane forward. "Mr. Muldoon, if the driver and automobile are not at the station waiting for me, I will remain with you."

"You've an automobile! You're a rare one, truly." *From wealth and yet generous and kindhearted. May yet change me opinion of her.*

"Since you had the presence of mind even in your fear to wire the depot before we departed, it is possible that you will find your son immediately." She rose and supported her weight on the silver-handled stick. "I will not sleep tonight without knowing your boy is safe."

"Aye." Mick altered his bag's position and supported Dora's elbow until the conductor escorted her down the steps.

"Thank you," Dora told the conductor. "My friend will bring my satchel."

Mick transferred Dora's satchel from her hands and slung both bags over his sound shoulder. "This is your only bag?"

"Yes, for I sent my trunk ahead."

He exited the car one step at a time while his desire to bolt down the platform in search of Liam tortured his soul with every second. "Let's go to the depot office and ask 'bout me wire. Hoping to have an answer for whether anyone has spotted Liam. Let me help you."

"No need. I can do just fine on my own. I will follow behind you so you may hurry."

Mick scanned the area, grateful for the thinning crowd of arrivals. Passengers milled about the edges of the station, some commenting on the architecture and decor as they passed. This was Mick's first visit to this newfangled Milwaukee Road Depot in St. Paul, and he needed a moment to get oriented to its layout.

The clock in the tower chimed twelve. Already noon? He spied the office door, and hastened toward it, while digging in his sack for his employee card. Dora's bag frustrated his progress. He couldn't be impolite to her and not carry it.

Mick's hand shook as he banged on the door. His heart thumped hard enough to burst out of his chest. Hurry, hurry.

Someone opened the door. Mick pushed past them to get inside, clutching his card, and offered it to the person. He expected it to be Milton, the old conductor and friend from a line back in Iowa who he'd sent the wire to regarding Liam.

Instead, Bailey slapped Mick's shoulder. "Mick Muldoon. Good to see you again. You here about your wire? Milton isn't working today."

Mick took a deep breath to calm himself. "Bailey, do you have Liam?"

"No. But he was here. Guffey noticed him when he arrived at the depot not more than two hours ago."

He grabbed Bailey's shirt and shook him. "Did he see where he went? Why did no one think to keep Liam here? Guffey didn't wonder at him being alone—"

"Release me shirt." Bailey seized Mick's hands. "I understand your fear, I do. We didn't receive your wire until after Guffey saw him." He tugged Mick's hands from his lapel. "Boys do wander. We thought you might be nearby, and so didn't worry. But I'll help you. I sent Guffey to the police station down on 3rd Avenue to be sure they received a description of Liam, his age, and they're looking out for him. Take a seat, will you?"

"No." Mick couldn't breathe. Panic drowned him with every passing second. "I must find me boyo!" He clutched the bags against his chest.

From the doorway, Dora spoke. "Thank you, Mr. Bailey, for your kind offer to help." She glanced at Mick. "Please do check that the police are involved, and we will go in search of the boy ourselves. Mr. Muldoon, come." Dora adjusted her cane and held out her free hand.

He scurried to Dora's side, and she looped her arm through his. "We will find your son with God's help."

"Aye." He tugged Dora toward the office door. "By all the saints, we must."

17

SANTA IN ST. PAUL

Saint Nicholas—it must be him.
Mick

St. Paul, Minnesota

Mick and Dora exited through the door below the clock tower. Mick halted Dora beneath the awning to gather his bearings. To their left, a major thoroughfare stretched through the city, bustling with pedestrians and carriages alongside the newfangled automobiles, mixing in all directions.

He clenched his jaw. It was nearly twenty years since he'd resided here. St. Paul's Depot renovation and recent building boom made the city almost unrecognizable to him. How would he ever find Liam in this mess of humanity? How could he catch up to his boy with Dora slowing him down? *I must go quickly.*

"Dora, can you wait for me inside the depot? 'Tis sure to be a long and difficult search."

"Mr. Muldoon, I do not see my driver, and I will not slow you down for long. But I am concerned for your health. How is your chest pain?"

"None. If I could run, I would. If I could fly, I would. Me only concern is finding Liam."

"Yes, let us go." Dora supported herself on her cane and stepped forward. *So be it.*

Further down the sidewalk, two unkempt men chewed something, and propped themselves against a metal railing attached to the depot's brick wall. One man in his early twenties narrowed his black snake-like eyes at Mick and Dora. The older brown-skinned man appeared relaxed and nodded at Mick. He was the same height and build as his chum, Josiah, decades ago in New York City.

"Pardon me, young men." Dora pointed her cane at them. "Have you seen a ten-year-old boy wandering around by himself? He has . . . What color hair?" She turned to Mick.

Mick's tongue was stuck to the roof of his mouth. He swallowed and licked his lips. "Like mine. Wavy like mine but redder. He's this tall. By all that's holy, can you not help me?"

He held his hand about four and a half feet above the ground. He rubbed his chest. His heart pounded like a marching drum, but without drumsticks to control the beats. He gulped in deep breaths.

"Saw one boy earlier. Did you see him, Moses?" At Moses's nod, the younger man scratched his chin. "We could help you for a price. A little something might help us recover our memory."

Mick fisted his hands. "Me boyo's run away. Don't you understand? He's in this city alone." Before he could grab the snake-man and strangle his rotten little neck, Moses interrupted with a punch on the scoundrel's arm.

"Quincey, have some compassion. It's not the time to be taking advantage of a father who's mortally terrified for his son's whereabouts. Had a boy once myself, mister."

Mick cursed. "I'm trying not to be mortally terrified. Tell me what you know, won't you, fella?"

Moses tilted his head toward the main street. "Saw a boy

headed to that corner over yonder, past the apothecary with the sign that says, 'Chronic, Nervous, and Private Diseases Cured' in yellow letters above it. Maybe not where he went, but that's the way he headed. Lost sight of him once he went round that corner." He turned to the side and spat brown juice onto the sidewalk.

"Thank you, Moses. You behave as an honorable gentleman does." Dora held out some coins and dropped them into his palm. Then she glared at Quincey. "You should be ashamed, young man. You ought to allow your delightful friend to influence your heart."

Quincey jerked his face away and spat.

"I'm grateful to you, Moses. Let's go, Dr. Dora." Mick took a step before he glanced both ways to cross the street but was forced to wait for two carriages to pass by. "Come on, come on."

When the street was clear, the two hurried, with Mick's limp and Dora's cane, to the shop with the odd sign above it. He cupped his hand to the glass and peeked through the window. The apothecary store contained bottles of medicines in many colors glinting in the sunshine, tins of other items, and a shopkeeper with a blue apron answering questions from a rotund woman. No sign of Liam, but there was Dora, entering the shop. The jingling of its brass bell was loud enough to reach his ears.

He shuffled around the corner and entered a just as Dora asked the shopkeeper about sighting Liam earlier.

"A boy fitting your description poked his head through my door about an hour ago. I told him to move along, there was nothing here for a child."

Mick's hopes of finding Liam quickly dropped into his boots. He'd been there but was gone.

Dora turned toward him. "We are on his trail, Mr. Muldoon."

The shopkeeper aimed his thumb over his shoulder.

"Then I told the lad to go two doors down if he was looking for food. That's where the bakery serves meals at all hours. He thanked me very politely and left. I'd check there. Now excuse me, I have a paying customer."

Dora hobbled out of the shop. "We will find him. I believe he will stay on this main street."

Mick read the sign on the next shop 'Golden Grain Bell Beers.' No. He surveyed several men in various garb, all with hats, loitering about the lamp post. The next sign said, 'Dr. Nelson Co.' Did the shopkeeper lead him astray? "Where's that bakery?"

"Pardon me, young men." Dora waved to the group. "Have you seen a boy with wavy copper hair pass this way?"

A short, chubby man pointed across the street. "Think I saw him go that away. But can't be sure. Was earlier this morning?" He turned to another man nearby, who shook his head.

The men didn't agree on who, when, or what they saw. The confusing statements from shopkeepers and customers sent Dora and Mick zigzagging across the busy street.

He couldn't swallow or breathe with his pounding heart. Had they lost Liam's trail? Why did his prayers not work? Where were the saints today? Busy with some other disaster? *Don't have time to find me a priest.* "Surely, God, You must see where Liam is."

"Oh, He does, Mr. Muldoon. You can be sure of that. Let us pray." Dora grasped his hand. "Holy Father God, we need You to show us what You see. We know and agree that You can see Liam. We pray and agree in the name of the Lord Jesus Christ, Amen."

Mick quickly crossed himself. "Er, amen." *She prays this way?* Does God answer those prayers? His own prayers entangled with the treetops.

They dodged traffic back to the depot's side of the street. Mick scanned the buildings ahead. He abandoned Dora and dashed down the walkway to a sign which read, 'Central Restaurant-Meals at All Hours,' under a red-and-white striped awning. *This could be it.* He pushed his way through a small group of shoppers who stood in the middle of the walkway and hastened to the restaurant's entrance.

Several people exited through the only door, and Mick wanted to shout at their slowness. A smaller sign on the door read, 'Bakery and Lunches.' Was this it?

Dora caught up to Mick. "A man on the walkway just confirmed Liam came in here earlier. Did I not assure you his hunger would lead him, and that God would—"

Mick hurried into the diner and scanned the chairs, customers, and the counter where people sat. None were young boys with red hair. *Liam, where are you?* He whirled around to Dora. "He's not here."

"We are on Liam's trail, Mr. Muldoon. Hold fast to your hope. Ask God to show you where your son is. I must rest." Dora plopped onto a chair. "My apologies. Please continue your search. Return to me when you have your Liam."

What to do? *Can't think.* Should he ask God for help? Should he go ahead and pray without a priest? His heart couldn't take much more, he was sure of it. *I'm too old for this.* Maybe the police would find him? The only lifeline was to pray for a miracle, and for Liam's safe return. He closed his eyes. *God, it's me, Mick Muldoon. I've ignored you for a long while now, to be sure, and I'm that sorry for it. You gave me four living children, yet now I've lost one. Please, will you send him back? I promise to be a better Da.* He crossed himself. *In the name of the Father, the Son, and the Holy Ghost, Amen.* Mick's prayer made him a little less panicky and cleared his head. He opened his eyes.

"Da."

He twisted around. Liam.

Dressed in an enormous apron folded over at the waist and holding a large dishpan against his stomach, Liam grinned.

"Me precious boyo!" Mick burst into tears as Liam sprinted to him. "Never has God answered me prayers so quick."

Liam stared up at him. "I knew you'd find me, Da, because you'd be scared for me, and I did a foolish thing to come here alone."

"You knew I'd find you? I'd absolute terror and no such assurance but bless me soul. Although, I'm very angry with—"

"Hello. 'Bless me soul' got my attention there." A voice boomed from an exceptionally tall man grinning behind the counter. His blue eyes sparkled beneath bushy white brows, and his cheeks were plump and rosy. When he spoke, his long white beard tied with a leather string bobbed against his substantial belly.

Saint Nicholas. It must be him. Christmas magic traveled with the autumn breeze, bearing the gift of his lost son now found.

"So you come for your lad. Name's MacTavish. Owner." He stretched out his wide palm above the counter.

Mick shook it. "Mick Muldoon. Liam's da, as you thought."

"You've trained him well," MacTavish chuckled, jiggling his belly, "to work hard and be proud of it." He rounded the counter and ruffled Liam's hair. "He's a good and brave lad. Saw that right off. He entered, walked straight up to me, and said, 'Hey, mister, my name is Liam, and I'm very hungry.' Well, that about got me right there." MacTavish held his belly and guffawed, like Mick imagined Saint Nicholas would. "Then he ups and says, 'May I work for my break-fast? I know how to do a good job.' That did it. I handed him an apron and told him to get to work. Oh, pardon me for a moment." MacTavish stepped aside to ring up a customer.

"The breakfast was tasty, Da. He fed me eggs with ham

and buttery toast with strawberry jam." Liam smacked his lips.

Strawberries. Mick glanced back toward the door, where he'd left Dr. Dora in a chair.

Dora aimed her eyes skyward, then mouthed, *I told you.*

He chuckled for the first time since this awful ordeal began. Relief battled to overcome his fear and anger, and he'd no idea which would win the moment.

MacTavish returned. "As I was saying, this keen lad was bound to have a parent come searching for him. No wily street urchin would behave in such a way. Those types lurk about and dash away when I catch them at the garbage bins out back. Kept him busy while we waited." MacTavish winked. "Thought I'd give it a few hours, being near the depot, then head to the police on Third Avenue after I closed up."

"Bless you."

"My, my, I'll be sad to see him go. Was short staffed today. He was my God-sent helper." MacTavish knelt to make eye contact with Liam. "Did you learn a fine lesson today?" At Liam's nod, MacTavish smiled. "Brave lad, but your Da needs you home." MacTavish chuckled. "Off you go. Come in and see me when you next visit St. Paul."

"Good-bye, Mr. MacTavish, and thank you for the breakfast." Liam folded his apron and set it inside the dishpan he'd fetched. "Think I can leave these here on the empty counter, Da?"

"Aye. Liam. We'll have a discussion on the train home 'bout running away and your consequences for giving me the frights. Never been so fitful." He cupped Liam's shoulders and guided him to Dora's table. "Here's someone who wishes to meet you."

Dora clasped her hands and laughed. "I see you found each other. God is very good, is He not? Food always draws children, just like the loaves and fishes' story."

Mick believed she referenced a story in the Gospels. "Aye,

Dr. Dora. as you assured me to look for the nearest market or diner to find him."

"How did she know I'd be hungry?" Liam scratched his head.

"Because I know children, and especially young boys." Dora offered her hand to Liam, and he shook it. "Your father was beside himself with worry—"

"Aha." A tall policeman approached. "Well, and I see you must've found your boy."

Liam grabbed his father's hand then let go.

"Red wavy hair, about ten years-old, fits the description sent from the depot." The officer frowned and smacked his leg with his stick. "You the runaway?"

Liam scrunched his face. "But my hair is brown."

"Brown? Runaway he is. Mick and Liam Muldoon." He extended his hand to the officer.

"Officer Brady, and 'tis is a good thing you found him. Such a large city to be lost in, aye?" Brady waggled his brows at Liam. "You'll not do this again, will you now? We don't wish to be searching for lost youngsters and then find them in troublesome circumstances, do we?"

Liam faced the officer. "No, sir. Yes, sir."

"I'll give the message to me fellow officers." A commotion arose in the street. Brady turned away, and the door slammed behind him as curious café customers scurried to the windows.

Dora took a sip from her cup then smiled at Liam. "It is wonderful everything worked out for you both in this terrible situation. It might have been worse, if not for prayer."

"Yes, ma'am." Liam bit his lower lip and stared at Mick. "But why did the policeman say my hair is red?"

"Hush. Aye, Dr. Dora, it went better than I expected. You were very helpful to keep me sane on the train. I'm forever grateful to you—"

"I did not wish to leave you alone during your search. No need to thank me. There is a timepiece above the door saying two o'clock, and I must go. I wish I could visit with you, Liam, and get better acquainted, but I have an event I must not miss." Dora retied her hat in place, smoothed her veil, and resituated her cane. "My driver should be parked alongside the depot."

"Aye, Dr. Dora, we'll walk you back and see to it you arrive safely." He gave his son his own sack to carry. Mick took Dora's satchel. "If we're lucky, Liam, we might see what's happening in the street and get a good look at Dr. Dora's automobile."

"Da, did you come here only for me? Or also for Mam?"

Mick inhaled sharply and halted. He raised his brow at Dora.

She pointed her cane at the gathering near the road. "I will wait over there for a moment while you discuss things."

"Aye. And by all that's holy, Liam, I'm your da, and you alone are worth me search."

Liam's lips pressed together, then tears welled in his eyes. He shook his head slowly. "But I didn't get anywhere besides the restaurant. Mam could be lost. What if she's all alone? Or hungry, like I was. I came to get her, Da. We must, or I've failed her."

Mick knelt to Liam's eye-level. "Boyo, you're ten. If a grown man can't bring Mam home, 'tis a failure on me own part. You're not responsible for what's happened in our family. 'Tis up to me to fix it if I can. Do you hear?"

Liam clenched his fists by his side. "I hear you, Da, but I don't like it at all."

18

VISIT GONE AWRY

'Twasn't only your dress, Orla.
Mick

S t. Paul, Minnesota
    1900
        Mister Death's black cloak swooshed between two
of only three automobiles on the street. Two autos had
crunched doors and a horse cart with a wheel stuck at an odd
angle between them. Mick peered at the scene. "By all that's
holy. Was no one injured in this terrible smash up? Did you
see—"

Liam pointed at the spooked horses. "Lucky, aren't they?
If the cars had hurt them, they wouldn't be trying to rear up."

Why was Mister Death involved? Nothing for that evil
creature to steal away. Mick scanned Dora and Liam's faces
and then the crowd for those who might have spotted the evil
creature, but no one reacted with fear by his horrific presence.
Most onlookers craned their necks and pointed at the
accident.

Officer Brady blew his whistle. "Alright. Get along everyone." Onlookers dispersed to go about their business as Brady put everything to rights.

Dora poked her finger westward, across Milwaukee Road. "I have spotted my driver waiting for me."

As the three approached, Dora's driver stood at attention next to the vehicle. It was parked in the middle of a long line of carriages, carts, and automobiles in front of the train shed and freight house.

Mick and Liam shook hands with Dora, thanked her, left her safely with her driver, then strolled ahead to the depot.

"She was a nice lady, Da."

"Aye. Did you see her driver's face, Liam? All red and flab-bergasted he was. Unsure whether to acknowledge us. The looks of us must've confused him as to why we were Dr. Dora's companions."

"Because we got our work clothes on?"

"Aye, mostly." They passed the Third Avenue South entrance of the station and turned the depot's corner to the side entrance facing Milwaukee Road. *Mayhap Moses lingers.* "I'm eager to share me luck of the Irish and show you off, Liam, by thanking Moses for his help. The fella was leaning on these iron rails hooked to the brick wall."

"Too bad he's gone, Da."

They approached the station's entrance. "Must check the schedule then we'll have a long conversation 'bout never, ever, worrying your da again."

Liam opened the door. "I'm sorry. Do you see how fancy it is inside? Listen to my echo." He stomped his feet. "Hello."

"Boyo, enough." Conversations and footsteps of passen-gers, train noise, and Liam's playful calls created a cacophony. Mick's head pounded.

"Look at the ceiling. Did you ever think you'd see such a sight?"

"'Tis a sight, to be sure."

"I was afraid when I first arrived. I felt so small, like no one could see me."

A shaft of sunshine beamed a golden hue through a western-facing window onto the floor. Like the day the undertaker came to take away his Fiona and their babes. *Do You see us, God?*

"Why would they put windows so high up by the ceiling? No one can see out. Look at those lights. They're hanging metal and glass bowls. What about the shiny white floor? What's it made of? How did they make it? It feels like we're walking on top of a boulder, like those by our creek. Except this one is flat and smooth."

Mick chuckled. "Always a curious boyo. Marble."

Liam dashed to a plaque on one wall. He poked the brass plaque. "This says the station was designed by the arch, archit. What's that word?"

Mick inspected it. His eyes were always blurry now when he tried to read. "Architect. He draws plans for buildings. 'Twas built recently."

"But what did it look like when you lived here before? Was that one fancy?" Liam situated himself against the wall, tilted his head up, and surveyed the vast, ornate ceiling.

"Nah, 'twas different. Big enough. Wait here whilst I get the departure times." Mick turned back and shook his finger at Liam. "Then we'll have that discussion of what you did."

Liam squirmed on the bench. "I still want to know what we will do about Mam. Where did she go, and wouldn't she wish for us to visit her?"

Guilt assailed Mick's heart, and warmth spread up his chest to his face. "Umm, 'bout that. Mam never came here to me knowledge. I fibbed 'bout her to spare your feelings, thinking it was safer to mention the city being far away and full of jobs. Never imagined you'd try to find her."

"You lied to us?" Liam's mouth hung open.

"Aye, a fib. To spare your feelings." Mick rolled his neck to ease the tension.

Liam scooted further down the bench with his wide gaze locked on Mick. "I can't believe it. Have you lied to us before?" He pursed his lips, and a tear slid down his cheek before he swiped at it.

"No, never. I swear by all that's holy—"

"But can I believe you? How do I believe your words? Or promises? Or anything you say anymore?" Liam shook his head.

Mick's soul turned to ice from his son's mistrust. It froze his own heart around its edges like a winter's pond, and he was the one at fault for the freeze. "Wish now that I hadn't lied. Wouldn't wish you all to believe Mam doesn't love us like Bridget told Moira. I justified me lie with how you children would think ill of her for leaving us. Me own fault." Sobs cracked through the ice in his heart.

Seconds passed before his son's hand brushed his shoulder. He grasped it and turned toward Liam. "Please, forgive me. I need your forgiveness. I won't lie again to you."

"If you can forgive me for what I did, I'll forgive you. But I don't know if the girls will."

It was past nine o'clock when father and son entered through the gate to their home. Crickets sang their nightly tune to the beat of the twinkling stars. An almost full moon shone, creating midnight-blue shadows blended with deep forest green and outlining the foliage and roof of the home with its silvery light. The house interior lay in darkness except for one yellow glow from the rear window spreading onto the grasses.

Liam climbed the porch steps first and lay his index finger over his lips. "They're probably sleeping." He turned the knob and slowly opened the door.

Mick yawned and followed. The house was quiet. Lamplight lit the kitchen. "Either your Aunt Orla left the lamp on for us, or she's enjoying a cup of tea."

"Da. Where's Grey?" Liam set his bag on the floor and gazed around the room. "Shouldn't he be by the door? Or at least coming over to greet us? He must hear us whispering, even with his bad ears."

"Ah. 'Tis right you are. Maybe he's asleep under a kitchen chair nigh Orla. Let's get a looksie." Mick entered the kitchen with Liam.

Orla hunched over the table, head resting upon her folded arms, strands of her curly peach hair pointing in various directions. In front of her sat a cup of tea with two biscuits on the saucer.

Mick slung his coat over a chair and drew his face close to her ear. "What's happened to your hair?"

She jerked upright and knocked against the teacup. She lay her hand on her chest. "Saints alive, you gave me the frights. I've been tugging on me hair in me distress, that's what. Although I've two children of me own, I'm not created to be a mother. Especially not a good one. Why'd you think I'm here? Needed time away from home, but you didn't ask for me reasons before you tossed me into the auntie swamp—"

"Well?"

"Cara found a knife." Orla ticked one finger. "She cut Bridget's hair whilst she was napping. Wanted to give her sister a pretty, modern look. 'Tisn't pretty."

He grimaced.

"Next." Orla ticked another finger. "Bridget lost her boots in the creek."

"How—"

"And mayhap the worst thing of all." Orla ticked her third finger. "I took the girls into town today to replace Bridget's boots, and Moira wanted a new dress. She'll tell you the woeful story."

He poured himself tea and considered her list of mishaps.

"In one day? And I'm the accused trouble magnet in the family?"

Orla shook her head, causing the strands to bob like downy plumes. "Moira will never forgive me for the hulla-baloo I caused. Oh, and you must get a new rooster. I tore him asunder with the shovel—"

"Why?" Thank God he'd taken a chair during her tales. His day was almost tame compared to hers.

Liam rushed into the kitchen. "Grey's not here."

Orla pursed her lips, and her scars pinked with her flush. "Aye, 'tis the bad news. He's gone."

"Gone, sister?" Mick's mouth went dry.

She stood and reached for Liam. "Such a grievous thing, 'twas. Poor Grey. He refused to eat nor take a drink. I tried—"

"You killed him?" Liam flung open the back door, letting it bang against the wall, and dashed outside.

"I never did such an awful thing, brother. 'Tis another tragedy. Why did this occur whilst I'm here?" Orla smoothed her hair. "A boyo loves his dog fiercely. Something happened with our dog as well, before I came. What could I do 'bout it, I want to know?"

He clutched his hair. "Not a thing. Knew Grey was nearing his time to leave us." He rubbed at the stone weight pushing against his chest. "Poor Grey. I must teach that boyo to not run off whenever he's distraught."

"Liam's young. He has unruly emotions yet, and death is—"

"I spied Mister Death in St. Paul. He must've been there scouting for Grey." He held his breath.

"Mister Death is after animals now? Hoped you'd given up on insisting on that superstition. But the whiskey—"

"Nah, 'twas a warning, not the whiskey. Believed Mister Death was there hunting for one of us. Me guess 'twas to boast of his theft of Grey. A terrible misfortune for Grey, me very best companion. That wicked creature is giving me children their first taste of him."

She squeezed his hand. "Maybe the dog knew death would be better with you and Liam away? He's inside the barn."

"Could be." He fingered his day-old stubbled chin. "And now me son is needing me, for he's away to the barn to comfort himself with Rusty, by all that's holy, to find Grey lying there. 'Tis a woeful day. Very taxing to be a da at me age. I'm weary."

Orla ripped his coat from the chair back. "I'm not too weary or old."

"Need a bit of me whiskey for me back." He clamped down on the lump in his throat.

She donned her brother's grimy jacket and wrinkled her nose. "I'll be after finding Liam."

"'Tis grand of you, sister. But tell me, nothing tragic happened to Rusty, aye?"

"Saints alive, I believe not. I'll be . . ." Orla dashed outside.

"Disasters all around." Mick burrowed around in his carpetbag for the half-full bottle of alcohol and leaned against the tabletop. What was the worst on the list? Molly's desertion? Being evicted? Nah, 'twas Liam running away, and Grey's death. Dogs don't make dreadful demands yet give inexhaustible loyalty. Children were wonderful and affectionate creatures, although they weren't his friends or companions. Where might he find companionship?

———

The next morning, Moira served breakfast to everyone without her usual chatter or instructions to her brother and sisters. She kept her gaze averted and only nodded a thank you as she served her Aunt Orla. *What's this 'bout?*

Liam also avoided eye contact with Orla, although Cara and Bridget engaged with her. The younger girls appeared more curious than upset while they studied her naked face without her personal paint applied.

"Cara, me youngest macushla, I believe 'tis your turn for saying grace over our food."

"Yes, Da. Blesses us, Lord, for these thigh gifts for Richard Bouts to receive. What comes after?"

"'From Thy bounty through Christ our Lord,'" Mick whispered.

"Amen." Cara crossed herself and beamed.

Everyone ate and drank their fresh milk in silence, as Mick had trained them. Silverware clinked against their plates accompanied by birds singing from the apple tree near the open kitchen window.

Mick finished first and relished his hot coffee while Orla drank tea. "Tell me more 'bout yesterday then."

Moira's fork clattered onto the table.

He must proceed gingerly as he asked for details surrounding Orla's visit. One day was all it took for her to demolish his peace and comfort.

"Da, may I be excused?" Moira tucked her lips in and stared at the floorboards.

Clearly, we can't speak in front of the others. "Aye." Mick shooed her away. "Get on with your chores."

Liam scrambled to stand and sat down again. "May I go? There's lots to do."

"Aye."

Mick waited while his older children made a run for it. He'd never seen such haste to do the chores, and he scratched his mustache while Moira cleared the dishes.

"Do you want help, Moira?" Bridget asked, then popped the last bite of her toast into her mouth.

"Not today." Moira stacked the dishes in the metal sink. "I'll wipe them later."

Mick frowned. "Me brain is muddled. Isn't Mrs. Cook taking you to Mass?"

"It's Tuesday, Da. That's why you dressed in your work clothes. She's sick anyway." Moira left the kitchen for the common room.

"What? Why aren't you all getting ready for school then?"

"Because Auntie O says she is only here until tomorrow. Can I stay?" Bridget bounced in her chair. "I want to hear more of Auntie O's tales."

"Please let me and Bridget stay home?"

He scratched his beard. "Suppose we can make it a holiday."

Orla clicked her teacup onto its saucer. "'Tis very glad I am that someone likes their auntie. With such happenings yesterday, I feared everyone would want me gone."

Bridget's lip trembled, and her eyelids were puffy. "Horrible things happened. Still, Auntie O, it wasn't your fault. Though I'll miss poor Grey terribly. The rooster was your fault, but I never liked him. It was my fault about the boots—"

"Macushla, no need to go over the list of tragedies your Auntie O created whilst I was away, and only for a day." For once, he wasn't to blame for disasters.

Cara slid off her chair and stopped. "I'm sad too. Can I go?"

"Aye."

She climbed onto her auntie's lap, and Orla's eyes widened with the lift of her pale, unpainted brows, shifting the whitish disfigurements on her face.

Mick raised one eyebrow. "Cara, you also must ask for permission to climb onto a person's lap."

"Oh." She bit her lip.

"Come. 'Tis as near to a girl child as I ever was since young Kathleen." Orla repositioned Cara on her lap. "Bony bottom she has, yeah? Digging into me thighs. Does she eat enough?"

"Cara is small and slight for a six-year-old. She's more like Kathleen in that way." His throat tightened at the thought of Kathleen.

"She'll be our new little lamb, aye?" Orla brushed her cheek against the top of Cara's head. "A delicate child. Me boyos are big like their Pa—"

Bridget slammed her palm onto the tabletop. "What about me? Aren't I delicate? I want to be special too."

"Bridget, apologize—"

"No need." Orla shot a warning glance at Mick. "Aye, you're a special lady. Noticed it right away, I did. You're a shiny new American penny. We shall call you New Penny. As for delicate? Well, I'm proud to be your auntie, for you resemble me. You'll be tall and majestic, where no one can miss your presence, and if you keep on singing, no lady can compare with you. What do you think?"

"Are you making that up, Auntie O?" Bridget narrowed her eyes.

Orla upthrust her hands, just missing Cara's head. "And why would I be doing such a nonsensical thing? Can't be after fooling you. Each one of you are treasures, no matter what the townspeople say." She lay her chin in her palm and muttered loud enough for her brother to hear, "Wicked women."

Mick patted Bridget's arm. "Auntie is telling you the truth, macushla. You and your sisters ought to be created differently by God's own hand. Moira is serious, and you sing and dance. Cara wishes to draw pictures. Why must you all do the same things?"

"Hmm." Bridget lifted one eyebrow.

Mick twisted his mustache. *What all happened whilst I was away?* "Quick, Orla, whilst Moira is occupied, tell me 'bout shopping in town."

"First, the day began grand enough after I introduced meself to your girls. Had no troubles believing I was their auntie." She patted their hands. "Troubles came when I didn't know what to do with girlies. Thought they'd be easy compared to boyos. They didn't wish to go to school, and I was glad to know them better. Your little angels wanted to play in the creek at the end of your property beneath the trees by the boulders."

"I know where me creek is."

"And do you also know what imps your angels are?" Orla jiggled Cara and winked at Bridget. "Told me the beautiful dress I was wearing wasn't fit for the creek. I wore me blue day dress. I've changed since marriage and motherhood, but me wardrobe, not as much. Haven't many plain dresses, don't you know?"

"Think so."

"We collected some empty storage cans from the barn and headed to the creek—"

"Without Moira." Bridget smirked.

"Aye, Moira was a proper young lady and stayed home to work all morning on the laundry. She works too much. I can tell, aye. She's a bit moody, as well, and I know moody when I see it, don't you know? You should—"

"Run me own family? Rear me own children? Moira enjoys doing for others. Said so many times, and Bridget helps her when she needs it. Moira is grand."

Orla lifted a brow, then cleared her throat. "At the creek, the girls kicked off their shoes on the bank of cattails, hiked up their skirts, and waded in. It was all giggles and fun whilst they fished for pollywogs with their cans. Found me a spot under the tree to observe. Must've dozed off."

Cara giggled. "You snored like Da."

"I did not. I awoke to such a hullabaloo with Bridget screaming and Cara splashing her."

Mick growled. "Girls?"

Bridget made a face at her younger sister. "Cara snatched all the pollywogs. I told her to leave some for me, but she—"

"Big baby." Cara stuck out her tongue.

"Hush, girlies. Let Aunt Orla finish her tale."

"Well, Bridget pushed Cara over, and Cara tossed Bridget's boots into deep water, and they sank with a *kerplunk*. Bridget wailed they were her only shoes." Orla glowered at Bridget. "Since then, I found out otherwise. So I forced meself to wade in, though we never learned to swim, aye?"

"Aye, no need."

"Had me dress gathered up in me fists, showing me petticoats and unmentionables to all the world, I did. When the water hit me waist, I gave up me search for the boots. Couldn't see them at all, and boots aren't worth drowning for."

"Agreed."

Bridget lifted her leg above the tabletop and wiggled her foot. "See? I got new boots for Cara's meanness."

"And I got all the pollywogs, so there."

Mick scowled. "Cara, where did you put the pollywogs? Not in the kitchen sink again, aye?"

"No. They're in the can on the porch. I knew better this time. That grouchy Moira would've taken away my drawing time again."

"You must return them to the creek where they belong when Aunt Orla is finished."

"Yes, Da." Cara sulked.

Orla waved her hands. "Ho there. I've more to tell you. So, I slid backwards, climbing up the bank and joined the boots in the water. Changed again. Now we're getting to the worst part. The hubbub in town when we went to the mercantile." She chewed her thumbnail.

Bridget shook her head sharply. "No, Auntie O, you forgot the very worst part was Grey dying."

"Aye, right you are." Orla scooted her chair back, set the youngest Muldoon on the floor, then rose. "Need me more tea before I tell you more tale." She checked the kettle on the stove. "Still hot. Anyone need anything whilst I'm up?"

"No." Mick massaged his jaw. "Get on with it." Neither ranching, rail work, nor raising children took care of themselves in the best of times. And now he had an eviction to deal with on top of these petty squabbles.

Orla poured hot water into her cup and resettled with Cara. "Don't mind saying your townspeople are rude. It being smaller than a city, thought 'twould be a friendlier place. You only have one main road with only one choice of shopping for clothing." She dunked a biscuit into her tea and nibbled at it.

"Must you stall?" Mick raised his voice. "There're chores to be done around here."

"She's almost done." Bridget drummed her fingers on the tabletop.

Cara squirmed in her chair. "She should tell you about the lady in the store yanking Moira's new dress out of her hands."

"What?"

Orla nodded. "All because of me fashion choices, me thinks. Changed into me red dress. The train travel crushed me purple velvet. Only brought two other dresses, and one was wet from the creek. Figured the red might be questionable, but I'm taller and fuller than Moira, so couldn't borrow hers."

Bridget scowled. "The women were mean to Auntie O, Da. Moira ran out crying."

"Let me tell it." Orla huffed. "Well, and the ruckus happened when the shopkeeper got his wife involved in choosing something for Moira. He was nice enough for a man, but the woman? She looked at me and turned into a vicious, moral, b—" Orla stopped when Mick's mouth flew open.

"But beautiful woman." Orla dunked her biscuit.

"Mrs. Thompson." Bridget sighed. "She's the prettiest lady in town. Everyone says so. I want to look like her when I grow up."

"Aye. The beautiful Mrs. Thompson stuck up her nose,

told me shame on meself for being a bad influence on young Moira, and ordered us to leave. Don't you envy that kind of beauty, me Bridget. 'Tis a bad path with consequences you won't enjoy. The ladies inside the store certainly enjoyed that scene, yeah." Again, Orla dunked her biscuit but viciously bit off the end.

Cara bared her teeth in the snarl of a protective dog. "That's when Mrs. Thompson yanked the dress out of Moira's hands."

"The other ladies rudely clapped and cheered about it. I stuck my tongue out." Bridget exposed it to him.

"So did I." Cara copied her sister.

"Those women acted as if I was doing something terrible. Being protective of Moira, aye, but I'd never turn a twelve-year-old into meself." Orla shuddered and caressed the mark beneath her eye. "That overburdened girl of yours carries a heavy weight ever since her mam left, and now poor Moira is horrified by her tattered reputation in addition to everything else. And all because I wore me red dress into your backwater town, aye? Moira hates me."

"Hates? Moira never uses that word, sister."

"'Tis what she said." Orla chewed the last of her biscuit.

Bridget patted Orla's arm. "I heard her say so. Are Moira and Auntie O in trouble? What are you going to do to them?"

Mick moaned. "First Orla, 'twasn't the dress making the troubles. Well, not only your dress. You paint your face. Most unnatural, 'tis. Makes folks stare with confusion 'bout who you are. Macushlas, don't you ever paint your faces, aye? It causes scenes amongst good folk."

Bridget's brow wrinkled as she stroked her face. "I'm sure they paint their faces in vaudeville and the theater. But I won't if you let me have piano lessons?"

"Brother, I must paint to cover me disfigurements. I've also pale skin, pale lashes, pale eyebrows, and pale eyes. Might as well be a monster." Orla twisted a curl as it glinted with gentle copper lights in the morning sunbeam squeezing through the parted yellow window curtains. "Everything 'bout me fades away except for me hair. 'Tis me saving beauty."

"Girlies, go help Moira. All day. 'Tis your consequences from behaving so badly for your auntie. There'll be no playing until Moira says so." He jerked his head to the side and waved toward the living room.

Cara scrunched her face. "But Da, I wanted to draw pictures."

"First, return the pollywogs to the creek. Tonight, after the supper dishes, Moira may allow you time to draw. 'Tis up to her." Mick kneaded his throbbing temples. He could apply for that foreman job. What were the details? If he could transfer with better pay to replace the ranch's income, with maybe a foreman's job, he'd know where to move his family. Would Orla return to help them pack and settle? What about her own family? She never told him about her problems. He glanced at his sister.

Orla sipped her tea and studied him over the cup's rim.

The children liked their auntie. Except Moira. And Liam.

Mick couldn't be expected to work the small sheep ranch plus find a new job and look after his children, could he? He must give the ranch work to Liam while it lasted. He'd get a break from some of his responsibilities then. He also knew based upon family letters he received he was the only one who hadn't cut off contact with Orla. *Risk Moira's angst and ask.* "Sister, I could use your help when we move. Can you return to help us?"

"Don't see why not. No one wants me at home, but don't ask questions. Won't answer them."

"Reasonable enough." Mick's mouth twitched while the tension in his body eased.

———

Doyle Ranch, Iowa
   Late Winter, 1901

"The Night of the Big Wind is fading fast." *Oíche na Gaoithe Móre.* Blindfolded for his surprise party, Mick called to the children from in his chair in the common room. Did he notice the aroma of a cake baking for his sixty-second birthday or how the girls whispered? Giggling increased with footsteps within the kitchen. He scratched his ears under the bandana. He was glad they didn't tie him up as well.

What tasks for his new job had he completed? *Wired the Doyle attorney we're leaving. Transfer request sent to the railroad's expansion site. Must purchase a younger horse. Poor old Scout.* His loyal old horse wouldn't survive the long trip to South Dakota hauling the family in the cart. Mick's elusive goal was how to take the children far from their mother and make it seem like she cared.

"Da, Moira told me to guard you with all my skill as a young man, so you won't peek."

"Alright."

"Do you know what this is all about?"

"Well, 'tis me birthday."

"But what could be out in the barn? Bridget wouldn't allow me inside." Liam chuckled. "I didn't mind her orders because she did all my chores, and that's why I had time to fetch the packing crates from Mr. Thompson. Is South Dakota like Iowa? When does Aunt Orla come?"

"She'll be here soon." *Bright and curious is our Liam.* "I've heard little 'bout South Dakota, but the pay is grand working there as a Section Foreman. 'Tis me highest concern as your Da and provider. Housing is the next thing—"

Thump! A brouhaha erupted with strange scratching sounds on the kitchen's floor, urgent whispers, and chairs dragged around the floor.

Liam tapped his arm. "Da, you'll never believe—"

"Guessed."

"Pretend not to hear. They want to surprise you."

Since being a Da, Mick never imagined he'd be called upon to act as daft as a dirt clod so often. It was the one time it was admirable to have the trait of being thick-headed.

"*Oof!*" Mick grappled with a wriggly, writhing fluff ball with sharp nails digging into his lap. Amidst laughter and shouts, someone tugged off his blindfold in time for a pink tongue in a black and white furry face to lick his nose. He held the squirmy pup at arm's length for inspection. "Bless me soul."

Bridget hopped in her excitement. "He's Blackie. Isn't he cute?"

"I—"

Liam bent over Mick's shoulder. "He looks something like Grey, but with brown eyes."

"So he does." Mick glanced up at his son's gleeful face. This pup wasn't only for his own birthday gift. Brilliant Moira had found the one way to heal Liam's heart from Grey's passing.

"Bridget, come help me in the kitchen."

"Why does Moira always ask me for help?" Bridget sulked.

Mick glowered at Bridget. "Because she often needs it. Shall she always do all the household work alone?"

Liam took Blackie and set him on the floor. The puppy darted around the room and greeted each person with a lick and a nip. He sniffed back and forth near the front door and squatted.

"Grab him!" Mick rose from his chair. "Outside. None of that business in the house. We must teach him to behave as a gentleman."

Cara giggled. "He's not a gentleman. He's a puppy."

Liam snatched Blackie in the nick of time.

Mick forced a frown. "Only a gentleman puppy who's

236 | E.V. SPARROW

trained to mind his manners is allowed inside of me home. We'll make sure he knows what to do in our new home as well."

Cara followed Liam as he took Blackie outside.

Moira's voice echoed from the kitchen. "So you're good at training gentlemen to mind their manners? Auntie O could use you in her business."

He startled. "What do you know 'bout Orla's business?"

Something clattered and whispers followed the sound. "Just what she's told us. Da, there's something else for you, so stay put."

"I will. How old is this pup, Bridget?"

Bridget left the kitchen and shook out her apron. "He's three months old. My friend's dog had the puppies."

"Cake." Moira stood in the kitchen doorway. "Where is everyone? I lit the candles. Quick, if don't want the flames melting the glaze."

"Outside." Bridget peered through the window. "Blackie was the last pup they took from his mother." Her eyes clouded and her chin trembled. "Will he miss her? Will she miss him? She might wonder if he'll ever come home. Will she try to find him? He—"

"Can someone get Liam, please?" Moira moved in front of Mick's chair. The glowing cake highlighted her concerned face.

Mick rose. "Sure. Moira is ready with the cake, Bridget. 'Tis not the proper time for questions. For now, we've a celebration, and everyone's worked hard to make it a grand one. I'll be sure to tell your Mam where we're moving to, aye? I'll write to her." His heart ached in his chest. Would their mother's desertion ever stop robbing his children of their joy? It fell upon him to be the one to deal with their broken hearts.

19

HOUSEKEEPER'S SCANTY WAGES

'Tis us Irish who become lawless when left to ourselves, yeah?
Mick

T wo Years Later
South Dakota
Late Spring, 1903

After Judd turned off the lights in his saloon for the night, Mick and his new rail crew headed home. He had chums here for the first time and spent many evenings with them as though he could make up for the lack of friends in his married years. Two pals lived near Mick's home, and Flash was his favorite.

Yellow lantern light lit one window of Mick's house and spilled out onto the ground. A shadow inside moved along the common room wall.

Flash pointed to the window. "Did you see that?"

"I'm thinking 'tis Moira and not some thief. Blackie would nip a chunk from a thief's backside rather than let one enter me home. See you Monday on the rails."

"Night."

Mick focused on making no sound as he stepped onto the

porch. A black flash flew around the corner of the house. *Mister Death?* Gold light highlighted the porch, and he jerked backwards a few steps, nearly losing his balance.

"Da." Moira stood silhouetted in the open door, and whispered, "Glad you're home. Everyone is asleep. I was hemming your old work pants for Liam." She stepped aside and darted quick glances beyond him.

Blackie greeted Mick with a lick to his fingers.

"Is something wrong?" He drew closer to her, but she recoiled. "Ah. Pardon me breath."

Moira wrinkled her nose and fanned her face. "Earlier tonight something happened, so I put the lantern in the window." She scanned the porch and peered into the shadows.

He should ask her to explain what bothered her, although it was near midnight. "What something?"

"Let's talk tomorrow, after you've slept." She dimmed the lantern then carried it down the hallway.

"Aye, off to bed macushla. You must get your rest." He followed her with the light's aura, grazing the wall to steady himself on the way to his room. What was amiss?

Bright light through his muslin curtains the next morning awoke Mick. Dread washed through him and replaced the joy of a lazy Sunday, although he needn't rush off to work. He could get Moira into his room for questioning. *She needs her mother, but there's only me.* He grunted while he grappled under his bed, removed a fresh bottle stashed there, and took a gulp. *Time for a grim chat with me eldest.*

Mick opened his door and listened. No voices, only sounds from the kitchen. He poked his head further into the hall and searched both ways. He called out, "Moira? Are you there, macushla?"

A pause, then, "I'm here."

"Come here for a minute." He glimpsed himself in the mirror as he turned back. He hadn't changed out of his long johns. "Knock first." He shut the door and hurried to dress.

A light tap on his door came as he buttoned his shirt. "Enter."

Moira stepped through.

"Where're the others?"

"They're in the paddock while Liam gives Bridget riding lessons."

Mick sat on a chair under the window and indicated for her to sit on the bed. "We should expect hilarious stories of their antics, aye?" He attempted a smile. "Wished for a private chat with you."

She sat and faced him. "What are we chatting about?"

He fingered his moustache. He should have practiced this speech so it wouldn't feel like jumping into a snake pit. "Last night. 'Tis 'bout your behavior."

"My behavior?"

"Aye. Something didn't sit right. You were skittish."

Moira huffed. "You recall my discomfort? I'm surprised. You don't always notice things." She wrinkled her nose. "I shouldn't say it that way. You notice a lot of things, just not things about me. You depend on me but don't ask questions."

What's she spouting off? Was she being moody again? He did his best, didn't he? "Unfair, but I'm asking you now. Learned from your Mam at our last meeting to ask 'bout feelings."

She pursed her lips and stared out the window. "I heard men's voices near the house, and you weren't home. Then something moved in the dark, near the shrubbery, so I considered your gun. Blackie didn't bark or growl, which helped me calm down."

Mister Death? It couldn't be. *I'm the only one who sees him.*

She faced him. "But more than that, Auntie O said some things during her last visit that bothered me and gave me sleepless nights."

"Well, I trained you to shoot to defend yourself and give you security. But tell me 'bout your Aunt Orla. What did she say?"

Moira slid her gaze to her da and sneered. "Do you know what Auntie O is?"

He closed his eyes. If only he could vanish. He didn't want to answer. How could he have asked for Orla's help and expose his children to her ways in his home? *What's wrong with me?* Was he a simpleton?

"Auntie means well. I could see that. But she isn't particularly aware of her affect."

"Moira, try to understand. Orla is not a stranger to me, and I know her foibles. Although she'd never harm family, and her aid in settling us was a gift in our time of need."

"Yes, I know. I understand your reasons. Anyway, I realized that day in the shop back in Iowa that Auntie was, uh, peculiar. The women's reactions revealed more details. And what did you expect, Da? That the town would never speak of her again? They gossiped everywhere I went. The dire warnings and the judgements. Then when she thought I should know what happens between a man and a woman, well, I knew it's not what I want for myself."

"What?" He gawped. His lungs burned for air as dizziness swept through him. Anger flooded his stunned brain and fired up his face. He took a deep breath to cool it off then he sat down beside his daughter. "She'd no right. She overstepped, macushla." He scowled. "I didn't expect that. And I never suffered from the gossips."

She laid her hand on his arm. "You wouldn't, being with your crew. Men care much less about women like her than other women do. Numbness took over, plus we were getting evicted and leaving. There was no reason to say anything, especially when you were so happy to have someone help us. I noticed her admirable qualities as well."

Admirable? "I'm confused, macushla."

Moira laughed until tears ran down her cheeks and she held her stomach. "Your expression. I've admired her determination in providing for herself, though I'd never do such things, so I made some wonderful plans of my own."

The shock wore off with her reassurances. "Ah, you wish to be a housekeeper or marry and raise a family? That's all I ever wanted. To have a family and to farm. None of it worked out yet. Thinking it won't at this late date."

She shook her head. "But I've been a mother to three children. You mustn't feel guilty about having Auntie here. I'm not interested in doing what she does with men."

Remorse stuck in his throat like a stick. He smacked his forehead, hoping to break it loose. "By all that's holy. What Orla did with men in her younger years is not the same thing as marriage."

"What's the difference?"

"Love, macushla." Moira had never seen married love in action. How could she know? Had he loved her own mother? He'd lived with her out of wedlock. *I failed her.*

"Da, I love God and wish to serve Him and the church. It's the only thing I'm interested in. Plus, every Irish family has a priest or a nun. I want to be the one."

His palms dampened. Mick wiped them on his shirt. "So you don't want to marry or have babes of your own? What if I pay you to keep house for us?"

"It's not about money. I want freedom to live—"

"Could you not be a housekeeper for a wealthy family or become a nurse? Always dreamt of marriage, owning a home, raising a family, settling in one place in this vast and beautiful land."

"Again, those are your dreams, Da, not mine. I enjoyed cleaning the house and caring for everyone. But as a nun, I could expand my schooling and not waste the brain God gave me. Auntie O says I'm like her in that. I remember everything I read and mathematics. I'd have opportunities to be a teacher or a nurse and learn more about God without all the demands from home."

What could he say? Hadn't his dedicated, loving eldest daughter earned her freedom to be what she wanted to be? She'd carried so much responsibility in her young life.

Moira clasped his hands. "I could read about God for all my days and never discover everything there is to know about Him. Pray all day, and it wouldn't matter how long. And I'd finally have time for friends. There'll be many women around me. Will you please hire a housekeeper and give permission for me to go? It will be wonderful."

Wonderful? Mick's mouth went dry, and his insides shriveled like sliced apples in the sun's heat. "Not to me." His comment sounded sacrilegious. He growled after he said it, as his dreams evaporated for his first surviving daughter's future of marriage and grandchildren. What right did he have to hamper his eldest? Leaving Ireland freed him from wretched poverty, didn't it? "You're freed to fly upon your hopes after I hire a housekeeper." If he could find one.

"You're the best, Da!" Moira embraced him, planting kisses on his cheeks. "One more thing. Liam told me something for he's too embarrassed to tell you. Don't be angry with him for keeping it secret. Please promise me."

Dismay lodged his breath in his lungs, but he forced it away with a cough. "You've another secret?"

She went to the door and listened. "I walked in on Auntie O teaching him tips on how to hire ladies of the evening cheaply, and—"

"What?" Mick jumped to his feet, jarring his leg. Pain shot up his back, but he ignored it for the sake of the pain in his heart, which was hundreds of times worse.

"Well it's her business, isn't it? Really, sometimes you don't consider things very well. I mean no disrespect. We know you're very busy working and taking good care of us, and we're very grateful, but what did you expect would happen with her staying here?"

He dropped onto the chair, sunk his head into his palms,

and clenched what remained of his hair. "I'm a da in shambles."

"Not true. I'm sorry I shocked you."

He tried to contain his sobs without luck. She hugged his arm, and he sobbed in earnest.

Moira softly kissed his forehead. "Can you not be happy for me? I've decided what to do with my life. Isn't it noble and exciting? Who knows where they might send me? It might be to Europe, or maybe I'll stay here. Would you like that best? If they keep me here?"

This was new territory for him. A da ought to be happy when his child's dreams come true. Hadn't he wondered what they would choose to do with their lives? Moira made her choice but was it a good one? "If I could be sure 'tis what you want and not from Orla's influence."

She dropped to her knees and giggled. "I grew up on a ranch, remember? And around farm animals, so I guessed where their babies came from before Auntie O ever told me a thing about procreation. With animals there isn't any love involved. Right? With Auntie's activities, you said love's not there either." Moira grimaced and stuck out her tongue. "Blech."

He chuckled and wiped his damp cheeks with his shirtsleeve. "You're a wise one, macushla."

She pulled herself up on the edge of the bed. "Everyone's back inside the house." His precious girl turned toward him at the door. "Don't be too harsh on Auntie O. Her opinions are from her experiences."

Maybe he didn't do such a poor job of raising his children. *But that creature, Orla.* Could be her guilt keeping her from writing letters to him. And Moira, how long could he stall, and could he find a willing housekeeper?

He desperately needed a drink.

And freedom like Moira's. *I should enjoy me own life before 'tis over.* Hiring a housekeeper might be the best thing for himself. And everyone else.

———

Early Autumn

Outside Sully's Supply Store, Mick folded the newest edition of The Prairie News and thrust it inside his work coat. *Four months without a response from me advertisement.* Hadn't Moira said the situation frustrated her? *As I thought, not enough women nearby.* He twisted his moustache as he approached Wings tied to the hitching post.

Why had Orla quit writing? Mick massaged the concerns for her well-being out of his neck. "She would've told me if something truly bad happened, aye?"

Wings flung his head, disarraying his mane.

A chill wind whistled between the town's structures, announcing October's approach. Mick tucked his chin inside his collar. He mounted Wings from the block and urged his mount toward home. "The warmth of home awaits us."

Wings broke into a trot.

"Pull up. I swear you understand me words." He chuckled. "You long to gallop across the plains as do I. But me old back couldn't take it. Those days passed us by, Wings." *As other enjoyments have.*

Would he allow Moira to leave if he found a housekeeper? He'd never marry again. He had disastrous luck with love, although he desired it occasionally. What about the type of love Orla experienced, which Moira said was the same thing? *Confusing lust with love, me sister is.*

His thirst for a gallop increased as they neared his home, now visible on a hilltop surrounded by other homes the railroad recently built for its crews. He was glad he had a family to avoid living in a boxcar like the single men did. Life wasn't as lonely with neighbors nearby, but they needed more children.

A small, dark-clad figure rocked in a chair on Mick's porch. *Mister Death?* He pulled up Wings and squinted hard.

No, it was a woman with dark hair. Something about her was familiar. His eagerness to discover who awaited passed onto Wings, and the horse slightly increased his pace. Mick waved, as he drew closer to his home. "Hello, there."

The young woman stood with her bag. Dark green eyes and dimples appeared when she smiled. *Like Anne Brown.* She couldn't be because this woman was much younger. A teacup sat on the table with an empty plate. "Evening. Your daughter served me tea and rightly didn't allow me inside whilst I'm a stranger to her."

Though Mick had never met this woman, her voice and something else niggled at him. "By all that's holy. Are you young Beth, Anne Brown's sister? You have the looks of her."

"Aye, from Ireland. 'Tis such a lovely compliment saying I'm young, for I'm now thirty-nine." She dipped a curtsy, and her grin widened, deepening her dimples. "Beth or Bessie or Bess will do. I'm grown up, as you can see." She tossed her shiny, thick hair over her shoulder.

He was partial to dark, thick, wavy hair with copper glints, and those large green eyes lined with long, dark, pony lashes like Anne's. And Shauna, with the dimples. *Stop that, Mick. She's twenty years me junior.* "How is Anne faring these days?" Mick didn't dismount. He felt more in control of the situation from the height of his horse.

"Dead." She crossed herself. "Passed to heaven two years ago, God rest her soul."

A sharp pain shot through his heart as he crossed himself. *Anne.* "May Christ have mercy on her soul."

"Aye." Beth rummaged in her large bag and pulled out a piece of paper. "Anne made me promise to come and search for a Muldoon. She often claimed you were her hero and a good man. She told me Orla or Ed would do as well. I found you first."

Thank God 'twas neither she found.

"I got your address here in South Dakota from your brother Ed's letter to your brother Rory in Ireland. He gave me Ed's address, but Ed wasn't interested in helping me and gave me your newest address. 'Tis that sorry I am to hear your marriage to Molly ended in divorce." She clucked her tongue. "Such a shame."

His head spun from attempting to follow the letters she listed for him and how she'd heard of his divorce. "Right."

She thrust the paper back into her bag and sat. "So I'm here. Does your horse enjoy standing in place for hours upon hours whilst you converse?" Her eyes twinkled.

Mocking me? "What I or me horse does is of no—"

She burst out laughing like a singing angel. "Go on, 'tis me, Miss Beth Brown. I'm jesting, for we've long been acquainted." She tilted her head at the other chair. "Come and join me?"

Ah, she's a Miss then. And 'tis her own house now? He was unsure whether to admire her amusement at his expense and her presumptuousness, or to keep his distance from this young woman he wasn't that well acquainted with. He waited for his mixed thoughts to settle and didn't trust himself to speak.

"I've offended you. We always bantered in me family. Anne told me you liked it. Don't you recall? Must be too many years ago." She twirled a loose curl around her finger. "I'll tell you this. I've had an affection for you ever since the day of your wake with the rat and the basket." She burst out giggling again. "I know I'll never forget that night. You toasted to the cat and the rat who battled, and to Mrs. Gilhooley's battered basket saving the day. You then told the people they'd never forget your wake, and see? I haven't. Anne and I spoke of it often—"

"Aye, 'twas a memorable wake." He didn't need to urge Wings toward the barn. "I'll get Wings settled in his stall."

"Evening, Da." Liam approached from around the corner of the house in the twilight. "I finished storing the hay and the wood." He pulled off his leather gloves. "Heard a rumor we'll have a tough winter." He gawked at Beth sitting on the porch.

"Evening, Liam. This is Miss Brown, a family friend from the Old Country. She's here to . . ."

"Seek employment." Beth darted a glance at Mick and curtsied to Liam.

Liam removed his hat. "Good to make your acquaintance."

"Such a polite boy at the age of . . .?" Beth turned to Mick and raised her brow.

"Newly turned thirteen. He's very responsible and earns coin however he can for the family. He even travels to the nearby towns to watch worker's children, or on the farms when I'm home, and helps care for Wings and Blackie." Mick handed the reins to Liam. "Give Wings his nightly rub down, and he'll be expecting his oats. I'll take Beth, uh, Miss Brown inside."

In the kitchen, Moira offered a chair to their guest. "I apologize, Miss Brown, for a simple meal. If I'd known you were to be visiting, I would've planned something else."

Beth accepted the offered chair. "Well, and me apologies for arriving unannounced. But Moira, you served me with a lovely tea on the porch, and I'm glad to share whatever meal you've cooked. You're a polite and grand young lady of the house."

"Thank you." Moira flushed. "Our family is easy to please. How did you find us?"

"When I arrived at the Doyle ranch, your neighbor shared you'd relocated here without an address. 'Tis a very tiny town to be sure, and you were easy to find near the rails."

It was Liam's turn to say grace, but during the recitation,

Mick's mind wandered away to what he should do with Beth. What was her plan? He studied her with one eye. She was rather beautiful, if thin and tiny, until she came to the supper table with her hair pinned up revealing jutting ears. This flaw rendered her less attractive. *More like an Irish mouse.* Beth had quick mannerisms, along with her speech. She was docile as well like Kathleen. *But her accent, by all that's holy.* Was his ever so thick? Hers was endearing with a soft lilt.

Liam finished with the blessing, and everyone crossed themselves.

Beth then asked his children a rapid litany of questions about school, church, and friends, as if they still lived in Ireland's ancient culture and not in the middle of this wild, sparsely populated railroad town built on the Dakota Plains.

Moira upstretched her hand when Beth paused to catch her breath. "Miss Brown, pardon me, but Da has a rule of not speaking until we've finished the meal." She peeped sideways at Mick.

"Aye, we eat in peace till we're done. Except for requests for a dish to be passed. Eat your meal, girlies. There'll be plenty of time to speak with Miss Brown later."

"As you wish." Beth then focused on her bowl of ham, beans, and thick bread laden with butter and Moira's berry jam.

Mick dipped his bread slathered with butter and jam into his beans and searched his children's faces while he chewed. Bridget and Cara stared at their guest and giggled at Beth's chatty ways. Liam was engrossed with his food while Moira beamed. She'd been longing for her freedom. He understood that very well, didn't he? Since he tucked his spoon inside his empty bowl, Moira and Bridget stood to clear the table.

Cara turned to Beth. "You're from Ireland. I can tell because you talk funny, even funnier than Da does."

Beth clasped her hands in the air. "We're free to speak now, are we? Saints preserve meself, I thought I would rupture me brains with all the words rattling around inside. But 'tis your Da's rule, and so you should obey, 'tis true. 'Twill be a struggle for me at every meal if I stay here with you."

She wants to stay here?

Liam bent down to pet Blackie. "You get used to it."

"You do." Bridget clamped her head in her palms like a vise. "My brains swell all the time while I'm waiting for Da to finish eating. But will you stay with us? Moira wants to go be a nun for some reason. I know I never would. I want to sing and dance on stage, like in vaudeville. Do you know about it in Ireland? I hear stories about it. My friend Mary Ellen in Iowa, where we used to live, says—"

"Bridget." Mick knocked on the table. "Let Miss Brown gather her thoughts. She says her brain is full of them. Give her time to shuffle through and rid herself of some."

Beth's eyes flashed at him with glee. "Your children are delightful, Mick. Anne told me often how she imagined your children would be kind and loving and hardworking. How did you ever raise them so well on your own?"

Moira scoffed. "He didn't. First there was Ma. Next it was me helping him. Then our auntie was here. You must've known Orla. She left us to go start a new business, she calls it. If you really do stay here, I can finally follow my dreams. Right, Da? You promised."

"I'm sensing a prickly story." Beth gathered his empty bowl and cup. "Let me help clear the table, and if your Da says it's a story for me ears to hear, I'll listen well."

Her ears. They probably don't miss a thing. He tracked her slight figure to the kitchen as she followed the girls carrying the supper dishes. Then he glanced at his son.

Liam folded his arms, and his eyes held reproach.

"What?" Were his thoughts apparent? Was this boy judging his Da? What does a boy of thirteen know of loneliness? "I make me own choices, which I haven't yet made on this. I don't require me children's advice. I'll thank you not to be moralizing. It that clear?"

Liam directed his gaze at the tabletop. "Yes, Da. It's clear." He raised his expressionless face. "May I be excused? I have things to do and must get up early to travel to Bluebell. I watch the O'Brien children tomorrow."

He wiped his mustache. "Aye, you may go. And be sure to pack some of Moira's bread for the children if they be hungry. Not all parents provide well for their children."

"Yes, Da. Not all do."

Giggling echoed out of the kitchen as Mick selected a chair by the woodstove in the main room. Good thing he started a fire, for the evenings had turned cold. Soon they'd have howling blizzards blowing snow drifts across the plains, and even if he wished Beth to leave, it wouldn't be safe. 'Twouldn't be safe at all. His eager Moira could leave in a day or two, and Beth may stay on as his housekeeper. *I found someone. Upon me doorstep.* Beth was the perfect fit.

———

One month later, the morning arrived for Moira's send-off at the newly constructed and unpainted train station on the edge of town. The pungent aroma of freshly cut wood and sawdust hung in the air.

Beth twirled with her arms open. Her full plaid skirt swirled around her black-stockinged legs. "Such a wide-open place, the prairie. Do you miss the trees? I wish Anne could've seen where you live, but then I'd not be the one here with you, would I? 'Tis a glad day for you, Moira."

Mick rolled his tense shoulders as he studied his oldest.

Tall and poised, Moira embraced a sparsely packed flour sack, since she rejected his tattered carpetbag. "I can barely withstand my excitement." She turned to him with enormous eyes. "Can you believe it?"

"'Tis on account of your belief God set you free with Miss Brown's presence, aye?" His fifteen-year-old girl would be a novice in the convent.

"Yes, He did. And I want to be with Him."

Beth embraced Moira. "You must be eager for your new life." She turned away to tend Cara when she tugged Beth's skirt. "What do you need, little one?"

"I'm grateful that yours and God's plans seem to match, macushla." Mick sniffed and glanced at his new housekeeper. Accepting the post and tending his children contented Beth. Her presence erased his concerns for his household's welfare and avoided entrusting flibbertigibbet Bridget with the house and Cara. Bridget might outgrow her tendencies, but he didn't think so. She was so much like Little Lamb was as a child.

"Here it comes." Cara hopped.

"I hate the whistle." Bridget covered her ears. "Must it be so very loud? We can see that gigantic monster with no warning to blow out our ears. Da, can you fix—"

"I cannot."

Moira grinned at Bridget. "I might miss your flighty and funny ways, but probably not." She breathed deep. "My new life is only hours away. I hope to make lots of friends. I've never had the time. I should hug everyone goodbye." She reached for her brother and sisters.

Mick's brain and throat jammed with emotions of guilt, pride, dread, and joy, all mixed into a confused clump. He tried to choose only one emotion so he could speak to his parting daughter. He had no luck. He coughed to free his voice. "I hope you make many friends, macushla. Do you have everything? Your bag is half empty."

"I took sentimental things. Ma's doily, Bridget's quilt piece with the cross on it, the farewell card Cara drew. Plus a crucifix, and the *Key of Heaven* prayer book you and Liam brought back from St. Paul for my birthday. Oh, and my underthings.

The convent supplies everything else." Moira hugged him tight. "You did your best with us, and I'll not forget it."

Her body trembled in his embrace. "I wish Mam was here to say goodbye, but it's impossible." She swung her gaze to Beth. "Miss Brown seems a suitable replacement."

He restrained Moira when she tried to pull away. "Me precious girl, me macushla," he whispered into her ear. Then he thrust her to arm's length. "Are you sure you wish this? You're shaking."

Moira touched his cheek. "And you're crying, Da. Yes, I'm sure. It's not fear. I'm more joyful than anything." Her eyes sparkled.

Beth squatted to help Cara with her loose bootlace while Bridget chattered away with comments on the few disembarking passenger's clothing and Liam inspected the train, asking questions of the conductor.

Moira murmured, "Since I'm leaving, I want to say behave yourself with Miss Brown. Although you'll have a daughter who's a nun, it doesn't mean it erases all your sins or you can take advantage of God's good graces. He still pays attention."

His mouth dropped open. *Me daughter, as well?* "And what do you think I'll be doing?"

"I'm old enough to remember you lived with Mam without marriage at first. Goodbye, Da."

The hulking train awaited at the platform, with puffs of steam billowing from the black stack and swirling down around its wheels. Five other passengers grouped together to board it, and her plump escort, Mrs. White, disembarked.

"Good morning to you, Muldoon family. Today's the important day for Moira, aye? I'll take grand care of her on the trip." Her gray eyes crinkled around the edges with her smile.

Mick shoved his hands inside his pockets. "I know you will,

Mrs. White. After our first meeting, I sensed the church knows how to pick fine women as escorts."

"Thank you." Mrs. White beckoned Moira and retreated into the doorway's shadows as the whistle blew.

"St. Paul. All bound for St. Paul," the conductor announced from the top step. "Get your tickets ready."

"I must go. Mrs. White is waiting." Moira reached down to grab her sack, but Liam snatched it first.

"I'm sad you're going, but I'll come visit you when I'm old enough." Liam flicked his gaze to Mick. "Or I'll come with Da." He strode toward the steps with Moira's sack while the engine powered up with more coal fed into it by the stoker.

Mick drew nearer to the train so he could linger in this terrible, wonderful moment. Steam clouds rolled over him like he imagined happening in heaven for all his other lost darlings. His only comfort was from the difference he felt with this kind of loss because he could take a train. Not a forever loss. He tugged his handkerchief square from his pocket and dabbed at the tears trickling into his beard.

Moira appeared in a window and waved. She continued to wave as the train gathered speed. Her family remained huddled together under a gray, cloudy sky, while the train grew smaller, until the steam puffs and metal hulk disappeared over a knoll.

"Away to an exciting life, she is." Mick's chest tightened.

A stiff gust of wind whooshed across the platform, whipping their coats against their bodies, and bringing with it the aroma of autumn's first snow.

Beth squeezed his fingers as restlessness embraced Mick's heart.

20

WHEN DREAMS BETRAY

HER DREAMS AREN'T MINE.

Mick

Mid-Autumn, 1903

Beth's presence after Moira's departure comforted Mick's family. Her cheerful disposition, welcoming arms to his children, and her love of cooking couldn't be any grander. Being docile as a newborn kitten fit well into his schemes for his future. *I'm content.*

Mick entered the main room and headed for the front door while his dog rose and greeted him. "Morning there, Blackie. All set for the day?" Through the window, he glimpsed the sparse snow on the ground under a clear, dark-blue sky as it turned turquoise on the horizon. "All clear on the prairie—"

"Where's Miss Brown, Da?" Liam stood in the doorway to the kitchen holding a galvanized pail.

Mick outstretched his cup to Liam for a splash of Chrysanthemum's fresh milk. "Not sure."

"She's not in the kitchen. Did she leave us?" Liam's bright-blue eyes were wide.

"No. She's just awakened. Not to worry, she's with me."

Liam strained his neck in search of Beth behind his da.

Mick stiffened his shoulders. "Not following me. She must be in me bedroom."

Liam's expression switched from confusion, to comprehension, into anger, darkening his eyes. He switched his focus on the ceiling and thrust his hands behind his back.

"By all that's holy, me own boyo is judging me? I give you this once to tell me your opinion, then never will I welcome it on this subject again."

"I do have an opinion. It makes me tense—"

"Me own tension with this conversation is your fault."

Liam nodded to Mick. "I understand what her being in your room means, but how can you? Are you marrying her? She's—"

"Marry? Now, why would I do that? Been married five times, and none turned out so well, did they? More like tragedies. Most of me wives died. Beth asked to move into me bedroom, for she was tired of sleeping with the girls. Bridget talks and sings in her sleep and keeps her awake. We made an adult agreement."

Liam inspected Mick head to toe. Disapproval shone in his eyes.

He took a few steps toward Liam. "And what do you know of loneliness or hunger? You've been well provided for, yeah? A thirteen-year-old, born here in America—"

"Da, here's what I understand. We accept your whiskey drinking and why you do it. You've never been mean even while drunk, like some are. We mostly accept your decisions because we know you do your best. But Da, this thing you're doing with Miss Brown isn't right. Don't you care what God thinks? He created marriage—"

"You dare to be me priest?" Heat gathered from Mick's chest to his face. "And why should I care what God thinks? I doubt He's ever given me much thought. If He has, I haven't seen it at all."

Liam frowned. "You have your mind set against God and marriage, then?"

"She's not asked for marriage, nor does she expect it. Our adult arrangement suits us fine. You've spoken your mind, and our discussion is over. Remember me warning unless you wish to be on your own."

Liam's shoulders slumped. "I will." He turned back to the kitchen with his pail of milk, and Blackie followed.

"'Tis time to enjoy me life before 'tis gone," Mick called out. Didn't he deserve it? "All me chums go gambling and drinking till all hours." And he may occasionally enjoy a woman at the saloon.

"Morning." Beth edged up beside him, pushing a pin into her bun. "Enjoying life, aye?" Her face flushed as he observed her trembling lips. *Such soft lips.* She averted her gaze and straightened her skirt. "I wanted to be in the kitchen before the children awoke. I see me timing is off."

"Have we done something to be ashamed of?" *Have I a calloused heart?* "Liam is up and asked after you. Thought you'd left us. I put him straight 'bout our agreement."

Her crimson blush rose to her hairline, and she glanced into the kitchen.

"Change your mind, then? 'Tis a bit late for that, aye?" *Watch it Mick, you're close to behaving dastardly.* He winked at her to keep the peace.

She met his stare. "Amused at me expense, are you? You're a mind-reader now? One night, and you know everything 'bout me?"

"Now, Beth. Never said that."

She poked her index finger into his chest. "I hold to me bargains, I do, and we've made one. I best get breakfast."

"Aye. 'Tis why you're here."

Beth stomped off but turned at the kitchen door to glare at Mick. "Morning there, Liam," she called over her shoulder. "I'll be making your favorite breakfast today. What'll it be?"

Late Autumn

Beth stood at the front door holding Bridget's and Cara's coats and mittens, ready to hand over the items when they finished tugging on their boots. "'Tis a fine but frigid day, girlies. Bundle up. Not to worry though, you'll be inside your classroom quick as a wink."

Mick chuckled at the piles of clothing donning the girls as he laced his work boots.

"No, we won't." Cara's voice was muffled from the scarf covering her lower face. "We must walk for hours."

Bridget covered her eyes with her mitten. "We do. Walking for miles in the snow. Lizzy Burr says—"

"For today you must walk, but not for long, aye?" Mick tested his bootlaces and stood. "Liam's gone out early to look at a horse for you to ride to school. Make sure to give thanks to Miss Brown for her help and for your breakfast."

Bridget wound a scarf over her head, and face, then across her shoulders, mimicking her Aunt Orla swathed in scarves. "Da, why can't we stay home to learn our letters and numbers and history—"

"Sure, and who would teach you? Moira's gone. Miss Brown, here? She's got her own work, and I got work. Liam as well."

Cara lowered her scarf from over her mouth, while Beth finished buttoning her coat. "Bridget, don't complain. I like going to school. Just because Clyde and Harry are bad to us sometimes doesn't mean we should stay home."

"Bad to you?" chimed Mick and Beth.

"Cara, stop." Bridget grabbed Cara's arm. "We'll be late. Thanks, Miss Brown, for everything you do for us. Let's hurry, Cara." She opened the door and yanked Cara outside into the chill wind sharing its icy breath with Mick's front room.

He turned to Beth. "Have you heard 'bout a Clyde or Harry? Has Bridget told you anything 'bout children treating them bad?"

Beth closed the door against winter's advancing intrusion then kneaded her tummy. "You feeling queasy?"

"Feel fine."

"Well, 'bout a Clyde." She revealed her dimples. "Bridget said awhile back that she liked a Clyde Harlow. Thinking she wanted to marry him one day. You know how us girls are, always dreaming of marriage. Have you heard your girlies speak of their dreams?"

"Maybe." Always finding a way to bring up marriage. Mick glimpsed Blackie waiting by the front door. He rose. "Blackie wants out."

Beth sat on the entry bench. "Come to think of it, one day awhile ago, Bridget came home in tears. I asked her what had happened, and she said Clyde and his brother, Harry, were bothering her and some others." Beth shrugged. "Couldn't get anything more out of her. Even bribed her with new ribbons for her hair, I did. I'll ask me friend in town today. She always knows the chinwag 'bout everyone's business."

"Harlow, aye? I'll get her to tell." Mick grabbed his work hat and coat from the pegs above Beth on the bench, then slid his arms inside the sleeves with her help.

She massaged his arms. "Anne always told me you were a fine man. She was right."

"And me girlies were right. 'Tis freezing cold out."

"No matter. I'll go into town later today, if that's what concerns you."

He opened the door, then turned back to find Beth standing close behind him wringing her hands. He gave her a peck on the cheek. "See you tonight." *Why does she irritate me so?*

"Supper'll be awaiting."

Mick crammed his hat down tight. His steps crunched in the icy snow on the way to the barn to tack up Wings for their trek to the tracks, since his crew was beyond walking distance.

Wings whinnied from his stall. He knew his horse's desire. Mick was also eager for freedom, being all cramped in tight quarters.

He gazed upward. Filtered rays of sun slanted between scuttling clouds, giving hope for a clear day, but conflicting thoughts darkened his mind. Why did unease swim inside his soul?

'Tis your guilt, man. Mick stopped and swiveled around. "John?" Nothing but frozen white rolling hills, his home, and the barn. No humans in sight. No black robe of Mister Death. Why did his thoughts sound like his brother John's voice?

A shiver snaked up his spine. Marriage. "Bah, those reproachful green eyes of hers." She had agreed to their arrangement. "There should be no guilt involved at all." *I'll think on it later.*

———

The Chicago, Milwaukee, and St. Paul Railway Track

The steel crew sat on the berm next to the rails for their lunch time. Mick's gang consisted of Macedonians, Irish, Chinese, and some native men, and he sought out his favorite chum, Flash. The first time they met, Mick had asked him about his name.

Flash had removed his work gloves. "Blue Lightning is my Pawnee name, but it is now Flash."

"Who renamed you? Your original is powerful. The Irish like to rename themselves. Mine was Michéal, but I go by Mick." He held out his hand.

"I did not rename myself." Flash studied Mick with his glittering, dark eyes. "Your people and the crew renamed me."

Mick kept his hand extended. "Do you like what they call you, or not?"

"It is good." He shook Mick's hand, then removed dried meat, bread, and cheese from his sack. He stacked them on his lap. "My brother, Wolf Paw, is now called Wolf. The farmers renamed him when he became an Indian Agent."

He'd yet to meet Wolf, but Mick had heard about the agents. Was Wolf like Flash, with his notoriety for getting a job done, and his ease with keeping secrets?

Today, he wanted to confide his thoughts about Beth to someone. He gazed at the prairie, then cleared his throat. "Do you believe in curses?"

Flash swallowed his bite of meat. "Curses from what?"

Mick shrugged. "Don't know. Maybe from death?"

"Death curses? There are those who practice belief in such things. I do not."

"I believe in some curses. For example, the one following me since me birth. Death, that evil devil, steals all me wives and children with illness, or he did do so." He struggled with the lump in his throat. "Ah, but not the one wife who deserted us nor our children. Thinking Mister Death didn't curse us because I didn't love her."

Flash stared. "Not loving does not keep death away as you believe. We all have that death curse against us." He bit off a piece of bread.

Mick twiddled his thumbs. "But usually women I marry die. Beth thinks I'm daft. Well, if it's not too personal, I've been wondering something else. Do you have a woman? Here or waiting for you somewhere?" He adjusted his hat.

Flash chewed, then slid a sideways peek at Mick. "I live alone."

"I'm thinking 'tis the best way as well. Living without attachment."

He focused his attention down the line, on the rest of the crew haphazardly scattered as they ate and drank. The water boy arrived with his buckets and rationed refreshing liquid to the men. "Me son, Liam, wants to work for the railroad as a water boy."

"I have met him." Flash's gaze flickered.

Mick rested his arms on his knees. "Whilst we await our water, can I ask you another question?"

"If you wish."

"What would you do if a woman you shared a bed with and who loved you badly wanted to get married and you didn't?" His heart pounded in his ears as he watched blackbirds fly above the grasses. He'd detailed his arrangement without feeling better. *Guilty of sin, you are.*

Silence spanned for over a minute.

Mick turned to catch Flash studying him. "So what's your opinion, chum?"

"Why do you ask it? Do you care more for my thoughts than for the woman's who shares your bed and watches your children? If you do, you can fix it." He wiped his hands together, stood, and took his metal cup from his bag. "Is it easy to do bad or easy to do good? Your spirit knows the answer."

"Was afraid of that." *Think 'bout it later.* Mick rose to get water and join his gang.

———

Suppertime passed, the youngsters had gone to bed, and Mick rested in his favorite chair with his beloved whiskey. His skin prickled at the base of his skull. He shrugged to soothe it, but it didn't help.

The ceiling creaked. He straightened and scanned the dim room in the lantern's dull light from the table beside him. The shadows were the evil creature's best hiding places. Didn't one move? Was it Mister Death? Woodstove and chairs, coats on the wall pegs, and shoes beneath the bench. Dark windows, but nothing peeking between the muslin curtains. Blackie—alert, ears pitched forward, attention on the door, but no hackles. The dog turned his head toward Mick.

"Do you hear or see anything?" Mick kept his voice low.

Blackie stood, wagged his rear, and yipped.

"Didn't know you had conversations with creatures." Beth stood in the kitchen doorway folding her apron. Her dark hair hung loose in tendrils over her mouse ears. Her cheeks dimpled.

Mick's ears heated. "Well, 'twas me and him before me and you. He's a good listener." He shifted in his chair and indicated the one beside him. "If your work's done, come join me."

Beth's eyes widened. "That I will."

As if I never ask her. Irritating woman. What were evenings at home usually like? What did she do after supper? He didn't know because he was away at the saloon many nights. Uncomfortable niggles nudged his conscience. *Being away limits awkward conversations.*

Beth settled and heaved a basket of mending from the floor. Shaking one of his shirts from the pile, she dug around, found a coffee tin, and popped it open. She selected thread, scissors, and a thimble, laying them on her lap. "How's work on the track coming?"

Mick swallowed his sip. "Grand. Got a good crew."

"When do you expect to be done?" Beth spoke around the needle clenched between her teeth as she fondled the cut thread.

"Do you never stop working? Can't you sit without doing something? Thought you must rest in the evenings." Mick narrowed his eyes at her.

Beth yanked the needle out of her mouth and chuckled without humor. The needle shook slightly in her fingers, and she lowered it. "Oh, you did, did you now? And how does a housekeeper and whatever else I am to you do that with five people, meself included, to care for?"

Mick wagged his head. Confounded woman. Both appealing in her helplessness and fragility but revolting in her neediness of him. "Aye, you know what you are to me, and our agreement means there's much to be done in the house. Americans live free of convention. The railroad cares naught for what its men do. No eyes watching me every decision. Living unbound to any beliefs is accepted."

Beth squinted at him.

"You're a Catholic, yet you desire to marry a divorced fella the church who's excommunicated from the sacraments. Including no marriage allowed in the church. You know their stance on the subject, aye?" He took another swig and gave her a sideways glance.

Annoyance flashed in Beth's eyes before she lowered them. She threaded the needle, then pulled it to snip the length she wanted and knotted the end. "You gave me the tale of the tragedy that happened, but I'm not as content as you with our arrangement. Seems in your favor, doesn't it?"

Mick clenched his knees. "Woman. You have no benefit from it at all?"

"I feel there's more to be said, aye. Mayhap another day." Beth stared at her sewing project.

"Don't wish to hear it. It'll be for naught."

Beth rearranged the shirt and smoothed it. "Well then, I do rest or change me activities. Mostly during school days."

"Ah, 'tis good to hear." Relief for the change of subject washed over him. Wasn't he being a better gentleman?

"For instance, today while the girls were in school and you and Liam were working, I spoke to the head teacher, Miss Henley. The children's jeers startled me as I arrived, but I paid it no mind." Beth tugged the thread tight after a stitch to a ripped shirt sleeve.

He choked on his whiskey and coughed. "Jeers? What for?"

She shrugged. "Rumors 'bout us. Went to report Clyde. Two of the five boys at school are the Harlow brothers, but Miss Henley seems reluctant to act and poo-pooed the issue of how he treats girls, especially Bridget. I'm thinking 'tis because of the rumor we're intimate without marriage."

"We just settled that, and who cares what we do?" He wiped his mouth.

"Well, the town's upright women, though women are few. Anyway, Miss Henley, being an upright one, made excuses, and told me she was very busy, and not to worry."

"Unbelievable—"

"Exactly me thoughts. So, I went to the Harlow home and told Mrs. Harlow 'bout her boy's behavior, knowing she'd never hear of it from the school. Mrs. Harlow wasn't one bit surprised. I can assure you."

"Huh." *Mousy, meek, needy Beth did this?*

Beth flipped the shirt sleeve over and continued stitching. "For shame if our own Liam ever behaved in such ways. But Mrs. Harlow wasn't ashamed. What do you think happened next?" She stared at him.

"I hardly know."

"Mr. Harlow hastened up to us, holding a rake. He yelled at his wife for speaking with me and dared to call me a harlot. She yelled back she could do as she pleases. She was only his mail bride, after all. Then he swung the rake at her. We both ran, and their dog followed us until we came to the pond and were forced to stop on the bank."

Mick's jaw dropped. "Then?"

"His own dog, Brownie, attacked him." Beth guffawed holding her side with her free hand. "You should've seen the sight. The dog would've torn him asunder if I hadn't grabbed the rake," she sliced the air with the scissors, "and whacked

Mr. Harlow, with Brownie hanging onto his leg, whilst they fell into the pond."

"You did all that?" Where had her spunk been hiding?

"Aye. Mrs. Harlow whooped and said she was starting over, maybe in Oregon. The boys aren't hers. They've been horrible to her in so many ways and mistreat poor Brownie. The Harlows are mean-spirited, don't you know? She'd answered Harlow's advertisement for a bride and arrived in town about the same time I did. Wish I'd met her before. Wish she could've stayed so we could be friends. Not many townswomen like me."

"God Almighty." Mick gripped his knees as her actions sunk in. "Mr. Harlow seems a violent sort of man." His heart thumped. "You put yourself in peril going alone."

Beth wiped her cheeks. "True, that. But who ended up in the pond? We now have a new dog, Brownie, inside our barn, and Mr. Harlow needs a new wife. Are you proud of me?"

Mick stood. "Proud? What for? Overstepping into me parenting responsibilities? Or risking yourself with such a man?" Blood pounded in his ears, making them ring. "Why would you do such a thing, woman?"

"Why?" Beth scrambled to stand. The mending tumbled to the floor. With her face at his chest level, she thrust out her chin. "Out of love. Defending young girls who don't deserve to be judged for what we do in your home. Thought you might respect me more for protecting your children. Was I wrong to think you see me as a servant?" She stomped her foot. "You leave them in me constant care most evenings as well whilst you laze at the saloon doing God knows what."

"You're unreasonable. Our arrangement—"

"You're the unreasonable party." She shook her fist. "You have all you want whilst I'm left with very little of what you wish to give."

He flicked the air. "Awful troubles are what you give me."

He glimpsed white material moving in the hallway. The girls. "I'm off to the saloon."

Beth hissed. "Mick Muldoon, I'll take your rake after you, I will."

He spun away, grabbed his coat, and hurried out the door. *Who does she think she is?* He didn't ask her to defend his girls. He tacked up Wings and rode to Judd's Saloon in search of his favorite, Kitty. She would give him no challenge.

———

Hadn't most of Mick's wildest dreams of freedom played out well? His family thrived under Beth's care. His worries when Moira left were all for naught. He threw back the rest of his drink and collected the bottle and tumbler from one of Judd's polished round tables, then settled at the empty bar. Judd always remembered to leave him a bottle on the bar. *Stick to two drinks only, Mick Muldoon.* The amber liquid swirling in his tumbler had a relaxing effect on his nerves. He should've expected his bliss, and his Irish luck would run out. Maybe he should leave his faith completely. God had never cared much for him.

The clock on the wall behind the bar ticked loudly into the silent room.

Was everyone upstairs? He'd met his chums most nights and learned to play poker—winning at times.

Sure, 'tis grand winning extra coin. Mick thumped the counter in front of him like piano keys. More importantly, after finally putting down roots, the gang accepted him in a deeper capacity, and he made some friends at last. *Me chums don't feel guilty.* Where was the niggly, uneasy feeling coming from? Suppressed blame squeezed out of Mick's fierce grip and into his dreams where his departed, previous wives accused him of being a despicable man. He'd caught Mister Death lurking around home and at the saloon. What was that devil's scheme?

Without any of his chums present downstairs and no Kitty tonight, Mick tried to drown his conscience. He glanced up from his glass to the stairway and the closed doors along the upper floor, expecting one of his men to pop out and join him. They must already be occupied. Hadn't Judd abandoned him to work in his office in the back? He twisted slightly to stare at Judd's open door and startled.

Another girl, Siobhan, stood near his shoulder, her brown eyes painted with blue and a dark outline, her lips redder than her hair, and her pink satiny dress pulled low, baring her shoulders. She wasn't the one he wanted.

Siobhan caressed his nape then slithered onto the stool beside him. She flicked a peek upstairs and nestled her chin in her fingertips. "Evening, Mick. You're late arriving. Kitty's not here, I'm the only one left. What do you think?"

"Think I'll be staying right here on this stool." He swallowed a nip.

"Very well. I'll grab a glass and join you, being as Judd left you with a bottle." She lay her slim body across the counter, felt around beneath the ledge, and drew out a tumbler for him to fill.

He poured her a splash then scrutinized the shelf of colored liquor bottles on the wall behind the bar.

"Though 'tis bad for Judd's business and mine, I'm happy to sit cozily with you this evening. There's something you should know. Kitty left without notice, except to say she'd write to me soon. I know she's your favorite, aye?"

He stared straight ahead. "Could be."

Siobhan's bracelets tinkled, then she smacked her lips. "Shall I be telling you Kitty's whereabouts after I hear from her?"

"No business of mine."

"Even so, you may wish to know later. It'll keep." She

stroked his hand holding his drink. "There's something else you mightn't know, Muldoon. About Beth and me."

Mick slammed down his glass, slopping some drops onto the bar, and jerked his gaze to Siobhan. "Beth? What can you know 'bout her that I don't?"

Siobhan tugged her strap over bare shoulder. "First off, did you know we're friends? No? Judd doesn't keep us inside during the day, for our contracts say we are free to go 'bout. Beth and I were both scarce of friends and found some common things, like arriving in town the same week, and the women don't take to us. She'd be a simpleton to come to the saloon, so we visit at your home."

"What are you saying?" His hand ached from his grip on the tumbler.

Siobhan giggled. "Only that we chat 'bout the old country and our families there. And I know 'bout her feelings for you and what yours sadly are. Such a tragic story Beth tells of her sister, Anne, who idolized you for your attitudes 'bout family, marriage, and hard work. Beth's young mind formed an emigration plan when she heard of your last wife's desertion. Thoughts?" Siobhan pursed her rouged lips.

Mick shrugged and poured another glass. "A snake pit comes to mind."

"Beth braved many perils to spend her life with you. It seemed her dream would happen, but she made a stupid choice to join you outside of marriage believing 'tis only a matter of time before you fall in love with her, as she is with you, aye?"

"Her dreams aren't mine. What's your point?"

She drew circles on the polished bar top while she swirled her glass in the air with her other hand. "Maybe to help you think on how you'd hate it if one of your girls found herself in Beth's position. She constantly speaks 'bout your children. and how much she loves them."

"Insolent girl."

"Mm hmm, meant to be. Hoping you'll treat her better, for all your sakes." She lay two fingers against his cheek and turned his face toward hers. "I never told Beth 'bout Kitty, but she suspects. I'm warning you out of Beth's friendship and respect for her girlish dreams. One of us should have them come true. Troubles might be coming your way from Kitty."

Dreams again. "From Kitty?" He tugged on his collar.

"You know, the one you visited upstairs?" Siobhan pointed. "On more than one occasion?"

Mick shrugged. "Didn't know we were an object of attention. We always snuck away when the place was cleared out with customers busy upstairs."

"Girls talk. Men aren't much better at keeping secrets. Watch your back is all I can say and marry Beth before 'tis too late." Siobhan slid off the stool and sashayed toward the staircase.

Mick couldn't get away from Judd's fast enough. *Consarn this creepy-crawly feeling.* He mounted Wings and rode home under the twinkling, mocking stars, whispering about his activities in the midnight sky. He couldn't detect any motion in the nearby shadows. No black cape flitted in the tall grass.

He shivered, and sensitive Wings snuffled. *Shake off these fanciful feelings, Mick Muldoon.* Should he ignore Siobhan and Flash's warnings? But Siobhan urged him to marry Beth quickly. Why would a bar girl care or think Kitty might make trouble? Siobhan mentioned a letter. Was he dealing with lies or truth, and if the truth, could it get him into misfortune? Maybe he ought to marry Beth, being urged to twice in the same day. If only he was a praying man. *Or believed God would hear me.* He'd think on it another day when his head was clearer.

21

DASTARDLY FROM BASTARDY

Something terrible is 'bout to happen, isn't it?
Mick

J udd's Saloon
    Late Winter, 1904
    Why couldn't Beth trust him to marry her soon?
    Wasn't his obligatory promise to do it enough to keep
the peace at home? He'd much rather leave God's restrictions
behind and live unfettered like the other men around him. *Me*
crew doesn't care that we aren't married. For once in his life, there
were men who accepted and respected him, not spurned him.

"Evening, Mick." Joshua, the town's livery owner, entered
Judd's and looked around. "Where're your chums?"

Mick shrugged. "They'll be along."

Joshua plopped onto a nearby barstool. "Give me regards
to your, er, woman."

"Fiancé." He stared at his almost empty glass. Why hadn't
his earlier explanations for avoiding marriage convinced Beth
of the terrible risks from Mister Death's curses? *Naïve woman.*

"Congratulations."

Mick threw back the rest of his first drink and set his

empty tumbler on a saloon's polished round table before him. But Joshua had made a point. *Where're me poker chums?* He stacked the cards and counted the five vacant chairs at his table. His tingling nerves dried his mouth. It required more wetting. *Something terrible is 'bout to happen, isn't it?*

He headed to the bar for another bottle and the second drink he allowed himself.

The crew filed through Judd's entrance after Siobhan approached Mick and handed him a fragrant envelope with its clear wax seal broken.

Flash selected a chair at Mick's table and peeked at the clock. "We were laying down bets for the past hour. The reason we are late."

Siobhan flicked the envelope Mick held. "Your name's on it. I opened it because Kitty addressed it in care of me. She told me to read it after three months passed. Kept it hidden under me bed."

Mick hesitated to open it. Could be Pandora's box again.

Siobhan clenched her fists and studied him. "Warned you, aye? Thinking you're to blame for her disappearance. Nothing but trouble, you are, and now the entire town will know."

Flash thumped the tabletop. "We heard the news. It was why we placed the bets in Hal Robinson's book."

By all that's holy, the something terrible has begun. Mick stood and forced his numb mind to catch up with the conversation. "Kitty accused me of something, and it's already bandied 'bout with bets placed? Before I ever read this letter?" How could they accuse him of involvement in Kitty's disappearance? He scowled down at Siobhan, and her dark eyes flashed malice at him.

Siobhan tapped her foot. "Well? Read it. She's in Chicago, and her finger points at you, Muldoon. Poor, trusting Beth."

"Did you know 'bout Kitty's thoughts before this letter?" He slid the note from the envelope.

"I suspected."

He scanned the few sentences of slanted script. His name stood out like a beacon from a lighthouse, warning of peril and rough sailing. Pregnant? Could it be true, but then, why would she lie? Mick stopped breathing. Would people believe Kitty's claims? What about Beth? The piece of paper trembled in his fingers.

In the silent saloon, his gang murmured around him and encouraged him to deal with Kitty's accusations forthwith.

Flash shuffled the cards. "Truth or lies are best faced with speed and direct speech."

Mick squelched a sob of terror or anger. He couldn't decide which. How could Kitty be pregnant with his child? "At me age, I'm too old to father children, aren't I?" His voice squeaked as he addressed his gang.

They nodded.

"But did you witness us together often? She says she told people stories 'bout our liaisons, did she? You knew of them?"

Joshua shifted on his squeaky stool. "Many men come here to do more than drink."

The men squirming in their seats and glancing at each other made Mick's thoughts fly in circles like scrambling horseflies. Why was she threatening arrest? "Surely you saw her with other men, her work being what it is. Does anyone care when a prostitute is with child?"

"You . . ." In a blink, Siobhan dumped Mick's fresh glass of whiskey over his head, and his chums at the table jumped out of their chairs to avoid the spreading amber liquid. Other patrons in the saloon guffawed, except for the girls. From the women's expressions, he must remember to watch his back in the dark on the way home.

Siobhan snatched Kitty's note from his hand as the liquid disaster preoccupied him. "Kitty says you stole from her. That's enough reason for arrest. Aye, did you read that?"

Mick wiped his face and neck with his handkerchief. "I'm no thief. But I deserved the baptism of me drink, I did."

Judd rounded the bar, then clapped Mick on the shoulder. "Rumor has it the townsmen might believe Kitty's story. Although it will all blow over, you'll see."

"So, the entire town has heard of it. I must speak to Beth." He snatched his leather hat from the table and rushed out the door. *Best set a wedding date, or I'll lose me housekeeper.*

———

Shelton's Jailhouse
Friday, February 12th, 1904

Later, when Mick again promised to set a date with Beth, it seemed the rumors' power fanned away her doubts. Then Kitty Donovan filed bastardy and theft charges against Mick, and the U. S. Marshal McGinty called him in for questions.

Mick's overnight stay on the hard mat without a pillow gave him a headache. He massaged his forehead as he inclined against the cell wall.

"Come on now, folks." Judd spoke outside the jail's window. "Hal Robinson has lots of bets for guilt. Are there any for innocence? Do that many of you believe Muldoon is guilty of theft? He's well known to you."

By all that's holy. Why was the entire town gathered outside the jailhouse window? *Proves the gossiper's influence.* "The town's founders failed to provide enough entertainment, and now 'tis me." Mick stood on the cell's bed to peer out the tiny window to view who was nearby.

"We've seen him with Kitty." Siobhan stomped her foot.

Joshua elbowed Siobhan. "He could be innocent. After all, the charges came from a saloon girl in hiding."

Mick couldn't make out the indistinct murmurs from the women in the crowd, but Joshua yelped. Was it only Judd and Joshua who believed he wasn't a thief? What about Flash? Did he believe Mick would steal? Embarrassing. What would the railroad do when they received notice of his arrest?

He slowly stepped down off the bed to the floor. His back ached with a fierceness. Whiskey was the only thing to put out the fire in his muscles and mind but it seemed to be the one to blame for these other fires in his life. *Aye, wish I could stop the drink.*

"Muldoon." Marshal McGinty approached, unlocked the gate, and it squeaked open. "Join me." McGinty ambled into his office.

Mick stood face-to-neck with the taller man he sometimes played poker with. "I'm not guilty. I can't father children at me age, and I didn't steal from her." Why was Kitty after him? He willed his breathing to slow and prayed McGinty couldn't hear his heart pounding then craned his neck to meet the Marshal's gaze.

"Kitty Donovan, the complainant, filed against you. As it stood, she accused you of bastardy plus theft from her treasury. But she's sent a note and dropped her accusations after the early birth of the child. I notified the railroad, so not to worry there."

Mick's knees collapsed, and McGinty grabbed his elbow to navigate him into a chair beside the desk. He breathed in deep several times, trying to dispel his dizziness.

"Seems you couldn't produce a child with its particular appearance, Muldoon. She'd been involved with a younger Chinese man in nearby Greely. We've arrested him for theft in the past. Known to the law, as it were. Aye, we'll find the father."

The marshal opened the jailhouse door and announced to the town his acknowledgement of Mick's innocence and that Kitty had dropped all charges against him. "Do any of you good people know the whereabouts of a young man by the surname of . . ." He glanced at the paper in his hand.

"Zhang? Hope that's how it's spoken. Last known address was in Greely. Please come into my office with any information."

Mick peered around the marshal. The crowd behaved as if McGinty hadn't addressed them, and a loud kerfuffle arose over the bets placed with Hal on Mick's guilt or innocence.

Judd nudged Hal. "Do those new bets count? I want to know. If they count, then I want my money." He yanked Hal by the collar.

Other loud voices added to the beginnings of a riot, and with the marshal's attention forced on the ensuing brawl, Mick slipped out unnoticed and made his way home on the crunchy layer of snow.

All the lit windows in Mick's house gave him a foreboding of more troubles to come, but he must risk it and enter. He stepped through the door, hat in hand, and hung it with his coat on the pegs, then Blackie greeted him with a lick on his hand. Would the hullabaloo about Kitty change into a family squabble? They must've heard the news. He turned toward the common room where Beth and the children stared at him and waited.

"Da." Bridget slid a glance at Beth. "We heard some troublesome stories about you and—"

"Someone named Kitty?" Beth put her fists on her hips.

His younger girls then pelted him with questions. Sidestepping the truth about his activities exhausted him. Honesty had become something to avoid.

Beth's typically cheerful manner altered after mentioning Kitty.

Mick cleared his throat. "You have nothing to say?" Odd to miss her nattering and chattering ways. Their engagement couldn't be at risk by the false, or mostly false, accusations of Kitty, could it? He'd never promised faithfulness to either woman. *Do owe more to Beth.* What did she expect from him? *We aren't in Ireland anymore.* They were on America's open plains, where they often accepted lawlessness. Although, he'd promised he'd marry her.

Bridget went to Mick, wearing her mam's comforting brown dress and shoes again. They weren't as big on her or as terribly baggy as a few years ago. She wrapped her arms around his waist. "So, Da, you did nothing wrong? You won't go back to jail? It's all lies?"

"Aye." *As for wrong ... not exactly. Bastardy.* Molly's face flashed in his mind. Then he noted Beth's sharp and hurried movements while she prepared supper in the kitchen. *She's not justified in her angst toward me. You devil's git, stop lying to yourself, man.*

Beth averted her gaze from him and stayed busy at the wood stove with her sparkling countenance dimmed. "Almost suppertime." She wiped her hands on her apron without glancing at Mick.

Cara skipped to the table. "I'm so glad. I'm hungry."

"Bridget and Cara, go fetch your brother." Mick shooed them to the door. "He should be home from carrying water for the crew by now, aye? Tell him to wash up and make sure to settle the horses."

"Both of us?" Bridget pouted.

"Aye, as I said. Take the lantern and Blackie. Don't be hasty, take your time" Mick glanced at Beth's back.

The girls skipped out of the kitchen, chattered for a moment about coats and mittens, then the door banged shut.

He approached Beth and touched her arm. "Dearest Beth. I have—"

Her upturned face tugged at his heart. Her chin trembled, and tears swam in her eyes. "Dearest, you say?"

"Aye." His ears heated. He took her hand, then knelt on one knee. He kissed her fingers. "I made you a promise last month, but do me the honor of becoming me wife and set a date?"

Her stunned expression gave him no clue as to her thoughts.

Will she slap me? Mick gulped and caressed her hand. "What'll your answer be?"

She burst into tears and yanked her hand away to cover her face. She sank against the prepared supper table then collapsed onto a chair. "I wish to say no, and slap you silly, Mick Muldoon. You took all the time in the world to make me feel beloved. Now you do so today of all the days we've been together because the truth 'bout your evening jaunts is revealed?"

What now? Mick grimaced. His heart sped like a horse running free to gallop on the prairie, but he'd just offered to shackle himself to her by marriage. "Beth? Are you rejecting me or what? I don't—"

Beth flew at him with open arms, knocking him off kilter. "Yes, I'll marry you, for heaven's sake, yes. You old lump of clay. But my favorite lump." She pressed her wet face against his neck while she entangled him in her arms. "Never thought you'd follow through with your proposal. That terrible agreement we made had me losing all me hopes."

"No doubt." *We need a ring.* He knew just the one.

"I was nigh to hating you, don't you know? I may yet distrust you for many a year."

He embraced Beth in return, then he lowered her arms to her sides. "I'll get the ring to seal our engagement. Give me a moment." He scampered to the bedroom, knelt on popping knees, and reached his hand under the bed. *In me metal chest.* That was where he stashed it. When his fingers touched a smooth, metal box, he tugged on it. Wiping off the dust, he flicked it open.

The front door slammed, and his children's voices alerted him to hurry.

He dug and fumbled through a stack of important papers, letters from Orla and Ed, old keys, and found the small, cloth bag buried beneath all the items. It would do fine. *'Tis me promise which counts, aye?*

Scrambling to his feet, he thrust the bag into his pocket. He headed to the lamp-lit kitchen, hoping for a happy celebration to end the day.

Beth turned at his footsteps, and his children waited for him at the table with quizzical expressions.

"Well, and you'll all be our witnesses of this joyful event. You'll see the answer to your questions soon enough." Mick jammed his hand back into his pocket. He beckoned to Beth, withdrew the bag, and presented it to her in his other palm. "Open it." He added a grin for good measure.

His heart warmed with the joy on Beth's face as she peeked inside. Molly's gold metal band shone dull in the gray light of evening through the window, and three awful things registered in his mind. He hadn't wiped off every speck of dirt and grass attached to it from when Molly tossed it out the window into the yard, it was probably two sizes too big for Beth's more delicate finger, and he'd prepared no good explanation for any of it.

She flipped it over in her palm after she had freed the nestled ring.

Holy heavens, I didn't have it inscribed, did I? Mick perspired around his neck and temples, and he squinted hard at the gold band.

Beth's green eyes swam with confusion after noting the tiniest bits of dirt and grass lying in her palm. "Where did—"

"Got it . . . Well, 'tis used, aye." Mick licked his dry mouth. "Couldn't find another in this tiniest of towns. There was no time to go into St. Paul or Chicago to shop there with the speed of events." His knees shook, and he almost knelt into a begging position. This tangle of events could delay the proceedings for a grand amount of time.

"Let me see." Bridget jumped out of her chair to rush over for a closer inspection, with Cara following her.

Oh no. Bridget was the worst possible child to get a better look, because she'd be the one to notice any details. But it was too late to stop her.

"Had it stored in me safety box." He held his breath and almost fainted.

Bridget's expression registered recognition, but she beamed at Beth. "You'll be the best new mother to us. We, we already love you." During her hug with Beth, she stared at Mick with narrowed eyes.

Mick tilted his head toward the hall and mouthed to Bridget, *later*. He cuddled Cara as she huddled against him and thanked him for her new Mam.

Liam had monitored everyone's reactions. He slid a quick glance at his father. "Glad to have you join our family, Miss Brown. You always make me laugh, and we have fun."

"Aye, she does brighten our days." Mick's knees still shook, and he pulled out a chair. "We can call you something other than Miss Brown now. What will it be, macushlas?"

Beth and the girls took their chairs. Her brow furrowed. "Should be a name each one of you is comfortable with. I have no ideas."

"Grand notion." Mick grinned. "Could be 'Beth,' or 'Mother,' or whatever you agree upon. Oh, and we can get the ring cleaned and sized to fit you. Can you wear it around your neck until such a time as we can travel?" He had handled this well, hadn't he?

Beth folded her hands on the tabletop and glanced at the family. "I do have a ribbon I can tie it on to wear 'round me neck." An odd-sounding giggle—more like a choked gurgle—burst out of her throat. "Dear me, makes me sound as if I'm hanging meself with it."

Bridget stroked Beth's hand. "It may feel like that for now, but Da will fulfill his promise to make it fit, Beth." She scowled at him. "Won't you? And very soon?"

"Aye. The ring must be made to fit you well as soon as I have the time in me schedule."

Bridget nodded at her Da.

"Well, now." Mick slapped his leg. "Beth's roast beef and mashie supper is losing its heat. Cara, 'tis your turn for blessing the meal."

After supper, while the girls cleared the dishes and Mick sipped his whiskey, chatting with Liam, Beth returned to the table. "You both must've heard that a new judge is moving just outside town? Mr. Muldoon, you can make me your missus when he does, aye?"

Mick spewed his swallow over the almost cleared-off table-top. He coughed while Liam pounded on his back.

"You took Da by surprise, Miss Bro—er, Beth. Evidently, he didn't know." Liam's lopsided grin belied his serious words.

"I can hear the both of you speaking' bout me. Me ears didn't choke. And I hadn't heard that. How did you?" Mick leaned back in his chair. His heart raced and his ears rang.

"The town's gossip, as always." Beth's expression and the sparkle in her eyes were like the barn cats after some spilled milk.

"If you're wishing to hurry things along, Beth, you've done the job."

Liam stood, scooted his chair under the table, and saluted. "A judge has rescued this Muldoon family's honor."

He never saw this odd happenstance coming, did he? Mick rubbed his chest, hoping to calm his heartbeat. He slid a glance to Liam, then to Beth. "I'll go speak to the judge when he arrives, if you don't beat me to it, girlie."

Beth cocked her head and dimpled. "Should I be enjoying your discomfort? For shame on meself. There's more. He's moving into his new home on Saturday."

"He is, aye? 'Tis grand." *If Mister Death doesn't notice, and me heart survives the week, I'll marry. If not, then no more worries.*

22

CIVIL MATRIMONIAL JUSTICE

And I'm in terror of Mister Death's curses
Mick

Mick's Home
A week after Mick spoke to the new judge, Cara and Bridget burst into the common room with excited chatter and carried bright yellow daffodil bouquets with the bulbs still attached. Bridget sniffed the bunches and extended them to Beth. "Look what we found for you. A bride's bouquet. We were going to make you a paper one, but this is better by far. We borrowed these flowers from Mrs. Gilchrist's front yard. She told us we could, Da."

Beth clasped her hands as in prayer then collected them from the girls. "The saints are smiling upon me, aye? I often prayed for a perfect wedding. Did I tell you me favorite color in all the world is yellow?"

"No," chimed the girls.

"Weddings must have flowers, mustn't they? Oh." She brushed grains of dirt from her dress and shook the daffodils to be rid of more.

Cara flapped a long length of ribbon. "We can cut off the

daffodil's bulbs and tie them together with this blue ribbon that—"

Bridget nudged her. "Let me tell it, Cara. It's from my friend's mother. Lizzie Callum told me her mother had a spool of blue ribbon we might use. You know *something borrowed something blue* from that saying? It's good luck to do what they say. Who started that? I wonder why it's supposed to bring people good luck on their wedding—"

"Bridget." Mick huffed.

"Oh, right. Where was I?"

Liam entered from the bedroom hallway. He inspected the bulbs. "Dirt's falling off them."

Beth lightly shook the bunch. "Girls, let's get the daffodils ready and put them in the sink. We'll bundle them into grand bouquets, and if there's any ribbon left, tie them in our hair. What d'you think?" She draped her arms on their shoulders and led them to the kitchen.

"Da, I'm wearing my Sunday suit." Liam splayed his hands over his chest. "What'll you wear? Do you have a suit? I've not seen it."

"Aye." Mick stood on shaky legs. Perspiration trickled down his nape, and he dabbed at it with his fingertips. "Kept it in me trunk, but I aired it out, and Beth ironed it. Quite the day we're in for, aye?"

Liam followed Mick to the bedroom. "You're doing the right thing. I'm happy for it."

And I'm in terror of Mister Death's curses.

They've gone daft as those daffodils. Mick beheld all his female family members dressed in Sunday clothes in shades of blue or yellow with blue ribbons tied in the girls' hair and Beth's bouquet. They waited by the wagon. Not stopping at beribboning themselves, they had decorated poor Wings with two bows tied to his forelock and bridle plus a fluffy ribbon attached to Blackie's and Brownie's necks. Poor creatures.

Liam jiggled his pointer finger at the scene. "Must we

leave those on them? Just look at Blackie and Brownie. It's funny when the girls dress up the kittens, but it's cruel to a proud sheep dog like Blackie. He's hunched up. I've never seen him ashamed before."

Mick snorted. "They do appear humiliated. Let's get those off the dogs as soon as the ceremony is over. But Wings' bows won't do."

Cara skipped up to him. Her braid swung back and forth, brandishing blue ribbon flashes. "Aren't we festive?"

"Aye, very. Although, I must fix this one thing. Who tied the bow on the horse's forelock, and how'd you do it?"

Bridget smiled. "Well, Cara fed him oats, and I sat on the porch rail so I could reach him. He was very cooperative."

Mick sidled over to Wings and unwound the ribbon from his forelock. "He must see where he's taking us, girlies. We can't sacrifice safety for good looks, aye? I'll leave the bridle decoration alone. No trouble there."

During the girls' disappointed groans and complaints about how they weren't as festive without the ribbons, Mick ushered Beth up the wagon's steps. "But 'tis a bright and nearly warm day for a wedding in February, aye? Cause for a celebration." He held Beth's free hand as she gathered her store-bought, green-sprigged dress's hem in her fist.

The veil Beth had sewn flew like butterflies in the breeze. She lifted it to stare down at him, a sparkle in her gaze. "Although hastily thrown together, and the dress and ring are ill fitting, I'm still the happiest woman in town." She blew him a kiss and dimpled.

"I'm glad for that." Mick checked to see if his children and both dogs had climbed into the wagon. "I'm truly sorry for being so difficult and contrary. Hoping we can put that all in the past, aye? Start things over between us?"

"Aye, praying so." Beth grasped his arm. "To the Justice of the Peace now, before you change your mind, and I must get the rake. Or use Brownie here, to latch onto your leg, forcing him to drag you inside."

The turnout for his wedding surprised Mick. It made for a more cheerful celebration to come. He'd expected his chums and a few patrons of Judd's Saloon but not the attendance of his crew. Many went home for the weekends.

Mick parked the wagon nearest the home's front steps, the space obviously marked with a barrel to keep it available.

Joshua sprinted over to roll the barrel out of the way for Mick to guide Wings into the space. "Good morning, Muldoon. Glad to see you made it. The other couple just left. Bets were placed again for if you'd show up for your wedding. There're going to be some mighty disappointed—"

"What?" Mick tugged on the brake then descended from the wagon.

"Truly?" Beth huffed as she stood.

"Beg your pardon, Miss Brown." Joshua flushed and removed his hat.

"Well, there'll surely be a wedding today, as you can see, and I'm glad they'll be disappointed." Beth climbed down backwards with Mick's and Liam's aid.

A short, curly-haired man approached the group. "Welcome. Name's Justice William Calhoun. Newly installed judge in the surrounding area and Justice of the Peace. You're my second wedding today, and there's another following. 'Tis best to do them all at once, don't you know. Until the town has a courthouse or a Town Hall, my home will do." He extended his hand to Mick and Liam. "Please. Your guests are already seated inside."

The girls hopped up the steps and disappeared through the doorway.

Calhoun waved at Mick's crewmen lingering near the horses and wagons. "Come on in, 'tis time, for you'll be witnesses to a wedding ceremony."

Here's to hoping Mister Death doesn't see. Mick surveyed the area around the building, but nothing alarmed him. *If the angels be watching, I'd best keep in their good esteem.*

Liam clapped his shoulder. "I'll be up front, Da."

On the top step, Mick turned to Beth. "I noticed something odd here. There're only me men in attendance today."

Beth picked at her quivering bouquet. "If you'd ever heard me complaints, you'd know that the likes of me offends respectable family women. None of your men's wives accompanied them, did they?"

He chewed his top lip and smoothed down his mustache. "Only three are married."

"And yet they came alone."

Mick studied her downturned face. "The wedding should change the circumstances for you then. I've treated you badly, haven't I?" He tipped her chin up with his fingertip. "And you don't deserve it. Forgive me, Miss Beth Brown from Ireland?"

A tear trickled down her cheek, but she met his stare. "Soon to be Mrs. Muldoon. It should change things, aye, but I fear people have long memories. I never should've . . . Well, you're making it right by making me respectable. So, we'll see. As for me forgiveness? Depends."

"Aha."

Her eyes glinted with mischief. "You must earn it."

"Well now." Mick waggled his brows. "There'll be a fiddler arriving to greet us at our home with tunes from the old country. 'Tis your wedding gift. Will that help me earn the first bit of forgiveness?"

Beth's jaw dropped. "Grand 'twill be, but 'tis the second bit. The first is our wedding itself."

Justice Calhoun waved at them through the open door. "We're waiting, you two. Not a good thing to dawdle on your wedding day. The piano player, Mrs. Sweeney, is getting impatient. We don't wish her to leave now, do we?"

"Piano player?" Beth turned to Mick. "He has a piano as

well. So, one woman accepts me besides Siobhan. 'Tis the third good bit."

He pressed his lips together. *Glad I hired Mrs. Sweeney.*

———

How could Beth be with child? Mick stared at her fitful movements as she removed her veil and dress in their bedroom and twiddled his thumbs. Hadn't they settled his inability to father children? But this was Beth, and he knew she was no bar girl and hadn't been with other men.

He plopped onto their bed and tried to breathe. "But Beth, they dropped the bastardy charge against me. The woman was involved with a younger man—"

"Do you or don't you believe me?" She wrapped her arms around herself and glared hellfire at him. "Didn't wish to tell you at first, thinking you'd believe I trapped you into marriage. Then the brouhaha with Kitty happened. You finally asked me to marry you without telling you of our babe."

He cleared his throat. "I know what you're saying 'tis true. Stunned me, is all. Seems impossible, doesn't it?"

"Aye, 'tis a miracle." She rubbed her belly. "I'm 'bout five months gone. Somewhat surprised you hadn't noticed."

Need me bottle. He thought she'd put on weight from leaving hunger behind in Ireland like he and Orla had done. He reached underneath the iron bed for the crate stored there and popped open a fresh whiskey bottle while he observed Beth tug on her nightgown.

"Surely, Mick, us being married will squelch the rumor mill's efforts, aye?"

"I fear it won't. Anyone who can count will still have the means to be offended. And the church doesn't recognize a civil ceremony." Heat built in his chest as harshness built in his thoughts. He shook his finger at her. "And you knew I didn't wish to be married. Yet here we—"

"Well, I wasn't the one to force your hand." Beth sat beside him. "Kitty was the culprit."

"But you knew you were with child and withheld it from me. And you always hinted at marriage, aye? Told you tragedy always befalls me marriages, and I feared harm would befall us. Marriage brings out the curse from Mister Death. Staying unmarried and childless keeps that foul creature away, don't you grasp that? I ditched him once with Molly's and me little ones, but will I do it twice? Me Irish luck doesn't run well that way." He tipped the bottle to his mouth.

She sprang to her feet, and her voice shook. "I do see. I see clearly that you're touched in the head. Or 'tis the whiskey. You must promise me you'll give up the whiskey. Please, Mick?"

He snatched her hand. "Beth, I'm grouching, but I can promise you this. I'll give up me gambling and the saloon girls. I owe you that." He was nearly certain he could give those up, but he'd miss his chums. Maybe he could invite them to his home instead?

"And the whiskey?"

"Can't promise you that one. I'll try, though I can promise to not drink as often." Beth allowed Mick to situate her on his lap. He lay his palm on her stomach, and the babe bumped it. He gasped. He always cherished that sensation of growing life. "Another child." His thirteenth. *But an unlucky number, 'tis sure, aye?*

She nuzzled his neck. "Mick, thinking 'bout your fear of our expanding family, I'll light a candle and say prayers for our safety. Maybe you'll attend Mass with us? The children always ask if you'll come along."

Shauna's voice from decades ago echoed in his mind. She believed the exact same thing about lighting candles to pray, and he closed his eyes. Candles never did a thing, did they? Or the prayers that went up with them. But that wasn't Beth's fault. He couldn't discourage her faith in Christ, could he?

"Aye, Beth, you do just that." He enveloped her in his arms and kissed the top of her head then jerked upright. "By all that's holy. What will Liam and the girls say 'bout a new brother or sister?"

She giggled. "Me prayers will be for them as well. Let's wait to tell them. I'd like us to be married for a while. I know they can figure it out if they wish, but I'd like to wait."

Mick caressed Beth's throat. "If you wish. But our Bridget, she'll be onto us. Now kiss me."

———

Liam tugged on his boots sitting beside the front door. "Da, I haven't told the girls about the baby as you ordered me. You two finally got married, I'm glad for that, and I hope you tell them soon. Bridget knows how to sniff out a secret. I do hope Beth gives me a brother." He slid a glance at Mick before he laced up his shoes.

"We'll tell them soon enough. You've too many sisters, then?" Mick chuckled.

"Yes." Liam slipped his arms into his coat sleeves. "Off to work. That water doesn't gather itself into the buckets for the crew. I'm riding Thunderstorm this time because the gang is too far away laying track. The girls don't need to ride him to school on Saturdays."

"You're a wise boyo, purchasing Thunderstorm with an Indian agent." He knew Flash's brother, Wolf, could help, but Liam volunteering to be part of it put his gift of observation and curiosity into the workings of things to good use.

"Thank you, Da." Liam closed the door behind him.

Mick stood at the window to witness Liam mounting their newest horse. He had no trouble with Thunderstorm, unlike the girls. In time, they would learn how to handle him.

Liam glanced at the window, and Mick bowed. "Me girlies may have trouble with a spunky horse, but he's still a good one. Aye, Blackie? Wings is perfect for pulling the wagon, Thunder is just right for riding."

"Talking to yourself again, Da?" Cara tickled his side.

"Didn't see you there. And what of it? Lots of people talk to themselves. It makes us better listeners."

"Bridget says it's on account of the whiskey. She said Beth says you're drinking even more whiskey. Is that right?"

"Wasn't talking to meself because of the whiskey. Was mumbling 'bout our new horse to Blackie. He's been a friend for many a year." *These children don't know how to mind their own business.* "Now get along with you and help Beth and Bridget make the beds."

If only Mick could get Beth to focus on what he was doing well, holding to his promise to be faithful and no more gambling. She shouldn't expect him to give up the drink. Beth knew of his drinking before they married. He desired a splendid future as a family, but risky childbirth frightened him. *Will they survive Mister Death? Mick, stifle your worries.* He would fight that devil with all his strength if he dared to come near them.

Mick massaged Blackie's ears while he leaned his head against Mick's leg. "Be glad you're a dog. You've no worries 'bout tomorrow, aye? There're too many in the Muldoon home to be certain of the future and no way to control it."

23

MISTAKING MISTER DEATH

Will they send me away to an insane asylum?
Mick

Mid-Summer, 1905
Unbelievable, me losses and gains in life. Mick held fourteen-month-old Finn on his knee as they sat in the shade of the front porch. Bumblebees buzzed around the rose vines tangled on the rails, birds flitted between their newest neighbor's saplings from last season, and Finn giggled with his da's jiggles, making his voice jump.

Mick couldn't help but grin. "You like that game, me little boyo? I know another you'd enjoy. All the others before you liked it."

The screen door creaked open, and Bridget stepped through. "Hey, Da. Do you want some lemonade? It might taste good. Maybe." She glanced behind her then back to him. "Cara's making it."

"Aye, bring it out for me when she's readied it."

"I will." Bridget disappeared into the house, but Blackie and Brownie slipped through the opening, and onto the porch.

The dogs licked Finn's bare leg, and he squealed.

"Come on boyos and enjoy the shade with us." Mick turned Finn facing out toward the prairie and the neighbor's home across the way. "Lookie there, macushla, we have the start of a neighborhood. You and your baby brother, Callum, will have school chums your own age."

How in heaven's name did Mister Death not find them as he'd dreaded? Had that demon forgotten to harass Mick Muldoon? Was the devil weaker in America? If anyone had told him he'd be a da again at the age of sixty-two, of not one but two more sons, he'd have laughed himself silly. *They'd have sent me away to the insane asylum for sure.*

Instead of laughing about it, Mick tried to appreciate his youngest boys. Hadn't he always grieved over the losses of his other children? Why did he now struggle to enjoy fatherhood?

Exhaustion. Simple, terrible, exhaustion. Mick yawned. "And Beth's demands. She shouldn't nag me into giving up the drink, and she nags me 'bout attending Mass." Mick twisted Finn around making his arms flap, and his son giggled. "I've fulfilled most of me promises since we married."

Finn squirmed to be let down, but he might get splinters in his knees from the porch.

"When you're walking steady, macushla." Mick resettled Finn's bottom onto his thighs and upturned Finn's tiny left hand. "Open up your fingers and I'll show you another game. 'Tis called Oops, Johnny. Don't ask me why. Here we go."

Finn pressed back against Mick's chest and stared up at him. His bright blue eyes sparkled with eagerness.

He unfurled Finn's fist, held it flat, and tapped the tip of his thumb then slid his own index finger down Finn's slope between Finn's thumb and forefinger. "Oops, Johnny." Then back up to the tip of Finn's pointer finger, and down the slope of his middle finger. "Oops, Johnny." Mick repeated this game with each finger to the pattern of Finn's chortles and kicking legs until Bridget and Cara arrived.

Cara delivered the lemonade. "I remember you playing

that game with me. It felt so funny between my fingers. Oh, and Beth took baby Callum with her to bed to take a nap. Bridget and I agreed to cook supper. Will you go to Mass with us next Sunday? It's been a long time since you did. Father Egan says—"

"Maybe." Mick shrugged. *Or maybe not. For it requires confession.*

"Hand me Finn. He's rubbing his tired little eyes." Bridget extended her arms.

"Aye, and he needs a change." He patted a spreading wet spot on his breeches above his knees. "By all that's holy."

"Right." Bridget wrinkled her nose.

"I'll take me lemonade out to the barn." Mick lifted his glass. "I must check on some things. Thank you, Cara." He gave her a one-armed hug.

Cara yawned, and he joined her. "Da, I think I'll nap with Finn as well. Callum wakes everyone up so much at night."

"Aye. He's only four weeks old. 'Twill take time for him to settle." He took a sip of Cara's lemonade after she left. He puckered his lips and cringed. Had she forgotten sugar?

A shriek came from inside his home, then Bridget went to the door. "Not to worry. Cara tripped over Finn's wooden horse and slipped on his ball, but she landed on the chair. She's fine."

"Consarn it." *'Tis a death trap in there with the toys.* Why couldn't Beth keep it picked up? Someone could get injured, and it shouldn't be a risky thing to enter one's home. Beth was probably more exhausted than anyone, but he was much older and worked hard every workday. What about nights with his chums? He shrugged off that uncomfortable conviction.

"Blackie and Brownie, away with me to the barn." Mick headed down the steps, around the side of the house, and toward his secret stash.

As he strolled to the barn, he turned and glanced back for the dogs. Blackie stayed at his heels, but Brownie wandered off toward the corral. "Rescued him from that mean Harlow family, but his loyalty isn't absolute like yours, aye, Blackie?"

He bumped into the clothesline of wet diapers and infant dresses. His own work shirts flapped against his face. He swiped at the shirts as if they were descending wasps out to attack some beetles. "Consarn it. Beth will threaten to starve me if I dirty her clean laundry." He set his glass on the ground and re-pinned a few corners of loosened shirts.

How could Mick tolerate his household's situation of young, growing children for several more years? He'd be nearing his eighties. *God's blessings, they're called.* Those precious boyos deserved a better da, didn't they?

———

Late Summer

Mick studied Bridget as she hummed a hymn from church to Finn while she rocked him so Beth could nap with Callum. Wasn't it right that Sunday naps had become a Muldoon family pattern? Liam got his wish for a brother plus another, he did. "'Tis a picture postcard. With a church song for a lullaby."

"We missed you again at Mass today." Bridget's eyes held condemnation at times for her da, making him jittery.

"Someone needed to care for Callum so Beth could attend." He stretched out in a chair at the table and read the same sentence in the newspaper three times. The niggle of guilt from his neglecting Mass crawled up his back and neck like a pesky, prickly insect. He twitched his shoulders. He'd cut back on his drinking since he worked the books and not the rails, hadn't he? Sleeping without nightmares remained his challenge.

"I guess so, Da."

Mick caught Bridget glaring at him as she set Finn in the highchair. *She's only fourteen and understands nothing.* How had he ever raised such moral children? First, it was all the fault of their church going with the neighbors when they were young, and now Beth.

"Tend to Finn, Bridget, and leave me to attend to me paper."

"Did I bother you, Da? I only wanted you to know—"

"Your thoughts expressed on your face are as loud as your words. They're enough to niggle at me without bringing up missing Mass again. Stop it." He peered over the paper at his middle daughter.

"Well, in that case, speaking of being bothered by the niggles, I do have a question for you. Why don't you go with us? Or call me *macushla?* I miss it. Did I do something wrong, Da? Are we not your darlings anymore? You never even call Beth that, and she's given you two sons. I'd think you'd be grateful to her."

"Just last Sunday I called Callum macushla. You weren't present to hear it." Ire at Bridget's questions and criticism smoldered inside him. His reaction was unfair, but how could he battle his irritation? Sleep would help.

"Da." Bridget regarded him. "Your face is all red."

He crunched the paper's edges in his fists. His ears heated up with his efforts to contain his anger at his daughter's righteous words and force back the unrighteous words he didn't wish to utter. The paper quivered.

Tap, tap, tap. Finn banged a wooden spoon on the highchair's tray, breaking the spell of exasperation.

Mick slapped the paper down and rose. "I'll try to remember to call you macushla. Now, 'tis time I go check on Beth." What was wrong with everyone? Shouldn't they all be celebrating the fact that Mister Death hadn't come near the littles and had left Beth entirely alone? And no bright flashes of God's own angels fighting Mister Death for two years. But how could they know? He'd never spoken of these things to his children. His children and Beth wouldn't know to count the good in their world. It exhausted him to be vigilant. *No easy task to guard the littles against that trickster Mister Death.*

"What's wrong, Da?" Cara studied him.

Mick changed his direction at the entry to the bedroom hallway and headed to the back door with Blackie following him. *Away to me quiet place to get a nip and a lie down.*

Why did Beth not understand how helpful the whiskey was in getting him comfortable enough to snatch a few winks of sleep between Finn's wails and newborn Callum's feedings? Sharing a room with a newborn infant taxed his nerves like piano keys out of tune.

He hadn't imbibed as much lately. His secret stash of whiskey in the loft amongst the hay bales was a brilliant idea for him to avoid drinking.

Beth's flock of chickens bustled across his path on their way to the coop. They clucked loud enough to awaken the household. *Hope no one heard.*

Hadn't Flash, Mick's self-appointed keeper at work, caught him twice this past week dozing off on the handcar? Pumping it down the tracks and out of the crew's sight hadn't been helpful. Humiliating. Mick's disappearance alarmed his men. How was he supposed to get a midday lie down? What good was a job managing a section if he couldn't be awake for his gang? He'd give the devil all his chums, except Flash and Judd, for a solid five hours of sleep.

A slowpoke hen with her peeps darted past, almost beneath Mick's feet. "Look out there, you old biddy. You must keep up with the others, or your brood could get crushed. Poor things. Victims of an older mother. God created parenting to be done when you're young, not past the age of forty." He'd never guessed another twenty years was so much worse.

What would happen to his own brood if he didn't pay

attention looking out for Mister Death every minute of every day? That devil would dare to wreak havoc without Mick's vigilance.

Mick and Blackie entered the barn, where the shadowed interior cocooned them like a cozy blanket. With Wings out in the paddock, their milk cow, Buttercup, in the pasture, and Liam on Thunderstorm in town, the barn was silent and perfect for a lie down.

"Down, Blackie. Don't want you up above."

Blackie obeyed by settling at the foot of the ladder.

He glanced to the top of the twelve-foot ladder leaning against the loft, shook it to check its steadiness, then climbed the rungs.

He shimmied a hay bale away from the far wall, grunting with the effort. He only needed enough room to grapple for his bottles. He tapped cold, hard glass in the narrow space and removed his favorite drink from hiding.

Rustling sounds echoed in the loft, and he waited. It couldn't be Mister Death. There wasn't a black robe. Rats? Where were his two barn cats? Mick slowly peeked over the edge of the loft. Nothing moved. He allowed only orange and white tabbies in his barn to easily distinguish them from the shadows. Never the black ones. Not after mistaking them for Mister Death in that barn incident back in Minnesota.

Imagine mistaking black cats, or anything else, for Mister Death. *Dimwit.* He returned to his hiding spot, laid atop some bales and noted the level of his liquid comfort. "Counting sheep to make me sleepy never worked, bah. Humming to meself only kept Beth awake. Then there's nothing to keep the terrible nightmares away, aye. Only you in a bottle."

Mick sipped a bit more, and his eyelids drooped with whiskey's relaxing effect. He dozed off.

———

"Mick Muldoon!"

He jerked upward so fast he almost flipped off the bale he slept on. He tried to focus his blurry eyes toward the shriek. Beth. "Consarn it. Did something happen to the children? And how'd you find me?"

She scowled. "Nothing happened. Blackie gave me your whereabouts by waiting for you at the base of the ladder."

A dog's loyalty isn't always a grand thing. "Ah. Well, is it supper time already? Must've been snoozing." He swiped at his face and eyes then squinted at his wife.

Beth clutched the ladder until her fingers turned white, keeping her head and shoulders above the loft. "Have you been drinking? When you promised you'd try to give it up?"

"Nah, you're imagining things. I needed a nap in a place where I could relax in peace. We haven't been sleeping at all with Callum fussing every night."

"That's not why I yelled at you or why I'm angry." Her accentuated words warned him, while she pointed at something near his feet.

He stared in the direction she indicated. Mick couldn't deny the empty bottle glinting in the lowering sunbeam which shone like a beacon through the open barn door. He couldn't give it up completely. Hadn't he already tried?

"Well? What do you have to say for yourself?" Beth's green gaze impaled him against the bale he sat on.

"Nothing. Anything I say will make our stalemate worse." He shrugged. "You want something I can't give, and I want something you wish to be rid of."

She chewed her lip.

Blackie yipped.

Mick rolled the empty bottle with his boot.

Beth took a deep breath as tears welled up. "I agree we've a stalemate on the whiskey." Her voice wobbled. "Let's discuss your lack of Mass attendance. Although you can't take communion, or go to confession, you're allowed to step inside a church, aye?" She thrust her chin up. "You promised me you'd go, and you went twice. Not only that, but you've gone back to the saloon many nights, and you promised not to gamble. Are you—"

Mick cupped his hands over his ears. "Holy heavens, woman. Of all me wives, you're the only one to nag at me until I'm a nub of flesh and not a man at all. Will you stop?" He knew he behaved like a *slíbhín*, but he was too worn out to care.

His jaw dropped when he read Beth's lips and recognized the muffled names she used. Unbelievable names from an innocent woman. He lowered his hands as she disappeared below the loft's floor, and after her footfalls faded away, the barn became hushed and empty. As empty as Mick's weary soul. The very thing he had relied on for strength only seemed to weaken him.

———

One evening after Mick's shift, his home life didn't improve. The family had their supper, but instead of typical lively banter after they'd eaten their fill, the children left the table with his permission. Later, inside their bedroom, Beth threatened to leave him.

"I didn't wish to be married to a drunk. 'Tis not what a girl's dreams are made of. But you wouldn't listen. We believed you were too old to father children, but now we've two sons. You're never home with us. You use me like you did your precious Kitty." She sobbed, startling baby Callum, who fussed in her arms. "I'm trapped here with you. There's nowhere else to go. You must stop drinking every night, Mick Muldoon. I already asked Father Calhoun what to do 'bout it a few months ago. He's—"

"You what?" *I'll not be condemned by a holier-than-me priest.*

"I started confiding in him when you returned to the

saloon most evenings. We formed a bond of trust, and he helps me manage—"

Mick rushed out of the room, yanked his coat from the peg, and slammed the door. His only desires were for peace and time with his chums in the saloon. That's where he headed.

The next night as Mick opened his front door, it barely squeaked. He'd remained out late because he'd dozed off during the card game. Late enough to be sure everyone had gone to bed at home as well.

Blackie scrambled to his feet and growled low.

"Shh, Blackie, 'tis me."

The dog backed up for Mick to enter the main room and shove his boots under the bench below the peg hangers. He hung his coat up, which dropped to the floor. His vision wasn't what it once was. Dizzy waves threatened to push him over, so he steadied himself with his hand on the bench. "Lay down, Blackie. I'm off to me bed." He had trouble getting his tongue to work for some reason.

Blackie returned to the rug by the front door.

Mick used the wall for better balance and wobbled in his stocking feet down the hallway to the bedrooms. He entered his room, but the furniture swam in what little moonlight shone through the curtained windows. He squinted at the shadows and blinked to set the objects to rights.

Something black shifted in the moonlight.

He peeked between drying diapers on a crisscrossed line stretched from the bedpost to the dresser.

Lit by the window's open curtains, a silhouette hovered over baby Callum's crib.

Mister Death. Mick lunged for Mister Death, but the demon jumped toward the bed with an unholy screech. His cloak flapped over Mick's face as they tousled on the mattress.

Baby Callum wailed from his crib, spurring Mick on with his attempted rescue.

Mick twisted beneath the cloak's fabric while he strangled the howling Mister Death as hard as possible. He attempted to flip Mister Death over to gain more control, but he knocked the demon off the bed.

Mister Death hit his head against the edge of the dresser and lay still and silent on the floor between the bed and the furniture's base.

"I can't believe I finally bested him. The evil—"

"Da, stop!" Liam grabbed Mick's arm and wrenched him away. "You've hurt Beth. What have you done?"

Mick toppled against the bed. "Beth?"

Bridget rushed over to the dresser and set down a flickering candle. She lifted wailing Callum from the crib, as Cara cuddled crying Finn and his teddy on her hip.

Mick rubbed his head. "What are you telling me? 'Twas Mister Death. By all that's holy, I don't under—" He stared at Mister Death on the floor, and in the flickering candlelight the devil's face was Beth's, lying still with a gash oozing blood from her forehead. He redirected his blurred gaze to his five children in the room. The older ones glared or cringed away at what they had witnessed. He swiped his face. "I thought 'twas Mister Death."

"Who?" asked Liam. "Never heard of him. Why didn't you recognize Beth? She's your wife."

Bridget whimpered and her chin trembled. "She's wearing Mam's old nightgown. I recognize it."

Liam knelt and checked her breathing. He held a handkerchief he'd snatched from the dresser against Beth's wound. "Thank God, she's alive. But I think you knocked her out. Who were you talking about?"

"No one. Was confused. How did I do this thing?" Mick's heart pounded fast and hard while his brain attempted logic.

"Too much whiskey, Da, like Beth says. That is why you did such an awful thing to her." Cara retreated from near

Liam and swayed back and forth with Finn on her hip. She backed up farther into the doorway.

Bridget retrieved the candle and held it above Liam. Her nose ran, and her eyes glittered with tears in the candlelight. "You never really loved Beth, did you?"

"What? I—"

"Da, hold your handkerchief against her head." Liam rose and swapped places with Mick. "I'm getting the doctor. I think she needs stitches."

Mick whispered into her ear. "Dearest Beth, come awake. You did nothing to deserve such a terrible thing. You truly have done nothing wrong, ever. 'Twas all me own fault."

Beth's eyes fluttered open, then she moaned.

He caressed her shoulder as he pressed on the wound with his other hand. "Don't move yet. Liam's gone for the doctor. Rest, now."

"Shh, it's alright, little one." Bridget caressed Finn's head. "Mama is sleeping on the floor. Da is here with her, so let's put you to bed. Cara, we can put Finn in your bed and Callum in mine."

Mick reached out toward them. "Thank you, macush—"

"You'll be in big trouble when the doctor sees what you did." Cara sidestepped his hand after she snatched Callum's blanket from his crib. She hurried after Bridget, then slammed the door.

He fondled Beth's hair stuck to the wound, already bruising with reds, blues, and purples. Once more, Mick pressed his handkerchief against the gash. The doctor probably would report this attack by Beth's deranged husband. He could justly end up back in jail. Or worse. How could he speak of what he thought he saw? Would they send him away to an insane asylum? *Christ, I beg of You, have mercy on me.*

24

BY OUR SINS

And why should this stun me?
Mick

The *Jailhouse*
Late Summer, 1905
A song sparrow with rust-brown and gray striped wings hopped along the narrow window ledge between the iron bars a few feet above Mick's face. It rotated its head, searching for breakfast. Yesterday morning, Mick had spotted a glossy web in the corner.

He flipped over to face the wall and closed his eyes. *Caged, I am.* He deserved it. Beth's assault charge would surely stick, for the doctor and Mick's own children witnessed his shameful conduct. How had he succumbed to this lowest of low behaviors for a husband? His age should make him wiser and not the complete fool mistaking Beth for Mister Death. He must've drunk more than he should've.

Now, he would do anything to squelch the recent horrendous memories. How could he desire a thing that brought such terrible troubles? *Dr. Ross warned me whilst on the Mona.*

Then, Orla. He stretched to relieve his cramps. He could try counting sheep again.

Clang, clang, clang.

Mick banged his elbow as he twisted on the ticking mat. "Consarn it." His muscles complained with a spasm. After he settled into a sitting position, he glared at Marshal McGinty.

With a smirk, the marshal jiggled the metal mug he'd used against the cell as an alarm. "Frightened you, did I? Judd fetched someone for you."

"Judd?"

"The saloon owner."

"Yeah, I'm not a blockhead."

A tall salt-and-pepper-haired priest stepped through the jail's entry door toward Mick's cell. His bright blue eyes flashed with dismay. "Glory be. Mick? I'm agog. What did you do, man?" John's mouth hung open as he surveyed his brother's cell.

"Only this. Consarn it. 'Tis only what's needed to deepen me humiliation." Mick squeezed his eyes shut and flopped onto his mat, then repositioned himself onto his elbows. "Me favorite brother shows up in this American railroad town. How and why, for heaven's sake?"

John folded his arms. "Marshal, please open the gate, will you?"

"No." Mick sprang up, ignoring the pain. "Don't let him in. You do, and you'll have a murder upon your head."

McGinty suspended the iron key near the padlock. "You'd kill a priest, Muldoon?"

"Me brother worries I'd be the one to hang for murder." John shook his head.

"Huh?" McGinty frowned then shrugged. He turned the key with a *clink.* "Irishmen. Can't get a straight answer from one another. Our wit isn't always understood, aye?"

John entered and inspected the tiny space and its window. "On me way to Seattle's St. James Cathedral, and Bishop

O'Dea." He rocked back on his heels. "And you're on your way to a dungeon abode, aye? What I'd like to know is how you've found the path of evil men more desirous than God's."

Mick dropped onto the thin, stained mattress and hung his head. *Bested me again, God. Unbelievable. You sent me beloved John.* "Won't greet you with a hug. Not had a bath in days."

"True, that." John wrinkled his nose.

"You see, Father John, I've found God's the weak one. He's good at besting me, but not good enough against Mister Death. God's ways and law never worked for me, don't you know?"

"You truly believe that?"

Mick waved at the ceiling. "The God of me youth has jilted me at His altar of love, abandoned me in me marriages, and allowed death to victimize me more than He should. So 'tis not a wonder nor all me fault I've ended up here. God fashioned me body with its flaws, so I always endure pain. And terrible nightmares that refuse to go away. I use what nature gives me for numbing it all. Whiskey. Blame that for—"

"Ah, Mick, me sniveling poetic brother. God isn't impressed with your fancy defense."

Heat rushed up Mick's chest to his face and ears.

John gathered his robe in his fist and drew face to face with Mick. His silver crucifix swayed between them like a timepiece's pendulum. "Never blame the drink. 'Tis the coward's way. You're nothing near to a coward, you're not."

"I am. I am so. Needed me drink for courage." Mick veered his gaze away from the crucifix, landing it upon the cage of immovable rods preventing him from blessed freedom. He'd lived free for decades. Being held in captivity was far worse than living under Crown rule. Or struggling as a single father with life passing him by.

John sat beside him. "I've heard countless confessions, don't you know. The drink is blamed by men who use it for unfastening God's arrows of shame from their souls. You must tackle your weaknesses, man. Take stock of your life and mend your choices." He drew Mick against his side. "Repentance is the pathway. Be clever, me favorite brother, and forsake your destructive ways."

Mick shrugged off John's arm and rose to pace the cell. He studied his scuffed boots and counted his steps, attempting to avoid John's words. The painful, truthful arrows found their target in his soul. Was it too late to mend his terrible actions?

"Well?"

He turned back to John. "What 'bout Mister Death's curse? Surely, you believe in curses. The Night of the Big Wind cursed me when I was born, you know, for Ed witnessed it."

"Cursed you?"

"Apologies for me delay." McGinty approached, carrying a tin tray laden with tea and biscuits. "From Mrs. Baker. Shouldn't keep a priest waiting. Fortunate you are, Mick, by Father John's timely visit."

"Very kind of you." John stood. "We're brothers as well."

McGinty froze. "Another jest?" He scanned the men, then at Mick's wagging head, he secured the tray between his hip and the bars. His keys jingled and he fumbled to open the gate.

John accepted the tray.

"Call for me when you've finished." McGinty clanked the door shut behind his exit.

John transferred the tea tray onto the bed. "Did you expect this?"

"Didn't expect anything 'bout this day. Marshal and Mrs. Baker gave me preference out of politeness to a priest. Good marks with the church are what they're after."

"Let's not tell him it won't matter, aye?" He poured out a cup for Mick and handed it to him with a few biscuits.

"Thanks."

John's silver crucifix glinted in a shaft of sunlight

squeezing between the window bars. "You must confront the brutal facts of your life, although you believe in curses. What's required of you is an unwavering faith in God and to make your confession."

Should he confess his shameful life of sin to John? His brother was trustworthy, and he didn't question John's love for him. Hadn't he been shamed enough without going into the particulars of his arrest? But if anyone could understand and empathize with him, it would be John.

John sipped his tea, keeping his attention on Mick.

Mick munched on a soft shortbread biscuit, relishing its buttery flavor. "Mmm. Best thing I've had whilst locked up. Mainly they only serve gruel."

"Well, what'll it be? Will you tell me what's happened?"

"One thing I must know. Are you wishing to behave as me Father John or as me brother in this conversation?"

"Both."

Consarn it. Mick fidgeted with a small piece of short-bread, crumbled it, and arose to sprinkle the pieces onto the narrow windowsill. "You're not me first visitor, you know. 'Twas a little sparrow this morning." Visions of Ireland flooded in, to the day he first considered emigrating to America, when another sparrow on his cottage doorstep searched for insects. Chills bristled the hair up his limbs. Was this sparrow another sign? He must make massive changes again in his wretched life. Perspiration trickled down his temples, and he turned toward his brother.

John rearranged the empty teapot, cups, and the saucers inside the tray then took it to the locked gate. "Hallo there, Marshal, we've finished."

McGinty brought a chair and placed it beside the cell. He unlocked the gate and grasped the tray. "Brought you a seat in case you'll be staying with him longer. Shall you be?"

"Aye, for a while yet." John carried the slatted wooden chair inside.

The Marshal spun back to the brothers. "Forgot to mention, Muldoon, a telegram came from a convent saying Sister Elizabeth will arrive tomorrow. God sure has it in for you, aye? First a priest then a nun." He chuckled. "I'll be at my desk should you need me."

John raised a brow. "Sister Elizabeth?"

"Me eldest daughter, Moira, took the saint's name. It took me time to adjust to it."

"A surprise 'tis but a blessing. Another of us in the clergy. What Order of Sisters is she?"

"Franciscan."

"She teaches then. Fine aspiration to educate our young-sters. Your last letter to me was many years ago explaining why you couldn't come to Mam's funeral. I understood why you avoided ships."

Mick shuddered. "Gives me nightmares still, that trip on the *Mona*. 'Tis sad I lost touch with you. But I hadn't attended Mass for years, nor confession, for the shame of me choices. And mostly because the church wouldn't allow me the sacraments as a divorced man. Don't wish to get into that discussion with you, do I? Thoughtful neighbors and friends took me children to Mass."

John grinned. "God bless them."

"Aye. Good people they were." Mick propped himself against the rough, icy, brick wall behind him. "I lost touch with most of our family except for Orla. She needed family when everyone turned against her. I understood why 'twas so."

"Ah. But I never turned against her. She chose not to answer me own letters. But tell me of your life. I'm with you for the day, and we have time." John scooted onto the chair McGinty provided for him. "Get comfortable, give me your excuses and whatever else you've been doing since your last visit with me at St. Mary's."

Mick wrapped his arms around his knees to stretch some

of the stiffness out of his back. "The warning you gave us upon our leaving Ireland was warranted whilst we were in New York City. We came across terrible prejudice and troubles there and criminals within our own community. Do you remember I wrote you 'bout the miracle of Ed finding me after receiving a beating on the docks? I was never so glad to see him. Or to leave a place other than Ireland. The earth called out to me soul, and 'tis when life changed for the better, at first."

For the next several hours, Mick described his never-ending search for work, of his loves and losses in Minnesota, the persistent nightmares, then his battles with choices. He purposefully included his sightings of Mister Death and the angel's light and their battles, then the ensuing havoc. That wicked demon was partly to blame for his current condition, wasn't he?

"I see."

"I'm that glad you didn't flinch or scold when I told you of me fear of Mister Death attacking Beth and our children. That's what led me to this place. Halting Mister Death before he harmed Callum, but it wasn't that demon."

"And I haven't lived your life or seen these things, have I? All the same, God sees and knows everything. Let Him be your judge."

McGinty interrupted to bring water then again to bring fresh bread with butter and soup with meat and vegetables. "Mrs. Baker supplies meals to inmates when I request it."

Mick inhaled the aroma. "These are a welcome indulgence."

"Hoping so." McGinty nodded at John then shut the barred gate.

"'Tis that glad I am that me presence as a priest blesses you." John handed Mick a bowl with a chunk of bread.

They crossed themselves and recited the blessing.

John gathered his supper. "You mentioned Mister Death's

presence in your life. It reminds me of our Grandfather Muldoon. He had the gift of sight, no arguing with it. Your sight seems to be a bit narrower though. Have you noticed?"

"I spoke of God's angels as well. What d'you think of that? Is it possible to see them?" Mick dipped his bread.

"Aye. Many report experiences with God's ministering angels. More than you'd expect. You're someone who sees them." John collected a spoonful of vegetables.

"You're saying God sends them to me?"

John studied Mick then laid down his empty spoon. "Could be. For don't you know, just as you see Mister Death personally, the Lord Jesus Christ sees you personally?" He waved at the low ceiling. "He's not far above us, letting us run wild as we wish, nor does He pay no mind to our actions. His Spirit lives inside us and holds us to account. Parents do this as well. You get a fair warning then may the saints preserve you. You've received your warnings. Beware of what's to follow."

Mick chewed his lip.

The brothers finished their supper in silence.

"Marshal, we're done." Mick set the tray in front of the gate but left their mugs of water by the bed. He returned to his bench. What might be next? Could John help him? "Can you vouch for me release?"

John shook his head then bowed forward. "I will say this. Your view of life differs vastly from reality. Your troubles began in your thinking." He flicked his temple. "Whilst wondrous love found you more than once, I've never seen a man suffer your tragic number of losses and misfortunes. A magnificent, terrible game played out until you've ended up broken and locked inside this cage, aye? Is this a good life?"

"You know I despise it."

John indicated the cell around them. "You believe God is ignorant of what you've suffered. That He doesn't feel your pain at all. You're wrong. He felt His one and only Son suffer and die for the entire world who might believe in Him. You've suffered the loss of three wives and nine children. God doesn't ignore that or count such things as nothing."

"But I didn't willingly give up me children like He did with Christ. Always wanted to fight Mister Death from stealing me children to no avail. That evil scoundrel always wins. I wasn't strong enough and neither was God." Mick scowled.

John cocked his head. "But our own strength isn't sufficient, for 'tis never been so. We're to use His strength for living. Sin changed us from immortal to mortal. If we didn't need Him, His Son never would've died, aye?"

"Me head is dizzy." Mick rested against the wall. "You've switched into the priest's job."

John chuckled. "And I'll speak as your brother with it. This is me truth. I sacrificed married love to serve God. But what's the reason you abandoned married love?"

"As I told you, love never worked for me. Not as it should." His voice wedged in his throat, not from yelling at John but from the heartbreak he normally doused with alcohol. He gulped water from his mug.

"True."

"Me experiences are pitted against your arguments, Father John. Love in any form never worked. Only pain and misery came from it, one way or the other."

John leaned within inches of Mick's face. His eyes darkened from gentle, light blue to intense midnight. "But God and I have this against you, Mick Muldoon. You have used a woman as a prostitute in your own home with your children as witnesses. You pretended it wasn't so. You refused her marriage disguised as an agreement until it suited you to protect yourself. What was in your heart for Beth? This country's laws and the church laws were founded to protect vulnerable women like her, and she used an American law to justly make her accusation against you."

Mick shrugged. "Yes, I'm guilty of the mistaken violence. Not guilty per the agreement between us. We—"

"Enough." John stood. The large crucifix swung and twisted with his movement. "What woman in Beth's situation would rather continue being treated so? Can you imagine if this happened between Mam and Da? What if Da had been the drunkard and you were born into that? Or if he was wicked to Mam, continually used by him for his selfish desires? Would you justify his selfish choices against her?" He thumped Mick's chest.

Orla's face, then her story, flashed through Mick's mind. He'd been so upset by her abuse and her entrance into prostitution. *And yet I treated Beth no better.*

Mick clapped his hands over his face while pangs of guilt hit their mark in his soul. He couldn't douse it or ignore it or reason away any of these awful events. He was truly and unavoidably guilty. Sobs wound their way up from his gut to his throat and burst forth. His cries broke free, and he howled louder than the wolves on the prairie.

Marshal McGinty rushed in. "What's happened to him?"

John folded his arms. "He's faced himself. At last, me brother has agreed with the heart of God. All will be well in his soul."

Several moments passed while Mick allowed guilt, conviction, and remorse free rein to wash him clean with absolution before God. He now embraced truths which he always hid from himself. "I'm a wretched, miserable man who let losses and unbelief beguile me into a pit of despair."

"We've a Savior who understands man's condition." John stared down at him, gripped his shoulder, and Mick faced him. The whites of John's eyes were pink, but he smiled. "What'll you do now?"

"Stop drinking, if I can." Mick wadded the ends of his shirt and stared at his knees. He sniffed back more tears.

"And?"

Mick puffed out a shaky breath. "Treat Beth with love and respect."

312 | E.V. SPARROW

"I believe you're contrite and ready for your confession, aye?" He handed over a square piece of white fabric.

Mick wiped his face with it. "Where'd you get this?"

"It'd surprise you what we stash inside our robes, but 'tis a story for another day." His John sat beside him.

"Were you weeping for me?"

John enfolded Mick in his arms. "Whilst your tears were for cleansing, me tears were of joy. Welcome to the land of the believer, Mick Muldoon. The church taught you and me that God is omnipotent, omniscient, and omnipresent in our lives, aye? And do you agree with God now, regarding your sins? You're contrite and you'll confess?"

"Aye." He offered John's handkerchief to him, but he shook his head. "But I have a question before we continue, Father John. Are you telling me this, that although God can rebuke the wind and the waves, He doesn't always? And when He doesn't stop the storms in me life, I must embrace the winds of tragedy and death, even Mister Death, as not a curse but as a warning from God? Sounds like a cracked notion."

"Aye, not exactly His warning, but His allowance of sin's consequences in our world."

Mick nodded. "Give me the Act of Contrition then. But you must convince Beth I'm contrite. Will you meet me family and smooth the way?"

"Aye."

The brothers crossed themselves, and John led them both first in the Our Father, and then the Apostle's Creed. "I believe in God, the Father Almighty, Creator of Heaven and earth; and in Jesus Christ, His only Son Our Lord, Who was conceived by the Holy Spirit . . ."

———

A few days later, Mick stood at the base of his home's porch, a light breeze tickling his scalp as he kneaded his leather hat's brim. *Putting this off won't do.* He couldn't avoid entering his home. *You've been a slíbhín.* How could he face his family after his attack on Beth, accidental or not? Would his macushlas accept his apologies?

Through the open kitchen window, dishes and silverware clinked, accompanied by Finn's giggles. Then a burst of laughter from the girls. Beth sang a tune with Bridget and Cara.

His stomach growled. He slid his silver pocket watch from his smelly vest. Just past suppertime.

The door opened, and Liam called out, "Got to tend the horses first." He focused on the latch, then turned back toward the porch stairs. His gaze froze on Mick, then his eyes darted around. "Da."

He licked his dry lips. "Evening, Liam. They released me."

"Yes. Father John visited us yesterday."

"He said he would speak with Beth, and without her pressing charges, the Marshal couldn't keep me." Mick forced a grin, but his lips quivered. He tugged on one end of his moustache.

"I'll join everyone after I feed the livestock." Liam opened the front door and held onto the handle. "Go on in, Da."

"Best get it over with, aye?" Mick dragged his feet as he climbed the steps, imagining a guillotine hanging above his home's entrance. He stopped before the doorway, turned to Liam, and ruffled his son's hair. "I'm proud of you. Don't ever be like your own Da. Be a better man."

"Yes." Liam hurried down the stairs without a glance back.

The household noises hushed. Mick shifted around and found all three females clumped together, staring at him with a mixture of fear, anger, and disgust on their expressions. His knees collapsed, and he hit the floorboards with a jolt.

Jarring his back into a spasm, he panted in pain and slammed down his hands until he was on all fours. *Groveling like a dog, I am.* He sobbed and choked and couldn't gather appropriate words for an apology, although he must. "Dear God. I . . ." He gulped. "Forgive me." His hands swam in his vision, as though underwater. "Terrible. Disgusting. Horrible."

Clothing rustled, and Bridget spoke near his ear. "Golly, Da, we still love you." She looped her arm around his neck. "Just don't ever do that again, like you tell us. Don't repeat the same mistakes."

"Right, Da." Cara knelt on his other side, and clung to his arm. "You scared us, but we love you."

The three embraced. "Thank you. I'm not deserving of your forgiveness." Mick slowly tucked his legs beneath him to stand while the girls helped lift him. He wiped his face with his shirt sleeve then searched for Beth.

"Beth went down the hallway." Cara pointed.

"Sweet macushlas, thank you, for your forgiveness. I must speak with Beth alone, aye?" He rested his palms on each of their heads. "We'll join you shortly." At their nods, he headed for the bedroom.

He poked his head into the girl's room and found Finn asleep on Cara's bed then went ahead to his own room.

Beth stood near Callum's crib with her back to the door, staring out the window.

Mick crept past sleeping Callum and grasped Beth's delicate hand to turn her around. He kept his voice low. "I'm forever grateful to you for dropping the charges against me for that accidental attack. I hope you can forgive me one day." He kissed her palm then glanced up.

She pulled her hand free of his grip, giving him a view of her purplish-blue bruise, jagged stitches, and swelling skin around her eye.

Mick whooshed out a breath, and tears welled up at the damage he'd done. "By all that's holy, Beth."

"Appears worse today." She carefully brushed the area with her fingertips. "I do believe you're sorry, for our Father

John convinced me of your contrition. But 'tis also true that I'm paying the consequences of me own making. I sought you out and mistakenly thought you'd love me in return." She laid her finger against his parting lips. "And I can blame me hero all I wish for turning out to be a slíbhín, but 'tis me own fault for believing in you sight unseen."

Mick's knees gave way, and he plopped onto their bed. "Beth, I never wanted—"

"Hush now. 'Tis clear." She turned away to stare out the darkening window. "There's one final thing. I'll not be your cozy blanket in your bed again. You've told me and shown me at every step together what you think of me, and I foolishly held fast to me girlish dreams. Can't blame you for that part."

He grabbed Callum's crib rail, to steady his shaky legs as he stood. "But . . ."

She swung back to him—her green eyes dark as cedars. "Please sleep elsewhere whilst I mend me heart. Take the quilt, will you?"

Mick tried to swallow with a tongue as dry as a dust cloud. "We'd a Mick Muldoon tornado swirling around us, aye?"

Tears lined Beth's lower lashes. She hugged herself, then turned away. "Aye, and the settling tornado dust cloud reveals a barren marriage."

25

BENEFITS AND BLESSINGS

Not cold and dirty, or barefoot with shabby clothes.
Mick

E leven *Years Later*
         Early Summer 1916
         Noisy children playing nearby added a sparkle of
joy to the fine day. The railway's completion brought many
new inhabitants to Mick's neighborhood. Robins scampered
for worms in the grasses, and goldfinches chirruped in his
neighbor's older saplings that show off their first blossoms. *'Tis*
as if nature rejoices 'bout a surprise only it's privy to.

The past several years since his release from jail still
haunted him. He was guilty of the charges, and undeserving
of her mercy. *Or other good things in me life.* Although, the tragedy
worsened by Beth's disappearance with Finn and Callum. He
doubted he'd ever know where they'd gone without notice.
Please, Christ, have mercy on them.

He turned to his weekend guest, Orla, rocking beside him
on the porch. "Thinking 'bout being married so many times,
sister. Wanted once and done. Fate gave me a trouncing with
never keeping a woman. Took me years to understand God's

ways. All those times He sent me help and I never recognized it as His love. What would've happened without Him sending our John to me in jail? It was hopeless." *Forced me to face the truth.* Getting free of whiskey's grip had not been easy.

"You'd be drinking still." She raised her gaze from her page of the newspaper. "Do you miss whiskey's numbing power over your pain?"

Disregarding the ache in his back and legs, he shifted his slight weight on the chair's seat. "Aye, for pain's more intense as an old man. Won't return to the drink, although I'd welcome something to dull the pain and all that creaking and snapping in me joints."

"Wished I'd welcomed our John's interest in me when I was young. Maybe I'd have straightened up earlier. John could've influenced our poor Ed as well. To think, 'twas always Ed's life which worried me. Nigh twenty years ago was the last time I saw him."

"Our own brother." Mick shook his head.

"Wish you could've seen his face when he first spied me waiting for the men on the dock in those days. Ed turned snow white then blood red when he climbed off the ore barge with the crew. Have you heard from him lately?"

"Nah, he lost interest in me. Gambling and gold were his loves. Last I heard, he was wagering away on some riverboat on the Mississippi River." Mick's rocking chair squeaked with each movement. "What 'bout your fancy living? You were after it like a snake on an egg. Thought the '84 fire on Whiskey Row took you. It frightened me into fits thinking you'd be dead."

"Had nightmares for months. Needed dire things for God to catch me attention, aye? Desiring wealth was where I messed up. God values faith, hope, and love, and He gave those to me. That's true extravagance."

"Aye. Hope fulfilled is potent. Isn't it odd we can be so wrong 'bout what God is? Your faith's altered you, like a caterpillar into a butterfly. No offense intended. If our family could see you now, they'd open their arms to you, aye? Wish they could know how you've altered."

She took a deep breath. "I understood their feelings. You never deserted me, and I've never forgotten that. You've been a devoted brother."

"Aye. Tragic how I thought whiskey was me strength. It led me down a dark hole and betrayed me into harming Beth. Unbelievable."

"And aren't all of us betrayed in some way by our feelings?" Orla returned to rocking. "Aye, the drink is the Irishman's curse. Still no word on Beth and the boys? Nothing ever came to light?"

"Reading me earlier thoughts? Not a thing." Mick pressed against the pain in his chest, certain it was heartache.

"'Tis a crying shame, that." Orla shook her head and swatted at a bumblebee hovering near an overgrown, trailing rose that wound around the porch rail beside her. "Maybe one day there'll be news of what happened."

I'll die never knowing what. "Their disappearance still causes a blackness in me soul. Liam promises to never stop searching. He says he'll find them with God and His saints' help." Mick refolded the newspaper on his lap but kept the pages in order. Even the latest rumors of the United States government's discussions of possibly entering the war in Europe didn't suppress the glorious day. He slowly inhaled late spring's aroma, and the occasional pain he experienced in his chest increased. He whooshed out his breath then drew it in slow and deep. The pain faded within a few moments.

Orla brushed his knuckles with her fingertips. "Brother, thinking I'll be returning to me home soon. Been away too long, and I'll be missed. Hoping me family will be glad to see me now. But you shocked me into being a statue, telling me of your church attendance and no more whiskey drinking." She tightened her white bun at her nape. "I think me hair turned a shade lighter because of it. They won't recognize me back home. I'd not have believed the changes in you if I didn't see it for meself."

"Me own mirror reminds me daily. Old age has its benefits."

She studied the hydrangeas against his porch. "Wished I could have seen the children. I'll always think of them as such. Doesn't matter they're adults in their twenties, for always children they'll be in me mind."

"Mine as well."

Orla rose to inspect the blue and lavender flowers. "May I cut a few for your table?"

"Aye. There's a vase in the kitchen cupboard near the sink, upper right, in the corner."

"Perfect." Orla entered the house.

Blackie, resting beside his chair, raised his graying muzzle, and his ears perked forward. He scrambled onto his stiff legs to stand. *Yip!*

Mick lowered his spectacles and searched for the dog's object of excitement.

Liam approached the gate to the yard and waved. "Afternoon, Da. Hiya, Blackie." He opened the gate. "I parked down at the store thinking I'd walk on foot up the hill to surprise you. Have some news."

"I'm still unsure 'bout that automobile of yours, boyo. Wouldn't you prefer a tall, hefty horse like our Wings?"

Liam grinned. "Sure, if Wings were alive. I'll take you for a ride, then you'll understand the appeal of an auto."

Mick cringed. "Riding along at the speed of twenty horses sounds as terrible as sailing in a coffin ship."

Blackie hobbled over to Liam then yipped again when two women carrying portmanteaus drew close to the picket fence at the end of Mick's yard.

"Hallo, Da." His grown daughters, Bridget and Cara, cried in unison. They giggled together as they spied Liam with

Blackie then entered the yard to stoop over and greet their loyal pet.

Orla stepped onto the porch carrying the vase. "Thought I heard angelic voices. Glory be, 'tis like opening Christmas gifts to see you all here. And wasn't I just saying—"

"Such fun." Bridget called out. "We didn't know you were here visiting, Auntie O, nor did we plan to meet up with Liam, but here we all are. It reminds me of last month, or maybe it was only two weeks ago, on a Friday night, when a bunch of us Ma Bell girls accidentally met up at—"

"Hello, Auntie O." Cara waved. "We had a fantastic time visiting friends and their families in Chicago."

Cara's got to have her say.

"They took us to the theater and to a new restaurant which serves ice cream for dessert."

Liam bowed and removed his hat. "Aunt Orla, glad to see you."

Mick rose from his rocker and stood on the top porch step. "Hold up there, macushlas. Let me inspect you all. 'Tis me privilege to enjoy the grand sight of you all together."

"Jobs keep us busy, Da." Cara smoothed her hair.

Bridget almost matched Liam's height. A striking woman, as Orla had predicted, dressed in a light-blue drop-waist dress swinging above her ankles, a matching hat, and a graceful pearl necklace dangling over her chest. The funny new style of pointy lace-up heels gave her an air of sophistication. *No more clunky work boots for this daughter.* Her favorite women's magazine could feature her on its cover. *Wasn't it McCall's?* She'd always enjoyed reading it but left them strewn about the house, irritating their tidy Cara.

Liam wore a button-up white shirt, necktie, and a vest under his jacket. The silver chain of the pocket watch Mick gave him for Christmas hung across his stomach. A bowler hat covered his copper waves. *No bedraggled or shabby farmer is he.*

He studied Cara. Although only a few months earlier she took a job at Ma Bell's, she'd changed the most. At twenty-two, she'd long ago left her childhood, yet he sensed another alteration in her today. What was it? She wore her curly auburn hair wound tight in a bun at the nape of her neck. *No more girlish braids.* She was a working woman like her sister. Cara batted her lashes and exaggerated rolling her shoulder. Cheeky creature. Maybe her bright yellow striped dress added to the brightness in her expression.

His heart almost burst with pride. Unlike his other children's odds, these four, counting their own Sister Elizabeth, had not only survived as Irish American offspring, but they'd also thrived. *Neither poor, nor starving, nor ill. Not cold and dirty, or barefoot with shabby clothes. These're me living treasures, and I have God and America to thank for it.*

Bridget curtsied low. "Are we acceptable, Da? Can we approach your throne to give you hugs? It was a tiring journey, you know."

"Plus I want tea." Cara tapped her stomach. "Do you have any biscuits left?"

Orla cringed and glanced at Mick. "That he doesn't, for I ate them all, I did."

"Being your favorites." Mick waved them forward. "Come, come. You must have news for me, macushlas. Me neighbor, Mrs. Lang, baked me a fresh apple pie. It's still warm from her oven."

"A neighbor?" Bridget giggled. "Is she sweet on you? It would be delightful if—"

"Oh, ho. That could happen, right, Da?" Cara clapped.

Mick sighed. "Doubtful."

After their hugs, everyone entered his home. Blackie trudged behind them, and the girls hurried away to the kitchen while chattering with Orla.

Liam hung his jacket and hat on a peg near the door. "Can I tell you my news?"

"Come, let's leave the women be and sit on the porch whilst we await the tea." He returned to the rockers.

The men settled in, and Liam bent forward. "First the good news. I've been promoted to section foreman. It's a fairly good pay raise, and Laura is proud and pleased. She's the best wife I could imagine. I hope to make her as happy as she makes me. You've met her sister's young girl, Christy? Well, she remembers meeting you and already asked after Blackie. She's coming out of her shyness after only two weeks with us. We tried explaining to her that a baby brother or sister will join us by Christmas, but she's a bit young to understand about infants."

"She's a sweet and bright little girlie, and you've got a kind heart to raise her as your own."

Orla placed the stack of plates on the table between the rockers. "Christy was a delight to meet at your wedding last year. She calls me Auntie O as well."

"We've not regretted our vow to care for her after her family tragedy. And the other good news is I collected twenty-five signatures on the pension petition to the railroad on your behalf. You ought to get it, Da, after forty-five years of service to them. They owe it to you."

"Join you in a minute." Orla left them again.

Mick stopped rocking. "That may be, but I'm skeptical they'll see it that way."

Liam twisted around to peer at the screen door and hunched closer. "Quickly for some sad news. I discovered that Beth died ten years ago. I'm sorry for it, but I know how to search for the boys. I told you God would show me. There's a woman, Beth's neighbor, who says Finn and Callum were sent away to an orphanage or an asylum after her passing. I promise I'll never stop searching until I bring them home to the family, Da. You know I won't. They'll be eleven and twelve by now, and they'll set out on their own in a few years."

Mick scrunched his shirt with both hands. "Pain is searing

me heart. I don't know what to say." He stretched up his hand to Liam's cheek. "I'm that sorry 'bout them all. God forgive me for me part in this family devastation." Tears trickled into his mustache.

"Da." Liam knelt before his father. "God forgives you. We do. God will help me find them. He answers our prayers. It takes time."

"Aye. I know it."

Liam rose and paced as he monitored the door. "I made inquiries in western South Dakota and in St. Paul and got a telegram yesterday from St. Joseph's orphanage in St. Paul. They have a Finn listed there around his age."

Mick struggled to rise from the rocker. "A Finn Muldoon?"

"No surname." Liam laid his hand on Mick's shoulder. "We shouldn't get our hopes up too high, but it might be him. Finn isn't so common a name, is it? There are only a few scattered on the rosters I've heard about. I'm praying I'll get to them both while records exist and that they're registered under their given names."

His heart raced, but his head was numb.

"It's disheartening, Da, but also hopeful to find pieces of the puzzle. I'll go as soon as I can to see if he's our Finn. Say a prayer for me."

"Aye. I'm grateful to you. I am. At least I've a few answers I've awaited and wondered 'bout." *Dear, God, can You return them to us?*

"Here we are." Bridget set the tray beside the plates. "Did you say you wondered about it? Be patient, our favorite men. I'll bring the kitchen chairs out. Such a beautiful day, isn't it? I'm so happy the neighbors planted those fruit trees, Da, they're so lovely in bloom. Are they planning to share any of their fruit or allow you to pick some? I've always loved all kinds of fruit, especially plums. Are those—"

"Chairs, Bridget," Cara called through the screen.

"What? Sorry, my hunger's yelling too loud at my brain. I'll grab the chairs, and you grab the apple pie."

The girls returned and poured out the tea for everyone. The very air radiated celebration and excitement, but Mick couldn't fully connect with the festivities. Bleakness hung over him with Liam's news of Beth and the boys.

"Da, I met a man." Cara's eyes gleamed. "At Ma Bell's. His name is Thomas Kelly. He's a fellow employee, I should say. We've been talking a lot after work, and he asked me to go to a play next month. I'll invite him to meet you first, Da. I think you'll like him."

Joy covered the bleakness in his heart. His Cara met a man. "And if he isn't a good one, you'll be hearing it from me. I'm glad for your excitement, macushla. Invite him to visit me shortly."

Bridget clapped. "Isn't that fantastic news? Don't you worry about him going to war, Cara? We may never join it. I know there's talk, but what good is talk? Why, the other day, I tried to clear the line from a talkative person for a call—"

"The war in Europe?" Orla flicked her hand. "'Tis a terrible thing. We had too much of it in Ireland."

"Aye. War is caused by evil." *And it's one of Mister Death's favorite weapons.*

Cara elbowed Bridget then reached for a slice of pie. "Aren't you here to tell Da that thing?"

"It's not news yet." Bridget stared at her cup and blushed. "It's more of a feeling. You see, William asked me how I see my future, if I still want to join vaudeville or if I want to get married and raise a family. I mean, we're not really courting or anything like that—"

Liam chuckled. "Bridget. If a man's been asking you those questions, you'd best believe he's wanting to court you. Is it William Sheehan?"

"Yes, but I still do want to try joining vaudeville. Sally told me there're auditions in St. Paul next spring. She read about it in the paper. Don't you think I should at least try out before I marry? I heard that Sarah Mulhern tried out and they accepted her for a magic act. Can you believe it? Nothing about her is magic. Did you know . . ."

Mick relished his scrumptious pie and tea, but as he listened to his children and how they loved and protected each other, he relished them most. His daughters supported themselves much better than he could, for he was aging, and his energy at work lagged these days. Liam was the best one to protect them from unworthy men.

His offspring cherished each other, and even though they quarreled, what more could a Da wish for? He'd joyfully witnessed his oldest son marry, adopt his wife's neglected niece, and was soon to be a father to his own child. *I'll be a grandfather. And such a privilege 'tis.*

Hadn't his own John helped him to understand his blindness about God, to confess, and then be redeemed from a destructive path? One filled with selfishness and depraved living. Mick shuddered. If he'd remained on that path, he would've missed what he experienced these past years, and especially what he witnessed today. Truly, God Almighty was more than he'd imagined. *He is mightiest to save me from prison, alcohol, and curses, especially those of Mister Death.*

EPILOGUE
REJECTED AND ACCEPTED

By all that's holy, I hope our Sister Elizabeth wears those masks mentioned
Mick

A lmost *Two Years Later*
Liam's Home
Mid-Autumn, 1918

The sun hung low behind the tree line between the earth and cloudless sky. Mick opened the yellow checkered curtain while he scanned beneath his new bedroom's window to the right and left. His daughter-in-law's prairie violets up against the house's foundation had recently lost their soft lavender blooms. Laura told him she'd planted several because she wanted to attract regal butterflies.

As he imagined the fluttering sight next spring, Mick grinned. She'd also provided a mass of orange, yellow, and pink chrysanthemums, which she'd cut and placed within a vase atop his dresser. *She's a thoughtful woman.* But how did he end up as an uncomfortable burden on Liam and Laura?

He swiped his moist face. How could a railroad betray a man's forty-five years of loyalty, draining their crews' blood, sweat, and strength to build an entire country only to reject him for a pension in his feeble years. *Tossed aside, I was.*

Mick tightened his fist full of fabric. The railroad had tossed every laborer aside in their old age. *Macedonians, Chinese, Irish, tribal men.* Anyone who broke their backs laying track for them.

He kicked his boot against the wall. *Rejected . . . you're stuck on that track, man. Get off it for your own good.* Liam's petition with thirty signatures should've done the trick. Didn't Mick have a wonderful family? Hadn't they welcomed him three hours ago with his favorite persimmon cookies? They'd readied a grand bedroom for him then reassured him living alone in a declining town during an influenza epidemic wasn't in his best interests.

He tugged the window sash down and sagged onto the bed Laura had prepared for him.

"Ganda, did you fall off your bed?" Rosy-cheeked and ringleted Christy hopped to him in her white dress, carrying her doll.

"What? Ah, did you hear a thump?"

"Yeah. Are you hurt?"

He straightened his shoulders. "I'm not, thank you. Hit me boot against the wall."

"Oh." Christy patted his yellow and blue quilt with one hand. "It's so pretty. Mama made it for you. She made me one too. You want to see?"

"Aye, Christy." Mick's tension faded with the joy of the little girl.

She slid backwards off the bed onto the floor. Christy skipped to the doorway, while the pink bow gathering her black curls on top of her head bounced like a grasshopper fleeing from a bird.

He chuckled.

She twisted around. "Come on, Ganda."

I wonder if me little Minnesota Maggie would've been like this girlie. Something about her made him think so.

Christy pointed at him. "You look funny." She swung back around near the door into her room. "Are you scared?" She sucked on a loose strand of her hair. "There's no monster in there. No yelling or hitting. Or scary face." She wagged her head, bouncing her bow again. "Daddy looks under my bed before we say prayers."

She can't be speaking of that monster, Mister Death, can she? Haven't seen him in years. Mayhap from her life before Liam and Laura. *Her dreadful stepfather and her mother's death. Hope she'll forget one day.* "Aye, you're right. No monsters would dare to live in such a grand place. I'll tell you a secret, shall I? You caught me earlier remembering a little girl from many years ago."

"Oh." She whispered her part of the secret. "What's her name? Can she be my friend?" She took his hand with her damp fingers.

Mick breathed in deep. "The little girl? Sure, and she would like that, but she lives far, far away."

Christy hopped on one foot with her doll raised in the air. "Where?"

Laura entered the hall and wiped hands on a flour sack towel. "My conscience, Christy. Are you bothering your . . ." Her face scrunched up to match her cloth.

"Ganda." Mick grinned. "'Tis been her name for me since last year, and I proudly claim it. I do." He lifted his adopted granddaughter. "You're a slip of a thing, like me sister Kathleen."

Christy hugged her doll and stared around the hallway. "What's a slip? Where's Kathleen?"

Mick stroked Christy's shoulder. "She talks a lot for such a young child. Doesn't she?"

"I guess so. When we took her, she was already speaking. My sister was a talker until she married that awful . . ."

A loud hissing from the kitchen startled Laura. "Our

rupper is sooking. I mean, well, in a minute it will be ready. I .
. ."

*Did better this time at not pointing out her mixing up of words when
she gets flustered.* Mick offered his hand to his granddaughter.
"Christy and I will go outside whilst you finish cooking supper.
Shan't we, macushla?"

She sang to her doll. "A mashla, a mashla, Ganda calls me
mashla. Dolly, I'll call you Mashla."

Laura hurried down the hall and called out, "Thank you,
Mick."

He escorted Christy to the screen-covered porch and
marveled at his son's home. Nothing like the boxy white board
homes the railroad had provided himself with only two rooms
and an outhouse. This one had a separate kitchen area, a
living room, three bedrooms, and a fireplace, not a wood
stove. He and Christy had their own bedrooms, and Liam
spoke of adding another for the baby in the future. *'Twill be a
veritable mansion one day.*

Blackie hobbled to him and Christy, and he patted his
dog's graying head, much like his own silver hair. *A content dog
to live this long.* Didn't contentment lengthen life?

"Blackie." Christy squealed. "It's cold. Go inside if you
want to. Mama said. Do you want to?" She opened the door
for Mick's dog. "Go on in."

The dog ambled past her and licked her arm on his way
into the house.

Christy wiped it off. "Dog kisses are icky. Can you get the
wagon, Ganda?"

"That I can." Mick rounded the home's corner then found
the wood and metal wagon parked beside the shed. He tugged
on it a few steps until the muscles in his back cramped. He
lifted and carried it to Christy waiting at the base of the porch
steps.

"Ganda, Daddy's home. Come see. He has mail." Christy

grasped his pant leg as Mick set the wagon beside a grassy patch.

Liam clicked the yard's picket gate shut, then turned. "Hello, my girlie. Da." He shifted some papers from his hand to his armpit as Christy ran to him with her curls bouncing her bow free to land on the dirt.

Christy burst into tears. "It's dirty. Don't get dirty. He doesn't like it." Her murmurs turned into wails.

"He won't do anything, darling, because he isn't here." Liam lifted her and cuddled her. "Remember?" His face flushed as he stared at Mick. "You live with us now. He's gone."

Infant cries from inside the home startled Christy.

"Did your brother wake up from his nap?" Liam kissed the girl's head.

Christy nodded against Liam's chest.

Mick patted his granddaughter gently on the back. "With your Da, Blackie, your Ganda, and God's angels, nothing bad will harm you."

Christy twisted around and held her arms out to Mick. "Hold me." She clamped onto his neck and whispered. "He gets mad. Dirty is bad." She poked her thumb into her mouth.

Mick's knees shook. He couldn't breathe, but he wanted to yell and something more. *If I could find the man he'd—*

"Some people have bad ways, right?" Liam raised his brows. "They say bad things and do bad things to others, Christy. But what did we learn about God's ways?"

Christy popped her thumb out of her mouth. "God is good. He does good things. Bad things make Him sad. He doesn't like people doing bad things."

"Right. But you added that last part on your own." Liam winked at Mick.

"And God's angels watch over us."

Mick kissed the little girl's arm. "That they do, macushla."

"And they can kill the bad people." Christy punched his shoulder. "And—"

"My conscience! Whatever are you saying to that sweet child?" Laura scurried down the steps with the nearly one-year-old James. She awkwardly shifted James to Liam, then snatched Christy from Mick. "I was so happy she ventured outside to play, but making her cry? Kalking about tilling and thorrible hings to a three-year-old." She glared at Mick then Liam. "How could you?"

Terribly unfair. Mick's heart thudded in his ears. *Keep your mouth shut, man.*

Liam raised his hand. "We never said those things to her, Laura. Don't know where she heard them. We were comforting her, and you came out at the worst time." He ruffled baby James' fine, coppery wisps of hair.

"I came out at the terfect pime."

James yawned, and his rosy cheeks matched his curls. He blinked and grinned over Liam's arm at Mick.

"Mama, they didn't say bad things at me." Christy hugged Laura's shoulder and stared at the gate. "The scary man did."

"Not Ganda?" Laura's mouth dropped open, and she flushed.

Mick shook his head.

"My Da never would."

"Not Ganda. The bad man." Christy darted glances around the yard. "Can he find me?"

Mick couldn't swallow for the horror stuck in his throat. He raised his eyes to the darkening sky. *Christ, have mercy on her, and help the child forget her earlier life.*

A thin trail of smoke fluttered out of what Mick guessed was the kitchen window. "Is something cooking, Laura? Appears to be overdone."

Laura shrieked. "Sour upper!" She passed Christy to Liam and rushed up the steps into the house.

With both of Liam's arms full of children, Mick gathered

up the hat and the mail from the ground near Liam's feet. "Ah, I see today's issue of *Railway Age* magazine is here. Will be glad to read it." He waved an envelope. "And a letter from our Sister Elizabeth. That's a joy."

Liam pressed into Mick's side, passed James over to him, then shifted Christy onto his shoulders. "I asked our Sister Elizabeth to help me investigate orphanages for the boys. There could be an update. She sends me what she finds. If it sounds likely, I'll go by train. It's sad nothing has panned out, but I'll find them as I promised, Da. Never fear."

"Let's open her letter now, shall we?" Mick tried to around James' wiggles without success. "We'll need the knife."

The little girl giggled and pinched Liam's oiled, copper strands between her fingers. "Let's go fast, Daddy! Go, go."

More billows of smoke drifted from the window with the stench of burnt meat.

Liam twisted around. "It must wait for now, Da. You won't make any prickly comments about the supper, right, Da? Laura is sensitive about her meal preparation skills. She only has one. Heat everything on boiling hot to catch up for forgetting to get the food cooking earlier. Each moment grabs Laura's attention, and time gets away from her, you see. It's her adorable way of living life. And my apologies for her accusation. She's protective of Christy for good reason."

"I understand. Hope to win Laura's fine opinion with time." Mick inserted the enticing letter into his pocket. The wait would be terrible. Then again, nothing could be done today.

The men climbed the steps as Liam wagged the periodical in the air. "There's a news article in the magazine we should discuss after the children are in bed. Christy's had enough frights for the day. But it's not about the war."

Mick brooded. What could be more frightening than war? *Death. Boyos disappearing.*

After Laura opened the windows and smoke from the stove had almost cleared from the home, Mick hid his cough while the entire family prepared for supper.

Liam placed Christy in her chair at the laid-out table, and she rose onto her knees. She fumbled with a fork and spoon, which clinked against the bluebird-patterned plate. She froze and peeked at Liam.

A disheveled Laura, dark ringlets coming loose from her bun, rushed in with a tray of what could be a chicken. She swiped at her damp tendrils stuck against her cheek.

If he imagined the shape of the meat lump forty shades lighter, it made sense. Mick stood, still unsure where to sit at the dinner table. *At the end?* Or was that Laura's chair? Where should he put baby James? He regarded the baby in his arms.

James stared at him and tugged on Mick's protruding gray mustache, making him wince. He waited to see where Liam and Laura sat.

Liam took his seat at the head of the table, and Laura stared at the burnt offering and twisted a loose clump of her hair.

In the silence, the wall clock ticked loud enough to blow a tunnel for the railway. Mick laid the rumpled envelope from his pocket on top of the magazine Liam had set on the sideboard.

Do we eat that thing sitting on the platter? Mick glanced at Liam. "Shall I keep baby James with me?"

"No, sorry. Laura holds him and feeds him at the table with us." Liam smiled at his wife. "Is supper ready then?"

Laura nodded then circled around Christy's chair with her arms out for James, not meeting Mick's gaze. "I'll take the baby."

He handed James to her and shifted his feet.

"Da, your chair is across from Christy."

"Wasn't sure. You got six. Never had so many empty chairs to choose from." Mick's ears burned like the chicken. *Shouldn't be embarrassed.*

Laura settled the baby on her lap and tied a bib she pulled from her yellow apron pocket around his neck.

"Yellow must be your favorite color, Laura. I see you use it in your decorating." Mick smiled.

"What? Oh, I do like it." Laura sulked and kept her gaze on the baby.

"Bridget and Beth liked yellow as well." Mick brushed his palms against his denims. He needed a drink for his dry mouth, but not whiskey.

Liam cleared his throat. "Are we ready—"

"Pardon me. I have something to say. If I don't, I may lose me courage."

"Ganda." Christy waved her hand. "You can't talk until you eat all your supper." Her dark-blue eyes widened to twice their normal size.

"I'm the one who made that rule little girlie. Well, me Da made that rule, so I can be the one to break it once. I wish to . . ." Mick stared down at the mashed potatoes and peas on his plate. "It's . . ." He lifted his fork and pushed a few peas around. "Never in all me days did I think I'd live this long."

"We're glad you did, Da."

Mick squelched down tears and poked at the mashed potatoes. "Thought for sure Mister—uh, with all me troubles I wouldn't last, but I did to an old age. All me children are married and gone. Cara in California with her husband, Bridget traveling the country singing and dancing, our Sister Elizabeth ministering in the church. Now you two got stuck with me when me town fell apart. Hooligans moving in." He swirled the potatoes into a circle. "Pensions are becoming the thing. Believed the railroad would take care of me after all me years with them. They didn't. I'm bitter, I admit. Seemed it was a good job. By all that's holy, 'tis come to this day, where me child and his wife are me parents, and I don't like it. Not at all."

Laura gasped. "I'm sorry about earlier. I rust jeacted when Christy cried."

Mick raised his gaze to her. "Aye. But I couldn't imagine a better place to live in all the world. Laura, your hospitality gave me a comfortable room. You trust—mostly trust—me presence inside your home with your children." He wiped his cheeks. "Maybe I never saw this day coming, nor never wanted it—"

"Da. You took care of me and my sisters for years." Liam leaned in. "It's my turn. I'm happy to do it. So is Laura."

Mick couldn't see through his tears, so he concentrated on the green peas and nodded.

"Are you done, Da? Supper is getting cold, and Laura worked hard at putting it on the table. Let's say grace."

It thrilled Mick to discover a grand way to eat burnt meat. His idea of pushing it through the potatoes by sticking peas into the potato blob and eating it all in one bite helped mask the smoke and crunch. The meat also softened enough to chew it.

Mick rose to clear the table with Laura, but she frowned at him. "Laura, allow me to be useful. It'll help me feel like I belong here and doing me part, and we can be done quickly. I'm eager to read our Sister Elizabeth's letter."

After Laura and Mick had finished supper clean-up, Liam had said nightly prayers with Christy, and Laura had put James to bed, Mick joined Liam in the parlor.

Liam finally slit the end of the envelope with his letter opener, which contained Moira's crucial message. "I'll read our Sister Elizabeth's note first, then we'll switch off. You've been so patient with our wait."

"Inside meself, I've been nervous as a racehorse at the gate, me boyo. Weren't you as well?"

"Yes, but I was thinking of honoring Laura's hard work at

putting supper on the table and all her other chores." He slid the letter out of its cocoon and scanned it.

"Me heart's been thudding fast, 'tis sure." Mick situated himself into a stuffed armchair next to the fireplace, glad for a warm spot. He clenched the chair's arms.

Liam grimaced. "No updates this time, Da. I'm sorry to disappoint you."

Mick relaxed his grip. "Ah well. As disappointed as I am, me soul is that glad you won't be giving up the search for our boyos. With your sister's aid 'tis even better odds, no doubt."

"Yes. Much better chances with her working with me whenever her church duties allow her the time. Here's the magazine opened to the article you should read."

Mick grasped the printed periodical from Liam's outstretched hand. He slid on his spectacles. The blurred, grayish smears came into focus:

The danger of contagion is most serious in crowded places. For that reason, it behooves the railways to take every possible measure to the end that they may not serve in any greater degree than necessary as an agency in spreading the disease. Crowding in passenger trains should be avoided as much as possible. The presence of an influenza victim in the midst of a crowd is exceedingly serious. A car added here or there will no doubt help considerably in many cases. Insistence on open windows and ventilators is a positive necessity. Notices should be placed in the cars that anyone having to sneeze, or cough, should do so in his handkerchief; and what is more important, instructions should be issued to the conductors and trainmen looking to the enforcement of these things. Spitting in passenger coaches is still occasionally seen and is a particular evil in smoking cars. It is not only a most obnoxious habit, but under the present conditions, it is positively dangerous. The present signs in cars on many railroads saying that spitting is against the law are almost a joke. Such signs should explain in far more emphatic terms how obnoxious and dangerous spitting is. Trainmen should be instructed to remonstrate with those who persist in the habit. The situation is exceedingly serious, and no steps should be left untaken to remedy it. (To your question: *I copied the article from the actual magazine word for word*).

Mick yanked off his spectacles and slapped the magazine onto his lap. "You must read this. They focused on spitting and spreading disease. What taradiddle is this?"

"Not nonsense. As a foreman, Da, they've apprised me of the influenza epidemic. I'm sure you've heard the rumors or read other articles about it?"

"Aye, heard, but truth be told, I've been busy packing and moving in here. 'Twas a hard choice to become a burden upon you which kept me from worrying 'bout anything else."

"It's one reason Laura and I wanted you here, to keep you safe during the epidemic."

That devil Mister Death is at it again. Mayhem is his middle name.
"Da?"

"Aye? Oh, and I thank you for caring for me with loving hearts. Yet, a man has a terrible time giving up independence as he ages."

"It must be difficult." Liam exchanged the magazine for the letter from Sister Elizabeth. "She writes about the Catholic Church's involvement with the influenza and what her Order of Sisters is specifically doing to help the public. You'll be proud."

Sliding on his spectacles, Mick smoothed Sister Elizabeth's three pages and held each page at arm's length to read it. Thank God for her fine penmanship.

"You two create a homey picture." Laura settled onto their chesterfield. "What are you reading, Da?"

"Our Sister Elizabeth's letter." *So Laura's forgiven me?*
"Anything interesting?"

"Well, now." Mick wiggled in his seat to face Laura directly. "I'm only just hearing more 'bout the Spanish influenza. She writes how they're making masks for patients and others, and the priests aren't taking the trains to visit parishioners for a while. There're also some nuns who've taken to visiting the sick in their homes, and they're calling them District Sisters for doing that in twos and threes. They go to everyone, not just Catholics, and they're working in hospitals as well. Have you ever heard of such things? I know I haven't."

"That's important work."

Mick's heart thudded with concern for his oldest child. "By all that's holy, I hope our Sister Elizabeth wears those masks mentioned." What if she catches the deadly illness? He extended the letter toward Laura. "She writes more 'bout it, should you care to read it. It made me heart nearly stop."

Laura's eyes widened as grasped the letter. "You helt your start fop? I mean—"

Mick chuckled before he could rein it in. "Me heart is fine."

Liam sighed. "Laura, my da is dramatic. He feels his emotions, granted, but it's his way of expressing himself. Right, Da?"

"Aye. Me heart seems good and strong with a lot more squeezes left in it as well." *If Mister Death, all armed to the hilt with the wicked influenza, can't find Moira or us.* "God's holy angels will keep us safe and may they do so in all the foreboding times."

Laura laid the letter on her lap. "You know, I believe our Sister Elizabeth is the bravest woman I know. She's facing chenormous hallenges. Like Christy here. More than a body should ever have to."

Mick gripped the chair's arms. "Aye. 'Tis truth. She and Christy. Both innocent of doing any harm to others yet facing the evil in this world with courage. Christy had violence from a man who should've loved and protected her yet she trusts us." He indicated the letter on Laura's lap. "Our Sister Elizabeth faces plenty of evil with faith, especially hell's unseen and vile creature, Mister Death."

"Good point, Da. And they're doing it all with hope, trust, and faith."

Laura smiled. "And don't forget love, you two. Love for God and others is the strongest motivator in the world."

Mick's vision blurred with tears. Here he'd believed all along that evil was the strongest. Stronger even than God. "I've believed a terrible lie all of me life. And letting it rule me nearly destroyed it." He turned to Liam. "Me boyo, I would've perished in a terrifying, dark place all alone. Much worse than in the belly of the *Mona*, aye. I chose to douse me fear of death and pain with me whiskey when I could've chosen faith and life instead."

"Da, we understood your struggles and daily saw your pain. You had your reasons for the whiskey." Liam knelt before his father. "Have faith I'll find our lost Callum and Finn. God will show me where they are. You'll see. It'll be the last wound to your heart that He will heal."

"Me macushla. Me boyo." Mick kissed Liam's forehead. "By God's mercy, whom I ignored for many a year, He gave me forgiving children, aye? You all showed me the way of escape from me fears and freedom into this joyous life by your gracious love."

The End

AUTHOR'S NOTE

My parents had me baptized and raised me in the Roman Catholic Church. The purpose of this novel isn't to promote or degrade my Irish Catholic heritage and faith, it is to include and salute it for introducing me to faith in the Lord Jesus Christ and the Holy Trinity.

As a young child, I urged my parents to take me to church because I liked the music. It didn't matter the service was in Latin. The reverence for God surrounded me. Jesus was on the cross behind the altar, and He looked so sad. I didn't understand His crucifixion, nor had I read the Bible yet.

At sixteen-years old, faith in Jesus became personal. I understood His sacrifice for me on that cross for my salvation. After I lost my high school friends who had no faith, the new ones who loved and accepted me attended every church in our small town. I attended a "Hallmark Channel" church by my high school and invited my friends from all the other churches to our youth group events. It created quite a stir among the adults, but I was happy to be together. We all loved Jesus Christ. My new friends described me as "ecumenical," meaning *representing several different Christian churches.* Exactly— definitions matter.

Although *Muldoon's Misfortunes* isn't a memoir, nor meant to be, it uses pertinent facts and history derived from my family's letters, photos, and documents. I must confess this up front—I didn't intend to write about my great grandfather. I planned to write a book about my grandfather, who I knew, respected, and loved. He will have his own book, as Book 3.

As with so many aspects of my life, the unexpected happened and God reordered my plan.

When an opportunity arose to write a short story on any topic relating to America's heartland, I immediately thought of an incident my 102-year-old grandfather had told me. It became South Dakota Foreman, in the *Heartland Treasures* anthology published by JV Publications.

I learned how to write an Irish character, use some details from Grandfather's story, and have since toned down the accent in Mick Muldoon's book. One critique group friend said, "I think you found your lane." They then encouraged me to write historical fiction novels.

You may know that research is foundational for historical anything. I dug through all I had in my possession. I hired my niece, Aerie, and my daughter, Hannah, to research more. They unearthed some gems via the internet and Ancestry. Many unexpected details surfaced and, boom, my great grandfather expected his own book. I used some aspects of his life in *Muldoon's Misfortunes*. Since the writing of this book, we've discovered more details. I may use them in my other two books if needed.

All towns are fictional, but the region is correct. I cited dates that are varied from actual to typical ballpark.

Here's a list of documented facts, and/or rumors about the character, Mick, inspired by my great grandfather. I created Orla based on facts about my great aunt. My grandfather inspired the character of Liam. My great grandmother's characterization helped to invent Molly from the little Liam knew about her. All characters are at minimum partially fictionalized.

Marriages: Rumor has it that Mick was married six times. Three in Ireland, where his wives and children all died from typhus. A church fire destroyed the records, but recently my cousin Vicky and her husband discovered more records through Ancestry. Often, England destroyed Irish records. His three marriages in America are documented. I fictionalized Mick's marriage relationships.

Children: Mick had ten children from his three American marriages, and rumors of six children in Ireland. In Minnesota, four died of tuberculosis with his first American wife. He became a father again at age 62, and 64, with his last wife. We estimate he fathered sixteen children in total.

Multiple divorces and multiple families: Two wives divorced him in America, and he raised four children as a single dad. Liam, my grandfather, was the second of the four. He will have his own book, Book 3 in the series. Liam's mother deserted the family when he was eight, and I didn't cite the reason he told us for that. He did runaway to find her, but I created those details.

Liam did quit school and began working to help support the family around the age of thirteen by what we call "baby-sitting" for families on nearby farms or railroad workers. Unusual for the time, but he insisted he did and told some tales about it. He was a "water-boy" for the rail gangs by age fifteen, he said, and told some whoppers about that. More details will be in Book 3.

Arrested: My researcher, Hannah, discovered Mick's arrest record. We'd not heard of the charge of "bastardy." We couldn't find more on his length of time in jail, but he posted bail and married his sixth wife, who had accused him. I invented a story surrounding this using the timeframe. She also disappeared with their two young sons. More on this in Book 3.

The tragic facts and many misfortunes about my great grandfather stunned me. *Muldoon's Misfortunes* formed in my imagination. Mick persisted in hoping to forging a life in America and survived, lived to eighty-five, but also dealt with so much death. I created an entity, Mister Death, for Mick may have felt cursed, as many Irish people are superstitious. How could a man deal with repeated losses like his? How did his Catholic faith come into play within his heart and mind? What must he have done to cope? I learned about the whiskey drinking of our great grandfather from my brother, Ray, which made some sense, so I moderately used Mick's drinking in the book.

In photos I have of our great grandfather, it appears he has scoliosis or something similar, and I expounded on that. Things I knew about Liam's relationship with his dad formed a dynamic because their letters are affectionate. None of his children spoke ill of him. This impressed upon me that Mick valued a relationship with his children, which endured the challenges he faced.

Mick's brother and sister: Yes, they came over together from Ireland about that time. One relative died on a ship earlier in that century, but I substituted it as their sister, Kathleen. Coffin ships were a well-known problem. Around 1868, the British Parliament addressed the issue when it started to pass laws for protecting passengers. Together with improvements of new ship designs, it shortened transatlantic journeys and made them safer.

Orla, the character of Mick's sister, was exactly who I wrote her to be, a madam. My brother, Ray, told me a little about her. She'll have her own Book 2 in the series, for she demands attention. Mick was the only family member who didn't disown her. How could he? He valued survivors.

Tenant farmer: My cousin Vicky gave me the exact location of the lane in Ireland that went through their land. Without giving the family name, we once held standing in the

British Empire, with land, a castle, and a title. Someone lost it all and it reduced the family to tenant farmers. Mick purchased a farm in Minnesota and left it behind after he lost his family. He requested to be buried next to his Minnesota wife and children. I have photos of that.

The railroad: Mick worked for the exact railroad I cite for forty-five years. Liam wrote a petition with signatures, which I still have, for his father to receive a pension. The railroad denied it because they didn't offer pensions yet.

Mick's last years: He moved into the home of Liam, his wife, and niece. I fictionalized many details for his great niece's story, but her situation was tragic with the loss of her mother.

The rest of the story is my vivid imagination and using superstitions. I never expected my childhood years, while being raised in the Catholic church with Irish priests and nuns, would come alive again within the dialogue of my own novels.

God has the best ideas. I always ask Him what He wants, or what He will do, because He forever surprises me with His unexpected presence and powerful, persistent love.

GLOSSARY
IRISH WORDS, HISTORICAL REFERENCES, CATHOLIC TERMS

an Gorta Mór
The Great Hunger, one of Ireland's worst famines from 1845-47.

Aye
Affirmative, ever, forever, always.

Bean Sidhe
(In Irish legend) a female spirit whose wailing warns of an impending death in a house.

Bodhran
A round drum with the appearance of a tambourine. It has a rounded stick called a "beater" similar to a spoon.

Boyo
Boy or man (used chiefly as a form of address).

Cobs
A powerfully built, short-legged horse.

Coffin ships
Any of the ships that carried Irish immigrants escaping the Great Irish Famine and Highlanders displaced by the Highland Clearances. Coffin ships were crowded and disease-ridden, had poor access to food and water, resulting in many deaths as they crossed the Atlantic. The cheapest way to cross the Atlantic, but with 30% mortality rates.

The Crown
The government of England (and therefore any countries ruled by England).

English landlord
Specific reference to *English* landlords in this time frame, who owned land and required exorbitant rents from their poor Irish tenants.

Fenian
A member of a 19th-century revolutionary nationalist organization among the Irish in the US and Ireland. The Fenians staged an unsuccessful revolt

in Ireland in 1867 and were responsible for isolated revolutionary acts against the British until the early 20th century, when gradually eclipsed by the IRA.

Gall-luch
A rat.

Hooligan
A violent young troublemaker, typically one of a gang.

Land Rights
The inheritance method in 1700-1800 Ireland was the "stem family system." The Irish Catholic could not "own" the land. One child inherited control of the family holding renting a parcel of land from an English overlord. Occasionally the oldest son didn't inherit "the farm." Most Irish Catholic families were large, and the plots of land were too small for dividing among all male offspring, or the businesses too small to support many. Other children were forced to live a celibate life at home helping on the family property, take a menial job with very little hope of ever getting a piece of land, or they immigrated.

Macushla
Literally, my pulse (mo + cuisle), used as an affectionate form of address, like "darling."

Moors, or moorland
A tract of open uncultivated upland; a heath.

Mummers
Performer, actor in pantomime.

Oíche na Gaoithe Mire
The Night of the Big Wind, a powerful European windstorm that swept across Ireland beginning in the
afternoon of January 6, 1839, causing severe damage to property and several hundred deaths before moving across northern England. The worst storm to hit Ireland in 300 years.

Reticule
Women's small handbag, originally netted and typically having a drawstring and decorated with embroidery or beading.

Shillelagh
A thick stick of blackthorn or oak used in Ireland, typically as a weapon

(club).

Slíbhín (sleveen, sleiveen)
An untrustworthy or cunning person.

Snug
Small, private room or compartment in a pub.

Tam, (tam o' shanter)
Round woolen or cloth cap of Scottish origin, with a tight headband, wide, flat circular crown, often with a pom-pom on top.

Tenant farmer
A person who farms rented land.

Tuama
A tomb or grave.

Catholic Terms

Absolution
Formal release from guilt, obligation, or punishment.

Act of Contrition
In the Roman Catholic Church, a penitential prayer.

Apostle's Creed
Sometimes titled the Apostolic Creed or the Symbol of the Apostles, is a Christian creed or "symbol of faith". The creed most likely originated in 5th-century Gaul as a development of the Old Roman Symbol, the old Latin creed of the 4th century. It has been in liturgical use in the Latin rite since the 8th century and, by extension, in the various modern branches of Western Christianity, including the modern liturgy and catechesis of the Catholic Church, Lutheranism, Anglicanism, Presbyterianism, Moravianism, Methodism, and Congregational churches.

Catechism
A summary of the principles of Christian religion in the form of questions and answers, used for the instruction of Christians.

Confession
A formal statement of admission of guilt.

Confessional, or booth
An enclosed stall in a church divided by a screen or curtain in which a priest sits to hear people confess their sins.

Confirmation
A church practice that falls into the category of what the Anglican Catechism calls "rites and institutions commonly called sacraments." A sacrament in the Catholic church deepening baptismal life.

Convent
A Christian community under monastic vows, especially one of nuns.

Come, Holy Ghost
A Hymn, sung in other Christian churches as well, including Methodist, and Anglican.

"Crossed themselves"
Making the Sign of the Cross over themselves.

Crucifix or crucifixes
A representation of a cross with a figure of Jesus Christ on it.

First Communion
(Especially in the Roman Catholic Church) the occasion on which a person receives the Eucharist (a Catholic Mass including the Holy Communion) for the first time, often celebrated as a religious ceremony for children of about 7 or 8 years of age.

Franciscan
A friar, sister, or lay member of the Christian religious order founded in 1209 by St. Francis of Assisi, or of an order based on Franciscan rule. The Franciscan orders are noted for preachers and missionaries.

Key of Heaven
(Catholic), prayer book published in 1874, John Milner. It also includes devotionals.

Laity
Parishioners, or church members distinct from the clergy.

Last Rites
(In Catholic and Orthodox Churches) rites (prayers and ministrations) administered to a person who is about to die.

Nun, Sister
A member of a religious community of women, especially a cloistered (living in a convent) one, living under vows of poverty, chastity, and obedience.

Order of Sisters
In the Roman Catholic tradition, religious institutes of nuns and sisters (the female equivalent of friars and monks).

Our Father (prayer)
Also called The Lord's Prayer.

Penance
Voluntary self-punishment inflicted as an outward expression of repentance for having done wrong.

Priest, or Father
An ordained minister of the Catholic, Orthodox, or Anglican Church having the authority to perform certain rites and administer certain sacraments.

Protestant
A member or follower of any of the Western Christian churches that are separate from the Roman Catholic Church and follow the principles of the Reformation, including the Baptist, Presbyterian, and Lutheran churches.

Purgatory
(In Roman Catholic doctrine) a place or state of suffering inhabited by the souls of sinners who are expiating (atoning for) their sins before going to heaven.

Rectory
Residence of a rector or parish priest.

Rosary (worry pearls)
Prayer beads. In the Roman Catholic Church, a form of devotion in which five (or fifteen) decades of Hail Mary are repeated, each decade preceded by an Our Father and followed by a Glory Be.

Sacraments
(In the Christian Church) a religious ceremony or ritual regarded as imparting divine grace, such as baptism, communion or the Eucharist and (in the Roman Catholic and many Orthodox Churches) penance and the anointing of the sick.

Saint Christopher

The patron saint of travelers venerated in Roman Catholicism, Eastern Orthodoxy, Lutheranism, Oriental Orthodoxy, and Anglicanism.

Saints

Verb: formally recognize as a saint; canonize: A person acknowledged as holy or virtuous and typically regarded as being in heaven after death.

Sign of the Cross

A Christian (Catholic) sign made in blessing or prayer by tracing a cross from the forehead to the chest and to each shoulder, or in the air.

ACKNOWLEDGMENTS

Dear Father God—You always do the unexpected, and You do the same surprising things for my characters when they need You. Please continue helping them encounter Your unexpected presence in their lives.

Thank you again, Mama. Your wisdom of how you dealt with me as a young storyteller led me to embrace my calling and life as an author.

Without the brilliant mind and dedication of my daughter, Hannah Hagen, and her love of research, there would be no historical fiction books with my name on them.

I'm grateful for the contributions of my niece, Aerie Sandusky, who, although without blood ties to this branch of the family, spent multiple hours digging for details I could use.

Thank you to my granddaughters, the older grands, who believe in me writing books. One says she wants to be an author like me.

My original critique group partners were the catalysts for this novel, or I would have continued writing short stories. Big hugs and a thank you to authors and writers — Elaine Faber, Dee Aspin, Ellen Cardwell, Judy Pierce, Suzi Kneedler, and Susan Wright.

A special thank you to Sandy and Denise Barela and the entire Celebrate Lit team for your support and interest in my manuscript. You encouraged me to continue forward on this author journey and accepted me as a member of your publishing family. Editor Liz Tolsma, your comments with lovely words warmed my heart like no other, and your editing helped me magnify aspects of this story.

Dearest Ireland, you've embraced me warmly every time I've visited, and you can expect to see me again. Your history is egregious for multiple centuries. Yet you've sent America millions of your people seeking more from life and independence, where they've often flourished. Including my own family.

ABOUT THE AUTHOR

E.V. Sparrow is a short story writer turned novelist. Her readers encounter God's unexpected presence through her character's escapades. Her own adventures she wrote about involved traveling in over twenty countries. Sparrow lived on an Israeli kibbutz, worked for the U.S. Army in Bavaria, and hopped a freight train for a weekend.

Her father's family's immigration from Ireland, their letters and documents, and some family stories inspired her current historical fiction novels.

In E.V.'s personal and church life, she ministered through prayer, worship, mission teams, and in Divorce Care and Singles. California native relocated to North Carolina, E.V. Sparrow and her husband enjoy family time with their grandchildren and exploring their new state.

instagram.com/erin.sparrow.world

ALSO BY E.V. SPARROW

THOSE RESILIENT MULDOONS SERIES

Muldoon's Minnesota Darling (Prelude Novella)

Muldoon's Misfortunes (Book 1)

Madam Muldoon's Garden (Book 2) — July 2025

Salvaging the Muldoons (Book 3) — July 2026

Made in the USA
Middletown, DE
16 July 2024

57346266R00215